END

of the

RACE

A Novel

JUDITH KIRSCHT

Paperback ISBN: 978-1-09835-215-8
eBook ISBN: 978-1-09835-216-5

END
of the
RACE

Chapter 1

2007

Annika swam into open water, each stroke breaking the early morning silence, scattering the reflection of the surrounding forest. She turned on her back to watch her wake settle, and the wavy image of the woods returned to surround her. She inhaled evergreen laden air sharpened, now, with the bite of fall, then turned again and felt the last month wash away behind her as she swam.

Rhythm replaced thought, her body slipped into a time lost from memory. Emptied of all but the water. No one urging her on, no lane markers, no whistles, no yelling crowd. Only her body releasing the weight of grief. She rolled over to take in the sky, but instead her eyes fell on the wood and glass house on the lake shore, the morning sun glinting on its windows, the broad lawn, the sun-warmed dock. Their house. Brian's and hers. Their wedding present from Uncle Joe, built for a woman who flew through the water, rendered weightless by speed—and victory.

She was again an eight-year-old on another dock, one where she wasn't supposed to be. The Wolfson's—a name she wasn't to say—with Brian. Laughing, pushing each other into the water. *"Come on!"* His words rang and her body followed, skimming free, until water mixed with laughter cut short her flight, and Brian had to turn around and hold her up while she choked.

But the image vanished, yanked away like a child from a busy road, and she was left staring at the house, hollowed now by the loss of the baby from her womb.

Then as she watched, a small figure in a nightgown burst from the door and ran across the grass toward the lake. Sadie. Annika laughed and swam toward the shore as her daughter leapt from the dock and paddled toward her, heedless of the gown. She whooped as Annika rolled her onto her back. "You should put your swim suit on, silly." She laughed, tickling her.

"I couldn't find you and then I did!"

A six-year-old answer, making perfect sense. Annika spun her daughter, reliving, for a moment, the children she and Brian had been.

"We get Daddy today!" Sadie exclaimed between sputters.

"Today!" Annika echoed, tossing Sadie toward shore. Brian's departure in the middle of her grief had left her floundering as though some essential part of her had dropped away. Horrified at her helplessness, she'd fled to the water and training, but her body would not respond. She'd cast around and found no one; her connection to the world had come undone. Her family? Her marriage to a Wolfson made her an outsider there. The Wolfsons? Brian was the Wolfson, not her. Friends? No time. But it hadn't mattered. They'd been complete, needing only each other and the water. Even Brian's Uncle Joe, who'd coached them since they were eight and ten, occupied a place outside their union. *It's a trip*, she told herself, just a sailing trip. Just two weeks. Tonight he'll be here. The hollowness will be gone.

Together she and Sadie swam for the beach, then ran for the warmth of the house. "Go get dressed, and I'll fix breakfast." She stripped the sodden nightie over Sadie's head and sent her off with a smack on her naked behind, then toweled dry, pulled on jeans and a sweater, laid out Sadie's clothes and went down to fix breakfast. Energy that had been missing flowed as though released from a damn. As though he were here already.

"Do we leave soon?" Sadie scrambled down the stairs, pulling her sweater over her head.

"As soon as we eat and you feed the turtles." She set cereal on the table, and Sadie climbed into her chair.

"Why'd he go without us?"

Why indeed? "Because ..." She searched for an answer that would satisfy a six-year-old. "Some old friends asked him to go on a sail trip—friends he met in college." She kept her voice light, hiding her bewilderment. Nothing had been right since the baby's loss. His words of comfort had been a tight-wound imitation of himself. And over and over he'd gone off, then he'd come back apologizing, muttering that when they got back to training they'd be okay. Then he goes off for two weeks. Just like that? "You met them," he'd answered her astonished look, giving her a couple of names that meant nothing. He'd run into one of them—Nils?—at a convention in Ann Arbor, he said, and he'd asked Brian to join them. Sailing from Maine, no less—out of Bar Harbor. "I'll leave you a training schedule. You'll be up to it soon. You don't need me for that." He'd turned defensive at her continued incredulity.

She looked at the training chart that hung on the refrigerator.

"OFF TO THE OLYMPICS!
CHINA 2008!"

blazed in red across the top. Her last chance. Her thirtieth birthday loomed. Twice—three times—and again—she'd forced her body, willing it to move beyond a warm-up crawl. She sighed, shook off the feeling of having gone crosswise to her life, and handed Sadie her juice. "Some day, when you're grown," she told her, "you'll know how good it is to go off and be young again for a little while." In truth, moments like the one on the Wolfson dock—all stolen—were all she knew of carefree as a child. She'd envied Brian the life she'd dare not mention at home—a place competitive swimming had taken her, welcoming its demands, each prize a guarantee

3

of her place in a world free of the grasp of the Berglund house. And always there was Brian, an essential part of that escape. For a moment this morning's swim came back, bringing a hint of some long forgotten time, but it was gone in a flash.

"Why?"

"Because it keeps you young." Words that were Brian's mantra. Great grandson of one of Frontenac's founding families, captain of his high school swim team, youth, for Brian, was one long adventure—swimming, sailing, kayaking, and love of the race. For her, it was an enemy camp she leapt into behind her father's back. She raised her eyes and looked out at the glint of sun off the water, feeling again its siren's call. They had no use, back then, for the quarrels that split the adults, creating barricades and forbidden territories; they lived for water, woods and wind. Always racing for a place beyond.

"I want to grow up!"

"Funny isn't it?" She picked up Sadie's dish and carried it to the sink. "When you're little you want to grow up, and when you're grown up, you want to bring back childhood." Brian's ten-year-old face rose up, grinning, and she felt her own face grinning in answer. They'd won their heats in the state meet. *"We're off to the Olympics, you and me!"*

"Can we go now?" Sadie jumped down from her chair.

"After you feed your turtles." Annika smiled. She could still feel the rewards of life away from the house on Browning Street. She looked around her living room, with its stone fireplace, beamed ceiling and soft-stuffed chairs for collapsing. She sighed, contentment wiping away unease. Escape she had. And victory. That day at the nationals rushed forward. Four years ago.

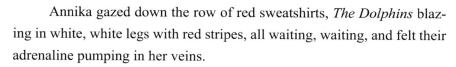

Annika gazed down the row of red sweatshirts, *The Dolphins* blazing in white, white legs with red stripes, all waiting, waiting, and felt their adrenaline pumping in her veins.

"Okay, Annie, you're on!"

She leapt from the bench at Joe's shout and headed for the blocks as the announcer's voice echoed, "200 meter freestyle!"

She pulled on her cap and goggles, then stretched and spread her arms, taking Brian's wind into her lungs along with her own. It was a ritual now. They'd done it ever since they'd won their first heats.

"Take your marks ..."

She stepped onto the starting block,

"Set ..."

She crouched, her arms stretched behind her ready to swing ...

The gun boomed.

She swung her arms, her body following, barely cutting the surface of the water, then began to stroke, picking up the momentum of the dive, her mind riveted to the end of the pool, the moment to curl for the turn, push. She was ahead. The air from many victories lifted her, the feel of water rushing past. And again ...

Her cheering team filled her ears the last meters before her hand touched the wall, and her mind released its hold. Brian was jumping up and down, holding her sweatshirt. The nationals. She'd won the nationals.

She gazed around the living room again, still euphoric. Swimming had given them this—and Sadie, too. *"Now for the Olympics ..."* she could hear Brian call, but the words brought the jolt of loss, tears of frustration. She drove them back. This time she'd make it. For them all. Tomorrow

Brian would be back, and her body would respond. They'd get it back. They had before. After his crushed leg ruined his chances, after her first pregnancy had made Sydney impossible, after Athens—

With a jolt, she was back, touching the wall, so sure, gazing up at Brian and Joe—but their eyes were on the clock—unbelieving. The name at the top wasn't hers. A half second?

"Tough break, sweetie." It was Joe reaching down to pull her from the pool.

Brian was gone.

Sadie's voice from the stands filled the empty space.

She could do nothing but sit as though waiting for the next breath to come. In the locker room, then their hotel room, Wrapped in terry cloth, staring into emptiness.

His face appeared, turning rage and grief into a leaden lump.

"Sorry. So sorry." His eyes beseeched." He took her icy hands in his. *"On to China!"*

———

But not quite. Fate intervened once again. She was pregnant.

"But you can't be, Annika. The trials!" His voice was incredulous, bewildered though he was forever impulsive, impatient with prevention.

"What about them?" she protested. "I can still train. I trained with Sadie, didn't I?"

He turned to look at his daughter, who was deep in a book, mouthing the words. His eyes softened. "Another miracle?" He drew Annika into his arms. "Promise?"

She'd trained that first time until she was eight months along and was back at it before Sadie was a month old, getting stronger, beating her times over and over. She'd been so sure this time would be the same—the car seat sitting beside the pool, throwing a towel over her shoulders to nurse. Brian finding her there, grinning at her enthusiasm ...

"I'm ready now." Sadie stood beside her chair.

She gazed down at her daughter's dark curls and soft cheek. So perfect. Pain choked her as the memory of the lost baby rose. She pushed it away and looked at her watch. "Good. Go get your book, and we'll be on our way."

As she drove through the farm lands and cherry orchards that lined the road, the anchorless floundering of the last weeks dissolved on the road behind her. She just needed him back, training, the sound of his voice. As she approached the village of Virgin Lake, the land changed from open fields and orchards to woodlands once again, bringing the smells of evergreens and water. In less than an hour, she pulled in to the parking lot at Traverse City Airport. "Here we are! Come on Sadie, let's go find Daddy."

"Outside! I get to see!" Sadie insisted as Annika started for the terminal.

"Okay. I guess we can do that." She turned toward the chain-link fence where they could watch arriving flights land.

"Is that it?" Sadie cried some fifteen minutes later, pointing to a small jet approaching the runway.

Annika consulted her watch. "Maybe." She felt her heart swell as the plane rolled toward them. They would be whole again, glad of each other.

The plane turned and taxied toward the terminal. Sadie was jumping up and down in anticipation as the attendants rolled the steps into place. The door opened and passengers began to descend to the tarmac. Sadie rose to her toes, waiting to wave and shout when she spied him. The stewardess and pilots emerged. Annika stomach knotted as she stared at the empty staircase.

Sadie's heels hit the ground. "Where is he?"

Annika studied her watch again. "Maybe that isn't his flight. Let's go check."

But the arrival board in the terminal matched the itinerary in her pocket. "I guess he missed his plane," she told Sadie, who was watching the passengers collect their luggage, her face clouded in confusion. But surely he would have called if he had. She pulled out her phone to check. It was on. No calls. "Let's go see when the next Detroit flight comes in."

Reluctantly, Sadie let herself be turned away from the baggage claim.

"Three hours. Well, I guess we wait. Let's find a place to sit."

Sadie raised her shoulders and let them fall, her mind clearly consumed with disappointment.

Once seated, Annika busied herself with her phone. The Boston flight had landed in Detroit with plenty of time to make his Traverse City connection. The next Boston flight wouldn't come in to Detroit until late afternoon. Why hadn't he called?

"I have to pee," the small voice beside her complained.

"Okay, let's go take care of that." She was happy to be moving. She was a lousy sitter. "And we'll go get your book from the car."

But once at the car, she was loath to return to the building. "How about we go to the beach? Or we could drive out to the lighthouse." Anything to drive away the jolt of his absence.

"The lighthouse." Sadie was firm.

Annika glanced at her watch again, calculating the distance to Mission Point. They could make it, and it was better than waiting here. "Good. Let's go."

Two hours later, they'd made the jaunt up the peninsula and, thankful for the thinning of summer traffic, climbed the tower to the light. Annika gazed at the land that had encompassed her life—the open arms of Traverse Bay, the vast stretch of Lake Michigan beyond, the golden ring of sand along the water's edge. Above the shoreline, the woods were splashed here and there with the colors soon to come in full. The vastness had always overwhelmed her, calmed her churning emotions, reduced her to a mere speck, brought peace. Today it anchored her; lessened the sense of being cast adrift.

"I'm hungry now," Sadie proclaimed after a few minutes of marching around the balcony.

"Okay, let's go get ourselves a hot dog.'

Annika dawdled as much as possible finding a café, but still they were back in the waiting room by five-thirty. Sadie frowned at her book and squirmed. She was clearly in no mood to sound out letters.

"I'm going to get coffee," Annika told her. "Do you want to watch for Daddy's plane? It's almost time."

Sadie jumped down eagerly. "How long?"

Annika checked the board and her watch. "About long enough to get my coffee. Let's go."

A half hour later, empty cup dangling from her hand, she watched the last of the passengers descend to the tarmac.

"Where's Daddy?" Sadie demanded. "Why isn't he here?"

Chapter 2

Annika stared at the empty tarmac. She'd fallen into a void. Her mind could find no toehold. "I don't know."

She took out her phone and stared at it. Call who? The college friends he'd mentioned were just first names—Nils and …? What? He said she'd met them at *Cottage Inn*, a favorite hangout. She could smell the pizza, see the pitchers of beer, the deep booths, and a ring of faces that, except for Brian and his brother, Jonathan, she didn't know. She remembered feeling she didn't belong. No more.

She switched to voicemail. Nothing.

"Are you going to call him?" Sadie's voice was high and tight.

Annika blinked. "Right." She clicked in the numbers, then tightened her jaw as the call went to voice mail. "Brian, call me!" She said into the void, then clicked the phone off and turned to her daughter. "I guess his phone is off. We'll go home. Maybe he called there." There was no reason on earth he'd do that when she carried a cell-phone, but Sadie was nodding. It was good enough for now. "Come on."

As she drove north, Annika's mind emerged from confusion and began to track. She had to remember the names of the men he went with. They'd been members of the U Michigan sailing club—a membership she, on a swim scholarship, working for her room and board, couldn't afford. Nils what? In the ring of faces, she saw a lanky blond—a Nordic last name. She ran through a list of Johnsons, Jensens, Stevensens but nothing clicked. The other name? She concentrated on the road, letting her mind rest. Dominic. Yes. But no last name came attached. Brian's yearbooks were at home. There'd be pictures.

The hope calmed her, and she glanced at her daughter who, as though sensing her mother's state of mind, had fallen silent. In the mirror Annika could see her gazing out, wide eyed, seeing nothing. She looked helpless, vulnerable. And Annika had no reassurances, nothing to give her. Failure drove her mind, insisting she focus.

What happened? Had the boat capsized, gone aground in a storm? Lost at sea? What was the name of that town? Bar Harbor. Yes. That was it. *Don't be silly*, she scolded herself. *He's just missed the damned plane.* She pulled over and dug her phone out of her pocket, but it had nothing new to tell her. So … *so don't get in a twit. Calm down or you'll frighten Sadie.* She glanced back again. More than she already is.

The afternoon light had reddened by the time Annika pulled into the drive. Once released, Sadie ran for the house, waited impatiently for Annika to catch up and unlock the door, then raced for the phone. Annika could tell by the way her heels hit the floor that the machine showed no messages.

She put an arm around her shoulders. "It's all right, baby. We'll just wait until he calls, then we'll scold him for not calling. For worrying us."

Sadie looked into her face as though examining every line. "He never did before."

"True. But usually he's just late from work. He doesn't have to count on airplanes to get home." But why hadn't he called? To say where he was, at very least?

Sadie frowned at the inadequacy of the answer but allowed herself to be led away on the promise of tomato soup and grilled cheese sandwiches.

An hour later, when Annika finally got her to sleep after reading two extra stories, she settled herself at Brian's desk with his itinerary. Several airline phone calls later, she knew he had boarded both the Boston flight and the flight to Bar Harbor, Maine, but there was no record of his boarding either of the return flights. She sat back. So he got there. Then what?

Facebook. His favorite way of chatting with the swim team he coached. They shared an account, though Annika rarely logged-in. She went to the swim club's page and scrolled through the timeline and notifications. He'd made no posts, even to answer questions posed by his team members. Someone even asked where he was. Would he be back for the meet?

She sat back with a huff. The meet? Yes, sometime this week. She couldn't remember the day. Who'd been coaching for Brian the last two weeks? *Stop it!* She shook her head to scatter the return of panic. *Don't be a ninny.* Uncle Joe would have taken over. Brian hadn't said so, but he must have or Joe would have been on the telephone. Not pleased. Understatement. It was Brian's uncle who had driven them hour after hour, meet after meet, she and Brian joining each other's energies to drive away fatigue. Until the day it ended.

～

White-faced on the hospital bed, his leg raised in traction, Brian's eyes begged her to say it wasn't true. He hadn't broken their dreams.

She shook her head, her brother's jeers still ringing in her ears. *"Wolfson chicken-shit!! Bet you can't! Bet you can't"*

"It's my fault!" She took an angry swipe at the tears dripping unbidden. "Eddy called me a traitor—warned me to quit ... I tried to tell you ..."

"What the hell were you doing?" Uncle Joe's yell preceded him into the room. *"Damn fool...!"* He cut himself off when he saw her there. "Sorry ..." he muttered, then turned his attention to the bed. "Look at you, strung up like a jib." He shook his head and blew a raspberry.

"It was Eddy's fault!" Annika fought tears."He dared him to climb the mast."

"What mast?"

"The …" She broke off, fishing for the name "… the old schooner that's moored in the harbor."

"Who's Eddy?" Then he waved the question away. "Doesn't matter. Who cares, anyway? A big meet a week away, and you have to answer some damn fool's dare?"

"I'll be ready for State," Brian protested. "Eight weeks they say. Then I'll be right as rain."

"Says you," Joe muttered, turning away.

"I will! I'll get back!"

Joe turned back at the desperation in Brian's voice. "Okay, sorry to blow," he muttered. "I was counting on you to spark the team, that's all. We'll manage." He patted Brian's shoulder, shifting from coach to the father he'd always been for Brian. "Eight weeks isn't the end of the world, I guess. Just do as the doctors say for a change, okay?"

He turned toward Annika. "Guess you'll have to swim for both of you." He grinned and gave her a pat. "Take care of him, will you?"

She'd nodded and smiled at him, in spite of the weight that dropped at his words.

As though she'd known he wouldn't come back. His knee had been too damaged. The leg would never regain its strength. But it didn't kill his drive. He joined Uncle Joe as her co-coach, all his hopes shifting to her. And she'd taken them. Taken their spirit into her body and flown, beating record after record. Until Athens. She'd missed. For both of them. By a half second, though she'd beaten that time in training a dozen times.

She got up, shutting off that day. Surely Brian would be back in time for the meet. But the increasing wrongness drove her to pacing the floor to get her thoughts to track. She needed to talk to someone. Someone who knew more. Maybe Carmen and Karl. She picked up the phone again, but again didn't dial. Why would he call his parents and not her? She'd only raise the alarm if she called now, and she wasn't ready to add his mother's to her own.

She made herself a cup of tea. Warming her hands around the cup, she gazed out at the lake where a full moon cast its trail across the dark water. She turned away. No time for fear. The yearbooks. In the storeroom.

She checked on Sadie, then headed for the room behind the garage where their past was preserved in carefully marked boxes. She was thankful, for a change, that her rebellion against her own chaotic family had produced such a need for order. In five minutes, she had the yearbooks. Back in the kitchen, she made more tea and settled at the table with Brian's first UM book. She turned to the athletics section and stared for a long minute at her husband's fresh young grin. Relaxed. Glowing with his love of the water. No trace yet of the frustration that had stiffened the lines around his mouth. He'd failed to make the sophomore team, ending the hope that had lived on despite his bad knee. Tears rose, and she shifted her gaze to the other faces, then shook her head and went to the names. No Nils or Dominic. Pictures of the sail club showed only Jonathan and his bride-to-be, now ex-wife, Vicky. No others she recognized.

It wasn't until she turned to his senior yearbook, to the sailing club, that she had better luck. Brian was there, but not Jonathan. He'd quit. She remembered now. He didn't like racing. A couple of other faces looked familiar, though—the long, lean blond, and a round and swarthy face she'd seen at *Cottage Inn* that day. She scanned the list of names. Nils Svenson, Dominic Costello. Yes. Those were the names. But the White Pages told her they were too common to be much help. She plodded through them looking for Maine or Michigan residents, then sat back and asked herself why she thought they were from Michigan—back then, to say nothing of now, ten years later. She returned to the memory of the group sitting over pizza and beer—saw the two of them punching each other, one teasing the other's Boston accent. Which? She shook her foggy head, her eyes burning. She had to quit. Tomorrow.

In the gray light of dawn, Annika woke and found herself on the couch, still fully dressed. *Brian.* She sat up with a jerk. Her head was splitting. Sadie mustn't find her like this. Stumbling to her feet, she climbed the stairs and looked in at her sleeping child before heading to the shower where she stood motionless, letting hot water stream over her.

She had to call someone. Her mind fixed on his mother's round, serene face, graying braid hanging down her back, clay-smudged denim jacket that covered her ample breasts. Carmen might remember. Brian brought friends north on weekends; Nils and Dominic might have been among them. So why didn't she remember them better? She turned off the water and stood frowning, trying to place them on the lake or beach. And couldn't. Well, she didn't come home any more often than she could help. Whenever she opened the door to her father sitting slumped, staring at the television, to her mother's stress-hollowed face, her escape into the Wolfson world and college felt like the betrayal Eddy had accused her of.

She pulled on jeans and a tee-shirt, looked in on the sleeping Sadie, then returned to her bedroom and sat down. This time she dialed her mother-in-law's number then realized she didn't know whether Brian had told his parents about the trip. The voice that responded was heavy with sleep. Annika glanced at the clock and winced. Six-thirty.

"Carmen? I woke you. I'm so sorry."

"Annie? Oh ..." There was a pause. "Is something wrong?" Carmen's voice cleared with alarm.

"It's just that Brian evidently missed his flight home."

"His flight? What ...?" Her foggy voice seemed to only half take in Annika's words. There was the sound of shuffling, as though she was sitting up. "What flight?"

"Oh, I'm sorry. I thought … he went on a sailing trip. From Bar Harbor."

"Bar Harbor? Whatever for?"

Annika opened her mouth but no words came. "I … to sail …"

"No, no, I knew he was going sailing. I told Karl he had no business going off so soon after … oh, I'm sorry Annie … but I thought … I just assumed he went from here …good grief …" her voice faded, and Annika saw her in her mind, running a hand through her hair.

"No. Maine. He said it was a chance to sail the Atlantic."

"Oh. Well, I suppose, but …" She sounded exasperated now. "Now? It all makes no sense …" her voice disappeared into a mumble "and neither do I …"

"That's okay, Carmen, but the problem is he was supposed to be back yesterday, and he hasn't phoned. I just wondered if you had the phone numbers of the men he went sailing with. He said they were college friends. I was going to call and see if they are home or … or what."

"Oh." There was a long pause. "Oh, I don't know … do you have names?"

Annika frowned. Carmen sounded muddled, a sleepy version of her scattered self, but there was a sudden defensiveness in her voice that was new. "Nils Svenson and Dominic Costello—I think."

"Nils … Dominic. Sounds familiar … Jonathan might—" She cut herself off.

"Jonathan?" The scene at *Cottage Inn* came back. Yes, it made sense. Jonathan quit the sail club for the Sierra Club, but Brian turned to sailing when he didn't make the swim team. He wanted to race. That's what they were doing there. Jonathan was introducing Brian to some sail club members. But why did Brian say they were friends of his? She frowned, trying to remember. She'd just been a freshman tagging along that day, but she couldn't remember Brian hanging out with them after that. He was too

16

busy sailing and coaching swimming to hang out any more than she did—
which was not at all.

"Oh, I don't know … never mind … I don't remember them anyway." Carmen's words came in a rush.

Annika went silent, struggling to make sense of both the news and
her mother-in-law's rush to dissemble. "Would you still have their phone
numbers somewhere, maybe?"

"Oh, I don't think I ever had them. But I'll ask Karl if he knows
anything more."

"Okay." What had his father to do with it? Brian worked for Uncle
Joe, and Uncle Joe rarely spoke to his brother. Ambitious go-getter Joe and
ageing hippie Karl accepted each other with patronizing smiles toward the
brother who hadn't yet discovered the right course in life—or a terse, "not
my business."

"Look, Annie, don't worry. He'll show up, and we'll both bawl him
out for not calling. Promise."

"I hope so. Well, I'm sorry to disturb you so early, Carmen.
Thank you."

"That's okay. Let me know when you hear from him, Annie."

"Right." Annika sat frowning at the now silent phone, unable to
shake the feeling that her mother-in-law knew more than she said. What
did Jonathan have to do with it? She cast her mind back yet again. They'd
both been sailors, growing up, and she could remember Jonathan in a Sail
Club sweatshirt at UM. But he didn't like the racing crowd. Turned to kayaking, hiking, and the natural world the way his parents had and joined his
father's wilderness boat tour company when he graduated. Both Carmen
and Karl assumed that sooner or later Brian would come "home" to their
side of the family "when he grew up"—the way Jonathan had.

Carmen still treated Annika and Brian as a pair of kids, and they were
happy enough to separate themselves from the post-Vietnam acrimony that

divided Brian's father and Uncle Joe—a mutual contempt that had grown old, soft and fuzzy around the edges. They'd even managed to ignore the hatred of Wolfsons that consumed Annika's father, still raw and virulent despite the years. She could still see the shock on Karl's face the day Brian introduced her.

"Berglund. What Berglund?" Brian's father shot the words at her, and she could only gape at him.

"Karl," Carmen chided, "don't frighten the child." She took her husband's arm and led him to the kitchen, leaving her and Brian rooted in the living room listening.

"There are lots of Berglunds, Karl." Carmen's voice was a hoarse whisper.

"Not that many in Fontenac. I don't want trouble, Carmen."

"They're just children. What trouble can there be? It's time to heal, Karl."

"Tell that to Tom Berglund!"

They heard the back door slam. Carmen didn't reappear.

"What's he talking about?" Brian burst. "Who's Tom?"

Annika stood frozen, her nerve endings singed by the way Brian's father had spat the name. "Vietnam," she whispered finally. "Tom's my father."

"Oh." He fell silent. They both knew the power of that word to split the world—Brian's father from Uncle Joe, his mother from the whole yacht club side of the family. "Come on. Let's get out of here."

Annika shook off the memory. Karl's rejection had left its mark, but she was still drawn to the laissez-fair household of Brian's parents. She needed the wandering canoe rides through the marshes with Carmen as an antidote to the high-pressure life of competition. Carmen had always included her, a little tentatively but with a sort of universal maternal warmth. Still, there was something guarded about the whole conversation—she felt pushed away.

"Mommy?" Sadie called from her bedroom. "Did Daddy get home?

Annika came to with a start and looked at her watch. After seven. "Not yet, sweetie." She got up and went to her. "And it's time you were up for school." She crossed to the chest and began to collect school clothes.

"But why isn't he?"

Annika went and put her hands on Sadie's shoulders. "I'm trying to find out, but he just got delayed in Maine, I—"

"Where's that?"

"In the East. Remember Daddy showing it to you on the map?"

Sadie frowned. "He showed me Barbor."

"Bar Harbor. It's in Maine, which is a state. What state do you live in?"

"Michigan." Sadie's voice was firm and proud.

"And what town?"

"Fontenac!"

"Right. And Bar Harbor is a town in Maine. Now get dressed."

An hour later, Annika saw Sadie onto the school bus and returned to the house. What now? She poured herself another cup of coffee and forced her brain to focus on their college days. So they were Jonathan's friends. She picked up the telephone and punched in Jonathan's number.

"Wolfson Explorations," a pleasant voice responded.

"Hello, Karen, Annika here. Is Jonathan in yet?"

"No, he's off with a group, Annie. Can I help you with something? Do you want his dad?"

"No, I guess not." She paused, frowning. "On second thought, would you look in Jon's Rolodex for me? For the names Nils Svenson and Dominic Costello? Thanks."

She waited, tapping a pen against the phone.

"Nothing," Karen reported. "But Jon carries a lot of numbers on his phone that never make it to the company Rolodex."

"Would they be on his computer? The reason I ask is that Brian went sailing with them and was due home last night. He didn't show. I wanted to see if they got home or know anything."

"Oh. You'd think he'd call, wouldn't you?" She tutted. "Men."

"Amen to that," she agreed, though it was unfair. As Sadie said, Brian had always let her know where he was.

"I don't know the password for his computer, Annie, but let me look through my email contacts."

"Thanks, Karen. That would help." Annika sat. Brian's clock ticked in the empty house.

"Sorry," Karen reported a few minutes later. "Nothing there."

"Okay. Well, thanks for trying. When will Jon be back, Karen?" Her head was beginning to ache, a sure sign of frustration.

"Tonight. He's due around five. Do you want me to call his cell? He can't get a signal very often, but I can try." Karen sounded concerned now.

Annika thought a moment. "No. Not yet. Let me see what I can find out on Brian's computer, first."

"Good luck."

"Thanks." She put down the phone and took her coffee to Brian's study, but the phone rang before she'd taken a seat. She picked it up.

"Hello, this is Annika."

"Morning Annie. Our boy have jet lag?" Uncle Joe's voice boomed with his usual heartiness.

"He ..." She struggled to find words. "He's not here, Joe. He ... must have missed his plane ..."

"Huh! Are you serious? Well, that's ... So where the hell ... He didn't call?"

"No, and I was trying to find out ... Do you know the friends he went with?"

"He didn't say. Just said he had to go." Joe gave an impatient sigh. "He's got a meet Friday."

"I know."

Joe was silent for a long minute. "Why the hell did he think he had to go on that trip anyway? Do you know?"

"Not really, Joe. I ... it surprised me, too."

"Huh. Well, let's hope he makes it back in time. Give him hell for me, will you?"

"Right," she responded into the dead phone. That was Joe, always half-way to the next item of business, like a sailboat catching the next puff of wind.

She turned back to the computer, then frowned as she waited for it to boot. She felt like a snoop. Facebook was one thing; they both used the same account, but what kind of wife went through her husband's email?

But that's what she was going to do. She sat up as the home screen came up and found his password in the notebook they shared. His email account showed some 3000 messages. She blew a raspberry. Brian was an impatient computer user, always racing through his messages without bothering to file or delete them. She scanned the most recent, mostly promotional stuff from athletic companies, yacht club newsletters, and swimming blogs. A couple from Joe were about summer meet schedules and entrance fees. Not many. None were from Jonathan. The Wolfson family carried on most of their business in person or on the telephone.

She tried searching by name. Three messages popped up under Nils Svenson. The most recent was very brief.

"Confirming your arrival on 9/9. Check in at the Bar Harbor Marina." It was a response to Brian's message giving his flight arrival time at the Hancock County-Bar Harbor Airport.

The earlier one, read,

"Affirmative. Wolfson notified us you would be coming in his stead. We'll be sailing on the Wayfarer on the tenth from Bar Harbor. Notify us of your arrival."

Annika frowned. "Wolfson" had to be Jonathan. That fit with Carmen's half-finished statement that Jonathan might know more. So the invitation was originally to Jonathan? But if they were friends, why refer to him by his last name?

She scanned down to Brian's message. *"I understand my brother, Jonathan, has notified you that I'll be sailing in his stead on your September trip."*

Again Annika frowned at the formality of the whole exchange. Not a bunch of old college friends getting together. That Jonathan, who was more and more taking over his father's business, couldn't go sailing in September made sense. The rest didn't. Again she reviewed her memory of the scene at the *Cottage Inn.* She and Brian were the newcomers there, she was sure. Later? She shook her head. No answer presented itself. Well, at least she knew the name of the ship. *The Wayfarer.*

She typed in Dominic's name and came up with nothing. After another hour searching various blogs and forums Brian subscribed to, she quit in exasperation. Time for a swim.

Chapter 3

Brian

1984

Brian braked his bike. Ahead, where the creek alongside the path drifted into a pond, a girl in a red swim suit was hopping in and out of the water, dodging around a pair of boulders. "What are you doing?"

She jumped and turned. "Catching tadpoles." She wiped a hand across her brow, leaving a smear.

He recognized her now, her wide-set blue eyes, the halo of frizzy red hair. "You're Eddy's sister." Younger than he was by a couple of years. Eight, maybe. He'd seen her in the playground after school, flying off the monkey-bars, practically doing handsprings. Not like a girl. He'd been going to talk to her, but then he saw Eddy Berglund calling for her and backed off. He had to catch the bus, anyway.

But he'd kept watching her, the way she moved—like on springs. He leaned his bike against a tree and headed down the slope. "You'll never catch them that way."

"Got two, already." She picked up a jar and thrust it at him. "You a friend of Eddy's?"

"My brother is." Which wasn't exactly true, though he'd seen Jon with him a couple of times, in spite of Dad's warning. "I'm Brian." He studied the jar. "That's pretty good. Want some help?"

She blinked, then raised her shoulders and let them drop. "I guess." She gazed around at the pond, the woods, the creek, as though looking for an answer, then pointed to the boulders. "You chase them around to me."

He shook his head and laughed. "Never heard of getting them that way, but okay. Here goes."

Fifteen minutes later, soaked to his knees, Brian gave a huff and climbed the bank. "Aren't you numb? That water's like ice."

She shrugged. "Some. I don't mind." She joined him and studied the jar where a half dozen tadpoles dodged about. "That's enough."

"Enough for what? What're you ..."

"Annieee ...!" A faint voice from the beach beyond the hill interrupted him.

"Gotta go." She jumped up and looked around.

"You're Annie?"

"Yep." She peered around into the rushes. "Do you see my flip-flops?"

He spied them under a bush and handed them to her as the call came again. "You'd better scat. He sounds upset." He watched her slide into the sandals. "Where're you supposed to be?"

"At the beach is all." She picked up the jar, then looked up and grinned at him. "Bye. That was fun with two." She turned and splashed across the creek and up the hill.

"See you at the beach!" he cried after her.

She waved, crested the hill and was gone.

Brian retrieved his bike and followed her until the sand sucked his tires, then, tossing the bike aside, climbed to the top of the hill and gazed down at Lake Fontenac's public beach. He only came here once in a while, looking for his town friends. The Wolfsons had their own beach, so there was no reason to. Sometimes in the afternoons they followed the sun over to the Lake Michigan beach, but not in June. Lake Michigan was too cold still, and except for one or two hardy kids up to their knees in the water, most of the people below weren't swimming in Fontenac yet either. He spied her—Annie—at the far end, holding her jar up to Eddy. Brian frowned. Was she always attached to him? He didn't mess with the older Berglunds, though he wasn't sure why, except Dad didn't care for them. He didn't see anything wrong with Annie.

As he watched, she set the jar down on a blanket, turned and ran for the water. In three seconds she was under and in another three emerged, shooting to her feet with a yell of glee. Then she swam a circle before running for shore. Brian gave a belly laugh, echoing her delight. That's exactly what he did, exalted in defying the cold. Now she was shaking water on Eddy, who'd spread out on a towel. He gave a howl and pulled her down, tickling her.

After watching for a few more moments, Brian turned back down the path, collected his bike and headed toward home. The June sun was gathering heat as he emerged from the woods into the abandoned orchard behind the old stone house. There he spread his arms and legs, whooping as he let his bike run free down the final hill.

The noise brought his mother's head up from the carrots, a fist full of weeds in her gloved hand. "There you are. Your Dad's looking for you." She eyed him from muddy feet to tousled hair and wiped her other hand across her brow. "How the devil did you manage to get so wet?"

"Oh." He looked down and waved toward the woods. "Just the creek. Was chasing a frog."

She gave a small huff. "Did you catch him?"

He shook his head.

"Well, no point in changing, I guess. They're down in the boathouse, likely as wet as you are."

"Getting out the *Giselle*?" He ran for the road and the water beyond without waiting for her reply.

"I'm here!" The boathouse door crashed against the wall behind him.

"So you are." "About time!" came simultaneously from his father and older brother, the first with the hint of a smile, the second with a scowl. They were standing on either side of the sailboat, which they'd already lowered into the water. Her mast lay across the rafters over their head.

"I didn't know you were going to get the boats out," he protested to his brother's scowl.

"It's okay," his father said. "Go ask Mum for a couple buckets of soapy water with sponges and rags. I'm going to leave you guys to scrub this lady down."

"We already checked the hull," Jonathan bragged.

Brian stuck his tongue out in answer and banged back out of the boathouse.

By the time he returned with buckets of suds, his father had opened the waterside door and was giving Jonathan instructions on examining the lines and sails. "I'll be back in a couple of hours—I just have to check out boats for the weekend. Then we'll set the mast and give her a whirl." He headed for the Zodiac that floated by the dock, *Wolfson Wilderness Adventures* blazing on its side.

"Can I check the motor?" Jonathan called after him.

"No. Wait for me on that." He jumped into the boat and gave the starter rope a yank. The roar drowned Jonathan's mumbled "nuts" as he turned back to the boathouse.

Brian watched the bright yellow inflatable speed toward the channel that connected Lake Fontenac to Lake Michigan, then followed him. "He said he'd take me with on a tour this summer."

"When? When'd he say that?" Jon jumped into the sailboat.

"Last summer. When he took you. He promised."

"Yeah? Well, he will then. Come on, let's get her cleaned up, so we get a sail today. Hand me that pail."

"You get the stern; I'll get the bow," he said as Brian climbed aboard with his own pail.

"Okay." He eyed the job, then started scrubbing. "Don't see how she gets so dirty doing nothing but hanging here."

"Yeah, and below deck, too," his brother agreed. "Yike!"

"What's wrong?"

"A nest. Squirrel, I think. Or something."

"Mouse, probably. Anything in it?"

"Naw."

"You getting the mildew off okay?" His brother called a few minutes later.

"Yeah." He liked it when they worked by themselves and his brother treated him like a friend. Whenever Dad was with them, Jon paired off with him like Brian was some kind of extra piece that didn't fit anywhere.

Two hours later, the *Giselle* sat gleaming in her berth, her sails spread on the lawn in the noonday sun.

The bell pealed from the front porch of the house across the road. "Lunch!" Their mother's voice floated after, and they looked at each other in surprise.

"I thought you said we had to get our own lunch this summer," Brian commented as he kicked off his shoes on the screened porch.

"Mm. You do, but one good turn deserves another. You've been working hard."

"Yeah. We're ready to step the mast and set the boom," Jonathan agreed, coming in behind him.

"You wait for your dad for that," their mother ordered. "Don't be getting too big for your britches. And leave those soggy clothes out there."

"Bet we could do it," Brian mumbled as they climbed the stairs to their dormer rooms after dry clothes.

"Yeah and get our asses in a pile of shit, too," his brother retorted, heading into his room.

"Yeah." He looked out at the sun-dappled lake and sighed. He didn't like waiting. It was going to be a good summer, going with Dad up Fox River on one of his fishing tours. He'd show him what a good pilot he was, not a mumbling idiot which he felt like when Jon was around. And he'd sail the *Giselle* this summer, too. He took the tiller last fall and did fine. He laughed as he remembered the feel of the wind and water under his hand, playing them together, air filling his chest.

"Coming?" Jon stood at the door in shorts and a dry T-shirt.

"Yup." He yanked open the drawer as his brother clambered down the stairs. *Dummy, why are you such a behinder?* He yanked out a pair of shorts, grabbed a T-shirt and within a minute was racing down the stairs.

But the afternoon was half gone before their father's boat roared up to the dock and dinner time before they had the mast secured and the boom in place.

"Good job, boys," their father said, examining the *Giselle* where she floated. Anchored to her buoy. "We'll rig her tomorrow."

"Tonight!" Brian insisted. "Why not tonight? It doesn't get dark until way late."

"The lines are all ready," Jonathan chimed in. "I checked them this morning."

"So are the sails," Brian added.

Their father looked from one to the other. "Okay, okay, let's go see whether your Mom is ready to feed us." He led the way up the lawn and across the road to the house, rubbing his hand along the stone balustrade and checking the doorframe for rot, as he went in.

Something on the old house was always rotting, everything except the stone. His father loved that stone. "Your great grandfather built this house, and there she stands, beautiful as ever."

It wasn't beautiful, really. Its windows didn't fit, and the stairs were always needing boards replaced. Not like Uncle Joe's, all shining glass and glowing wood. But you couldn't say a word against it to Dad. He loved telling pioneer stories about the Wolfsons who homesteaded the land, pointing out the old apple shed or the water tower. Pictures of long-dead Wolfsons hung all over the house.

Their mother turned from the stove when they clattered in, shedding their shoes on the porch. "About time you got hungry. Go get washed."

Their father went over and put his nose over the simmering pot, then kissed her. "Smells good."

"Just chili." She stood back and took in his face. "You look tired."

"Ah, two boats in bad shape, one with a rip. That last trip was hard on 'em." He went to the sink to wash his hands. "Had a couple of hotdog-gers who wouldn't ship the motor and use their oars up river where it gets shallow. Must have grounded their boats a dozen times."

"You get too many of those these days." She popped a tray of torti-llas into the oven.

"Seems like. They don't understand why they don't get a fish the first thirty seconds they put their poles in, either." He sighed and took his seat. "Life's always a goddamn race."

"Don't take them next time," Jonathan offered, setting bowls for chili on the table.

Their father smiled. "Well, if I had a magic wand so I could tell ahead of time, I wouldn't."

"You don't need to rig that boat tonight, Karl." Their mother spooned chili into crockery bowls. "The boys have all summer. They can wait a day."

"But then Dad will be off on a trip, and we'll be waiting forever," Brian objected, reaching for his helping.

"It's okay, 'Mella, " their father said, taking his. "It won't take that long, and they're anxious to get sailing. Don't blame 'em. I could use a good run, myself—air out the system." He picked up his spoon and dug in.

"In the big lake?" Jonathan asked, his eyes widening with hope.

Their father laughed.

"For heaven's sake, Jon, stop forever pushing," their mother burst, pulling the tortillas from the oven and sliding them onto a plate.

"You need to warm up on Fontenac first," their father said, reaching for one. "Ouch!" He snapped his hand back. "Then we'll give it a try. Tomorrow we sail out there." He pointed his spoon toward the lake out front.

"And I get to sail her, too," Brian declared between slurps.

He was greeted with silence filled only with the sound of spoons against bowls.

"I suppose I promised that, too?" his father asked, finally.

"Yep." He took a tortilla from the plate and dipped it into his chili, then glanced up to see his mother and father exchanging a look and heard his mother mutter something about "big mouth."

They didn't think he could.

Chapter 4

Brian

1987

It was a perfect morning. Brian trimmed the jib as Jonathan brought the *Giselle* closer to the wind, then leaned back as the boat heeled and sped up. The wind numbed his face and pulled at his hair, and the rush of water past the hull filled his ears. He laughed.

"Coming about!" Jon cried, swinging the tiller.

Brian released the jib sheet and ducked to the other side as the boom swung over his head. He grabbed the other line, and the jib filled again as Jon controlled the mainsail. Perfect. He glanced at his father who sat amidships, smiling. He grinned and pulled the jib in as his brother brought the boat close to the wind again.

"Take it easy," his father called. "This isn't the World Cup."

Jon grinned and fell off a hair. Just a hair.

"Okay, let's jibe," their father called as they neared the south end of the lake.

Jon fell off the wind and the boat slowed. "Ready?"

"Ready!" Brian answered as the wind came over the stern and the boom swung. They managed her with barely a quiver, and Jon gave him a thumbs-up and a grin. They were good, that's what.

When the boat approached the end of the lake, Brian shifted impatiently. "Let's take her to the big lake!"

"Yeah!" his brother joined the plea. "Just for a bit, Dad. Okay?"

Their father looked at his watch.

"It's early! We can be back by lunch, easy," Jonathan urged. "We're already at the channel almost."

"Okay, but we come back when I say. No arguments."

"Right," they chorused.

Jon swung the boat into the wind, and Brian jumped to lower the mainsail so the boat was ready for their father to fire up the engine for the trip through the channel.

Fifteen minutes later, they emerged into the open water of Lake Michigan and hoisted the sails again.

Brian felt the boat lift under him as the sails filled, and the water hissed against the hull as his father trimmed the sails. The noonday sun glistened on the endless stretch of blue. Across from him, Jonathan minded the jib, eyes on the telltales but matching their father's every twitch of the rudder. There was a shudder and flap of sails as the *Giselle* left the protection of the shore and the keel met deep water. His father swung the tiller, Jon pulled the jib line, and the *Giselle* gathered her skirts and took off. Brian was left with nothing to do but move from port to starboard and watch his father and brother as they tacked out across the water. A perfectly attuned team.

For a while, Brian sat back and closed his eyes, feeling the June wind, still edged with spring ice, numbing his face, smelling of sails just released from their long winter storage, hearing the whistle of the Giselle beneath him as she plunged into the summer ahead. He itched to feel the tiller under his hands, but knew it was too soon to ask. He could only watch theirs, imagining his own on the rudder, his eye on the telltales.

The boat slowed as his father fell off the wind. "Okay, Jon, take her."

Jon grinned and slid off his seat, handing off the jib as he reached for the tiller.

"Let me now!" Brian reached for the jib line, but bumped Jon's arm instead ...

The tiller swung free, the boom met his head as the Giselle lurched into the wind, and he hit the frigid water.

He woke, shivering, his head splitting, aware only of the vibrations of the motor under his blanket clad body—motoring through the channel. *You're done for.* He turned to the wall, shame blotting memory.

"Brian."

The name came out of some distant fog, and he became aware that the boat was rocking in place.

"Brian? You all right?"

A hand on his shoulder. His father. He tried to shake his head, but pain halted the motion.

The hand pulled him onto his back. "Look at me, Bri. I need to know if you're okay. That was a nasty bump."

He opened his eyes and stared at the concern in his father's brown ones without words because there were none.

"It's okay, Just a mistake."

"Yeah," his brother's voice came from above. "My first chance and he has to go ruin it."

"Come on, let's get you inside." His father put an arm around his shoulder, helping him to his feet. He shrugged it off, then, his head buzzing, had to grab the guard rail to keep from falling. "Get into the dinghy and give me a hand, Jon."

Together they lowered him, helpless as a babe, into the skiff. Pain swept him into a hole of shame.

"Oh Lord, what happened?" his mother cried when she saw him.

"He got himself knocked overboard like a dumb shit," Jon spat and headed for his room.

"Karl?"

"Got cracked by the boom. I'll have Dr. Stephens take a look—"

"No!" His cry cracked against the windows. "Leave me alone!"

They went away and left him to his shivering. Vaguely he heard his father call to Jonathan to tend to the boat.

"Let's get you dry." His mother stood before him with dry shorts and shirt.

The rest of the day passed in a haze. His mother driving, Dr. Stephens asking questions, driving home again. None of it mattered. He'd never get to sail the *Giselle* on the big lake. Not now.

Early the next morning, he woke blue, his head throbbing, his chest heavy. Jon's bed was empty, and he found them all in the kitchen, already at breakfast—which meant his father was leaving on a trip.

"Hello, sailor." Dad smiled at him. "How are you feeling?"

"Okay," he muttered and slid into his chair.

His mother was eyeing him with concern. "How's your head?"

"Just a little achy," he lied and reached for the cereal.

"Dr. Stephens says you're to stay quiet for a couple of days," his father said.

"Why? I'm okay." He poured milk on his cereal. "Where're you going this time?"

"Up the Fox again, I'm afraid. It seems to be the favorite trip this year. For a week this time."

"Fishing?"

"Yup. We got the *Lightning Pup* down, so you can get her ready, but you're shore-bound today. Got it?"

"Okay." Brian winced. Outside, the branches waved in the morning breeze. Perfect day for sailing.

"Just take it easy like Dr. Stephens ordered and be careful. Stay where your mother can keep an eye on you." He reached for another piece of toast. "Understand?"

"Yeah."

His father frowned at his impatient tone. "Every sailor gets knocked in the head once, Brian. Just a lesson learned. You're a good sailor—until you get reckless." His father pushed back his chair and rose. "Gotta go. Jon, you ready?"

Brian's head shot up. "Where's he going?"

"He's going to help Billy and Papa with boats and supplies while I'm gone."

"I'm all set." Jonathan rose, wiping his mouth. "Just need my shirt."

Then his mother was on her feet, too, giving Jon his lunch and kissing their father.

Brian ducked his head and spooned cereal in silence. He could feel his mother's eyes on him and eventually looked up.

She smiled. "You'll get your turn, you know, and you'll probably wish you were back on the *Lightning Pup* again with nothing to do but feel the wind in your hair."

"Yeah?" He gave a sigh. "Well, I guess I'll get at it then." He shoved his bowl away and got up.

"Nah, nah, buddy, you heard your dad. No sailing. And besides, you're on dishes this morning."

"I thought I was supposed to stay quiet!"

She laughed and gave him a pat. "I think you can manage dishes."

JUDITH KIRSCHT

He grumbled his way through the job, then wandered down to the dock, where he sat dangling his legs, staring across the water, nothing moving in his head, which had settled into a dull ache.

"Brian? You okay?" his mother called from across the road.

He dragged himself to his feet and waved. "Just resting," he called and went back to the boathouse, forcing his arms to go through the motion of hosing down the hull, rigging her, digging out the sail. Finally, he laid the sail out in the sun and hosed it down, then opened the lakeside door and backed the boat out, pulling it around to the dock.

The breeze teased, and the boat rocked softly in its bed of ripples. He looked up to see his mother standing on the lawn watching him.

Giving a wild yell of frustration, he raced down the dock and jumped into the water. The shock of cold took the weight from his limbs, and he surfaced with an exuberant yell then swam for the float.

When he climbed to its deck some twenty strokes later, he turned, shook the water from his hair, and waved at his mother, who twirled her finger beside her head, then settled in a lawn chair with a book. His headache was now a mere hint of itself. Brian stripped off his wet shirt and lay down on the sun-warmed boards as the residual motion of the air tanks dwindled into the stillness of noonday.

"Brian!"

His mother's yell roused him some timeless space later, and he raised his head.

"Let's get the kayaks out!"

Brian blinked in surprise at this violation of his father's orders, then grabbed his shirt, dove before his sun-soaked body could protest, and swam for shore.

"You're pretty fast," she commented, as he got to his feet a few yards from the beach. "Are you swimming on the team again?"

"Yah." He took the towel she handed him.

36

"Get yourself dry clothes first, then we'll go. Your dad won't mind if I'm with you and we stay along shore."

Five minutes later he was back, warm and dry. Together they carried the family kayaks out of the boathouse to the lawn, rinsed the winter's grime from their hulls, and sorted through the paddles, looking for their favorites.

"Here you go." His mother handed him his lifejacket.

They carried the boats to the water, shoved off and climbed in. He knew where they were going. He leaned into his stroke and felt the hull lift and skim the water, breaking the glassy surface into fans of rivulets. They rounded the headland and paddled toward the reeds that marked the swampland where Lazy Man's creek flowed into the lake. That's where the heron, ducks and water birds hung out, and the deer came to drink. He was approaching fast, digging his paddle deep when his mother's arm shot up in warning. Too late, he saw the dappled fawn among the greenery at water's edge. Startled by his movement, she was gone.

His breath escaped, and his chest caved. *Ruiner. Always the ruiner.*

"Just wait," his mother said softly. "They'll be back."

He shipped his paddle and closed his eyes, letting his boat drift. The weight was back. He rarely kayaked with his mother because he couldn't bear the inactivity of it, but today it felt like a relief to let himself sink into the lazy motion of the water, the sun on his back, lulling him deeper and deeper ...

A motion from his mother brought his head up, wondering how much time had passed, and he saw the fawn and mother approaching. The doe stopped for an interminable time between each step, her head rotating, her ears twitching. He couldn't imagine that kind of caution and wondered if his mother had brought him here on purpose to witness it. He didn't mind. Not today. He let himself sink into the acrid smell of rotting leaves. They watched the pair, then a chipmunk, then a pair of geese, then the empty reeds, the only sound the buzz of insects, the rusty call of redwing blackbirds.

The next morning, his mother relented and let him sail. "Be back in an hour, or I'll call the rescue boat."

"I will. Promise."

"Where's your watch?"

"I'll get it." He ran to his room, grabbed it, and raced downstairs and out. The sail lay where he'd left it on the lawn, wet now with dew. He should have put it into the boathouse for the night. *Shit! Dummy!* He picked up a corner and pulled the sail behind him toward the water. When the weight suddenly lightened, he turned in surprise. She'd picked up the back end.

"Everybody needs a hand once in a while."

He grinned, relieved she hadn't heard his language. "Okay." He jumped into the boat, and she waited there while he attached the sail and raised it. They stood together watching it flop in the breeze.

"A bit soggy," she remarked.

"It'll dry in no time. Thanks." He untied the boat and grabbed the mainsheet and rudder. "Give me a push?"

"Aren't you forgetting something?"

"What now?"

"Your lifejacket, buddy." She raised a hand before he could answer. "Yes, yes, okay, I'll get it." She headed for the boathouse and returned with his jacket.

"Ready?" she asked when he'd buckled himself into it. "Bye!" she gave the boat a shove with her foot.

He swung the rudder hard, watched the sail fill and was off. He looked back as he sailed past the float and saw that she stood watching. She gave a wave, and he freed a hand to return it. He wondered, for a moment, whether she ever felt left behind, but she didn't seem to. She'd rather be puttering in the ponds, the reeds, discovering a bird's nest, following a water snake. Then the wind caught the sail, and the *Lightning Pup* took off downwind. Everything vanished except the tiller under his hand.

He let her run until he found himself nearing the cove where Uncle Joe's dock jutted into the lake, and Uncle Joe himself was working on his speedboat. "Ahoy!" he cried, releasing a hand to wave.

"Ahoy yourself!" his uncle answered. "She's looking good!"

Brian jibed, bringing the boat around into the wind. "Yeah," he agreed, drifting a few feet from the dock. "Jon says you're going to let ten-year-olds race this year."

"You want to sail and swim both? I'm counting on you for the swim team."

"Sure. Why not?" He shrugged.

"'Cause I'll work you to death, that's why." His uncle climbed out of his boat and came to the end of the dock.

"That's okay."

His uncle frowned, considering. "I don't have many ten-year-olds sailing Lasers, but okay—we'll give it a try. Bring her over next Tuesday, and we'll see if we have enough boats to make a go of it."

"Over at the main dock?" His uncle ran sail races from the Wolfsons' Lake Michigan charter business.

"No, no, here. We'll sail on Fontenac—much better sailing for the little guys." He nodded at the *Lightning Pup.* "Meanwhile, you show up for swim team day after tomorrow, okay?"

"Promise!" He swung the rudder. "Bye!" He laughed as the boat caught the wind, his heart glowing with his importance to Uncle Joe's swim team. And a sail team too!

He tacked into the wind, back and forth, back and forth until his muscles responded automatically to shifts in the pitch of the boat, losing himself in the rhythm of it. When he passed his own house, no one was on the dock. She'd gone back to her garden or potting shed. He chuckled and went on past his grandpa's white shingled, many-windowed house with its wide green lawn, then rounded the bend to the public beach.

He came off the wind, slowed the boat and studied the group of kids on shore and puttering about on paddleboards.

He was almost past the beach when he saw Annie throw her towel on the sand and race for the water. She dove, came up and swam a dozen strokes before standing up and shaking the water from her hair.

"Ahoy!" he cried, before he'd even thought about it. "Annie!"

She looked around and waved, then swam toward the boat with swift, clean strokes.

"What are you doing here?" she grabbed the gunwale.

"Just sailing by," he said. "Want to come?"

"What? Sailing?"

"Sure."

"Never did that."

"That's okay. You don't have to do anything, just ride. Come on, you can swim at our beach."

"Your beach." She laughed. "You have a beach of your own?"

"Back there." He gestured behind him.

She followed his nod, and the smile fell from her face. "That's Wolfsons'."

"Yeah. So what?"

"You a Wolfson?"

"Yeah, so …? That doesn't matter. Come on!"

She glanced back at the beach as though looking for someone, then again at his eager face.

"Just climb over the stern," he urged.

She gave a sudden laugh and a kick, bringing her up over the back end of the boat. He let go of the rudder to give her a pull and the boat flopped about in a dizzy circle, making them laugh all the harder.

Chapter 5

2007

Annika's long strokes failed to perform their magic. The sense of things gone wrong tightened her arms, threw off her rhythm. The evergreens crowded the shore, chilling the water. She turned back toward the dock. She had to be doing—find him. Not wait for Jonathan. The odd tone in Carmen's voice had taken up residence in the back of her brain, as though the answer lay somewhere in that household.

When she'd toweled dry and dressed, she pointed the Jeep along the lakeshore toward her in-laws. The Wolfson land was a quarter mile of woodland, beaches and farmland between Lake Frontenac and Lake Michigan, remnants of the square mile homesteaded by their ancestors in the nineteenth century. Whenever she drove within its bounds, Annika heard her father's rage when she'd announced she was going to be on the swim team. The Wolfson Yacht Club swim team.

~

"What did you say?" Her father reared up in his chair, his bony hands clenching the arm rests.

Out of the corner of her eye, Annika saw her mother come to the kitchen door, wiping her hands on a dish towel, her sister, Stephanie, hovering behind. She didn't need to look to see the scowl of alarm on both of their faces. Her mother had told her to leave the telling to her, but Annika'd gone and blurted it out when he'd asked what she was going to do with her summer. "I said I'm going to be on the yacht club swim team. Mr. Wolfson asked me." She watched his face redden. "The other Mr. Wolfson!"

"So just like that you're going over to the Wolfsons! Deserting your family for the rich yellow-bellied …" He waved his arms in frustration and disbelief.

Annika gripped the back of the chair that stood between her and her father. "I'm not! It's not that Mr.—"

"Don't backtalk me, young lady—" Tom Berglund rose to his full height. *"You're a Berglund! Hear me? Your father fought! Fought! Came home half-crazy and without a leg and those lily-livered bastards stood jeering at us—jeering at us!"*

"Tom!"

He stopped at his wife's cry and licked his lips. "She knows that, Maggie, and she goes and joins—"

"No!" She gripped his arm, cutting him off. "It's Joe Wolfson's team, not Karl's."

"That makes no difference. A Wolfson's a Wolfson, cozy in their castles while we crawled in the jungle. I didn't raise my kids to kiss ass with that crowd."

"No, Tom. Joe Wolfson went to Vietnam, just like you."

Annika's muscles relaxed at the calm, firm tone that had so often stood between her father's explosions and a fate that came only in nightmares. But never had that rage been directed at her. The knot in her stomach remained.

"Not like me, Maggie. He was an officer," her father muttered, but the steam had gone out of his voice. "They're still rich bastards."

"She only wants to swim, Dad. That's all. Just swim,"

Annika felt tears of gratitude at her nearly grown-up sister's support.

"On a Wolfson team! And who's going to pay for you to join the yacht club, sweetie. Tell me that!"

"I have a scholarship."

"A scholarship? To a swim team? Godamighty, what's the world coming to? You have to have a scholarship to swim with the rich kids when all around you there's free water! How'd you get hooked up with that bunch, anyway?"

Annika froze. She didn't dare mention Brian or swimming off the Wolfson's float. "Just from kids at the beach. I was racing with them." Well, it wasn't a lie, quite. She did race with kids at the beach.

"Give her the chance, Tom. Joe Wolfson's done you no harm."

With a huff, Tom Berglund sank back into his chair. "Well, I don't like it. She'll be thinking she's one of them. You just wait."

"No, I won't. Promise," Annika almost shouted. "I really won't!"

～

And here she was, Annika Wolfson, passing the many-gabled white clapboard house of Markus Wolfson, founder of Wolfson Charters, who she now called "Papa" as the rest of the Wolfsons did. She now knew him as the first Wolfson to forsake farming for the water, starting with a couple of pontoon boats that toured the lake, the rivers, and the Lake Michigan shoreline.

She also knew him as an old man who held his family together with the force of his personality. At his annual Labor Day picnic, just past, his rugged sun-baked jaw had clamped as he perused his family, sitting at separate tables on the wide lawn, his wife Melissa moving from one group to the other, denying the split. "Okay Joe! Karl! Time to see if you can still race those crates down there!" He did it every year, and every year, for an hour, Joe and Karl became kids again, chasing each in their old dinghies with yells and jeers and laughter. And on shore Papa drew Melissa close and watched, the house's glassed-in porches glittering in the sun behind them. Now she could hear the sound of a mower, probably Papa himself, from the wide lawn between the house and the lake.

Was she a Wolfson now? Adopted by Uncle Joe, who had, in turn, forsaken pontoon boats for yachts big enough to plow the big lake. It was Joe who'd gotten her scholarships. His was the glass and steel mansion that dominated the shoreline at the far end of the property. A childless widower, he'd taken Brian and then her under his wing then added a much younger second wife, Suzanne. Joe *was* a rich man, surely, but also her mentor since that fateful day she'd first jumped into the yacht club pool.

It was Karl, Joe's younger brother, who'd been her father's closest high school friend until the day they graduated, when her father exchanged cap and gown for an Army uniform and Karl went off to college—and joined the protest movement. She never knew whether he was in that jeering crowd, but it didn't matter. Karl's betrayal remained an open the wound. Her father's bitterness rose in her whenever she was buried in the PTSD-shaped lives of her family. But Karl was Brian's father. And it was Karl who'd rejected the life of wealth and returned to the family's pioneer roots.

On the other side of the road from Papa's, the ancient orchards of the original Wolfsons stretched in the sun, the barn and outbuildings bleached gray, the gnarled old trees buzzing with dragonflies and honey-bees. Ahead, a lone grove of oaks surrounded the original stone farmhouse Karl and Carmen now occupied. Brian's home. Her-in-laws. She was family. Traitor?

Annika turned in at the drive of the old house. She loved its grass-encrusted stone walkways, moss-covered patio, high-beamed ceilings and time-blackened stone fireplace. She'd felt, in the house and its occupants, a comforting reunion with the land. Its chronic disorder, which drove Brian crazy, was, for her, more comfortable than the sharp modern lines of Joe's and Suzanne's.

No one answered her knock at screened porch door. She opened it and knocked again on the interior door. She was answered only by the parrot's "Hello there! Hello there!"

A wet nose on her bare leg turned her around. "Morning, Bruno, where did she go? I bet she's out back, isn't she?"

Bruno's tail thumped against a porch chair.

Annika went around to the potter's shed and found her mother-in-law vigorously mixing a tub of clay. "Good morning."

Carmen's head jerked up. "Annika! Lordy, you scared me!" She picked up her paddle again. "Just a minute until I get this stuff … can't leave it …" Her words were sucked into the motion of her arms and shoulders.

Annika stood watching the paddle, her tongue frozen against the sides of her mouth.

"There," Carmen announced. She lifted the paddle, covered the tub, rinsed her hands, and turned around. "Now. What brings you … oh, no, don't tell me that boy hasn't called yet."

"He hasn't, and I'm worried. The Bar Harbor airport says he got there, but …" She paused at Carmen's shaking head.

"That still doesn't make any sense!" She broke off head shaking and crinkled her nose. "Hold on." She pulled her cell phone from her apron pocket and dialed.

They both stood listening as the relay took the call to voicemail.

"No cell service, as usual." Carmen gave a huff. "Well, he'll be back tonight, and I guess we'll just have to wait."

"Jonathan?"

She nodded. "He's up on the Fox." She turned back to her work table.

Annika gazed at her back, at a loss on how to go on. Was it Carmen's muddled brain or did she know something? "Why?" She waved a hand, brushing away her own question. "I mean I'm confused about this whole thing. He said he was going sailing with old friends from college, and it turns out they're Jonathan's friends … but Jonathan didn't run with that crowd …" She let her voice trail off.

Carmen turned and spread her hands. "Well, they're brothers."

Annika blinked. Whatever they'd been once, they were hardly buddies now. Jonathan's life was the wilderness, Brian's the swim meet. Papa and Melissa pulled the family together with barbeques and holiday feasts, but on a day-to-day basis, they had as little to do with each other as their father and Uncle Joe. Papa could command the condescending peace that reigned between the two factions, not the relationship Carmen was suggesting. "If you know anything, Carmen, please tell me. I'm frightened."

Carmen wiped her hands. "Come on, let's have coffee." She took Annika's arm and led her out of the shed, then turned and closed the door. Stuffing her hands into her apron pockets, eyes on the path, she led the way to the house, then, with the same preoccupation, started the coffee pot. It wasn't until they sat opposite in the breakfast nook that she seemed to make up her mind.

"All I know is Jonathan was scheduled to take a group up the Fox, but then Karl told me he was going instead—that Jonathan had been invited to go sailing. As you can imagine, Karl wasn't pleased that Jonathan was taking off that way." She stopped and stared at the daisies on the ancient oilcloth table cover. "I thought it was odd. Jon and Karl just don't stand each other up. But then at the last minute Karl said Brian was going instead. On the sail trip." She threw up her hands and rolled her eyes. "That was even more wrong, so soon after—" Her eyes widened. "Good grief, I didn't even ask. How are you doing?"

"I'm okay, except for this …" Annika's voice faded off as she realized how thoroughly anxiety had driven grief into the background.

"Well, I don't know what he was thinking, going off that way." Carmen frowned, staring at a fly knocking against the windowpane. "What was so important he'd do that?"

Annika spread her hands. "I don't know. Did Jonathan say anything about who he was going with?"

"No. When you asked about them this morning, that was the first time I'd heard those names since Jon's college days."

"He hasn't gone sailing with them before?" Annika frowned. The whole thing was getting stranger and stranger.

"Not that I know about. And not in season." Carmen got up to get coffee.

"Not from Bar Harbor?"

Her mother-in-law gave a huff. "I don't know anything about Bar Harbor. I didn't know he was taking a flight until you called. I just assumed they were going out from here. Why on earth wouldn't they?" She thumped the cups down on the table then swore as they slopped. "I don't understand any of it," she finished, retrieving a cloth from the sink to mop up. "Victoria might know more about those friends."

Annika started at Carmen's use of her ex-daughter-in-law's formal name, then remembered that while she was accepted as a local kid, even though she was a Berglund, Carmen had always treated Jonathan's wife as an alien intrusion. "Why would she? Is Jon still in touch with her?"

"Not that I know of, but she was in the university sail club, back then." She wrung out the cloth, "So she may know those names you mentioned—and where they are." Carmen returned to the table and sat down.

Annika looked at her watch. "Do you have her address or phone number?" And why didn't she have it? Why had she let Vicky go off without trying to stay in contact?

"No, but Papa or Joe probably do. She's big in the Traverse City Yacht Club, so they still connect with her once in a while." Carmen took a sip of coffee and managed a half smile. "Papa even likes her."

Annika winced. How could a family so given to flying apart remain so stuck together? It was as though the world had split in the Sixties, and she and Brian, each bonded to one side and drawn to the other, were fated to cobble, or re-cobble, it together again—or live on a tightrope between the two.

Vicky's and Jonathan's marriage had failed in that attempt. She and Jonathan found each other in the college sail club and stuck together when he quit sailing and went off kayaking with the Sierra Club. But then they moved back to Fontenac and the tangle of family. Annika liked her. They came from different worlds but shared the frustrations of finding their way among the Wolfsons. But there was so little time. She was in training, at the pool hours every day, and Vicky got fed up trying to create a middle ground. "Jon doesn't see the big deal. It's normal to him. But I can't find a place to be." She'd thrown up her hands. "Carmen thinks I'm a debutant, and she always will. I'm done, Annie."

And so she'd left. Annika missed her. She hadn't realized how much she counted on Vicky to ease her way into the wilderness side of the family—or how much she wanted that. But not today. She rose and took her cup to the sink. Carmen stayed gazing out of the window. "I'll stop and ask Papa. He was out mowing when I passed."

Her mother-in-law roused herself from whatever thoughts had so absorbed her. "Do that."

"Thank you, Carmen. You've been a help."

"I have?" Carmen turned her head. "I think I've only confused things further."

"It helps to talk to someone. But I've got to move along if I'm going to go to Traverse City and back before Sadie gets home."

"Right. And I need to get to that batch of clay." She rose. "Let me know, though, Annika." She frowned. "I hope Jonathan hasn't gotten Brian into something."

Annika stopped. Chilled. "You think he might have?"

Carmen shrugged. "Not really, but it's all very … unsettling."

"That's putting it mildly." She gave Carmen a hug and headed for the door.

The mower was silent when she passed the senior Wolfson house, but she found Papa washing up in the garden shed.

"Morning!" He shook water off his hands and reached for a towel. "Glad to see you about again." He gave her a sharp look. "You're still white as a sheet, though. What brings you out?"

Annika smiled at his habitual warmth, distracted for a moment from her task. "I'm doing okay." She paused for several beats. "Well, the fact is Brian … he went on a sail trip out of Bar Harbor. Did you know that?"

"Hell no. Why'd he do that?" He tossed the towel aside. "When?"

"Two weeks ago." She paused at his frown. "He wanted to sail the Atlantic, Papa, which was okay, but … but he hasn't come back and I don't know where he is." The words came in a rush.

Papa frowned. "He didn't call?"

"No, and his cell-phone goes to voicemail."

"Hmph." He turned for the house and beckoned her to follow. "He would have called."

"I know." The reassurances of others dissolved in the face of this simple truth. Brian always called, even if he was just late for dinner.

The old man opened the kitchen door and held it for her. Without further comment, he went to the phone and punched in numbers. "Joe? What do you know about this sail trip Brian went on?" He voice had lost its easy heartiness. "Oh, yeah?" He listened for a moment. "So Annie told me. … yeah. I know. He didn't say anything else? … Why the hell did he want to go all the way to Bar Harbor to sail for God's sake? … But why now? It was a hell of a time to leave Annie …"

The sound of the two men's bewilderment brought a sense of connections coming apart. Where was she in this tangle? Where did it start?

They jumped together from the float, but Brian swam off in a different direction, and she paused, uncertain.

"This way!" he cried. He headed toward a distant Wolfson dock, and she could do nothing but follow until they stopped beneath the deck shoes of a burly man with dark curly hair like Brian's. "Meet Uncle Joe."

"This is Annie," Brian announced. "You have to put her on the swim team. The girls' team."

"I do, huh?" The man put his hands on his hips. "Hullo, Annie."

"She's fast. Really fast," Brian insisted.

"Yeah? And do you want to be on the swim team, Annie?"

She nodded, only vaguely aware of what it was about.

"Uncle Joe runs the swim teams at the Club."

"What club?" She shivered, suddenly afraid.

"The Yacht Club, silly!"

"Oh." She shook her head. "I don't go there." That was Wolfsons.

"Sure you do!" He turned to the man. "Uncle Joe, tell her. Tell her anyone can be on the team."

"If you're fast enough," Uncle Joe agreed. "I tell you what. Let's see you race Brian to …" he gazed about, "… to that buoy off the headland." He pointed. "You can dive off the dock."

"Right. Come on, Annie."

She'd never raced when it mattered, but Brian seemed to fill her with air. They collided at the buoy, exploding air in laughter.

⚓

That was the beginning. The day she'd discovered she could fly.

"Yeah? Well I'll let you know what I find out." She came back to the present as Papa punched the disconnect and turned to her. "All Joe knows is that Brian was filling in for Jonathan. He's supposed to be at the pool today. They have a big meet Friday."

"I know. And Brian was anxious about it."

"So who are these guys he went with? Joe says they're old college friends." He picked up the coffee pot.

"Nils Svenson and Dominic Costello. They were members of the UM sailing club. I think I met them once, but Carmen says they were Jonathan's friends."

"Hmph. Local?" He poured two cups of coffee and handed her one.

"I don't know. I looked through Brian's stuff and couldn't find anything except pictures in an old yearbook." She sank down at the table. "Carmen says Brian went instead of Jonathan, and I found an email about their meeting at the boat, but ..." Her voice trailed off.

"But what?"

"The message didn't sound like old friends, that's all. Too formal."

"Well we'd better ask Jonathan." He picked up the phone again and lowered his big frame into a chair.

"He's up on the Fox," she told him as he dialed. "No cell service. He'll be back tonight. Their names aren't in his Roladek. Karen looked for me."

He knit his heavy brows and his blue eyes drilled into hers. "What's going on with him? Joe says he's been in a mood. Wouldn't talk."

The habit of privacy Annika had developed over the years, dissolved at the compassion in the old man's eyes. "He's been different ... since I lost the baby."

Without warning, she was in the bathroom again, bleeding, cramping ... Brian's face rose up blank with shock. *"No no ... Annie! NO!"*

He'd swept her up, driven for the hospital like a madman. But it was too late. It had always been too late, the doctor told her. Miscarriages were common in the first trimester—nothing she could have done. Brian had stood white-faced, shaking his head. His hand, when he touched her arm, was cold. He struggled for words, but none came. Then he'd bolted. There was no other word for it. Bolted, muttering that he had to get Sadie, leaving her staring at the empty doorway.

She struggled to keep her voice steady. "I don't know, Papa, ..." She broke off. "He wouldn't talk to me either, and ..." She hesitated then went on. "He wanted me to get going ... to start swimming again ..." She raised her shoulders and let them fall.

"So soon?" He put a hand over hers. "To get over it, I suppose? He's like that. Like Joe."

"I guess ..." But that answer didn't fit. And over and over he'd disappeared for hours at a time.

Papa patted her hand. "A bad business. Melissa says you were pretty broken up."

Annika raised her head. "She was very kind." Brian's grandmother, who usually treated Annika as though she and Brian were the same children who had run in and out of her house for cookies, had suddenly treated her as an adult—a woman.

He nodded. "She was worried. But we told her you were strong. You'd get back on your feet."

"I have," she said, though it was a lie. The hole inside remained empty. "But now ... this ... I don't know what to make of it all."

He took a drink. "Nor do I. It doesn't set right, I'll tell you that."

"Carmen thought Vicky might know those guys. She was in the sailing club."

"Hm! She might at that." He pushed himself to his feet and went back to the phone. "Joe?" he barked a moment later. "Look under the Traverse yacht club and see if we have Vicky's number, will you? She might help track down those guys." A few minutes later he jotted down some numbers. "Got an address?" He jotted some more. "Thanks. I'll let you know what we find out. ... Yeah. Let's hope." He disconnected and turned to her. "Here you are."

"Thanks." She took the paper. "I keep trying to remember the day I met them—whether Vicky was there. I don't think she was."

"Well?"

Annika shook her head. "Just trying to get a fix on why we were there—with them."

"Well, let's see if she can shed some light on it." He punched in a number, and Annika could hear the voice-mail message. Papa hung up and dialed another number. "Maybe she's at the Club," he explained as he waited for an answer.

Annika gazed at him, forever wondering at the energy that never deserted him and grateful that he'd seized the initiative as she grew increasingly confused and bewildered.

"Morning. Markus Wolfson here, from Frontenac. I'm looking for Vicky Wolfson—no, Hargrave, it'll be. Vicky Hargrave." As he waited, Annika wondered how well he'd kept in touch with his grandson's ex-wife. "Ah. Too bad. Would you ask her to call me when she gets back? Markus Wolfson." He gave her the number and put the phone down. "Hm. She's at home today—doesn't work Mondays. So why didn't she answer? You young people's habit of screening calls is a giant pain."

"She might have been in the shower or gone shopping." Annika looked at her watch.

"Okay. I'll try again later."

"No, don't. I'll go. If I talk to her in person, I might remember more about what Brian did with the sail club."

"Go to Traverse?" He sounded doubtful. "Sure you're up to that?"

"Yes. I'll ask Carmen to meet the school bus and keep Sadie for me." She rose. "Thank you, Papa. You've been a help. I'll let you know what I find out."

"Or if you remember anything."

"Oh. I did find out the name of the ship—from that email. It's the *Wayfarer.*"

"Good." He made a note. "I'll see what I can find out about her."

Chapter 6

After a brief stop at Carmen's to make arrangements for Sadie, Annika headed for Traverse City. As soon as she was on the open road, she began to wonder why she was squandering two hours to talk to someone she could, eventually, get by phone. To fill up the hours until Jonathan returned? Because she couldn't think of anything else to do? No, she decided, because she missed Vicky. The svelte and beautiful Vicky had intimidated her when they were the new brides of the Wolfson boys, but she'd counted on Vicky, married a couple of years ahead of her, to clue her in to the split that ran like a scar between the branches. And Vicky was at home in the yachting world. She was an Easterner—a Bostonian, in fact. Maybe she'd known the others at that table.

An hour later, she pulled up at a new wood and glass condo complex on the Traverse City waterfront. This was it. No one answered the bell. Damn. So why did she think she'd be home? Why should she be on her day off? She stomped back to her car in frustration.

"Annika?"

She turned.

"It is you!" Vicky, her arms loaded with grocery sacks, slammed her car door with a hip. "What brings you down here?"

"Hello! Thank goodness. I was afraid I'd missed you." In that moment, the sun glittering off the water behind a lovely blonde in beige linen capris, Annika's mission seemed incongruous. She was at a loss about where to start. "Something ... I need to talk to you, if you have time."

"Sure." Vicky frowned, puzzled. "Come on up."

"Let me help. Is that all?"

"Yep." Vicky handed over a sack.

They mounted the stairs to the apartment, a vision in glass, chrome and black leather, dashed here and there with orange and rust throw rugs and bright pillows. Vicky busied herself putting things away while Annika gazed out at the scattering of boats enjoying the September day. Older people reveling in the absence of summer crowds. The scene seemed to laugh at her panic, and she turned away.

"Coffee?"

"Yes, thank you." She watched in silence as Vicky filled and started the pot then crossed to her. "Brian went sailing with two friends of Jonathan's ... and I'm hoping you know them ... because he didn't come home."

Vicky's eyes widened. "What? When?" Her brows puckered. "Sit down and make sense, Annika. Please." Her voice held the concern of the friend she'd been, and Annika sank to a leather cube, only to jump up again.

"Sorry. I'm better this way." She ran her hands down her jeans to calm herself. "Jonathan was supposed to go sailing out of Bar Harbor with two men ... Nils Svenson and Dominic Costello. They were in the sailing club at Michigan ... but Brian went instead." There. She had it out. "Do you remember them? He said I met them at *Cottage Inn.* I don't remember whether you were there." She paused, her eyes a question.

Vicky frowned. "I don't remember that, but they were sail club people ..." She crossed the room and sat on the couch. "But I wouldn't have thought Jon would be ..." She frowned. "He sailed with the wet-bottom crowd, the 440s. Only once or twice on the big-lake trips."

"I think … it had something to do with introducing Brian. They were racers. Brian wanted to race." She paused as more memory returned. "I was on the swim team, and he couldn't be, with his bad leg …" Her voice faded.

"So he turned to sail racing."

"Was one of them from Boston? Do you remember?"

Vicky stared at the wall as though searching memory. "Nils. Dominic was from Chicago. They were always joshing each other … sailing the Atlantic versus the Great Lakes. Long distance sailors as well as racers, both of them, always up for the next challenge."

"That sounds like Brian." The words popped out without thought, but it was true. His eyes were always fixed on some distant star. It excited her, lifted her from her own sense of limited possibilities.

"But not Jonathan. He wasn't into racing, or big boats. So why would he be going …?" Vicky shook her head. "And Brian went with instead?" She waited for Annika to go on.

"From Bar Harbor. Yes. He was due home yesterday. He wasn't on his flight or the next one, and he hasn't called."

"That's not like him, is it? Especially when …" She stopped, searching for words. "Jon told me about the baby, Annika. I was away and couldn't come. I'm so sorry." She patted the couch beside her.

"Thanks." Annika crossed and sat down. "It was so sudden … we'd just told the family I was pregnant … when I lost it." She stumbled at the last word. "But I'm okay now. Dealing with it …" She choked.

"Right." She squeezed Annika's hand. "You don't look yourself."

"I'm really okay, but this has …" She stopped, unable to find the words.

"How did Brian take it?"

"Losing the baby? Not well. He was … thrown. Well, we both were. Like he didn't know what to do … all his confidence … just zapped. He kept running off and coming back. Then he announced ..." She waved a hand. "... this trip. Out of the blue."

"Impulsive. Well, he was always that." Vicky's eyes drilled into hers. "Sounds like things weren't going too well."

"He had his heart set on the China Olympics—" She broke off, startled at the pronoun she'd used. But it had opened a door, letting her mind go back. One day, the enthusiastic Brian was back, cheering her on, the light in his eyes making her fly again. The next, he'd be a ferocious version of himself, hands on hips at the end of the dock—"*Stroke! Stroke! Harder! Harder!*" The voice that had made her blood race carried a new tone—one that stiffened her arms and turned her rhythm to churning. "He was driving me like his life depended on it." His face rose, standing above her, eyes burning with some need from deep inside, something that had nothing to do with her.

"Did he know you were pregnant?" Vicky sounded surprised.

"Yes." She remembered well his bewildered look when she'd told him. Not understanding how this could happen, though he was the one who rejected protections. "He wasn't too happy ... no, that's not right, more thrown off course. But I reminded him that I trained when I was pregnant with Sadie, which made it okay." She gazed out the window at the sunlit bay. "Except it wasn't. I was slower this time."

"And he didn't like it," Vicky finished for her.

"Well, not enough to vanish, for heaven's sake." Annika pulled herself back to the present. "And I was getting faster ..." her voice faded as she groped for memory.

"But then you miscarried." Vicky jumped up and went to the kitchen, returning with filled coffee cups. "It does seem a strange time to go off like that." She returned to the couch. "Brian is a driver. I always admired that in him." She laughed as she came back and sat down. "In fact, there were times when I thought you and I had married the wrong brothers."

Annika slopped coffee. "What?"

"Don't worry. Nothing like that." She patted Annika's hand. "There was something about you that didn't fit the mold, that's all."

"Of an Olympian?" Annika was half offended.

Vicky nodded. "You're a beautiful swimmer. I love to watch you, but ... it's not the same."

"What do you mean, not the same. I've been headed there all my life—almost?"

"I know, but ... you're different, somehow. Anyway, I don't see why he was pushing you so hard if you were pregnant. That's all."

"There was something missing. From me, I think." She stood up. "Anyway, it has nothing to do with this. Would you have the addresses for those guys, Vicky? Some way we can contact them?"

"Right." Vicky frowned. "I don't know. Three of us women sailed with them once, up to Georgian Bay. It didn't take long to discover they didn't invite us along to pull sails." She made a face. "I don't think any of us went again." She paused, thinking. "I might still have their phone numbers, if I can find them ... but they would be Ann Arbor numbers, Annika. What good would that do you?"

"I don't know, but they might—"

"No, wait a minute ... I was secretary of the club for a while. The membership list might have more." She headed for the door. "Wait here. I'm going to my storage locker."

Annika paced as she waited. Her hands were cold and her mind full of Brian's stricken face when she'd begun to bleed. To her it had meant he wanted that baby, so something in her was relieved. They'd rushed to the hospital, but it was too late. She'd wakened from a drug induced doze to see him sitting there with his head in his hands.

Her cell phone cut off further memories. "Hello, this is Annika."

"Papa here. The harbormaster called. At Bar Harbor. The *Wayfarer* is in dock. Came in Saturday."

She sat down. "Saturday." Her mind spun. "The timing would be right. Does he remember how many were aboard?"

"He's not sure. He says he chatted with Svenson. Seemed to know him, and he remembers another man tending the sails. He didn't see anyone else, but there might have been someone below deck."

"But he didn't see him." Annika frowned.

"Nope. But he did say that ordinarily they wouldn't sail without at least a third man. The *Wayfarer* is a fifty-footer. He also said the Bar Harbor Yacht Club would have an address and phone for Svenson, so I called and got that."

"Oh, good," she exclaimed. "Wonderful. Wait ..." She turned to find her purse, took out her pen and grabbed a pad from the counter. "Okay, ready." She jotted down a Boston address and phone. "Thank you so very very much, Papa. I'll let you know what I find out."

"Do that. At least they're not on the high seas. Which is some sort of relief, I guess."

"It is." She said goodbye and punched the disconnect just as Vicky came back. "Papa just called. The boat is in dock, and I have the address and phone for Nils Svenson."

"Great, because all my list shows are Ann Arbor addresses." Vicky waved a paper, then crossed to the couch and sat down again. "So call."

Annika looked at the note and stared, frozen.

"Now." Vicky handed her a land line phone. "Use this."

Buoyed by her support, Annika sat down and punched in the number. She watched silently as Vicky picked up an extension. It rang and rang.

"Sun Time Charters," a female voice sang out just as voicemail cut in.

"I'm looking for Nils Svenson. Is he in?"

"May I say who's calling?"

"Annika Wolfson."

"One moment, please."

"Svenson here," a gruff voice barked.

Annika jerked in surprise. "Hello. This is Nils Svenson?"

"Speaking." The voice clipped.

"This is Annika Wolfson. I'm looking for Brian—my husband."

"Yes?"

"He went sailing with you," Annika began, thrown by the mono-syllabic reply. "This past week—and he didn't come home. Do you know where he went?"

"Couldn't tell you." His indifference was edged with impatience, or something else she couldn't identify.

"Well, did he come back with you? Get off the boat at Bar Harbor?"

"Sure. Headed for the airport—or I assumed that's where he was going." The voice was flat.

Something in her wanted to yell, *I don't believe you!* She looked instead at Vicky who was shaking her head, her lips pursed.

"Sorry." Nils' voice was a period and the phone went dead.

Annika stared at it.

"He's lying." Vicky's voice was certain.

"For sure. But about what? And why?"

Vicky shook her head. "I don't like that man. That's all I know."

"Ditto. And I'm going to find out. Their trip is sounding less and less like a joy ride." Annika jumped up and began to pace.

"I agree. So … what are you going to do?"

She swung around. "Go. To Bar Harbor."

"Not alone you aren't. Look, I come from that country. Give me a day to clear my schedule, and I'll go with you."

"Would you? That would be … a relief." Annika grinned.

"Absolutely. That man made me cringe." She got up. "Just give me a day to clear the decks."

"Right. I'm not going until I talk with Jonathan in any case. He gets back tonight."

"Good. I want to know what he has to do with that guy." Vicky made a face at the dead phone in her hand and put it down.

Annika glanced at her watch. "I need to go. Carmen is keeping Sadie for me, and I won't get back until dinner time."

"How is Sadie? I miss her."

"Growing." Annika smiled. "Learning to read! It's great fun to watch." She sobered."But confused. She wants to know where her Daddy is." She rose. "She'll be frightened if I don't get back. How am I going to reassure her this time?"

"Tell her it's just a mix-up, I guess. I don't know."

Annika sighed. "Neither do I, but …" She headed for the door. "I need to go."

Vicky followed her. "It was good to see you again."

There was a sincerity in her voice that made Annika turn, surprised. She'd never thought she shared more with her fashionable sister-in-law than their position as outsiders in the clan.

Vicky smiled at her surprise. "I've missed our talks."

Annika gave a laugh, realizing how much better she felt. "Thank you."

Chapter 7

Brian

1990

Brian swam in murky waters, batting away fish, eels and branches, sinking deeper, flailing now against a current that was sweeping him into a hole ...

He woke with a start, already throwing back the covers, fleeing the bed, and stumbled—his left knee refusing his weight. He caught himself with a curse, then stood staring out of the window at the snow covered orchard just emerging from darkness. Just a day. Three months of days, but he was winning. Defeating the eyes that didn't light up when he insisted he would race again. Again and again, he rocked onto the bad leg, ignoring the pain, until it responded to his weight.

He crossed the room to the treadmill and began the first workout of the day, his mind fixed on the weekend's meet. Lulled by the rhythm of his feet, thoughts wandering back into the fog of that day, still filled mostly by the accounts of others. He remembered leaving the pool with Annie, encountering Eddy waiting for her on the wharf, yelling at her to *"leave that Wolfson shit alone!"*

He yelled back at him, then it all went fuzzy, faded into the nightmare, battling fish, being swept toward a hole ... waking as the fish became pain, and he couldn't move at all. Annie's face above him, saying something he couldn't hear. He locked his eyes on her, pulling himself away from the hole. "Where … what happened?" His voice sounded hoarse, a muttering.

"You tried to climb the rigging of *The Empress.*"

"Wha …?"

"It was my fault. 'Cause I wouldn't go with him. He dared you."

Her face receded into fog.

"Don't tell them it was Eddy … please …"

The next time he awoke, his parents' faces had replaced hers. Exasperated, worried.

"Breakfast, Brian!" His mother's voice broke through, returning him to the present.

Damn. He wasn't dressed, as usual. "Okay," he answered, dismounting and scrambling for his clothes. He'd get a shower at the pool.

He grabbed the rail and descended the stairs, forcing his bad leg to perform by muttering at his knee—*grab, grab, grab.*

"Morning," She eyed him critically. "Eggs?"

"I'll fix 'em," he said. He'd cured her of treating him like a cripple as soon as he got home from the hospital.

"No time," she answered. "Come on, it won't kill you to let me do it. You make the toast."

He glanced at the clock and shrugged. No point in arguing when she was right. "Guess I'll have to take Jon's car," he commented, pushing the lever on the toaster. After a term at UM, Jon had given up having a car on campus and bequeathed their father's old Jetta to Brian with a dozen orders on its care.

His mother glanced out the window, then up at the ceiling where they'd heard the shower go on a few minutes before. "I guess." She frowned.

The toast popped, and he buttered it. "There's no way I can wait for Dad, and I've been driving for a week. The leg's fine with it."

She smiled. "Reading my mind, huh?" She put a plate of eggs in front of him. "Okay, but be careful. It's icy, and you're a novice driver, like it or not."

"But I learned at the hands of a master," he quipped and dug into his breakfast, remembering the spells, not long but frequent, spent showing his father how attentive and careful he could be. It was a good time. His mother sat across the table lost in her own thoughts, but watching him, nevertheless.

"I love the confidence that's grown in you since Jon's been gone."

He looked up, surprised.

"And the way you've come back from the accident is great. Truly impressive."

"But?"

"No buts. I just hope the accident makes you realize you don't have to live in Joe's world, racing to be number one all the time."

"Stop blaming it on Joe, Mother. He had nothing to do with it."

"Mothers worry. It's incurable."

"Don't." He jumped up before she could go on. "See you after practice." He dropped a kiss on her graying head, grabbed his backpack and the keys to the Jetta, glanced at his cane and rejected it, then headed for the garage. He'd helped Dad shovel the drive, last night, too. Things were coming along fine. He'd suit up today, though he probably wouldn't be fast enough yet to swim in the meet this weekend. Annie would be swimming though.

School hours dragged. There was too much time for worrying, then feeling that downward pull. At lunch his eyes sought Annie, but didn't find her. He was heading toward the swim team table when he spotted her just coming out of the food line clutching a paper bag and a carton of milk. "Yo!" He waved, and was relieved when she grinned and headed his way. Everyone thought of them as a pair even though she was just a freshman—which was okay with him, but he was never quite sure about Annie. Sometimes she was with public beach friends who had nothing to do with the teams, and there was always the threat that her brother might win. She might desert the Wolfsons. Eddy'd graduated in June, but he still hung out with the high school crowd.

"Whew!" she exclaimed, taking the seat opposite. "Algebra test this morning."

"Did you ace it?"

"Ha. But I passed, I think. If I could get over being scared stiff, I might even like the stuff."

"Keep that a secret." He attacked his hamburger.

"You coming to practice today?" she asked, following suit.

"Yeah. It's time trials."

"Is Joe going to let you swim?" She took a bite of ham sandwich.

"He said he would."

They ate in silence, letting the racket of the cafeteria fill the space between them.

"Eddy picking you up?"

"Uh uh. He got a job. Out at the motorcycle place on the highway. They let him test cycles for the repair shop."

"I bet he's cool with that."

"He loves it." She gave him a long look. "You won't be bothered with him anymore, I don't think. He's totally into learning the repair trade."

"Good."

"Anyway, I'm taking the bus. The city bus." She gathered her paper stuff as the warning bell rang.

"I have Jon's car. I'll take you."

"You're driving?" Her brows shot up. "That's great! Maybe you *will* be ready for State."

Two hours later, they were at the yacht club pool, swimming side by side. Usually boys and girls trained separately, but today was time trials for State. He felt the old energy returning. The leg was clumsy, but he could keep pace with her during practice, and his endurance was coming back. If the doctors would turn him loose, he'd been down here working out before school every day. He knew Uncle Joe had only kept him on the team to be kind, but he'd show him.

The whistle blew for the end of warm-up, and they climbed out and into their sweats. Joe joined his assistant at water's edge with a list of races in his hand. He led off with freestyle, and Annie was in the first heat.

Brian whooped at her. *"Stroke! Stroke! Hit it! Hit it ..."* and it happened. That old feeling of feeding each other energy. *"H'ray!"* He read the time on the board. *"Look at that! I bet it's a record!"*

"I could feel you!" she exclaimed, climbing out of the pool. "I could. Like always!" She threw her arms around him.

"Okay, okay love birds," Joe said behind her.

She broke free and turned.

"Damned good!" Joe exclaimed. "A personal best, I think."

Annie clasped her hands and jumped up and down, then turned again and gave him a hug. "I'm so glad you're back I could—"

"Annika Berglund please come to the office. Annika Berglund."

Annie sank back on her heels, frowning, then grabbed her towel and sprinted for the door.

He was alone.

Behind him Uncle Joe called the breast-strokers to the mark. Brian kept his eyes on the girls' locker room door. Just a phone call, he kept telling himself, but he couldn't shake the unease. Joe called another race. Still no Annie. He grabbed his sweatshirt and headed for the lobby.

"Where's Annie?" he asked Julie, the receptionist.

"Went to get dressed."

His heels hit the floor. "Has to go home?"

Julie nodded. "Bad news, I think."

The door to the girls' locker room sprang open, and Annie rushed out, her face white as a china doll's in the frame of red curls.

"Eddy's dead!"

The words hit him in the chest, his brain refusing the meaning. "What?"

"He's dead ..." She choked. "His motorcycle ... skidded ...I don't know ..."

"I'll take you home."

She shook her head. "Steph's coming ..." She turned and ran outside, the door swinging shut behind her.

He stood staring at it. Rejected, helpless, abandoned ... he couldn't put a name to it. Gone. Eddy. He didn't hate him, didn't even know him, not really, though his jeering dare came back. But dead? He felt Julie staring at him. "Bad shit," he said and turned back for the pool door.

"Annie went home," he told his uncle.

"Home? Why?"

"Her brother was killed. Motorcycle accident."

"Damn!" Joe huffed. "Just happened, huh?"

Brian shrugged. "I guess so."

Uncle Joe shook his head. "Kids." He walked away toward the deep end and called for the boys' team.

She'd be with her family now. Sealed up. A Berglund. No way could he go there.

"Hey Brian! Let's go!" his uncle called.

He swam badly. The rotten leg would only move at half speed, and the rest of him flailed, missing the rhythm that pulled things together. He swore and ended up flailing all the harder.

Chapter 8

2007

Annika drove north, her gratification at finding an ally, a friend outside the Wolfson clan, faded as the cold memory of Nils Svenson's voice returned. Fear rose, but she still couldn't picture Brian as the victim of foul play. Exuberantly self-confident Brian, master of his world, his family the masters of Fontenac, was anchored deep in its history, unshakable. She still carried a picture of him standing on the hill behind the old orchard, sun glinting off his hair, Jonathan beside him, his hands on his hips.

She was ten, standing between the brothers, smelling dry summer grass, the orchard below still blooming despite age and neglect, the blue of Lake Fontenac spreading beyond, circled by forest.

"Can you imagine all of this before cars and people, telephones and television?" Jonathan waved his arm, his eyes misted with some distant vision. "They cleared all of that," he pointed to the orchard, "with hand saws."

"Come on, Annie, let's fly!" Brian took off, his arms wide, soaring this way and that down the hill,

Annie followed him with her eyes, the stone house below ready to catch him, the distant houses of Papa and Uncle Joe surrounding him, and wondered what it would be like to grow up in such a nest. Believing you could conquer anything.

~

But instead of reassuring, the memory of Brian's heedless charge left unease behind. Better think about what she was going to tell Sadie.

An hour later she arrived at Carmen's door, no further ahead. The sound of voices carried her around to the shed again, where Sadie sat, clay to her armpits, molding small animals.

"Did you find him?" she cried, jumping up and heading for Annika.

Carmen caught her arms before she could cast them around Annika's middle and held her tight, her eyes asking the same question.

"Not yet, sweetie." Annika stopped as Sadie caught her lip between her teeth, her eyes wide and filling with tears. "But we're looking. Papa and Aunt Vicky are helping." She raised her head and looked at Carmen. "Their boat docked Saturday. I talked to Nils Svenson. He *says* Brian headed for the airport."

The lines of her mother-in-law's face tightened as she read Annika's expression. They gazed at each other in silence, then Carmen turned away. "Come on." She led her granddaughter toward the sink. "Let's get you cleaned up."

Annika watched without thought as Carmen rinsed the clay from Sadie's arms, dabbled at her face, dried them both off and removed the apron that had protected her school clothes. "Show Mom your zoo."

Sadie shook her head. "They're dumb."

"No, they're not." Carmen, her hands on Sadie's shoulders, turned her toward the bench, where Annika joined them.

"They're good!" Annika exclaimed, pointing to a small figure. "This is a rabbit, right?"

Sadie nodded, but said nothing.

"Is that a giraffe?"

She clamped her lips. "A donkey." She turned away. "I told you they were dumb."

They both watched helplessly as Sadie headed for the house.

"I talked to Karl," Carmen said, as they followed. "Asked him what he knew about that trip."

"And?"

"Not much, I'm afraid. Just that Jon was adamant he had to go. Karl asked him what was the big deal, but Jon just said he needed a break."

Annika suppressed a four-letter comment and looked at her watch. "Karen says Jon gets in around five."

Carmen glanced at the wall clock. "Four thirty, already! Good grief." She led the way back to the house where they found Sadie curled on the couch with Bruno.

Annika crossed the room, wishing she'd never taken Sadie to meet that plane. "Don't be scared, baby." She gathered her daughter in her arms and felt her stiff body give way to tears. Rubbing her back, Annika's eyes met Carmen's in a helpless plea. "It's just a puzzle we have to figure out."

"I tell you what," Carmen began, crossing the room. "You and I are going to clean up and get supper while your mom goes to talk with Uncle Jon."

"Will Uncle Jon know where to find him?" Sadie twisted her face from Annika's breast.

"I don't know, honey," Annika told her, "but he knows more than we do. He knows the men Daddy went with."

"Oh." Her body relaxed a little as she considered it.

"So let's let your Mom go see him." Carmen held out a hand.

Annika threw her arms around her mother-in-law, which she'd never done before, and gave her a hug. "Thank you."

Ten minutes later, she opened the door of Wolfson Explorations and followed the noise through the displays of fishing tackle, tents and backpacks to the boat shed, where she found Brian's father, a lumberjack of a man, shoving kayaks onto racks.

"Hello?"

"Ho!" He turned and gestured to the boats. "Sorry. Working off my frustration. Where the hell is he?" He put his hands on his hips. "Brian, that is. What have you found out?" He glanced up at the old clock that kept a rusty version of time on the far wall.

Annika followed his eyes. Five o'clock. She turned and searched the lake through the open door of the boathouse for any sign of the Kodiaks coming up the lake from the river mouth. "Their boat docked Saturday, and Nils Svenson says Brian headed for the airport." She turned and read the puzzled frown on his still-young face. "Papa found his phone number, and I talked to him, but ... I don't believe him. Svenson, that is."

"No? Why not?" He drew off his work gloves and headed for the door that led to the docks.

She followed. "He was almost rude—indifferent. Not like Brian was a friend."

"Hmph." He headed for the end of the dock and gazed toward the headland where the boats would first come into view. "Damn. There's been something fishy about this whole thing from the beginning."

"Carmen said they were old friends of Jonathan's—from college."

"Yeah. Said she remembered them." He shook his head. "I don't, but that doesn't mean much. There was always a mess of kids around. You didn't know them?"

Annika shook her head. "I met them once on campus, that's all."

"To be honest, I thought he had a girl somewhere—Jon, that is. Didn't know why he just didn't say so. But then he said Brian was going instead, so that idea washed out ..." His voice faded, and a moment later he pointed to the spots of yellow that had emerged in the distance. "Here they come." He turned and took her arm. "Let's wait in my office until he sends the clients on their way. If they caught anything, they have fish to deal with. It'll take awhile."

Annika paced Karl's office, coffee cup in hand, as minutes ticked away on the ancient clock. The room was a jumble of peeling wicker furniture, its faded striped cushions strewn with brochures and an antique buffet that held a coffeemaker, leftover doughnuts and more brochures. One wall held books, ranging from ancient hardcover to new paperbacks on Michigan history, wilderness, wildlife, trees, flowers, and fishing. There were even a few old tomes on hunting, though Karl and Jonathan didn't hunt. The room's centerpiece was the battered desk of some long-dead Wolfson topped by the foreign intrusion of a computer.

Karl had gone to help Jonathan unload and batten down the boats, and Annika watched them from the window, trying to fit the scene with her own growing terrors. They wore their worn flannel shirts, jeans and vests like skin, unlike the fishermen who surrounded them, sporting microfiber high-end gear. Jonathan was a slimmer, younger version of his father, and they moved as a team. For all the office suggested indolence, they went from shaking hands to packing fish in ice with a smiling ease that belied its efficiency. They were one with the forests and water and inspired trust.

The whole defied any suspicion of underground intent. But neither did Wolfson Charters, over on the big lake. Their offices were as sleek as this one was weather-beaten; Joe's energy was loud and fast-moving, his boats built for speed. Life there was a sport—and it suited Brian. The voice of Nils Svenson didn't fit either world. She shivered and turned away to pace again.

The next time she looked, the two were alone on the dock, closer to her now, and Karl was speaking to Jon, his face stiff, intense. She saw Jon jerk. She could hear his exclamation through the glass. They headed for the office, and a moment later, the door banged against the wall.

"Annie—" Jonathan struggled for words, his face drained of color. "What's happened?"

Karl followed him in and closed the door.

"I hope you'll tell me! Brian's missing. That I know. The rest ..." She felt tears about to engulf her and fought them back. "Their boat docked two days ago—and Nils Svenson says Brian headed for the airport. But no one saw him. Who the hell is Nils Svenson, Jon?"

Jonathan, white faced, waved a hand. "A guy I knew back in college ... I see him now and then ..." He turned and walked to the window, then back, then to the desk, as though trying to find a direction that would answer her question.

"And Dominic Costello?"

"Same. They have a business together." Jon frowned and shook his head, as though to free his thoughts.

"What sort of a business?" Karl's voice was sharp.

Jon's shoulder jerked. "A charter business. Sailing the Atlantic Coast—to the Outer Banks, the Keys, the Caribbean ..." He stopped pacing, finally, and stood facing them. "I ran into them at a convention last year, and they said I should come sailing sometime." His voice had lost its panic now. "One of those vague invitations you pay no attention to." He shrugged again, this time rotating his shoulders as though to loosen the tension. "But then they called—wanting to know when I was going to come." He snorted. "I didn't even remember saying I would ... didn't take it seriously. But they said this was their last trip of the season. I should come."

"So why did Brian go instead?" Annika asked.

"Oh ... he offered." He glanced at his father. "I shouldn't have said yes without looking at our schedule. And Brian said he would."

"He didn't mention he had a meet?" Annika asked.

Jon shook his head. "When is it?"

"Friday."

"Well, he should have been back. It was a chance to sail the big water. You know Brian. Impulsive. Always up for an adventure."

Annika turned away from his nervous improvising which sounded wrong though it matched Brian's own words.

Karl looked at her. "Strange timing though. Annie'd just lost the baby."

"Yeah." He frowned. "Did you check the airport, Annie? The flights?"

"I did. He didn't take them."

Jon let out a long hiss. "Well, at least he's on shore."

"Is he? I don't know that. Nils Svenson didn't sound like a friend. I don't believe him. The harbormaster only saw Nils and Dominic. He knows them. Didn't see anyone else on board."

"What do you mean, not like a friend?" Jonathan frowned.

"Like he wasn't interested that Brian hadn't shown up home. Brushed it off. Saw him go and that was it—no more." Nils' tone came back, and she shivered again.

"Better call him, Jon," Karl urged. "See what you can find out."

"Call the other one. Dominic. See if he knows—or will say—more," Annika urged.

Jonathan pulled out his phone. After thumbing through a few screens, he shook his head. "Don't have it. Guess I only talked to Nils." He thumbed again, then put the phone to his ear.

"Hello? Jonathan Wolfson, here. I'm looking for Nils." There was a pause that stretched several beats too long. Jonathan began to pace, then stopped. "Nils? Right. I'm looking for my brother."

They could hear the man answer, but couldn't make out the words. Jonathan began shaking his head. "Well, he didn't get on that plane, Nils. No." … "Did he say he was going to the airport?" … "Well, what *did* he say? Come on, I'm standing here with our father and his wife. I need to know what happened to my brother!"

Annika made out something like "not our business" and heard the line click off.

Jonathan stared at the dead phone, then up at them. "Same damn thing he told Annika. Damn ..."

Annika stared at him, refusing to believe his helplessness. She'd counted on an answer. Some kind of answer.

"Get the *Wayfarer*'s route from the harbormaster tomorrow." Karl's voice was tight, his words clipped.

Annika looked at her watch. "I have to go. Sadie's waiting ..." But she had nothing to tell her. Nothing! "Keep looking, Jon, okay?" She hated the pathetic weakness of her words, but could find no others. She gave a wave and headed for the parking lot.

Dusk was falling as she started the engine then realized she hadn't told them she was going to Bar Harbor with Vicky. Why not? No answer presented itself, but she wasn't going back. Then her eyes were drawn from the softening colors of the lake to the lighted window of Karl's office. Karl stood there waving his arms at his son whose hands were raised in denial. As she watched, Jon left the office, slamming the door behind him. The office went dark, leaving her staring. At the other end of the parking lot, a car started and headed toward town.

Chapter 9

Annika arrived at Carmen's to find Sadie sitting in front of macaroni and cheese. She jumped up and threw herself into her mother's arms. "Did you find him?"

Annika buried her face in the child's neck. "Not yet, sweetie. Not yet."

"Why ...?" Sadie's voice swerved into tears. "You need to!"

"Yes. We do." She raised her head to Carmen.

"Jon didn't know anything?" Her mother-in-law looked as distressed as Sadie.

Annika shook her head. "He called Nils and got the same response I did." She set Sadie down. "Go finish your dinner now."

Sadie returned to the table and patted the chair beside her. "You sit here."

"Right. Have a plate with Sadie and me. Karl called just now to say there's a water board meeting, and he'll grab a bite in town."

Annika frowned, seeing the office scene again. "You didn't know about it?"

"Oh, I never keep track. He knows that." Carmen went to the stove and served up two more plates. "What's next, Annika?" she asked, taking her seat.

Annika hesitated. She was about to tell Carmen she was going to Maine, but the argument between Jon and his father added to her recurring sense that there was a layer of knowledge in this family she wasn't privy to. She needed space from the Wolfsons. "I can start calling friends, but why would they know anything? Any ideas?"

"No, except I intend to grill Jon about that trip." Carmen drove her fork into her food.

"Please do." Karl might at least tell Carmen what he was yelling at Jon about.

They ate in silence, listening to the ticking of the old cuckoo clock on the wall behind Annika's head. The sound marked passing time, her lack of action, lack of answers. Beside her, Sadie pushed food around on her plate. "Carmen," she said when she'd had all she could stand, "this is so good of you. And keeping Sadie, too. But I have to get home and see if there are any messages. I haven't been there all day and ... who knows ... something may have happened." She put her napkin down. She looked at Sadie's questioning face. "I need to put this girl to bed. Tomorrow's a school day."

"Sure." Carmen's mind seemed elsewhere. "I'll call if I find out anything."

"Okay. Come on, Sadie."

"Can I take my animals?"

"Not until they dry, honey," Carmen answered. "You come get them tomorrow, okay?"

They drove home in the twilight, and Sadie leapt from the car and raced for the house the moment Annika stopped in the drive. By the time she got to the door, the child was jumping up and down. "Hurry!"

"Do you have to go potty?" Annika asked, turning the key in the lock.

"No! Daddy might be here!" Sadie rushed through the opening, calling for her father. Her cries echoed through the empty rooms. She stood for a long moment, then turned to her mother, her eyes brimming.

Annika swept her into her arms. "It's okay. It's okay, sweetie. You can cry." She carried the weeping child into the living room and sat in a rocker, saying nothing, letting the tears flow. Across the room, the answering machine blinked.

"It's hard, not knowing," she agreed when the flow had slowed.

"I missed my Grandpa day, too," Sadie mumbled.

"Oh!" Annika exclaimed. Sadie was almost the sole light in her PTSD-ridden father's life. "So you did. Well, I'll call Grandma later and see if we can go tomorrow. Now, let's get you into the bath, then I'll make you some warm milk."

When she had Sadie in the tub she returned to the telephone. Two messages blinked on the digital screen. She punched the first.

"Annie?" her mother's anxious voice greeted her. "Did something happen? Dad's waiting ... well, that's all. Let me know, will you?"

The second was from Vicky. "I got us tickets for tomorrow night. Ten o'clock from here, midnight from Detroit. Coming home the next night, getting into Traverse City around seven in the morning, Thursday. Let me know if that's okay. I hope Jonathan gave you some answers."

She sat down relieved. The calls anchored her in a world that moved from Monday to Tuesday. Calmed, she called her mother. "Sorry, Mom. I had to go to Traverse, and I didn't get back in time." She gave a grimace at her half-truth, but her mother had enough on her plate without trying to keep Brian's disappearance from her father. Annika could hear his response if he found out.

"The bastard's left you!"

What if he had? What if that was the answer they all knew and were waiting for her to tumble to?

"Well, I told him it was probably something like that," her mother answered. "But you know how your dad is when something doesn't go right."

She forced herself back to the conversation. "I am sorry. Has he calmed down now?"

"He's still grumbling, but he's okay."

"Can I bring her after school tomorrow?"

"Well of course! I'll tell him."

Annika hung up and stared at the picture of the three of them on the wall above the phone. *Why didn't it ever occur to me that Brian left me?*

"I'm all clean now!"

"Okay, sweetie, get dry and put on your pjs. I have to call Grandma W." She shook off the new shock and started to dial Carmen to ask if she could keep Sadie, then stopped. What was she going to tell her? That she was going to Bar Harbor and keep it a secret? No. Not good. Carmen felt like a friend these last two days, but … there was more … something they weren't saying. No, for this trip she needed to stay clear. She dialed her mother again instead. "Mom, I was wondering. Could you keep Sadie for a couple of nights? My plane leaves Traverse tomorrow night, and I'll be back early Thursday."

"Oh, I'd love to! A sleepover. You sure it's all right with Brian?"

Annika shrank in shame at her deception. Brian would never let Sadie stay with her parents because of her father's bouts of violence, and her mother knew it. She had to tell her … but not now. Not on the phone. "Yes. It's okay. And thank you. Vicky's asked me if I'd like to get away for a couple of days. I'll call."

"Well, it'll be a treat. And your dad's been real good for the last week or so."

"Glad to hear it. I'll see you tomorrow, then."

Quickly, she called Vicky and told her she was all set. She'd meet her at the Traverse City airport. Sadie appeared at her elbow, and she disconnected.

"Okay. You're going to Grandpa B's after school tomorrow, and you get to stay all night!"

"Really? Really and truly?"

"Really and truly. And for two nights. You can walk to school, too. Grandma will take you."

Sadie grinned. "We have to make Grandpa's brownies!"

Annika glanced at the clock and winced. "How about your warm milk?"

"I'll have it while we make them."

"Okay, let's get at it."

The clock said it was well past Sadie's bedtime when they put the pan into the oven. "Okay," Annika announced. "I'll take it from here. You have to get to bed."

"But I need to stay up! I need to stick the toothpick in."

"I can do that. I'll be happy to. You have school tomorrow, and you're going to Grandma's. That's a big day."

"I have to—"

"Go to bed," she finished for her.

Forty minutes later, she returned to the kitchen at the ding of the timer.

"CHINA 2008!"

The words blocked her way to the oven. "I'll get back," she promised. "Tomorrow."

The words didn't sound real but allowed her past the chart. She tested the brownies and removed them from the oven. Then she went to the living room and sank into a chair, voices threatened to flood the void. Despite her determination to block them, her father's voice came booming through.

~

"Ah no, Annie, don't tell me that!" Tom Berglund leaned back and closed his eyes. "Maggie! Tell her she's got no business marrying that playboy son of a bastard!"

Her mother, who had gone limp in shock at the news, pulled herself erect. "Well, they've been friends for a long time, Tom. I expected they might make it permanent some day."

"You did? You never told me that or I would've ..." He broke off, struggling to rise.

"And he's not a playboy, Tom. That's not fair—"

"Not fair!" He pulled himself upright and picked up his crutch. "I'll tell you what's not fair—her going off with that ... I warned you, didn't I? That she'd get to thinking she was too good for us." He headed for Annika, and she shrank back, but he veered off and marched to the kitchen.

Annika and her mother were left staring at each other, wordless.

"It's all right," her mother said finally. "He'll quiet down—"

"The hell I will!" her father yelled from the kitchen doorway. "You marry him, and you're a Wolfson. That's it. Not a Berglund. Stay out of this house!"

Annika met his glare. Was amazed she didn't flinch. Out of the corner of her eye she saw her mother shaking her head but didn't shift her gaze. "Goodbye then."

She turned and went out the door. Free.

The memory faded but the sense of finishing a life stayed with her. She hadn't gone back. She met her mother or Stephanie for lunch in town, called them at Christmas and on their birthdays. They called her. Until Sadie arrived on the scene, and her father decided he wanted a grandchild. Not her, just Sadie. A sort of a truce.

Her eyelids were sagging. Time for bed.

The next morning, after she'd gotten Sadie off to school, the empty house descended on Annika, paralyzing her. She forced herself up and into the lake, but her muscles refused to relax and the water stretched to an unreachable horizon. She couldn't get her wind. How did people live with this? With people disappearing. Children, husbands, wives. They did. She knew that. What did they do with this space that seemed to crush? She pulled herself onto the dock and stood there until her wet flesh chilled, forcing motion. Find answers. That's what.

She dressed and tore apart Brian's study, looking for she knew not what. She found nothing, but at least it took time and more time to put it back together. Then she went to the bank for money. She pocketed the bills, glanced at the ATM receipt, and the thought hit. Money. He would have taken money. She checked the receipt against the balance in her checkbook; it showed no decrease beyond the withdrawal she'd just made. Why not?

She raced home, booted her computer and logged onto their account. He'd made no withdrawal from the checking account, but the savings account was $10,000 low. She sat back and stared at the screen. Dear God … Half of their savings. Their hopes of paying Uncle Joe back for all he'd done—her scholarship, entrance fees, training camps, making Brian a partner—all for Athens, China, the Gold.

She stared at the number, her mind refusing to move. Withdrawn the day before he left. After frozen minutes, she turned away and put her head in her hands. She was cold. Ice cold. No accident, not lost at sea. He left. Given up the Gold? Not possible. She jumped up and went to stare out the front windows at the lake that was his life. His history and his life. Twelve-year-old Brian rose in her mind, standing over the old sailboat they'd found abandoned on the Lake Michigan beach, his face glowing.

~

"There's gold on Bear Island! I read about it in history class—an old shipwreck …"

"Really?" Annika sat down on the sand where they'd beached the boat and looked out across the water to the distant island.

"Let's go find it! The *Shirley Ann* will take us." He nudged the little boat they'd found abandoned on the beach. They'd spent half the summer repairing and painting, patching her sails, making up stories about this battered lady who'd been cast adrift by some faithless lover.

"That's too far, Brian. It's Lake Michigan. You're not allowed to come even this far."

"Nuts! We just came through the channel, that's all. Come on!" He gave the bow of the boat a shove, backing it into the water. "Want me to go alone?"

"No!" She jumped up and headed for the boat. "She's mine, too, so I get half the say." She splashed into the water and climbed in the stern.

"Sure." Brian vaulted in as the boat went afloat. "You get half the gold, too!" The summer breeze gave the boat a gentle puff, sending her out across the water. "You want to take her for a bit?" he asked.

"Me?" She eyed at the tiller. "Okay." She giggled as they switched places, making the *Shirley Ann* wallow into the wind. Once seated, she took the rudder in hand, pushing the boat into a tack. The sails filled. She'd never thought she'd be able to sail, much less have a boat. But she was good at it, for a novice. Brian said so. She nudged the *Shirley Ann* closer to the wind and laughed as the boat heeled and gathered speed.

Brian waved at a passing boat.

Annika pulled the mainsail in further. "Coming about!" She swung the tiller.

Brian ducked and shifted sides as the boat passed through the wind "Atta girl!"

Annika grinned as she settled the boat on the new tack. The breeze stiffened a bit as they went, and she let the sail out to ease the heel.

"Better let me take her, now," Brian called, shifting toward her along the gunwale. "We're gonna hit big water soon."

Reluctantly, she and moved forward, relinquishing the mainsheet and rudder to him. "That was fun."

"Yeah, and pretty soon it'll get better." Brian watched the telltales.

The boat gave a sudden thud and slowed at an onslaught of wind and water. "Oh!" she cried, clenching the jib sheet.

"Big water." Brian settled himself to resist the much heavier pull on the mainsail. "We've left the shelter of shore," he explained. "Now the fun starts. Let's see what this old lady will do!"

Annika turned her attention to the flapping jib and concentrated on slowing her gasping breath, calming her rapid heartbeat. *Have fun,* she ordered herself.

The glare of sun on water vanished like a light turned out. Clouds. Where had they come from? The wind came in gusts, almost jerking the rudder out of Brian's hands. The water pounded the boat. The island didn't get closer.

She stared fixedly at Brian as her mind raced with warnings they'd both grown up with of sudden storms on Lake Michigan. A gust yanked the rudder free.

"Duck!"

She slid from the gunwale and felt the boom graze her head as the *Shirley* swung wildly and icy water washed over her.

"You okay?" Brian yelled. "Hold on!"

She grabbed the gunwale and looked up at the sail, its homemade patches coming loose in the wind.

Brian reached past her and released the mainsheet from its cleat. The sail fell in a sodden heap. "Lower the jib!" he cried.

She reached up and unwound the jib sheet.

Released from the wind, the *Shirley Ann* righted for a moment, then began to pitch as the waves had their way with her. Annika gripped the gunwales. They had no life jackets. No one knew they were out here. They sank into the middle of the boat and held onto each other.

Annika opened her eyes to the ringing telephone. The Coast Guard had found them that day, but the terror of those hours at the mercy of Lake Michigan had never left her. The gold on Bear Island had transmogrified into Olympic gold, but the winds of chance still robbed them.

She punched the phone. "Hello?"

"Joe here. Any sign of Brian?"

"Nothing, Joe. I'm sorry."

"That's crazy. What's happened to him?"

He's left me. Her mouth froze, preventing her uttering the words. "I … nothing comes together, Joe. Nothing makes sense."

"You're telling me!" Whistles and echoing shouts drowned out his "Damn!" and the phone disconnected.

She stared at the dead instrument, and for a moment she was a part of the world that had swallowed him. Then the silence of the house wiped it out. For the next hour she paced, the unuttered words ringing in her head. *But he wouldn't split from the race for gold. He couldn't.* She stopped as the truth of it struck her. She and the Gold. One and the same. The raw truth sent her to the window to stare out at the lake. When had the water they loved swallowed everything else? Had there ever been anything else?

She turned and fled to the kitchen. Brownies to pack. When she'd finished that, she went to gather Sadie's things. As long as she kept in motion she was all right. Tending Sadie, finding toothpaste … He wouldn't leave Sadie without telling her. He'd snuck away. That wasn't Brian. She tried to convince herself she didn't know him, but failed. But why take $10,000? He wasn't a man for secrets. Except … She set Sadie's backpack by the door and sat down, forcing her brain to face the two weeks that followed her miscarriage.

Brian drove himself in bursts of energy, drove her to get back to work, put a new training calendar up on the wall, studied every swimmer scheduled for the Olympic trials. She'd hear him working the Nordic track for hours—frenetic energy to drive away—what?

Grief. That was the answer she'd given, but now … now what? She rose and went to pack her own bag, confining thought to the movement of her arms.

Chapter 10

Brian

1992

"You're just putting in time, my friend. What's going on?" Uncle Joe asked as Brian lifted himself out of the pool.

"Nothing," Brian muttered. "Just getting sick of getting nowhere." He reached for his towel.

"Talk like that and you really will go nowhere. Come on, give me a good sprint. A champ's 100 meters." Joe grabbed the towel from him.

"I'll pace you."

They both swung around in surprise to see Annika pulling on her cap.

"Annie!" Brian cried.

"What are you doing here?" Joe exclaimed.

"Mom told me to go swim." She put on her goggles. "To get me out of the house."

"Oh yeah?" It was only three days since Eddy died, and she looked drained.

"Well, it won't do you any harm," Joe assented, "That's for sure. Maybe Brian can pace you."

Annika grinned. "Let's see." She stepped to the edge of the pool.

Brian rotated his arms, his blood flowing again. "On your mark!"

"Set!" Joe cried. "Go!"

They flew through the air, their bodies barely skimming the surface as they hit the water, their strokes matching and matching and matching again. For a fleeting moment, he wondered if she was holding back, but flicked it off with a stroke. Annie was back. His muscles loosened. Nearing the end of the pool, they somersaulted as one person and shoved off for the second 50 meters as though wind driven, arriving together at Joe's feet.

Joe clasped his hands over his head. "Okay!"

Brian grinned, then shoved off again at a more leisurely pace. They counted off another ten lengths before the team began arriving for the daily workout. "I've missed you," he told her as they rested against the end of the pool.

"Me, too."

"You okay?"

Her face lost its light. "I don't know. It was so fast. Not real ..."

"Yeah."

"It was so good. He was out of school, which he hated, had a real job testing motorcycles, which he loved ... then POOF!" She clenched her hands.

"Annie, work with the B-team today, okay?" Joe had appeared over their heads. "Don't do any more than you feel like."

"Okay." She pulled herself from the pool. "See you later," she called back as she set off for the second-string swimmers.

"Brian, your time in the sprint was almost A-team. Keep it up and you'll be back in the game. Work with B-team, today. Lead off and pace them, okay?"

"Righto!" He turned and swam to the lane where the freestyle B swimmers were gathered and waited for Joe's signal.

On the other side of the pool, Annie had disappeared among the girls.

He spent the next hour beating his own time again and again. She was back. His heart sang with it every stroke. Joe was grinning. All was well.

But after he'd showered and dressed, he found her sitting on the bench outside the door, her hood up, her arms folded across her chest. "What's wrong?"

She straightened. "Oh, nothing … just don't much want to go home." Her voice wobbled.

"Your dad?"

"Never seen him like this … yelling, swinging at ghosts, damning everything. Stephanie tried to help, got too close and he knocked her right over …" She shivered.

"Come on," Brian laid a hand on her shoulder. "We'll drive up to the point and look at the lake a while. That always helps."

She gazed out at the snowscape and sighed. "Can't, Brian. Steph's picking me up, and Mom needs me."

"Thought she told you to go swimming."

"She did. She wants me away from him, but she needs us …" Annie blinked back tears. "Here's Steph." She rose, gave his hand a squeeze and was gone.

Sucked back into a world he could not enter. Her world. Ananie was only a visitor in his. *But she'll be back!* He told himself as he felt the hole opening beneath him. *Hold on!*

He forced himself to turn from the door and go to the exercise room, mount a treadmill and put it into action. *Move! Move! Move! Move!* The rhythm of his body took over, closing the hole. *She's back. She's back. She's back!*

An hour later, he drove to the physical therapist for his weekly checkup, feeling steady, in charge of himself, though the bad knee hurt like hell.

The therapist took one look at the rapidly swelling joint and frowned. "You're going to have to slow down, my friend."

"Can't. Have to get back on the A team for State. Swimming."

"You didn't do that swimming," He pointed to the now swollen joint.

"Treadmill. That's part of it. Part of getting back."

"How long?"

"An hour. Twice."

"Huh. No wonder. Okay, let's take a look." He prodded the knee, found the pain triggers, and sat back. "We're going to need an X-Ray." He stood. "The technicians will bring the machine. You stay put."

He left Brian to stare at his leg. *Dumb shit. What've you done now?* How was he going to explain about the hole—that he had to keep free of the void? He wasn't. They'd think he was a loony. No way.

By the time they finished X-Raying his leg, he'd steeled himself for the verdict. He'd find a way to make it, that's all. Find a way around it—whatever it was.

"Well, you're lucky, Brian," the therapist informed him. "You haven't pulled anything loose. But no more treadmill until I say so, okay?"

"Okay. But I can swim."

"You can swim. But nothing else—no machines—Okay?"

"How about machines that work my arms and shoulders? That's okay, isn't it?"

"Of course. But don't come in here telling me you tore yourself up on those."

"I won't."

"You're likely to. You need to find the patience to heal, Brian."

"I'll be careful. Promise."

He smiled. "I'm going to give you a shot of Prednisone in that knee. It should be better in a couple of days. Let me know if it isn't." He waved as he left.

He'd escaped the worst. Working his arms would do it. Keep him in motion. Arms were as important as legs. In fact, maybe his arms could make up for his leg. He remembered being amazed at the speed of handicapped swimmers who spent their days in wheelchairs. He grinned at the nurse who'd arrived with a syringe. Things were almost good.

Outside, the winter sun was already setting, and the slush from the day's traffic was beginning to freeze. He negotiated his way to his car with uncharacteristic attentiveness. No more trouble today. It's been a good day, remember? Annie is back. Don't wreck it any more than you already have. He reached the car, scraped the ice from the windshield, and forsook his usual cockiness about driving on icy roads.

He gave his mother a wave as he passed through the kitchen to distract her from his limp.

"Wait!" she cried after him.

"You have a letter!" She pointed to the table. "From University of Michigan."

He stopped and stared at pile of mail. "Yeah?"

His mother grinned at his squeak. "Go ahead. Open it."

He cleared his throat. "Yeah." This time his voice was normal, almost. He went forward and picked up the real letter that sat on top of the stack of circulars and bills.

He sat down and stared at the seal in the corner, ran his fingers over it. Then, aware that his mother was watching, he tore it open and took out the folded paper. He wished he was alone. With a huff he flipped it open.

"I made it!" He lifted his gaze to his mother's face. "Really!" He held it out to her.

She laughed as she took it, whether at him or in relief he couldn't tell. Her eyes lit up as she read the words. "Wonderful, Brian. Hooray for you!"

"Ha!" He reached for the letter to read it again. Slowly. He hadn't wanted to apply. He was going to community college. He'd decided that. Jon was going to U of M. He wasn't going to apply and not make it. He didn't need that kind of proof that Jon was better—all round better and always had been.

"Why are you so surprised, Brian? You're smart as they come. Your grades show it." She walked over and sat down opposite.

He shrugged. "I'm not ... like Jon, though."

She frowned. "What do you mean? Why should you be?"

He looked at the question in her eyes, then down at the maple table, following its grain with his fingers.

She waited.

"Jon's just good at everything. It comes easy for him. I botch things up." He raised his eyes, challenging her to disagree with the truth.

"Ah!" She sat back. "You're younger, honey, that's all. It comes with the territory." She got up and poured herself a cup of coffee, then returned and sat down again. "I was younger. Youngest of six, always chasing after, trying to catch up." She took a sip. "Then one day we were walking up to the church—all of us—all dressed up. I don't remember why ... yes, I do. My oldest sister, Liselle, was getting confirmed. Anyway, I stopped to watch a chipmunk and got left behind. And smeared my dress with dirt. I was upset, but then I wasn't. Decided I wanted to watch the chipmunk. My mother came racing back for me, totally exasperated, but I wasn't. I was happy."

He smiled. "You still like chipmunks."

"I do. And that," she said, pointing to the letter, "is your chance to stop comparing yourself to Jon and find out what makes you happy."

He heard his father's pick-up in the drive and met him at the door. "I got into UM!"

"Oh yeah? Great!" He shrugged out of his sheepskin. "Good going Brian, I figures you'd make it. So you're going?" He turned to hang up his coat.

Brian looked at him in surprise. "Of course! Why would I not?"

Laughing, his father turned back. "I suppose because you spent hours telling us you weren't going to apply!" He reached out and enclosed Brian in a bear hug. "But I'm glad you came to your senses. It's a good school."

Brian handed him the letter. "Uncle Joe says I should go into business."

"Well, it's not up to Joe, is it?" his father snapped.

"Who knows?" his mother tempered. "You have a while to decide. Try things out."

"Yeah. We'll see," he muttered, backing out of the nest of thorns mentioning Joe always created. He got up and went toward the stairs. "Gotta call Jim and Sam. They applied, too."

"Who the hell's kid is he, anyway?" he heard his father mutter as he climbed the stairs.

It wasn't until he went up to bed and was confronted by the pictures on his dresser—he and Annie standing beside the *Shirley Ann,* he and Annie holding their medals from the county meet—that it hit him with a jolt. He was leaving Annie. The *Shirley Ann,* Uncle Joe. Everything. "You have to come, too, Annie," he whispered. But she was only a sophomore. He sank to the bed.

"I'll come home on weekends. Every weekend, and we'll swim together. Promise." It would be enough. But how could she follow him there? The Berglunds had no money for universities.

A knock at the door turned his head. "Yeah?"

"It's me," his father said, opening the door. "Your mom says you didn't think you were good enough for UM. You're comparing yourself to Jon."

"I'm okay," Brian protested, annoyed that his mother blabbed about their conversation. "Must be wrong since I got in, huh?"

"Yeah. You're okay. You're smart enough. Remember that."

"I will. Dad, how much does it cost to go to UM?"

His father blinked. "How much? Quite a bit, actually, but we'll make it. Jon works to pay for books and entertainment, so that helps."

"I will, too."

"Good."

"I was thinking about Annie."

"Oh." He looked at the pictures. "She's what …a freshman?"

"A sophomore, but …" His voice trailed off.

His father nodded. "I know. Well, she's quite a swimmer, Brian." He stopped, considering. "Now this is a time I think you should talk to Joe. Maybe he can help her get a swim scholarship."

"Oh! Does that cover everything?"

He laughed. "Nothing covers everything, buddy, but it gives her a chance." He smiled. "Annie deserves that."

Brian looked at him surprise. His father had never talked about Annie or her family—never mentioned her except to say "Annie's at the door," or "Annie called." He grinned. "Yeah. She does."

His father waved and headed out, then stopped at the door. "And congratulations."

Chapter 11

2007

An hour later, her packing finished, Annika picked up Sadie at school and drove toward the Browning Street house, eyeing the lowering clouds that promised rain. As she approached the Cape Cod bungalow where she'd grown up, the usual dread descended. The white clapboard, green-shuttered cottage kept its place in a row of similar houses, and its picket fence remained unchanged, but every year the shutters faded in the sun, the paint flaked a little more, the fence lost another picket.

Inside, her father would be sitting in his recliner, the TV filling the room, covering the tension without bringing the house to life. The same green couch, glass-topped coffee table, and knick-knack cabinet would occupy their time-worn spots, and the same dried flowers lost a little color each month. The House of Phantoms, she'd called it in her crueler high school days.

Sadie began to chatter beside her, clutching the brownies. "… and if it's raining we'll play checkers and make a zoo with my … Mama! I forgot my animals! I have to go get them to show Grandpa!"

"We'll get them when I get back, sweetie. There's no time now." How much longer could she keep Sadie from discovering that she lived in a tangle of truces? That her grandparents never spoke to each other—or of each other for that matter

"But …"

"Then you can paint them before you show them to Grandpa." Surely she'd mentioned one grandparent to the other. Maybe she knew.

"Oh." Sadie's face cleared. "That'll be good."

Annika smiled and pulled into the drive. Tangled web or not, she'd not deprive her parents of the joy they found in Sadie. Had they brought light into their father's eyes when they were small the way Sadie did? Back when he returned from Vietnam without a leg? Eddy had, sometimes, when her father wasn't yelling at him. Her brother's face rose, twisting her gut. At least the yelling had been parenting—alive. Eddy's death had broken him all over again. Stephanie remembered a different man. At night, when they'd wakened to his screams and the house filled with the ghosts of dead men, Stephanie would hold her and tell her stories of those times. There was a picture of the man her sister remembered on her mother's dresser, alongside another of the three of them. Steph and Eddy grinning, holding her, an infant, between them. Sometimes, if she closed her eyes tight, she could feel herself being swung high in the air, but she didn't do that often. It just increased the longing for that father's return.

Sadie loosened her buckles and jumped from her car-seat as soon as Annika pulled to a halt, calling out as she crossed the shaggy grass to the front door. Annika picked up her daughter's backpack and followed, reaching the door just as her mother opened it.

"Well, would you look who's here!" She threw up her hands in surprise. "Tommy, come see what the wind blew in!" She swooped Sadie up in a hug.

"Whoa! Who are you?" her father cried as Sadie escaped her grandma's hug and ran toward him.

"Sadie!" Sadie cried, always ready for the game.

"No. Sadie's just a little thing."

"I'm bigger now!"

Tom Berglund lowered his face until he was nose-to-nose with his granddaughter. "Well, I'll be. You're right. You *are* Sadie."

Annika stood in the doorway and watched. Then sniffed. Pot. She looked at him again. He was different. The pleasure that lit his face wasn't a mask over underlying pain. Had he gained weight, too?

Sadie giggled. "And I brought you a present."

"Hm." He took the box. "Good thing. I might not let you in otherwise. Did you make these yourself?"

"I helped."

"Good. Well, let's see how you did." He opened the box and lifted the wax paper. His eyes widened. "They're all brown!"

"They're supposed to be! They're brownies!"

"Yeah? Well, isn't that something." He picked up a piece and took a bite.

Annika's mother chuckled and headed for the kitchen, but Annika remained at the door, letting the easy delight of the pair fill her.

Her father chewed solemnly as Sadie watched, her brows knit in question. Finally, he nodded. "Lovely. You did good. When are you going to do it all yourself?"

"When Mommy let's me. I'm too messy now, she says."

"Umhmm. Mothers are that way." With that he raised his head and looked at Annika. "Your mother's missed you. Wondered how you were getting on."

Annika winced at the deflection of affection, though it wasn't unexpected. Her father wasn't going to forgive her for the loss of his second grandchild a mere week after she'd told them she was pregnant. *"What the hell did you go back into training for? What's a piece of gold compared to a child's life, for God's sake?"* The words burned still, and she had no answer. "I'm all right." She turned away to escape his change in mood and went to the kitchen.

A strand of her mother's gray-streaked hair escaped from its bun and fell over her thin face as she dredged a roast in flour. "He's so much better, don't you think?" She looked up, beaming.

Annika's hurt dissolved at her mother's smile. At least she hadn't cut Annika out of the family. "Is it the pot?"

"Oh, yes. You can't believe what it's done." Her hands were quick and free, without the tension that had driven them for years. "He's even working—down at the VFW. Two days a week." She laughed. The light in her face made her look ten years younger.

"That's a real break-through. I can see what it's done for you, too." Annika smiled, knowing her mother still hoped he could recover enough to open the boat repair shop he'd always dreamed of. "What can I do to help?"

"Not a thing. I was hoping … can you stay for supper? He's nicer now—not so angry at you."

Annika doubted that, but nodded. "All right, but you have to let me help. Where are the potatoes?"

"In the pantry." She gestured. "He hasn't had a nightmare in a month. Can you believe it?"

"Really?" Could this house ever be free of maimed soldiers and butchered children that had inhabited it at night all her life? "That's incredible."

Her father appeared at the door. "We're off to the park before it rains."

"Okay," her mother answered. "Be home by five."

"Righto." The front door banged shut.

Annika watched through the kitchen window as they retrieved Sadie's bike from the garage and headed down the street. "Where's he getting it, anyway?"

"What? Oh, the pot? Stephie gets it for him. He read about it and nagged her forever. She finally found some."

Annika frowned, hoping that Stephanie, a nurse, wasn't endangering her career. Medical people knew where to get it, had known forever, but it wasn't legal in Michigan—yet. "Do you know where she gets it?"

Her mother laughed. "I ask no unnecessary questions, Annie."

"Right." She turned her attention to peeling potatoes.

Beside her, her mother dropped the roast into the hot pan, searing it. She poked it with the fork. "What's the matter, Annie?"

"Ouch!" The knife nicked her finger. She put it to her mouth and sucked before answering. "Why?"

"You're white as paper and just as stiff. What's going on?"

Annika pulled a tissue from the box and wrapped her finger. "Where's a band-aid?"

"In the top drawer, there." Her mother turned the roast and waited.

Annika washed her finger, dotted it with ointment, and wrapped a band-aid around it. "Brian's gone." She raised her head to meet her mother's widened eyes. "He went on a sail trip and he hasn't come home. That's all I know." She felt tears surge and fought them back.

"Well for ... just like that? Did you fight?" The kettle began to whistle, startling her into turning away.

Annika relaxed in the moment of reprieve. "No."

Her mother poured boiling water into the roast pan. She covered it and put it in the oven in silence. When she turned back her face had lost its radiance, settled back into its careworn calm. "Explain, Annika. Please."

"He's been in a mood since ... since I lost the baby ..." She struggled for words. "We both have. Then he just announced he was going on a sailing trip." She took a breath. "He hasn't come home."

"Oh, you mean he's missing? Where? Where did he go?"

"Out in the Atlantic—from Bar Harbor."

Her mother frowned. "That's strange. Why would he do that?"

"To sail the Atlantic. That's all I know." She felt her voice wobble.

"Dear God …" Her mother put an arm around her. "Does Sadie know?"

"Unfortunately. She went with me to meet his plane."

Her mother sighed and sank down at the table. "Poor baby." Then she got up again, this time headed for the coffee pot. She poured two cups and returned to the table. "I don't understand why he'd do that. Come talk to me."

Annika sat down and poured out the whole story, including the true reason for her trip with Vicky. Then she choked, unable to mention the missing money. The retelling had drilled a hole of certainty; the money only cast it in cement. Brian had left her.

When she looked up, her mother, arms folded across her chest, was watching her. Their eyes met, and Annika saw her own conviction mirrored there. Her mother gave a sharp nod. "Good." She slapped her hands flat on the table and rose. "Have to say that, Annie. Not good for Sadie, but … I don't have it in for them the way you father does, but Wolfsons aren't your people."

"Don't say that, Mom; they're just people like everyone else. They aren't bad just because they have money, and they've done a lot for me." She heard her own defensiveness and stopped. "I just don't know what's going on, that's all."

"Mm. And you won't, Annie. You're an outsider. You need to understand that."

Annika watched her mother in silence, then rose to help clear the table for supper.

"Or you'll get hurt. The way your father did. He thought Karl Wolfson was his forever best friend—years and years of growing up sailing, swimming, getting in trouble together—then boom! It's gone. Karl's not going off to Vietnam with him. No sir. He's off to college, and when your dad comes home without his leg, there's the likes of Karl jeering at him." She opened the oven, peered at the roast, and slammed it shut again.

Outside thunder rumbled, and the first drops of wind-blown rain struck the window.

"But it wasn't Karl, Mom. And Karl asks after him."

"Some hurts don't heal."

The front door slammed, and Sadie burst into the kitchen. "We fed the geese!"

Annika laughed in relief. "And rolled in the sand by the looks of you. Off to the back stoop to brush off. You'll spray sand on our dinner." She got up and followed the child out. "Stand still," she commanded, taking the hand brush from its hook.

When they returned, Tom Berglund was seated at the table, a cup of coffee in front of him. Her mother, at the sink cleaning more vegetables for the roast, cast her a warning look over his head. Annika gave a quick nod. She wasn't to mention Brian's absence. She turned instead to Sadie. "Go up and change into your play clothes before you do any more damage."

Sadie looked down at her school skirt. "It's okay," she protested.

"Now."

"And be quiet," her grandmother added. "Your Aunt Stephie is sleeping."

Sadie scampered off, and Annika joined her mother at the sink. "Steph's still on nightshift, then?"

"Seems to suit her." Her mother gathered the vegetables into a bowl. The scar on her arm, left from trying to block her husband's access to a knife, winked in the sun.

"She needs to get out and get a life," Tom grumbled.

"You mean get a man and get married," his wife jibed. "But she's got no taste for that. Never has. She's taken up writing. Did you know that?"

"No." Annika looked up, relieved and surprised. Her older sister's life was protecting her mother. Being on hand. And adding to her father's disability check. "Writing what? Stories?"

Her mother nodded. "She's had two published. Says she going to try a novel next."

"No kidding. That's great." So her sister had found an escape from the over-developed sense of responsibility that had run her life.

"Sadie says her father's gone." Tom Berglund slapped his cup down as lightning lit his face.

Annika froze. They'd forgotten Sadie's unstoppable flow of news. The deep rumble of thunder filled the kitchen and saved her from answering while her brain spun. "On a sailing trip. He had a chance to sail the Atlantic and didn't want to pass it up."

"Huh." The sound expressed his contempt for those who spent adulthood in such games.

"I'm going to check on Sadie," she said, wiping her hands. As she climbed the stairs, she heard the shower going. Stephanie was up. She went on down the hall and found Sadie, school clothes piled around her, pulling on shorts. The rain pounded the roof above their heads now, and with a crack, another flash of lightening lit the room.

"Wow!" burst Sadie.

"You got home just in time," Annika said, picking up clothes.

"Can you still fly to find Daddy?"

Annika watched her daughter buckle her sandals, her mind racing. "I'm sure it will pass by then, but I'm just going with Aunt Vicky for a couple of days vacation—not to find Daddy, Sadie." she said, finally. "Uncle Jon says I got the date of Daddy's trip wrong. He's not due home yet for a couple of days." Rain swiped the window, marking her deceit.

"What?" Sadie looked up. "How, wrong? We went to meet his plane—it was on a piece of paper!"

"I know, but I read the date wrong. So you can stop worrying, okay?"

"Yeah …" She frowned. "How'd you do that?"

"I guess I just wanted him home." She smiled, feeling like a heel. But she had to stop Sadie from drawing Tom Berglund into the search. "Come on, let me fix your hair." She reached down and pulled her daughter to her feet, then fished out the brush from her backpack. "You must have been rolling on the beach," she commented as she stroked.

"No … just a little."

The shower at the end of the hall had stopped, and she heard Stephanie's door close. "There, you look better. Go help Grandma set the table."

When Sadie disappeared down the stairs, she knocked on Stephanie's door.

"Come in?"

"Hi."

Stephanie's head emerged from her T-shirt. "Annie!" She pulled the shirt down. "Mother said you were coming. How are you doing?" She reached for her scrub pants.

"Not good. Brian's gone missing."

"What?" Stephanie stopped, her pants in mid-air. "What do you mean, missing?"

"He went on a sailing trip and didn't come home. From Bar Harbor of all places and no, I don't know why he went, but the boat returned and the other sailors say he went to the airport—but he didn't—or if he did, he went somewhere else."

Stephanie sat down on the bed. "That's too weird. What …" She broke off, shaking her head in disbelief.

"I think …" Annika stopped, unable to say it. "No, I don't, really, but mother thinks … and she may be right … that he left me. He took money."

A now distant rumbling filled the silence.

"Mom's not a fan," Steph said finally but without certainty.

"No, I know. And don't, for God's sake, tell Dad."

"Cross my heart. But what are you going to do, Annie?"

"I'm going to Bar Harbor with Vicky to try to get to the bottom of it."

"You're …" Stephanie frowned. "You need to let other people do that. Have you reported it?"

"Reported … to the police, you mean?" It had never occurred to her. "Not yet. Not now … until I know more. Whether he just left me."

Her sister gave a long sigh. "What a bitch." She put her feet into her pants.

"Mom says you're writing," Annika fought to change course.

Stephanie gave a small smile. "She thinks I'm going to be a great novelist." She stood and pulled up her pants, began to tie them. "But yes, I am … or trying it out, anyway. It just came to me one day that I might give it a go."

"I think that's super. She says you got a story published. Can I read it?"

"Sure. I'll dig it out for you. Just don't think you have to say nice things about it. Okay?"

"Promise." Annika sat on the bed. "Things seem quieter around here. Mom says it's the pot you've gotten for him."

Stephanie gave her a sharp look in the mirror as she drew the brush through her hair. "I hope she's not advertising that around town, but yes, it's made a world of difference."

"She won't. She's not dumb. And she looks as though she's sleeping at night. Where do you get it, anyway?"

"Oh, there's plenty around." She pulled her long dark hair into a ponytail, "but I get it from Jon."

Annika felt her heart jolt. "Jon Wolfson?" She choked on the words.

"Who else? The wilderness folk have access to that stuff. Always have." Stephanie looked at Annika with a puzzled frown. "Why the shock, Annie? I've known Jonathan since we were kids. He used to hang out with Eddy." She went to the chest and picked up her watch.

"He did? I don't remember that. Did Dad know?"

"Ha! Not on your life." She sobered. "Jon was at Eddy's funeral, though. I saw him, buried in the shadows by the door. He's an okay guy."

"He is." Why did the mention of his name here give her such a jolt? Everyone knew everyone in Fontenac.

"Even back then he had pot, sometimes. Bragged that his dad smoked." She pulled on her trousers. "Which didn't surprise us. His dad was a hippie in those days."

Annika smiled, her upset evaporating in the ordinariness of things. "He still is—he and Carmen both."

"Girls! Stephie? Annie?" Their mother's voice came from the staircase.

Annika went to the head of the stairs where her mother stood waiting.

"I forgot milk for Sadie. Could you run to Ralph's and get some?"

"Sure."

Stephanie reached out as she stood there and pulled her to her. "Bear up, okay? We're with you."

Annika felt tears gather. "Thanks, Steph."

"And good luck on your trip. I hope you find some answers."

Chapter 12

2007

The storm had passed, and the setting sun lit up a newly washed sky as Annika embarked for Traverse City. Her father had been talkative—to Sadie, Stephanie and his wife. Annika had been humiliated but grateful; exclusion was better than interrogation. Then, as she helped Stephie and her mother clean up, she felt a part of them, the phalanx of caregivers giving each other warmth and strength. How quickly that bond, or bondage, returned. The others seemed to feel it, too. Something restored.

They said little as they worked, but when they were done, her mother had turned and thrown her arms around her. "Good to have you home."

And Stephie had followed suit. "Take care."

"The story," Annika reminded her. "Do you have a copy?"

Stephanie suppressed a smile and turned away. "I'll get it.'

Annika's eyes had smarted with tears as she went upstairs to gather her things. She'd come so rarely, since she left for college, and been home only to sleep and eat before that. Wanting only to get away. She neatened up Sadie's scattered clothes, picked up her own suitcase, glanced at her watch and headed for the stairs. Sadie was bent over the checkerboard opposite her grandpa.

"I told him you were going east to meet him. Brian." Her mother had whispered in her ear.

Annika opened her mouth to protest, *but what if ...?* then stopped and mouthed a thank you instead. What ifs could wait. She crossed the room and dropped a kiss on her daughter's curls and looked across at the bent graying head. "Bye, Dad."

He looked up. "Tell that man he should be taking care of his family, not running off to play."

She'd smiled, unaccountably softened by the warmth that bled through the rancor. "I will."

Stephanie pressed a manila envelope into her hands, and it was over.

Now, as the mission ahead returned, she asked herself again what she hoped to gain. She didn't know, and it didn't matter. She had to go. Bar Harbor was the black hole that had swallowed him. She had to put her feet on that dock, look at that boat, confront the harbormaster. She had to give it shape, sound, texture. She had to make it real.

As villages, fields and forests passed in the dimming light, the pieces of the puzzle swam in her head, failing to cohere or make a pattern that satisfied. Jonathan. So much swirled around him. Why had she been so shaken that he was the source of her father's pot? The weed had been a part Carmen's and Karl's household that no one much talked about. Karl had it, so Jon had it. So what? Was it the connection to her own family, to Stephanie, that surprised her? Maybe. Steph was older than Jonathan and was always running home to help Mom. She'd never had much of a social life that Annika could remember. But again, so what? Everyone knew the Wolfsons and the split that frayed but never quite tore the family bonds. "That's what the war did," Steph had said, as though it was beyond humans to repair.

She arrived ats the airport with no answers and found Vicky there ahead of her, looking sleek even in jeans and sweater. "Made it!" Annika laughed, then burst into tears.

"Whoa! What's up?" Vicky put an arm around her shoulders.

"I'm so glad to see you," Annika mumbled, then laughed again. "And to be doing something."

"Yeah. I can imagine. Let's get through security and find ourselves a glass of wine. Then you can fill me in." She turned Annika toward the gates.

By the time they held full glasses and found themselves seats, Annika had pulled herself together. "Sorry to be such a ninny." She took a long slow sip. "I didn't realize how up-tight I was."

"Well, it's no wonder. Just sit back and close your eyes. We have almost an hour."

Annika did so, and for long minutes flight announcements and safety warnings filled the echoing space around them. She floated free of her life, in the hands of forces from her core, inaccessible but commanding. The presence of Vicky beside her drew her back to solid ground. "Jon and his father had an argument after I left. I saw it through the window. Then Jon banged out."

"When was that? After you told him Brian was missing?"

"Yes. Well it was Karl who told him; Jon was upset. Scared, too, I think. So he called Nils and got the same brush off I did." She stopped, considering her own words. "Odd, isn't it? I don't think Jon was any more their buddy than Brian was." She raised her shoulders and let them fall. "So I left. But I saw them through the window. Karl was waving his arms and shouting at Jon."

"Interesting." Vicky looked thoughtful. "Wonder what that was about."

Annika shook her head and sipped her wine.

"It sounds as though Karl knows more than he's letting on," Vicky mused. "Did he know Nils?"

"No, he said Carmen remembered him from Jon's college days, but he didn't."

"Hm. Guess it doesn't mean anything, then. I thought there might be some connection." Vicky sat back her eyes on some distant memory.

Annika glanced at her, bemused. "Like what?" Why did she think there was more Vicky wasn't saying? Was she beginning to suspect everyone of being in on some great secret?

Vicky shook her head. "Nothing specific, but in the tour business people get connected. Plus my generalized distrust of that pair—Nils and Dominic. They felt like trouble. Always seemed to be bragging about something they'd gotten away with." She wrinkled her nose and put her glass down. "Come on, we'd better get ourselves to the gate."

When they'd boarded, turning their phones off as the plane rolled down the runway, Vicky pulled out a book and opened it.

Annika leaned back and closed her eyes to think, but as the plane rose, releasing her, thought dissolved and left her floating.

"How's Sadie?" Vicky asked, a timeless space later.

Annika woke with a jolt. "Not good. Scared. I left her at my folks. Didn't want to tell Carmen and Karl where I was going." She felt the tightness growing around her shoulders again. "I don't know why."

Vicky turned at her words. "You mean no one knows?"

"My mother does, and Stephanie."

"But not the Wolfsons—or your father?" Vicky looked puzzled.

"No, except Sadie told him her daddy hadn't come home. Not a good thing."

"So your father still hates Brian." She didn't sound surprised.

"It's Karl he hates, mostly; Brian gets it as his offspring. But yes. He has a picture in his mind of coming home half-conscious and hearing the jeering crowd of hippies. He sees Karl there, though he wasn't, as far as I know. The picture never fades. He'll go berserk if he knows Brian has disappeared. He already blames him for the miscarriage—for making me train when I was pregnant."

"Making you?" Vicky's brows rose.

"In his eyes, yes. So I had to act as though he wasn't due home yet. Then I had to lie to Sadie, too … tell her I'd made a mistake."

Vicky gave a small groan. "Did she buy that?"

Despite herself, Annika saw again the mix of fear and pleading in Sadie's eyes as she'd turned at the door one last time. And turning away. "No."

Vicky grunted. "I wouldn't guess she would. She's too smart."

"They all are. When the Wolfsons find I'm gone, it'll all fall apart, but it was enough to get away." She leaned back. "And except for Sadie, I don't seem to care what they think." The words came on an expulsion of air. A letting go of something.

"That's a good place to get to." Vicky was quiet for a moment. "Do you think they'll follow you?"

"Who?"

Vicky shrugged. "I don't know. Jon, I suppose. It wouldn't be hard to guess where you went. It might be harder to explain why you didn't tell them."

Annika gave a short laugh. "For sure." She looked out into the night as the plane started to descend to Detroit. "Let's not think about it."

But the possibility that Jon might follow them stuck in Annika's mind as they landed and found the way to their Boston flight. When they were seated on the plane an hour later, she was still chilled at the idea. "Jon is getting pot for my father."

Vicky stopped in the middle of fastening her seatbelt. "Oh?"

"Steph gets it from him, and my dad's so much better for it." She snapped her seat belt in exasperation. "So why does it bother me?"

Vicky's brows knit. "I don't know. There's always been pot around in Karl's family. Jon always had it. I didn't like it, actually. It changed him."

"I remember. You complained about living with spacey people." She paused at the thought. "Is that why you split up?"

"Partly." Vicky gazed out of the window. "I always had—still have—this dream of being surrounded by family, and Jon's seemed so wonderful—so perfect. The family of founding settlers, still squires of that beautiful land. And Jon … he was a dream. Kind, fun, laid back ..." She smiled, then sobered. "But then you get in the middle of it, and it's a river full of snags. If you like Joe, Karl gets icy. If you like Carmen, Joe's pissed. And if you come in from the outside, you can never quite learn the steps." She sighed. "But I had Jon, and that was enough—until I found out I didn't. Family came first." She turned toward Annika. "Right? Yours is the same. Different but the same."

"Except that my family river has an alligator. Brian and I spent our childhood avoiding our families. How about yours?" In the year they'd shared the daughter-in-law role, Vicky'd never talked about them.

"Air," Vicky snapped. She turned back to the window. "My father is a banker. My mother a lawyer. I lived in a huge house filled with air. When I was little I had a nanny. There was a housekeeper, usually, but she had her own quarters and emerged twice a day to do her rounds." She turned from the window, making a dismissive noise with her lips. "That's a really banal 'poor little rich girl' story, isn't it?" She waved a hand. "Which is why I don't usually talk about it."

Annika shivered at the description and thought of the hours just spent in the Berglund house, so full of human voices, smells, so full of undercurrents. "Somewhere you got a lot of brains and—presence," Annika told her. "And warmth," she added, realizing the truth of it.

"Mm. Thank you, but I'm afraid I learned to be alone too early and too well. That seems to be my natural state."

"You'll find someone," Annika reassured her. "You're beautiful, poised—I can't imagine you not attracting plenty of men."

"I scare them off. And I don't seem to be looking." Vicky gave an impatient flick of her wrist. "Where did this conversation start, anyway?"

"With Jon and pot."

"Oh, right. The pot." She paused, thinking. "Does Brian use it?"

"No. Absolutely not. He's dead set against anything like that. Believes it's ruining amateur sports. A glass of wine or a beer at dinner is his worst indulgence." She sighed. "And he begrudges me that."

"I thought those guys might be the source, but if Brian doesn't use it, that washes out that idea."

"Would you have to go that far away to get pot?" Annika raised her brows.

"I wouldn't think so, but I'm not up-to-date either."

"Mm. Neither am I."

The flight attendant took over the conversation at that point. The plane began to roll, but the take-off failed to release her this time.

"I suppose we'd better try to sleep."

"Hm. For all of half an hour."

Annika looked at her watch. "Forty-five minutes, to be exact."

They leaned back and closed their eyes. How long had it been since she'd talked about anything but training schedules, times, meets, and strokes?

"Why does nothing we find out connect up with Brian?" Vicky's voice broke the silence.

The zigzags on the seat back danced in front of Annika's eyes. "Because he used the trip as a way to leave me."

"Oh, yes?" Vicky turned, frowning. "And when did you decide that?"

"He took money." Annika turned to escape the pattern. "Ten thousand. Half our savings."

"Oh. Damn." Vicky leaned back. The drone of engines filled the space between them. "But why?" She sat up. "Brian needs you—has always needed you. You're—essential to him. Beyond questioning. What's been going on to change that?"

"Nothing I haven't told you, but ..." She fished for words. "It's the swimming. Swimming was the magic, and something went missing. In my family, growing up, we all had to sort of dim out, stay under the radar, be careful, be quiet, walk softly. It was like none of us ever quite took shape. We were shadows. Look at Stephanie. Even now, Dad is the center of everything. She wants him back the way he was and ... never went on from there. Eddy kept trying to bust out of it ... turned wild, reckless. And ended against a tree." She choked and stopped. "For me, Brian was the magic key. *"Come on!"* he'd cry, and I'd fly free of the whole thing. I could stand up and shout, "This is me!" She laughed. "Not whisper. And every time I got a medal, it was another lock against going back."

"I never knew most of that," Vicky mused. "But it fits. You were always ... so bright ... like a brand new person." She winced. "A silly way of putting it, but, well, I thought you were naïve. My mistake. I apologize."

"No need. I was. But then—Athens—I missed by a half second. How crazy is that? I didn't know I could lose." She stopped at the words she'd never spoken before, even to herself. "I was really thrown. Lost. But then one day I watched Sadie splashing around in the water like a grounded fish—so like me I started laughing."

"Mm. But Brian didn't, I'll bet."

"No. He just kept saying *'China! China!'* until we both believed it." Annika frowned, thinking back. "Like he couldn't let himself be down." She looked out of the window into the blackness. "But I couldn't get back into it. I was slower."

"You were pregnant with your second. That's natural."

"True, but before that, even. I didn't get faster. It felt like the games were something I used to want."

Vicky watched her. "Okay. But that was bound to happen, sooner or later. Didn't Brian have other swimmers, youngsters he was training? Why was it such a big deal?"

"I don't know. We didn't talk about it ... but we'd always been—almost a part of each other." She tried to visualize his face, the intensity in his eyes. "It was as though I was him ... he was watching me, but seeing himself."

"He never got there, did he? To the Olympics." Vicky was studying her.

"No. That knee he screwed up in high school kept giving him trouble. He could never get his speed back." She saw his face again, white with pain, hammering his fist in frustration. "*I'll get it back! I will ...*"

Vicky sighed.

Annika gazed out at the stars. "He did a lot of dumb things in those days—impulsive. As though he was trying to prove something."

"Damn fool."

"But he was exciting. Free. I loved it." She smiled. "And he got the same kick out of me. Up until that half second at the Athens trials." She could still feel the bone-chill of training sessions that wouldn't quit. Brian holding the stop watch, the dead weight of exhausted muscles.

"And it's been eating him ever since?"

For a week Brian hadn't spoken more than grunts. He slammed out of the house in the morning, took his bike and disappeared, not returning until dark. She couldn't tell whether it was her own failure or his, but she sat pressing Sadie to her, terrified at what was happening to them. "No, he got past that," she said aloud. "I thought." Did he? She tried to bring the memory into better focus. "I relaxed. Got faster. Thought it was okay."

Annika gazed at the ceiling, absorbing the truth of her own story. What else was there? Besides swimming? Her mind was silent.

Beside her, Vicky lay back with her eyes closed. "It still doesn't jell, Annika."

Annika didn't answer. The certainty of his leaving was answer enough.

A long time later, Vicky's voice came out of the dark. "Forgive me for saying this, but worse things could happen to you."

Annika turned and stared. She was too deep in this situation to imagine any other.

Vicky shrugged at the question in Annika's eyes. "Forget it—just came to me." She sat back and closed her eyes.

Annika did likewise, unable to imagine a state other than her own. She woke to the flight attendant's voice, surprised that she'd dozed off.

Beside her, Vicky turned from the window. "You slept."

Annika yawned. "I guess I did. Did you?" She sighed when Vicky shook her head. "Because I dumped it all on you."

"Don't worry about it, Annie. You needed sleep more than I did."

They felt the plane begin its descent into Boston and said no more.

Twenty minutes later they found themselves searching for yet another concourse for yet another flight. It was two hours later before, gritty and dazed, they boarded the turbo-jet for Bar Harbor. They spoke little. Annika stared into the blackness, trying to give form to the town ahead, the harbor, and the ship that was their destination.

Chapter 13

Brian

1992

Brian watched as Joe picked up the envelope containing the names of swimmers whose times qualified them for the Junior Olympics. He exchanged looks with Annie, who sat across the room with the girls, remembering so many other days like this as they rose from State to Regional All Stars, and then from the Bronze to Silver to Gold on the USA team. Nothing could stop them—until he busted up his leg. He lost a year, and now he was a senior. This was his last chance for the junior tryouts.

Annie gave him a high sign as Joe opened the envelope. His uncle had entered his name, but …

"Ladies first." Joe smiled. "Annika Berglund, 100 meter freestyle, time, 1:05 minutes, and Susan Johnson, 100 meter breaststroke, time, 1:22. Bravo to both of you!" He flung his arm up in a cheer as he flipped the page, shooting a look at Brian before he continued.

"And here are the boys. Robert McMillen, 200 meter freestyle, time 2:15, George Stevens, 100 meter backstroke, time 1:10, and Larry Stewart, 100 meter butterfly, time 1:08."

He lowered the paper. "Bravo! That's a great representation for the Fontenac Club. And for the rest of you, keep swimming for next year. Those of you who turn eighteen will be swimming as adults now, a whole new ballgame, but keep up the good work here or at college—wherever you are." He turned and put the paper on his desk. "Okay, let's swim. The day's routine is on the board."

Brian sat staring at the wall of trophies behind Joe's desk, unable to move. The swimmers left; he sat in the bottom of a hole, the place he'd run from all his life.

Joe stood over him. "Coach Annie today."

Brian shifted his gaze to Joe's face. "It's over isn't it? For me."

"Not necessarily, but you need a break, Brian. A change of pace. And I've watched you work with Annie. You're golden together."

"Brian?" Annie stood at the office door. "It's my fault and I'm really sorry."

"What?" Joe swung around.

"I wasn't here on the boys' tryout day. My mom was sick, and I couldn't come."

Brian's laugh caught in his throat as he remembered the day, feeling the hole of her absence, driving his arms and legs like pistons, knowing he wasn't doing well. "No, no Annie. It wasn't you." He stood up, shaking free of the paralysis. "Joe submitted everyone's best times, anyway, not just that day's."

"Is that true?"

Joe nodded. "Sure. Tryout day is a training technique—to practice swimming under pressure."

"Oh." Her shoulders dropped.

"Now I've assigned Brian to you. Do well, and I'll send him to the Olympics with you as your coach. Go swim!"

"Can't I coach him, too?" Annie asked.

"No, he needs a break, Annie. He's been training too hard, and when you do that it can boomerang. Look at that knee." He pointed to the swollen joint.

"Yeah." Annie studied Brian's leg. "Okay." She raised her eyes to his face. "Let's go!"

He rose and followed, his mind numb, his legs moved because ordered to. For a half hour, he called out the routine printed on the board, the words traversing the blank space that was his mind. Slowly Joe's echoing shouts at other swimmers began to seep into him, lifting him.

He flopped his arms like a gull. "Fly, Annie!"

She laughed, and he jumped in the water to pace her. Her energy flowed into him. He was okay. He wasn't done. Just a bump in the road.

The whistle sounded, ending practice.

"Annie, Susan, Robert, George and Larry! Report to the office when you're dressed," Joe called. "Brian, you, too."

Fifteen minutes later, they gathered around him, toweling their wet heads.

"You're a team. Our team. Brian is my assistant." He smiled. "I'm going to pull together some names for each of you. Swimmers you're likely to meet at the trials and their times. That'll be your goal sheet. Brian will work with the girls; I'll take the boys, then we'll reverse. But you'll work with each other too, as the time gets closer. For now, we'll stick to the regular training times and use the first three lanes. Clear?"

They looked at each other and grinned. Brian laughed in surprise. He'd never coached anyone but Annie. Cool.

"Bravo!" Joe broke from his coaching voice and raised his arms in a cheer. "To all of you. You'll do us proud, and I'll see you back here tomorrow with bells on."

"Brian!" Joe called as they trooped out, "Need to see you for a minute."

Brian returned to his seat and Joe closed the door. "How's that knee?"

"It's okay. Just overdid it on the treadmill this morning."

"I thought Jim told you to stay off that thing."

"Yeah. Just anxious to get it back where it needs to be."

"I know. And it's taking you in exactly the other direction." He sat down with a huff. "You have drive, Brian. Lots of it. But it's past time you learned to control it."

Brian nodded.

"You have a gift. You and Annie both. Not only in the pool but in cheering each other on. Now, I'm asking you to spread that energy around to the other members of the team. Different but the same. Can you do that?"

"Yessir!" He grinned.

He felt good, going home. Solid. Settled. A place to be until his knee let him race again. At the sight of his father's truck in the drive, his new foundation melted. He hadn't made the team. Well, so what? His father didn't give a damn about racing anyway. He climbed out and slammed the car door.

"Didn't make the team for Junior Olympics," he announced as he passed through the kitchen. He continued on past them as they exchanged looks and went up to his room. When he'd unloaded his backpack and donned a sweater, he went back to face their sympathy.

"Sorry, Brian," his father said as he entered the kitchen. "Maybe that's a sign you should change gears. Stop racing and look around."

"No, I'll get back. Joe says I've been training too hard. He has me coaching the team. Says I have a gift."

"You have lots of gifts. Racing's the only one Joe knows."

"So says You!" Brian spun on his heel and headed for the door. "Always dissing Joe!"

⁓

"Let's go!" Brian cried for days and weeks as winter melted into spring. Annika dove into pool after pool across Michigan, his voice echoing with the cries of other coaches, in the hollow air of meet after meet, joining the cheers from bleachers filled mostly with families. He and Annie had only Joe, as always, but they had each other. That was enough. Annie won heat after heat.

"Let's go!" got him up before dawn in the morning to join her at the pool before class. They carried him through classes and back to the locker room and through his own workout until she arrived to swim once again until dinner.

Now the flags of the Junior Olympics hung above them, and that was his mother in the stands. And Stephanie sitting beside her. Stiff as high school freshmen who can't imagine how they ended up that way. He turned to Annie, who was shaking loose, and pointed to them.

A sound that was more shock than laughter burst from her. "Magic!" She turned and held up a hand for a high five. "Us!"

They turned as one and gave Joe, behind them on the bench, a thumbs up as the horn sounded.

"Stay loose," he whispered as she stepped up on the starting block.

"Loose, loose, loose," she muttered, rotating her arms.

"Marks!"

The gun shot eight swimmers into the air, and he began breathing with her, stroking with her, his rhythm joining hers, duck push kick, now, stroke stroke … good good good until the laps took on a life of their own. Push push push, she was edging out now, now, now, now … He was aware that his arms were moving in rhythm to her strokes, his mouth sending messages she couldn't hear, already cheering as she sailed through the last lap, touching the wall a full second ahead of the next swimmer. Annie

END <i>of the</i> RACE

grabbed the bar of the starting block, catching her breath as he caught his above her. Behind them, Joe's cheer was joined by others from the stands.

At home his parents watched, waiting for him to "grow up," come to his senses, and said little. As the summer sun warmed the waters, they forsook the pool to swim in the lakes. Fontenac in the morning, Michigan in the afternoon, exulting in the open water, soft breezes and vistas of trees and sand that had made swimmers of them in the first place.

Until one afternoon he came in from the bay to find that his mother had put a steamer trunk in his bedroom. Summer was over—for him. He was leaving. Leaving Annie.

Chapter 14

2007

By the time Annika and Vicky landed at the Bar Harbor airport, the clock read five am. Beside her, Vicky gave a huff of relief. "I'm going to dream of being lost in a maze of concourses."

Annika turned on her phone and checked for calls and messages. None. The Wolfsons hadn't yet discovered her missing.

They found a taxi and arrived at the village waterfront by dawn. The shape of land and sea appearing out of the darkness was surprisingly familiar. Annika felt her feet take root. Here, as at home, the land rose in mounds from the water, a firm if temporary habitat for humans. The water glowed, then shone in the rising sun. "Have you been here?"

"Once. Long ago. It's lovely, isn't it?"

"It is. So much like home."

"Mm. I'd never live anyplace not on the water." Vicky took her arm. "Come on. We need breakfast."

By the time they found a café and recovered from the night with pancakes and eggs, the sun was up, and the differences in the sea-washed town came to light. "The colors. They're so faded. Everything looks old and—sort of pallid."

"It smells different, too," Vicky commented. "You notice that particularly at sea. It's the salt water."

Annika sniffed. "You're right. Okay, off to find the harbormaster. He's on the town pier, according to the Internet." They passed a row of commercial fishing boats along the pier and found the harbormaster's office, where a weathered, jowly man looked at Brian's picture and listened to their story.

He nodded when they'd finished. "Well, I maybe remember him, but I didn't see him when they came in. Know Svenson. Been running his charter business out of here for years."

"But you didn't see this man?" Annika's voice was insistent, pushing against the chill that had seized her. "Svenson said he headed for the airport."

He shook his head. "He might have done, but all I remember is Nils and his mate hauling gear." He gestured to the pier.

"Can we look at the boat to see if there's any sign of him?" Annika asked, feeling her hopes for the trip dissolving beneath her. "We really don't understand where he could have gotten to, or if he arrived with them at all."

"Well, she's out there." He pointed out to the flock of moored craft. "But you can't board her, of course. Not without the owner's permission."

"That's Svenson, I assume?" Vicky asked.

"Right. Lives in Boston."

They looked at each other, stymied.

"Well, which boat is it?" Vicky asked.

"See that triple-decked yacht at two o'clock? The new one."

"Yes."

"Okay, next boat to the right. The ketch with the black sailbags."

"I see it. Thanks." Vicky smiled, and they headed back down the pier. "Well, that wasn't a lot of help."

"So we have to get out there. How do we do that?" Annika looked around as though the answer lay among the aging fishing craft. "Wait." She put a hand on Vicky's arm. "Look." She pointed past a row of racked kayaks to a clump of beached dinghies.

"Bravo." Vicky headed down the beach. "All we need is a pair of oars."

Annika browsed the row of boats until she found one that wasn't chained, a sea-beaten shell that had once been green.

Vicky arrived with a pair of oars. "Good thing some people are careless with their stuff."

They cast one look down the pier, but no one stood watching, so they stripped off their shoes and socks and dragged their craft to the water. Vicky rowed, and Annika played watchman, but no one appeared at the sound of their dipping oars. Soon they were looking up at the hull of the *Wayfarer.*

"Beautiful ship," Vicky commented.

She was indeed. Gleaming white in the morning sun, her sides reflecting the lapping water. Two masts rose high, sending shafts of early light into their eyes.

Vicky checked the pier one more time, then pulled the dinghy around to the far side and tied up to the ladder. "Let's go. Stay low if you can."

Annika clambered aboard and looked around, trying to imagine Brian on this deck hoisting sail, minding lines. The boat rocked gently as Vicky climbed the ladder. Annika's phone jangled, and she grabbed it quickly to shut it off. "Carmen."

"She's discovered you're missing. Are you going to answer it?"

"No. What would I tell her?" She turned the phone off, pocketed it, and joined Vicky, who was circling the deck, peering into portholes. Annika looked but could see nothing but empty surfaces—the galley, a table, gleaming brass and polished wood.

"We've got to get in," Vicky mumbled. She straightened from peering through a porthole and gave looked around, but Nils was a good seaman. There were no telltale signs of the voyage.

Annika straightened from her examination of the dim interior. "We'd better get ashore before the harbormaster spots us."

"Or someone comes looking for his dinghy."

The old man emerged from his office as they started for the beach, and Vicky quickly pulled behind the fancy yacht next door. "Hold the ladder," Vicky whispered, and climbed until she could peer over the deck. "He's gone," she reported, reseating herself.

They cringed as they rowed across the open water but reached the beach without further incident. They returned their stolen craft and pulled on their shoes and socks.

"Now what?" Annika looked around, unwilling to quit so soon. "Come on. I want to talk to that man again." Vicky followed as she headed down the pier.

"Is there any way to get to the airport other than the taxi?" Annika asked when she arrived at the open door of the harbormaster's office.

"Hmm?" He looked up from his computer, "Not to Hancock. There's a bus to the Bangor airport."

"Where will I find the taxi then?"

The harbormaster put his hands on the desk and pushed himself to his feet. Then he lumbered over to the counter and handed her a business card before raising the leaf and going to the door. "Go up to Harbor Inn." He pointed to a rambling stretch of white clapboard in the distance. "Alf usually hangs out up there if he doesn't have a fare."

"Thank you. That's the only way?"

"Yep." He turned and headed back to his desk.

"Look, I'm sorry to trouble you, but could you look up the exact time the *Wayfarer* came in?"

He sighed and reached for a battered log that lay on the counter. Sniffing, he shuffled through the pages, then peered over his glasses at the entries. "That'll be Saturday last …'bout four o'clock."

"In the afternoon?"

"Yes ma'am."

"That's about right then." She turned to Vicky. "Brian's flight was around six."

As they waited at the hotel for the taxi-man, Annika checked her phone again. She had a voicemail. After listening, she sat back and laughed. "Carmen just wants to know when Sadie's coming after her animals."

"Her animals?"

"Of clay. I guess that can wait. She'll just figure I'm off to the store or something and left my phone home."

"Good. And here comes our taxi, I think."

Annika eyed the weather-beaten Ford and the matching man who was getting out, lighting a cigarette. "And that would be Alf."

After Vicky made brief introductions, Alf studied the picture. "I remember him all right, but he was coming this direction, and it was a couple of weeks ago at least—not last Saturday."

Annika's limbs turned to lead at this final confirmation. Either he never got off that boat, or he lied to Nils about his going to the airport. Her gut told her it was the former.

"Let's check at Harbor Inn," Vicky suggested. "It's possible he stayed here, isn't it?"

"I suppose." She didn't correct the futility in her voice.

But the inn had no such customer. Vicky turned her attention to a brochure listing the town's hotels and motels. By lunch time they'd canvassed every one with no luck. "Food," she announced firmly and waved to the Sandpiper Café at the foot of the pier.

Once they'd settled at a table, Annika checked and saw she had two more voicemails. "Carmen again and ..." She stared at the number. "I think that's Wolfson Wilderness ... probably Jon."

"Let them stew," Vicky advised, flagging a waitress.

They devoured chicken croissants and tea, but food failed to fill the hollow. Soon they stood outside the inn, staring at the gleaming ships.

This time it was Vicky's phone that came to life. "Familiar. Probably a Wolfson, but I don't know which." She let it go to voicemail.

"Hello, Vicky, Papa here. I'm looking for Annika. Is she with you?" His recorded voice evaporated in the sea breeze. Vicky looked a question at Annika.

"Text him. Say I'm with you, but not where."

She winced as Vicky finished the text and clicked the phone off. "I hate to deceive Papa. He's a friend."

"I know. But he knows you're okay. Let that be enough."

"I guess it has to be. For now. So now they think we're in Traverse City."

"Maybe, but they won't get an answer on my landline."

"True. So they start getting upset and guessing where we've gone." Annika looked around, searching for an idea but found none. "We need help. It's time to stop thinking he might just show up. I'm going to report it, Vicky."

Vicky gazed across the parking lot without answering. "All right," she said finally.

Annika returned to the hotel desk and asked directions to the police department, and ten minutes later they'd walked the few short blocks from the waterfront.

"You know," Vicky said as they approached the door, "Jon and family aren't going to like this."

Annika stopped. "This? Telling the police, you mean."

"Right. Family business."

"Oh. I suppose." She stood, imagining their shock at the police arriving at their door. "But I don't know what else to do."

"No. You've done everything you can. I just wanted to forewarn you." Vicky took her arm. "Come on. I'm with you. It's time."

The officer at the desk listened to their tale, then nodded. "I'll have you talk with Lieutenant McCabe." She pushed a button on the intercom and waited for its response. "I have two ladies here who want to report a missing person." She listened, then flicked it off. "Right through that door."

It wasn't until Annika sat looking at the rugged lines of Lt. McCabe's face and the graying crew-cut that seemed to mark his occupation that her stomach clenched at the enormity of her decision. It couldn't be this big a deal. She gripped the arms of her chair to keep herself from fleeing. "We're from Michigan," she blurted, at a loss for a way to start. "Fontenac. My husband, Brian, went on a sailing trip from here and was supposed to get home last Saturday. He didn't, and we can't find him." She sank back in her chair.

Vicky stepped in with the details, and Annika let her attention fade, but came alert when she saw McCabe's face change at the mention of Nils Svenson and Dominic Costello.

"You know those names?" she interrupted.

"In another context." He waved a hand. "Go on," he prodded Vicky.

"That's about all, except nothing we know about Brian fits with any of this."

"He has a swim meet to run in Fontenac tomorrow. He would never miss a meet," Annika added.

"Okay." The lieutenant sounded as though he'd heard such stories every day. He sat up. "First of all, you need to know it's not a crime for an adult to go missing. They do it … well, not all the time, but frequently. Especially the old and mentally ill. So I have to ask, was your husband depressed or otherwise upset?"

Annika frowned at the request to tell more than she wanted to. "I had a miscarriage a month ago. He was upset about that, but he'd gotten over it. I thought. He wanted to get back to training. For the Olympics." She forced every word, hating it.

"Olympics?"

"Yes. I'm a swimmer, you see. I'd been training when it happened— the miscarriage."

"But you're the swimmer, not him."

"He's my coach."

He leaned back and put a hand to his chin. "All right," he said, sitting up. "That does seem an odd time to run off, but people do. More often than not, they turn up on their own, unless … they've had an accident of some kind." He pulled a form from a drawer. "Have you checked local hospitals?"

Annika and Vicky looked at each other. "No," Vicky admitted. "I'm afraid it never occurred to us."

"Well, we'll start there." He punched the intercom. "Lisa, check the hospital and accident reports for a Brian Wolfson in the last three days, would you?" He spelled the name. "And any other reports with that name attached. Thanks." He closed the intercom and looked at it for a moment without speaking. "As I said, it's not a crime to walk away."

"He took money," Annika blurted.

"How much?"

"Ten thousand dollars."

"His money?"

"Our money."

"That's a lot for a two-week sailing trip. Suggests he left intention-ally." He paused, but receiving no reply, went on. "So at this point, unless we suspect some crime was committed, there's not much we can do." He stopped and gazed at Annika intently.

McCabe opened another drawer. He drew out a leaflet and handed it across the desk. "Here's a brochure of some things you can do."

She took the leaflet, feeling abandoned. "Thank you."

"And we'll get more information from you, in case he shows up here. Do you have a picture?"

"Oh. Yes." She fished out the photo and handed it to him.

He studied it. "I'll send this along to the Coast Guard. Have you notified the Fontenac police?" He punched the intercom and asked the sergeant to make copies.

"Not yet, no," Vicky answered for her. "We were hoping to find some answers here. We will when we get home."

"Do that." He tapped his pen on the paper in front of him. "Do you have reason to believe some crime was committed?"

"Just that it all seems wrong. It doesn't fit." Annika insisted. "I talked to Nils Svenson on the phone, and he doesn't sound like a friend. He didn't seem concerned at all. Just brushed it off. And when Brian's brother called him ... and it was Jonathan who was supposed to go on the trip in the first place ... he brushed him off too." She stopped. "There's just more to it, that's all."

"You knew those names." Vicky had sat up in her chair.

McCabe gave her a sharp glance. "From another investigation; noth-ing came of it."

"About drugs?" The question sprang from Vicky's lips, and swung Annika's head round in surprise.

McCabe's eyes narrowed. "Why would you think so? Are drugs involved here?"

Vicky bit her lip as though regretting her outburst. "Brian never touched anything, but ... well ... I knew Nils and Dom—Dominic Costello—that's Nils' partner—in college. They were into pot and ..." She shrugged her shoulders. "Maybe other stuff ... I don't know. It just ..."

Annika stared at her friend, not believing what had just occurred. So that's what Vicky had been thinking when she told her Jon was the source of her father's pot.

"Have you asked Brian's brother ... Jonathan, is it?" McCabe sat up, hands flat on his desk, his demeanor changed from sympathetic listener to police officer.

"I haven't talked to him. Annika did, but ..." She shook her head. "Drugs never occurred to either of us. There's no reason to connect Brian with that."

The Captain's intercom buzzed. When he answered, they could clearly hear the sergeant's voice reporting that no Brian Wolfson had showed up at local hospitals. "Roger that." He hung up and turned back to them. "How about Jonathan?"

"I don't know," Vicky insisted. "We've been divorced for two years."

"But before that?" The officer wasn't to be put off.

"Just pot." Vicky was emphatic. "Nothing else."

"Okay. Well, in that case, we'll have a talk with Nils Svenson. And we'll notify the Michigan police. They'll have a talk with Jonathan."

Annika sat frozen. They'd just released a storm that could shatter lives and over which they had no control.

Chapter 15

Vicky walked quickly, head down, fists jammed into her pockets.

Beside her, Annika hunched her shoulders against the wind. The day had turned gray. "You're upset," she commented.

"So are you—or you ought to be," Vicky retorted. "And I don't blame you. Damn. I don't know why I said that."

"Well ..." Annika stopped, waiting for words to come. "It seems you're right ... or at least the police think so."

Vicky gave a harsh bark of a laugh. "They sure do." She stopped. They had reached the bay, where the scene had lost its color. She clasped her forehead. "God, Annie, they're going to be all over that family like bees to honey. I'm afraid I've put you in an awful jam."

"What were we supposed to do, Vicky? Just go on as though nothing has happened? Do people just ... vanish ... and everyone goes on?"

"Not that I know of." Vicky folded her arms across her chest against the chill and stared out at the masts that now waved and danced in the wind. "Let's find someplace warm to sit." She turned and headed for the now familiar Sandpiper.

They filled the silence between them by ordering pie and coffee. Vicky sat back. "I was married to Jonathan for six years, and I really can't see him involved in moving drugs. He's just not that kind of guy. Smoking pot around a campfire, sure. If he didn't have it, someone else would. But the hard stuff? And dealing? No way. When you said he's the source of your dad's pot, it stuck in my mind. Worried me." She sighed. "So it popped out. Sorry."

"Do you suppose that's what Jon and Karl were fighting about?" Annika stopped as their coffee and pie arrived. "Karl was angry, that much is for sure," she finished as the waitress left.

"Could be." Vicky picked up her fork. "Any charter business is crazy to get themselves involved with that crowd, and Karl would be the first to tell him so."

"But would he involve Brian in it? Brian is so dead set against that stuff, I can't believe he'd go."

"If he knew." Vicky stared out the window at the bay.

Annika followed her gaze and watched a cruise ship emerge from around the headland and approach the pier. A giant among elves, its very size spoke of the vastness of the waters beyond the bay.

"The Coast Guard," Vicky muttered, as though following Annika's thoughts. "The police mentioned them, and it never occurred to me ..." She pulled out her phone and began to punch buttons. "There's a station on the island, but it's way south ..." She looked at her watch. "I don't think we have time to go, but we can call."

Annika stared out across the harbor, trying not to listen as Vicky told the story yet again. The ugliness and reality of the possibilities rubbed her bones raw.

"They want to know if he filed a float plan," Vicky said behind her, clicking off her phone.

Annika blinked. "He being Nils? Filed with whom?"

"With his family, I guess, or maybe the harbormaster." Vicky pocketed her phone and collected her purse and coat. "Let's go ask him."

"But the boat arrived. What good does that do us?" Annika rose to follow.

They reached the street before Vicky answered. She put an arm around Annika's shoulders. "In case there was a 'man overboard' call to some Coast Guard Station."

"Oh, God ..." Her stomach heaved. Her feet moved of their own volition while her head spun. "What have we gotten into, Vicky?"

Vicky gave her shoulders a squeeze. "Don't make too much of it, Annie. It's only an unlikely possibility."

Annika glanced at Vicky's face, which denied her words, and said nothing.

They reached the pier and walked to the harbormaster's office once again. They found the master still deep in his computer.

"Hello, again," Vicky started.

He looked up."Hm? Oh. Any luck?"

Vicky shook her head. "We've come to see whether Nils Svenson filed a float plan."

"He usually does." He didn't move to look. "But we don't generally give out that information."

"We've just reported Brian Wolfson's disappearance to the police; I'm sure they'll ask you for it," Vicky insisted. "And I called the Coast Guard. They want to know."

"He's my husband," Annika added. "Surely I have a right to know."

He shifted his gaze to Annika and scratched his beard. "Well, sometimes, you know, people don't want to be found." He turned to Vicky as Annika sank back on her heels. "I'll be happy to cooperate with them—both of them if they ask."

"The Coast Guard *did* ask." Vicky's voice rose. "Would you FAX it to them, please?"

"Sure. I can do that."

"Thank you." Vicky let out an exasperated huff, and they turned to leave. "Wait ..." She crossed the room to the brochure stand on the opposite wall. "Here," she exclaimed a few minutes later, pulling out a leaflet for Svenson Charters. She glanced through it then returned to the desk. "Can you tell me which of these trips he was on?" She handed him the brochure.

He ran his thumb down the choices. "Must have been that one—Outer Banks Adventure—judging from the dates."

"Thank you. Does he ever vary the route?" Annika asked.

"Only for weather, far as I know." He turned to his computer, dissuading further questions.

"Were there only the three men? Aren't there usually more?" Vicky asked the back of his head.

He swung around and put his hands on his knees. "Depends. Only the three of them that trip, as I remember. Sometimes he picks up clients along the way—Boston, Atlantic City."

Vicky frowned. "Seems odd." She shrugged. "Thank you." She headed for the door.

Once off the pier, they sat on a bench to study the cruise course—a list of ports giving no answers. "Well, it's something, I guess." Vicky gave a sigh.

"Better than imagining endless high seas," Annika agreed.

Vicky handed her the brochure. "You keep this." She looked at her watch. "It's time to go find that taxi. He told us to be at the Inn at three."

"Okay." Annika rose. "Let me get a picture of *The Wayfarer* first." She pulled her camera from her purse and walked out onto the pier where she could get a better view and snapped the shutter.

"Lady?"

She turned and saw the harbormaster standing in his doorway. "Yes?"

"The police just called. Said it was okay to give you that plan, if you still want it."

"Oh, yes!"

Five minutes later, she headed for Vicky, waving the page. "The police called him," she explained, handing it to her.

"Super. Come on, we'll look at it on the way." Vicky started for the inn.

They found Alf waiting for them. Annika shot one last picture of the harbor, before getting into the cab.

"Why?" Vicky asked, as they pulled away. "Is that a picture you're ever going to look at?"

"Probably not, but I need it. It anchors my head."

"Good. At least this trip produced something positive." She yawned. "My sleepless night's beginning to catch up with me."

"And another one ahead." Annika drew the float plan from her pocket and stared at it, fighting to get her brain connected to her eyes.

"So the cruise goes as far as the Outer Banks," Vicky commented, looking over her shoulder.

Annika ran her eyes down the list of ports. "They're just names to me, I'm afraid. Have you been to the Outer Banks?"

"A couple of times as a child. I couldn't get used to my aunt and uncle, who had a home there." She laughed. "I remember feeling like a fish that's found itself in the wrong tank."

"Well, the fish part sounds right. What was wrong with the tank?"

"The all-day-cocktail-hour set. I came home thanking my lucky stars my own folks would have nothing to do with that." Vicky turned toward the window as the taxi slowed. "Here we are."

They settled in the loading area for the first of many waits ahead. Again they studied the list of ports. "It looks as though they chose small inlets and harbors, which I would expect, maybe picking up passengers," Vicky commented. "They might lay over in Nantucket or Virginia Beach. They were only out for two weeks ... but even so, they weren't spending much time ashore." Vicky frowned at the map as though it would answer some question. "Usually pleasure trips take more time ..." Her voice faded off. "But maybe it was just the three of them on a last sail before the weather turns. Nothing feels right." She pulled a magazine from her bag.

Annika studied the map, wondering how Vicky could read so much into it.

"Annie, did Brian ever talk about performance enhancing drugs?" Vicky's voice split the silence.

"What? All the time, Vicky, damning them. Not taking—ever. No way."

Vicky opened her eyes at Annika's vehemence. "Okay. I'm just stretching ... covering possibilities."

"That's okay, but—no. Can't be that."

The loudspeaker announced their flight, cutting off further conversation, but the question rankled, nonetheless. Brian raged at Olympic drug scandals. *"Who do those guys see when they look in the mirror?" "Why do we all have to come down to the level of the Russians?"*

They took their seats and gave in to fatigue, cat-napping until the plane descended into Boston. Once they'd deplaned, they found their Detroit flight on the board, then Annika turned on her phone long enough to check for messages from her mother. There were none, but Joe and Karl had both called, and together they listened to their angry pleas to call. She pocketed the phone again. "We need food, I guess."

"What do you feel like?" Vicky looked around at the offerings.

"I don't even know whether I'm hungry or not," Annika confessed.

"Okay, let's go light. There's a stand with wraps. Then we can sleep the rest of the way."

"Sounds like a winner."

They selected their wraps and were lined up to pay, when Vicky grabbed her arm and swung her around, away from the central area. "What ...?"

"Jonathan," Vicky hissed.

"Oh ... Are you sure?" She resisted the urge to turn.

"Yes. Just stand where you are." Vicky peered beyond her. "Okay. He's passed."

"Did he follow us?"

"I don't think so. I don't see how we could have missed him—at least at the Bar Harbor airport we'd have run into him."

"Unless he's going the other way ... but that can't be; he'd be at the Bar Harbor gate ..."

"Then what ... oh." Annika felt a chill. "He's come to see Nils."

Vicky nodded. "I suspect so."

They arrived at the counter and paid for their food.

"Maybe he's on a different flight," Vicky mused, taking a seat, "but I suppose that's too much to hope for."

"Not probable," Annika agreed. "And especially not probable on the Traverse City flight." She bit into her wrap. "Well, so what? I'm looking for my husband. He's looking for his brother. What makes us enemies?"

Vicky blinked. "Nothing, I guess." She shrugged. "All right." She took a bite.

"But I'd rather not talk to him," Annika conceded, "though I don't know why."

"Because you think he's up to something, and so do I." Vicky took a sip of water. "Eat. We've got a long night ahead."

When they'd finished, they approached their gate cautiously. There sat Jonathan, one leg crossed over his other knee, his foot bobbing in quick impatient motions.

"No such luck." Vicky looked around. "The Ladies Room." She took Annika's arm.

They stood in the anteroom to the toilets where they could hear the boarding call. When it came, they watched Jonathan board with first class, then crossed to the gate.

"We have to pass him," Vicky muttered. "Just pray, I guess."

But Jonathan was deep in his cell phone and had no eye for other passengers.

Vicky sank into her seat with a sigh. "We're blessed."

"Until Traverse." Annika heard a crackle as she kicked her flight bag under the seat and pulled out an envelope. Stephanie's story. As Vicky slept, she was transported into a Cinderella story, but not, for this heroine tends her crippled parents as her beautiful sister marries the prince. She falls in love with a sailor who vanishes, leaving her to mend her broken heart by nursing the sick.

Annika put the last page down and leaned back. *My God, Steph.* Her mind searched for words to give the shock shape. She didn't know her. Had never known her. Her protector. But not this person who released such passion onto the page. Where in her super-responsible, straight-backed sister had the writer hidden all these years? But maybe she hadn't hidden. It was Annika who'd disappeared.

Beside her Vicky stirred as the planes began its descent to Detroit.

Chapter 16

Brian

1993

Brian gazed up at the blue and gold University of Michigan flags, struggling for the certainty that had once been his nature. *You made it!* You made the UM freshman team, he told himself. And then the sophomore. You did fine in school. Kept training. Didn't go off wild and get drunk or do any of that other crazy freshman stuff. No crazy impulses. Kept your nose to the grindstone. Or swimming pool. And Annie's here now! A freshman. So you're a junior. What's so different?

"Marks!"

Brian stepped onto the block and crouched. *Imagine Annie!*

The crack of the gun sent him flying.

The rhythm of this body filled his head. He had it! Had it had it go go go go ... Now! He somersaulted and kicked off. The three other swimmers in his heat were alongside. *Go!*

His body gave a spurt, but the knee was dragging. *"Go!" "Now damn it!"*

Two swimmers passed him, then another and spurted for the wall.

"One forty three."

Nowhere close.

The sun hit his eyelids, forcing him awake. He rolled over, shutting it out.

"Hey!" his roommate yelled. "Don't you have class?"

"Go away."

Feet shuffled, kicked a footstool, a voice muttered something like "your funeral" and the door slammed.

Brian rolled over, eyed the drifts of dirty clothes on the floor, turned toward the wall again and went back to sleep.

"Brian, damn it, wake up!"

Jonahtan stood above him, "Get out of bed."

"What are you doing here?"

"Steve came and got me. Said you'd been in bed for three days."

"So what?"

"So what the hell's the matter with you?"

"Nothin.'" He rolled away.

"Steve thinks you didn't make the swim team. That right?"

"Go to hell."

"You gotta get up. Now."

"What business is it of yours?"

"I need you to crew for me."

"What?" Brian rolled over and blinked.

"Crew. At the sail club. We're racing the 440s today, and I need someone who knows what they're doing. That's you."

"Me?"

"Yeah. You get up now, and I won't call the folks."

Brian groaned and sat up. "Gotta eat."

"We'll stop on the way."

143

Brian pulled open a drawer and found it empty, then scanned the floor until he found a pair of jeans and a sweatshirt.

Forty minutes later, he munched the remains of his hamburger and gazed at the water. "You call that a lake?"

Jon laughed. "It's the best they can do down here. Come on."

He shifted his gaze to the row of yellow-hulled, white decked boats along the shore, rigged and ready to sail. Bigger than Lasers.

"They're pretty cool," Jon told him, leading the way down the line. "You can single-hand them, but they're faster with a crew. "This is ours." He turned to the sailor standing at the next boat. "This is my brother, Brian. Brian, George."

"Welcome. You sail?"

"Ha. He's better than I am."

Huh? He said that? Brian stepped forward and shook George's hand. "That's news to me."

"Launch your boats!" a voice called from the dock.

"Let's go!"

They shoved together as they had a hundred times before, then leapt aboard as she floated.

"Center board!"

Brian dropped the board as Jon hoisted the mainsail, eyes on the telltale. "Jib!" he called as the sail filled.

The boat lifted and Brian felt the wind in his hair.

"Head up!"

Brian pulled the jib tight and leaned back as the boat heeled.

"Coming about!"

He fell into the rhythm they'd perfected long ago on Lake Fontenac, and they came in an easy first.

Jon grinned. "Great to have you back."

"Yeah. I'd forgotten."

"Why don't you take a break from swimming and join the sail club? Do you good."

"This all the water they have to sail on?"

"No, some of them go over to Lake Huron, sail bigger boats. "

"Like the Giselle?"

"Yeah. I don't do that anymore, but I can introduce you to a couple who do."

"Yeah?"

Want to?"

"I guess ..." Today had been fun. And the big water. Fly away toward the blue horizon. He grinned. "Yeah!"

Three days later, Annie at his side, he sat around a *Cottage Inn* table with Jonathan and two men. They looked like men. Older than Jonathan. Not like college students, though Jon said they were seniors. A tall lean blond guy with a smile that said he was sizing you up, and a chunky Italian who made jokes. Nils Svenson and Dominic Constello.

"Welcome aboard!" Nils said as they waited for their pizza. "Your brother says you're a sailor."

"Yeah." He swallowed the addendum of not being as good as Jonathan.

"He's good," Annie added for him.

"Yeah? You sail?"

She shook her head. "I swim."

"You can't do both?"

The others laughed and Annie blushed.

"She's headed for the Olympics," Brian broke in. "Doesn't have time for both."

"A rising star, eh?" Dominic's tone was indulgent.

"Tell me about the club. Jon says you go out on Huron."

"We do. What Dominic here calls 'the big water.'" Nils laughed.

"You'll have to forgive Nils his ignorance," Dominic retorted. "He's a Bostonian. Thinks the Great Lakes are mere puddles."

The pizza arrived, shifting the conversation to the superiority of Chicago pizza over the eastern variety.

"What do you sail on Lake Huron?" Brian asked as he served himself a generous slice.

"A forty footer. But if you want to race, I'd go with the 440s on Baseline Lake. Jon says he took you on as crew last Saturday.

"Yeah, but I'd like to sail the big lake, too. Our family has a forty footer. I've sailed Lake Michigan a little."

"Sure. We'll come out and see how you do with the little guys first."

"Nils has been angling to get us into an east coast regatta. We'll be looking for crew if he manages it."

"That possible?" Jonathan asked.

"Depends on who you know." Nils gave a wise half smile

Brian felt his stomach contract and glanced at Jonathan, whose eyes had gone still. These were the kind of guys their father warned them against. "The racing crowd." Which wasn't true of Uncle Joe, who raced with a bunch of local guys. Or the guys at the yacht club he and Jon both raced with. But these guys fit their dad's description to a T.

"Stick with the 440s," Jonathan advised as they headed back to their coop. "Those two are smartasses because they sail bigger boats."

"Why'd you introduce me then?"

"Because they'll come watch you race the 440s and give you a leg up on qualifying."

"I don't like them," Annie declared. "Are you going to stop coaching me?"

"No way! But you're on the UM team now. They aren't going to let me stand over you the way we do at home. They have their own coaches. I'll be watching, but I need a distraction.

"Settle for the little guys," Jonathan urged again.

"On the itty-bitty pond they call a lake?"

"Don't be a snob. It's water, and all that coming about is good practice."

Brian laughed. "Okay."

Chapter 17

2007

Annika tucked the story away and stared out the rain-swept window into blackness. As she returned to the present, her joints stiffened with the nameless dread that was becoming part of her.

Vicky gave a groan and sat up, looking at her watch. "Yuck."

Annika glanced at hers. Four-thirty. "One more flight and we're home."

"From the frying pan ..." Vicky muttered.

"Into Jonathan." The plane hit the tarmac.

"My ex."

Annika shook her hands, attracting Vicky's questioning gaze. "They turned to ice," she explained. "Why? When did he become an enemy? What's he hiding? Or what are we hiding from him?" Her questions dissolved into a growl. "And when did I become a gibbering idiot?"

"You need coffee."

"And a Danish. A sugar jolt."

"Absolutely. Before we go to the Traverse City gate."

"Amen to that." Even the small plan calmed Annika enough to set the blood coursing through her veins.

As the plane rolled up to the gate, Vicky put a restraining hand on her arm. "Let everyone go by. Then he'll be way ahead of us."

Annika leaned back, time slowing to the pace of the line of passengers inching up the aisle. She came out of her daze when Vicky shook her arm.

"Where've you been?" Vicky laughed.

Annika yawned. "Cocooning, I think."

"Ready?"

They rose cautiously and peered forward. Jonathan's seat was empty. They gave a unified sigh of relief and moved up the aisle and gangway into the terminal, scanning the scene for Jonathan's familiar figure. He was nowhere to be seen.

"Looks like we've lucked out for another hour," Vicky commented. "Time for breakfast." Her voice was brisk with returning energy.

"Careful," Annika warned. "He may have the same idea."

"True. The restroom first. That's safe, anyway." She swerved toward the sign.

When they'd finished, Vicky stopped at the entrance, searching the passing crowd.

"Let's just go," Annika burst. "We're going to meet him sooner or later, and it really doesn't matter which."

"Okay. Better than playing hide and seek without coffee." She marched into the flow toward the Starbuck's where, undisturbed, they breakfasted on coffee and Danishes.

As they approached the Traverse City gate, they saw Jonathan jabbing his phone. Annika readied herself, then walked up to him. "Hello, Jon."

His head jerked up. "Hey! It's you!"

"What have you been up to?"

"Me? Where the hell have you two been? They've been searching all over for you." He waved the cell phone, then looked around and lowered his voice. "Someone went and called the police. About Brian."

"That would be us." Vicky took the seat next to him.

"You! Why the hell—"

"Cool it," Vicky barked, silencing him. "We've been to Bar Harbor. No one remembers Brian getting off the boat, and we're getting nowhere with Svenson."

"We decided we needed help, so we went to the police and reported him missing. Why not, Jonathan?" Annika took the seat on his other side.

"Why ...? Because it's nobody's business but ours! They're all over everyone up there!" He waved the phone again.

"So text them, and tell them where we are," Vicky retorted. "And tell them to cool it, too. The police are only trying to help. He's your brother, for God's sake."

"Where've *you* been, anyway?" Annika shot.

"Boston." Head down, he began to text.

They remained silent watching him until he hit the send button.

"To see Nils Svenson," Annika guessed.

"Right."

"And?" Annika asked when he showed no signs of continuing.

"He said Brian went to the airport. I accused him of lying and threatened him with the police. He finally said he ditched them at the Outer Banks."

"The Outer Banks." Annika frowned. "That's the turn-around point. So why did he lie about it? And how do we know that's the truth?"

"Says he just wanted us off his back. He's pissed about the whole thing—that I sent Brian instead of going myself, that Brian ducked out, that they had to sail back shorthanded."

"That doesn't make much sense. Why would lying get us off his back? Did he think we would just let it go?" Annika rubbed her tired forehead.

"I don't know. I think he didn't want questions about Outer Banks or anything else—and don't ask me why." He shoved the phone into his pocket. "He's really going to be pissed if the police show up. Did you give them his name?"

"Yes." Vicky studied him. "And they already had it. In connection with a drug investigation."

He swung his head toward her, his face frozen.

"That's when they got interested," Annika went on. "His name and Dominic Costello's had come up in a drug investigation, but I guess nothing came of it—that time."

"Oh, shit …" He buried his head in his hands.

They watched him in silence as the boarding call filled the space.

"Come on." Vicky stood.

They boarded and found their seats, watching as Jonathan, white-faced, did likewise ahead and across the aisle.

"So our boy is mixed up in drugs," Vicky muttered. She gave a sigh. "Let's hope it's only pot."

The plane began to roll toward the taxi-way as Annika studied the back of Jonathan's head, trying to fit him into her image of drug dealers, a skuzzy bunch that hung out in city streets. "Vicky, why would Jon have to go all the way to the coast to get pot? It can't be that hard to come by locally."

"Beats me. But it sure looks like he's in trouble."

They fell silent as the plane gained speed and lifted into the air.

"And Brian. Why would he send Brian, knowing how Brian feels about drugs?"

"I'd say it isn't like him—at all. But there you are." Vicky reached over and put a hand on Annika's arm. "Are you ready for your reception in Fontenac? If not, you can stay with me."

"I hadn't thought about it," She confessed. "But I have no choice, Vicky; I have to pick up Sadie."

Vicky sighed. "I suppose you do, but prepare yourself. There's a side of the Wolfsons you haven't seen."

Annika studied her. "You have?"

"You bet. I started hanging out with the sail-racing crowd at the yacht club. It's the way I grew up. I got myself on the team—mostly guys. All I did was sail, but there was talk ..." She shrugged. "Joe pulled me aside one day and told me I had to quit. 'The Wolfsons,' he explained, 'couldn't be having that kind of talk.'"

"Good grief."

"Yeah. Well, I quit and started going on the wilderness trips with Jon, and Karl started making comments about Jon's country club wife. Jon just laughed. That did it."

"So you left," Annika finished for her.

"So I left." She turned her head toward the window. "Too bad, you know. We loved each other. Carmen thought I was into the cocktail party stuff, but I wasn't. I just love the wind in the sails. Riding the wind."

Annika smiled. "That's how I feel swimming—or felt." She paused as a very different feeling—like joining the rhythm of the waves—flowed through. "When I'm racing, anyway."

"I know. And Brian feels that."

Annika chilled, as the present tense hit her as oddly wrong. *Surely not. He's somewhere!* "And Jon?" She fought to turn the conversation. "How did he feel about your love of sailing?"

"He understood. He loves to sail, too, but not to race. He thought I should stand up for myself and ignore the talk." She turned back to the window, as though remembering, then turned back. "But he didn't know … he was such a seamless part of his family, with his father … he couldn't imagine not belonging, really. And I was rubbing cross-grain with the whole family. So much for a dream of belonging. Sooner or later they'd buy into some rumor, and it would get worse."

"That's rotten, Vicky."

"I was pretty angry," she conceded. "But with Karl and Carmen thinking I loved the high, loose life of the rich, and Joe obsessed with what people would think …" She gave a raspberry. "It wasn't worth it."

"Well, I know how you felt. I was a Berglund, which was—still is—dangerous territory … Her voice faded as the scene of her introduction came back. "But it hasn't been that way for a long time." She thought back to her conversations with them in the last days. "Even Karl has changed— because he thinks I'm good for Brian."

"Which you are. But you may find a change today. Don't let them intimidate you, Annika. You're a normal, adult, very bright woman look-ing for her husband. And they should be looking too. Why aren't they?"

"Maybe they are. Jon is, apparently." She looked forward, across the aisle. Jon had his head back against the seat as though sleeping, but she didn't think he was.

"True. And scared spitless of something. Well, let's hope the police can get to the bottom of it, and damn the family."

"Amen."

They both leaned back and closed their eyes, letting the drone of engines fill the space where thoughts had taken flight.

When the plane rolled to a stop in Traverse City, Jonathan disem-barked and headed for his car without acknowledging them further.

"He's angry, that's for sure," Vicky remarked, as they descended the steps to the tarmac.

At the parking lot, they paused. "Look," Vicky said, "do you want me to come with you?"

"I'd love you to," Annika confessed, "but there's no need for you to go back into that."

"Well, can't say I'm eager." She studied Annika. "And I'm afraid it'll only make things worse if they see us paired off from them."

"Damn it, it's not *from* them. They're the ones ..." She broke off at the futility of it all.

"Just remember that. It isn't you." Vicky gave her a hug. "Call me."

"For sure. And thank you for coming with me."

"In other situations, I'd have enjoyed myself thoroughly." Vicky gave her another hug and turned toward her car.

Annika pushed aside Vicky's warnings as she headed out of Traverse City; she would have only Sadie and her own family to confront—for now.

Chapter 18

Annika drove along the bay, tension draining from her muscles as the line of motels gave way to pastures and cherry orchards and those, in turn, to woodlands, sand and blue water, their colors unblanched by salt. She opened the window to absorb the scent of sun-warmed grass and feel the autumn-crisped breeze on her face. Home. A good swim and a nap. She frowned as she realized that the word swim had somehow separated itself from training. What was happening to her?

But as she approached her childhood home, fear drove unease away. Her father. Her mother had told him she was going to meet Brian, and here she was. Alone.

The door burst open, and her mother waved, then spread her arms wide in welcome.

Annika went into them. "Is Dad here?"

"No, he's at the vet center. He goes there on Thursdays, now. He's helping collect for the Thanksgiving food drive." She kept an arm around Annika, guiding her into the house. "And Sadie's off to school. I told her you'd be picking her up. I hope that's okay?"

"Of course. How is she?"

"Quieter than usual. She's worried, but she's a sweetheart. How are you? What did you find out?" She led the way to the kitchen.

"That Brian got on the ship and maybe got off at the Outer Banks." Annika sank into a chair, grateful for the untroubled quiet of the house.

"Outer Banks? That's South Carolina." Her mother frowned in confusion as she poured coffee into two mugs.

"Right. It's where the boat turns around. They go from Bar Harbor to the Banks and then back." She accepted a cup and warmed her hands around it. "Thank you."

"And that's all?"

"Almost." She took a sip before continuing. "The harbormaster and taxi driver remember Brian when *The Wayfarer* set sail, but not when the boat returned." She paused. "So we went to the police and reported him missing."

"Oh dear." Her mother sat down with a jolt. "Missing." She sighed. "But you had to. I see that."

"It's scary."

Her mother nodded. "Caught me off guard." She sipped her coffee and set down her cup. "What did they say? The police."

"That they couldn't be involved unless foul play was suspected." She took a drink, wondering how much to tell. "But it turned out they'd heard the names of the friends Brian went with in connection with another case, so they're going to talk with them—the friends. And check with the Coast Guard. See if there were any distress calls from the ship."

They drank coffee in silence.

"Is Stephanie here?"

Her mother nodded. "Sleeping. Have you had breakfast?" she asked after the clock had ticked off several minutes. "Can I fix you something?"

"A piece of toast would be nice. That's all. The coffee's wonderful."

"Nonsense. You have to eat."

Annika gave in to the warmth of the sun on her back, the slim figure at the stove, the tiny daisies on her housedress.

"Here you are."

She roused and looked down at bacon, eggs and toast. "You're an angel."

Her mother smiled. "Wish angeling were so easy."

"Amen." Annika started to eat, but found her appetite fading quickly.

Her mother watched in silence until Annika put her fork down. "What do you want me to tell your father?"

Annika took a last deep breath of peace. "The truth. He'll be furious, but there's no point in keeping up a charade. Maybe he'll think I'm better off. He believes all the Wolfsons are scoundrels."

Her mother sighed. "But why, Annika? Why would he just take off like that unless ... but the boat came back. It was there?"

"Yes." She was tempted to go on and tell the rest, but decided her mother was better off not knowing about the drug connection. "I don't know, Mother, and that's the truth. I may never know." The words set loose a storm of outrage that had been growing silently somewhere deep inside. Elbows on the table, she pressed her fists to her temples. That couldn't be. Couldn't. Things happen for a reason.

Her mother reached a hand across the table and clasped her arm.

Annika took a deep breath, released her grip on her temples and took her mother's hand. "At least for now, that's where we are." The words eased the ball in her gut. "And we go on. You taught me that."

"I did? Never intended to."

Annika laughed. "Be glad you did."

Her mother gave a huff and pulled away. "That's pretty grim gladness."

Annika pulled the story from her bag. "This is wonderful writing. Mom. Tell her that for me, will you? Tell her she broke my heart but somehow healed it, too. I wish I knew how she did that."

"Maybe she'll let me read it."

"You haven't?" As she said the words, Annika realized her mother could easily identify the fictional characters in the story.

"She's been shy about it. Brushes it off as nothing. But maybe she will now that she's shown it to you."

"I hope so." And she did. It was not a bitter story, not at all. "Now I'm going home for a swim and a nap before Sadie gets out of school." Repeating her intent to swim was an assertion of some kind, which she didn't stop to question.

The glass and cedar house sat undisturbed, its windows gazing out across the lake as though the world was powerless to disturb it. Annika gave a sigh of relief, though what she'd expected she had no idea. Once inside, only the blinking message light signaled her absence.

She put down her bag and punched the button.

"Annika? It's me. Carmen. What on earth is going on?" Her shrill voice shattered the quiet. "Karl says the police showed up! At his office! Did you do this? Go to them? For heaven's sake, call me! We've been looking for you everywhere!"

Annika hissed through clenched teeth. Well, Vicky had prepared her. She stared from the instrument to the window where water winked in the sun. Carmen could wait. She'd have her swim first. The training schedule on the refrigerator challenged her, demanding. She turned away.

As she dove into the lake, the small child came back, the water washing away the confusions of life, bringing the exultation of freedom. She swam. The motion of her body fed her brain. She was strong. Sure. She stroked harder. Water slid past like silk. Flying. Then she slowed again, letting the water flow past more gently and swam on.

Her hand struck sand, startling her out of her euphoria, and she put her feet down. She'd swum all the way across the cove. Looking back at the house, she remembered the day she'd first swum that distance from a different dock. A mile. On a dare. A birthday party. Brian's. She'd been ten. As the memory faded, she was left staring across at their dock, as though Brian stood there, cheering her on.

The dock was empty. She splashed water on her face, returning to adulthood and started back across the cove, shifting from breast stroke to back crawl, in no hurry. When she turned again to freestyle to gain some distance, the dock was no longer empty.

Carmen stood, hands on hips, watching her. Annika waved. Her mother-in-law didn't return the gesture. Annika went back to swimming. She wasn't going to feel guilty. Swimming had once again given her what she needed.

"How long have you been here, for God's sake?" she cried as Annika pulled herself to the dock. "I left messages …" She waved an arm as words failed her.

"I know. I just got home, and I needed a swim." She picked up her towel and headed for the house. "Come on up."

"You went to Bar Harbor. With Vicky."

"I did." She held the screen door for the other woman.

"Without telling anyone." Carmen marched past her. "Where's Sadie? Did you take her?"

"She stayed with my folks. I'll pick her up from school." She went to the kitchen and filled the coffeepot. When she'd loaded the grounds and hit the switch, she turned to Carmen, who stood watching her. "Help yourself to coffee. I'll be back." She headed for her bedroom, wondering at her calm control. Liking it.

When she returned, Carmen was pouring herself coffee. She helped herself to a cup. "I went because I had to, Carmen. To see the boat for myself. To find out what I could."

"But why didn't you tell anyone?"

"I was afraid you'd stop me." She could hardly say she needed to get away from the Wolfson clan.

"So you went with Vicky. Jonathan told us. And you went to the police. Was that her idea?"

"It was not. Why would you think so? We need help, Carmen. Why are you so angry? Don't you want to find him?"

"Of course I want to find him! He's my son! But not with the newspapers blaring our business! The police showed up at Karl's office, for God's sake. In the middle of the morning business, as though he was some sort of criminal."

"To talk to Jonathan?"

"Who wasn't there, so they tackled Karl instead. Something about running drugs." Carmen smacked down her coffee cup. "Karl doesn't do drugs, Annika. Not even pot anymore. Whose idea was that?"

Annika met her glare, remembering Stephanie's story about Carmen's and Karl's hippie days. "The Bar Harbor police recognized Nils Svenson's name from an earlier investigation—a drug investigation."

"Which has nothing to do with Karl." She waved a dismissive hand. "But Sheriff Billy Constantine will always have his eye on the Wolfson business because he remembers Karl from his college days."

"He knew him back then?"

"Oh yes. They grew up together. A straight arrow, that's our Billy Constantine." She sniffed and picked up her cup.

"A Vietnam vet?" Annika asked on a hunch.

"You bet. A real patriot."

"Like my father?" Her voice was sharp in the quiet kitchen. She'd never seen Carmen in this mood and didn't much like it.

Carmen looked up, startled, then slumped. "I'm sorry. You were no part of all that, Annika, but ..." She shrugged.

"Neither was Brian—or Jonathan."

"I know. But Billy'd love a chance to nail Karl—he'll go to the papers with great glee." She put her head in her hands. "And the very fact that Brian went ..." Her voice died.

Annika watched her in silence, chilled by the idea that Brian was forever caught up in this family saga.

"Why did he go, Annika?" Carmen's head shot up. "Have you found out anything more?"

Annika returned her stare. "Why was Jonathan going? What had he to do with those guys?"

"I don't know." Her voice was barely over a whisper. "And I'm scared." She rubbed her face, her defenses gone.

Annika sighed, her anger softening as she looked at the crumpled woman. "So am I. It's time Jonathan came clean with both of us. Is he home yet?"

Carmen shook her head. "He came in and left—in a twit. Said he'd explain later. The police are looking for him. The police!"

"They can find Brian better than we can, Carmen."

"No, no, no ..." Carmen raised her hands in protest then broke off and sat staring at the rug.

"Jonathan talked to Nils Svenson—"

"You saw Jonathan?" Her head shot up. "Where?"

"On the way home. In Detroit. Svenson told him Brian got off the boat at the Outer Banks. That will give the police a lead."

"Why would he get off there? It makes no sense. Joe called—wild that Brian isn't here for a meet tomorrow ..." She put her hands over her ears, as though unwilling to hear more.

"Well, so are the rest of us, Carmen. So why not get help? Why is the family so upset?"

Carmen slapped her hands on her knees and rose. "You simply don't understand, Annika. The Wolfsons have a name. They're founders. And when Karl became a hippie and war protester …" She gave a bitter laugh, "Then came home with me—a wop from the depths of Chicago—" She choked. "Well, it wasn't nice. It's taken years for them to forgive me for leading Karl astray." She sat back, spent. "And there are people in town, like Constantine, who'd love to drag it all up again." She stood up. "So leave this to the Wolfsons from now on, okay?" She headed for the door without waiting for a response.

"Goodbye," Annika called after her and was left staring at the now vacant doorway. There was nothing she didn't understand about the bitterness left by that war. Except why it never healed. And what it had to do with Brian. Or her.

She glanced at the clock. Almost time to get Sadie. She'd better eat. As she made herself a sandwich, she pondered her mother-in-law's visit. Carmen was frightened. Not only for Brian, for Karl and Jon, too. And for herself. Annika had never seen old pain reopen the way she'd just witnessed. The town's resentment—hate even. She thought of her own father—a symbol of those times. But it was the war that left him broken. Carmen sounded as though the whole town was waiting to get back at Karl. Or the Wolfsons. Which? So Carmen had had her own fight for acceptance. She'd always seemed an odd combination of awe of the pioneer history of the Wolfsons, their attachment to the land, and aversion to the polished lives of the rest of the family. She exploded into Italian cooking with a vengeance Annika now understood. Neither of them had ever fit.

With an exasperated sigh, Annika shoved her food away. None of this brought them any closer to finding Brian. The clock said she would have no nap. She took Sadie's overnight pack from the car and put her things away, concentrating on the child who had to be told something. She drove to town and stared at the school, her mind still vacant. She heard the final bell , her mind still blank. How do you stop protecting your child? She got out and leaned against the fender, waiting for the flood to burst forth.

Sadie came out slowly, then spotted Annika and began to run, waving. "Mama!"

Annika threw her arms wide, welcoming the small body. "Hello baby!" She hugged her tight and felt her world regain balance. "I've missed you."

Sadie giggled. "Me too."

"Did you have a good time at Grandma's?" She put her daughter down and opened the car door.

Sadie nodded. "Grandpa taught me tricks." She climbed into her car-seat and began twisting her fingers as Annika buckled the straps.

Annika laughed. "Like this?" She shaped her fingers into a rabbit. Then a spider.

"That's it! How did you know?"

"Well, Grandpa is my daddy. He taught me, too." She closed the door and opened the driver's.

"Oh." In the mirror, Annika saw understanding turn to fear. "Where's *my* daddy? Did you find him?"

"I didn't, sweetie, but we're getting help now, from the police."

Sadie's eyes went big. "Do the police help find people? Good people?"

Annika glanced at her in the mirror. "They do. And I saw the boat Daddy went on. It's home safe."

"But what if he fell off? No one can find him then!" The words exploded in a sob, a sign she'd nursed this fear in silence.

"But the people he went with would know, sweetie. And they'd call the Coast Guard. We're checking with them, too." She thought of telling the child he may have gotten off at the Outer Banks, but the possibility that

Brian had left them deliberately was more than she wanted to pile unto a six-year-old.

They rode along the shore in silence.

"I think those men kidnapped him."

"What?" Her eyes shot to the mirror in astonishment, but her daughter sat with lips clamped shut, saying no more. "What on earth gave you that idea?" She pulled into their drive, switched off the engine then turned toward her daughter.

"Bad men do that."

Annika stared, then it dawned on her. "Did you watch TV with Grandpa?"

Sadie sobered, wide-eyed at being found out. "Just some."

"Uh-huh. I'll bet." She was more than familiar with the sort of TV her father watched. "Well, those are stories, Sadie. Not real life." She got out, went around the car and released the car-seat buckles.

Sadie jumped down and marched toward the house, "In real life daddies come home."

Chapter 19

Brian

1999

"Let's go!" He raised his hand for a high five as she came out of the locker room.

Annie laughed, returning the greeting then gazing around at the USA Swim flags. "It isn't real, is it? Just some magical dream …"

For four years they'd done it, apart and together, surviving the weeks between, living for weekends when he joined her in Ann Arbor. He'd survived his terror when she went off on field trips with her environment class, insisting she did better if she had a break. No one knew that those breaks sent him reeling toward the void. He joined the sailing club, made the team and sailed then sailed some more, happy enough to avoid the two creeps he'd met at *Cottage Inn.* He never felt his feet hit firm ground, though until she returned. "It's real." He reached over and gave her a pinch.

"Ouch!" Annika gave him a slap.

"Every day, week, year of it. And now you're here." He waved his arm at the crowded stands, then stood letting echoing din of voices swell his chest.

The loudspeaker came alive, calling the 500 Freestyle to the pool.

He threw his arms around her and kissed her. Right on the mouth. He'd never done that before, and it surprised him as much as her. "You're off!"

Mouth agape, she started to say something, gave a laugh instead, then turned and fled toward her lane.

He stood grinning at himself until the call to the marks, then came to and trotted to the benches behind the start line, arriving with the gun. His head moved with her body, his own muscles stretched as she stretched for the water, rocked with her rhythm, turned and stretched again. A beatific calm descended as he watched, reliving the feel of her lips on his, knowing exactly when she would pull ahead of the group, when that liquid stroke would speed up as others tired. One glance at the clock brought him to his feet, cheering, feeling Joe's hand clapping his shoulder from behind, turning his face to the stands to see his mother and Stephanie on their feet, yelling as Annika's fingers hit the wall. A record. Not just a personal record. A national record.

"You did it! You did it!" He cried running forward as the last swimmer reached the wall.

She gasped, then croaked a laugh as the times went up on the board, then reached across to receive the congratulations of the swimmer in the next lane.

When she heaved herself out of the pool, he was there, putting her towel around her shoulders, taking in her smell.

She spun around and threw her arms around him, laughing. "We did it!" And kissed him squarely on the mouth again, right there with their families watching.

～

Through his binoculars, Brian searched the undulating sea of mortarboards below, flashing gold as the sun caught their tassels. The magenta, purple, ochre and gold of faculty hoods on the stage at the far end of the football field gave magnificence to the scene, but the bobbing satin squares revealed no faces.

"Good grief!" he heard Annika's mother exclaim from her seat down the row. "How many millions are there? How will we ever find her?"

Brian watched the tall boney man beside her who searched through his army field glasses without responding. He'd rarely seen Tom Berglund, who lowered the glasses, his jaw clamped in disappointment, his hands landing on his knees. He was a stony crag of a man with a long, creased face, a jutting chin, and a thatch of fading hair that had once been red. The man had given him a harrumph of a hello, neither welcoming nor hostile, but acknowledging his presence—reluctantly.

"Just take a picture of the whole field, Mom," Stephanie told her.

"That's about as good as you're going to get," Mr. Berglund agreed.

The loudspeakers beginning the graduation program cut off further conversation, for which Brian was grateful. He couldn't not sit with them, since Mrs. Berglund had invited him, but he felt like a duck among geese. They didn't know what to do with him.

Two hours later, his seat raw from squirming on the bleacher bench, a cheer rose from the sun-baked field, and the air filled with mortarboards. It was over.

She was free. They were free. She could come home to Fontenac now. They had two years to get ready for the Sydney Olympics. He rose and cheered with the rest of packed stands and followed the Berglunds into the mass of sweating human flesh shuffling toward the gates. He laughed. Packed in like a sardine and he was floating. Insane and wonderful.

A half hour later, they spied Annika waving her mortarboard from Gate Six, their agreed meeting spot. He leapt forward then abruptly caught himself as Mrs. Berglund threw her arms around her daughter. It was their day, the Berglunds. He stood watching, his euphoria wilting in the sun.

"Brian!" She called. "Come!"

Released from purgatory, he dashed forward to give her a hug. He ached to kiss her, but the Berglunds stood behind him, watching, so he lifted her arms in a cheer.

"Come to lunch," she said, gripping his arms.

He tried for a smile. "No, no ... can't ..." He could feel Tom Berglund's eyes drilling into his back. "See you later ... I need to ..." His brain floundered for something he needed to do.

"I'll call," Annika said, having mercy on him. She smiled, waving her cell-phone.

He turned, stiffened his spine and turned. "Glad you could come, sir. You should be very proud of her."

Tom Berglund gave a startled "humph," and Brian turned to Mrs. Berglund without waiting for further response. "It's really cool you're here."

She smiled. A real smile. "So am I." Her handshake was firm, as though approving his bond with her daughter. He grinned. "She's a great lady."

He turned to Stephanie. "Good to see you." He meant it. She brought back the days when he'd tagged along behind Jonathan and his friends who hung out at McDonald's. She'd been nice to him.

"It's been awhile," she acknowledged. She paused and glanced at her folks, who were talking to Annie. "Take care of her." She gave his hand a squeeze.

With a wave, he extricated himself and headed for town. *Damn it, I could be friends with them if it wasn't for the old grouch.* He headed for the gym, flashed his alumnae card and talked his way in to work off the tension of the day, then finished it off with a few laps in the pool, his mind turning to the months ahead, swimming with Annie every day, no long weeks of absence in between.

To his surprise, his phone rang soon after he'd returned to his room. "Ho!"

"They're off for home," Annika assured him. "Steph has to work tonight."

"Meet me at *Cottage Inn*."

"It'll be mobbed, Brian. Come to my place. Everyone's off with their folks or gone home."

"Yeah?" The idea of having the student ghetto she lived in to themselves catapulted the day back into euphoria. "I'll bring pizza and beer! And a cake to celebrate!"

"See you in an hour!"

When he arrived, she'd changed into shorts and a blue and gold sun-top that set off her thatch of curls that had turned auburn over the years. She'd set the table for them in the communal kitchen, complete with a candle, which she lit upon his arrival.

He drew her to him and kissed her, letting his muscles turn fluid.

When it was over, she didn't pull away. "This is nice," she murmured.

"Mmm," he responded. "Let's do it all the time."

She laughed.

"I mean it," he said, pushing her back until he could look into her eyes. Her gaze sobered as she met his. "All you need to do is marry me."

Chapter 20

2007

Annika stared after the small figure, defeated. She caught up with her on the front steps and saw that Sadie's anger had dissolved into tears at the failure of the adult world. Her attempts to take her daughter in her arms were thrown off with renewed vigor, so she was left with nothing to do but unlock the door and watch Sadie stomp up the stairs to her room.

She leaned against the closed front door, absorbing the silence of the house, the glint of late afternoon sun off the water beyond the windows. But the counter was littered with the remains of her lunch, her suitcase sat by the stairs where she'd dropped it, the answering machine was blinking.

She sighed, crossed the room, and punched the button to play the messages. The Fontenac News, Traverse City Record Eagle, Fontenac Police—she shut off the machine and stood shivering at the sound of the impending wave of publicity. Not now. She had to sleep.

Picking up their bags, she climbed the stairs and went to Sadie, who was now curled on her bed hugging her stuffed duck, staring out the window.

"Come on, baby ..." She lay down behind her and took her in her arms. "We're going to be strong until they find him." She pressed her head into Sadie's curls.

"But why is he lost, Mama? Grown-ups don't get lost."

"Well, I guess they do, sometimes. Grown-ups can be dumb, selfish, confused, angry, just like kids."

"They should know better." She jutted out her chin, Brian's chin in miniature.

"True. Come on, let's get out of your school clothes and make ourselves some supper." She rolled Sadie off the bed as the doorbell rang. "Huh! Okay, get changed, and I'll see who's here." She made her voice light.

The peep-hole showed her the blue uniform of the Fontenac Police. She steeled herself and opened the door.

"Mrs. Wolfson?" The officer was young, blond and very tall.

"Annika Wolfson. Yes."

"I'm Officer Carlson. I'd like to talk to you about your husband's whereabouts, if I may." He stood very straight, his tone almost apologetic, like a boy rehearsing lines for the school play.

"Come in." She turned, and spied Sadie out of the corner of her eye, standing at the top of the stairs. "Wait in your room, Sadie, until I come get you."

Sadie didn't move.

"Go. Now."

She turned obediently, but not before Annika saw the tears of anger and confusion gather. She sighed and turned to the officer. "This way." Her tone was sharper than she intended, but she didn't correct it. She merely motioned him to a seat.

Carlson sat, pulled out a notebook, then a pen, then waited.

For what? She took a seat. "What ... do you want to know?"

"First I'd like to confirm some things." He flipped back a few pages. "Your husband is Brian Wolfson ... the son of Karl Wolfson?"

"Yes."

"And he disappeared last Sunday. Is that correct?"

"He didn't arrive on his flight, Sunday. But he'd been away for over two weeks. I don't know when he disappeared."

"Right. He went on a sailing trip I understand. Out of Bar Harbor." Carlson kept his eyes on his notebook, as though bent on plowing through the interview as quickly as possible.

"Yes."

This time he looked up. "Did you confirm that he actually got on board?"

"Yes, the harbormaster and a taxi driver at Bar Harbor remember him."

"But they didn't see him on the return."

"That's right." Why did she feel like a suspect? Was that the effect the police had on people?

He stared at his notes for a long minute before bursting forth. "Mrs. Wolfson, do you have any reason to think something happened to him ... other than he ... didn't return?"

Her mind shot to the missing $10,000, but her throat closed on the words. "Do I think he left me, you mean? No." And she didn't. Really didn't.

"Well—but he might he have had other reasons? Financial or personal?"

"Not that I know of. He has a swim meet tomorrow. He wouldn't miss that, not with State championships coming up."

"No trouble at home?" His color rose, but he persisted. "You didn't fight?"

"No." She wasn't going into the last month's tensions. Not to the police.

Another long pause followed. "Was your husband … involved in drugs?"

"Drugs." She was too tired for this. "Absolutely not. Never." Whatever Svenson and Costello were into had to do with Jon, maybe, not Brian. It was the man's uniform that made everything seem sinister.

Her head began to pound as his questions went over every bit of ground she'd covered again and again. Did she know Svenson and Costello? Had she been on their sailing trips?

"Officer Carlson, you'll have to excuse me." She stood up. "I haven't had any sleep, and I have a child to feed." She motioned to the door. "I don't know any more than I told the police in Bar Harbor."

"That's okay. I'm about finished." He clambered to his feet and closed his notebook. "Do you have any idea where we might find Jonathan Wolfson?"

She blinked. "He isn't here? He flew back to Traverse on the same plane I did. He was looking for Brian, too."

"His father says he showed up and left again." He put the notebook in his pocket. "You'll let us know if you see him?"

"All right."

He nodded and left, closing the door behind him.

"Mommy? Did they find him?" Sadie stood at the top of the stairs.

Annika turned, relieved to be free of him. "Not yet, honey; they just started."

"Well …" Sadie came down the stairs. "I wish they'd hurry."

Annika smiled. "Ditto. Meanwhile, let's eat. Are you hungry?"

"For pizza."

"Okay, you run and get the mail, and I'll tend to that."

Annika turned on the oven and took the pizza out of the freezer.

"Mamma!" Sadie stood wide-eyed, her arms loaded with papers and mail. "There are people out there! With cameras. They want you!"

Annika crossed the living room and looked out the window. "Damn," she muttered. Apparently Carmen was right. The local press rose to the Wolfson name like fish to fresh bait. And she'd sent Sadie into that. Alone.

"Who are they?" Sadie squeaked.

"The newspapers, Sadie." She put an arm out, drawing her close. "Did they try to talk to you?"

Sadie shook her head. "Just asked where you were."

"Good." She returned to the kitchen and put the pizza into the oven. "Wait here," she told Sadie and headed outside and down the drive, only to be greeted by a hail of questions and camera flashes before she could open her mouth.

She held up both hands. "Stop! Please!"

The crowd quieted. "You've no business here! You scared my daughter, and I have nothing more to tell you than I told the police."

"But you must have some idea what ..." "Your husband's the swim coach ..."

"Why'd he go to Bar Harbor ..." "Did you know he was ..."

"Why ..."

Questions attacked and buried each other.

"No!" The babble quieted. "Nothing more." She turned her back and headed for the house. *Damn! Vultures!*

They mumbled and headed for their cars.

Annika closed the door and leaned against it, imagining her trials of the last month spread all over the Traverse City and Fontenac County papers. No wonder Carmen was upset. Was this the work of the police chief ... what was his name? Constantine. Billy. Getting back at the Wolfsons? Was she right about that, too?

"Look!" Sadie exclaimed when she saw Annika. "It's Daddy!" She held up the morning paper.

"LOCAL MAN MISSING AT SEA?"

And there was a grinning Brian, front and center.

Sadie was mouthing out the words. "But he's not! Is he?" Her voice rose. "You said he wasn't ..."

Annika stepped forward and took her daughter in her arms. "No no, it's okay, baby." She rubbed the tangled curls. "I said the ship came back okay, and his friends would know if he fell overboard. The newspaper's just ..." She paused, searching for words. "Just trying to make a good story."

"It's not good! Why's it good?" Sadie pulled back.

"Whoa ..." Annika grabbed her hands. "I only meant a story people will want to read."

Sadie frowned.

"Like ... when we go to the library, and you pick out books to read. You like stories where scary things happen, don't you?"

"This is not like that." She pulled free and turned away.

"No. Not for us. But I guess it is for other people."

"That's not nice."

Annika heard tears in her daughter's voice and felt tears come to her own eyes in response. "I smell pizza."

They settled themselves to eat and the doorbell rang. Annika slapped the table in exasperation. "Stay here. I'm going to run them off."

She swung the door open, ready to yell, then her heels hit the floor. "Hello, Melissa."

"Are you all right? Markus sent me—he's on a tear."

Annika smiled at the diminutive silver-crowned figure of Papa Wolfson's wife, Brian's grandmother. "Come in. Yes, we're okay. Will you join us for pizza?"

"No no. I just … hello Sadie!" She caught the hands of the child who rushed her. "You eat. Pizza isn't any good cold." She patted Sadie's backside and sent her back to the table.

"My daddy's gone," Sadie told her after she'd climbed back into her chair. "He didn't come home and no one can find him."

"I know, honey."

"But the police will find those bad men who took him."

"No, no, Sadie," Annika admonished. "We don't know anyone took him."

"Markus is furious he wasn't kept in the loop—the police just showed up! He went storming after Karl and Joe, and he wanted to be sure you're okay."

"I should have called. I'm sorry." She'd included Papa and Melissa in the excluded Wolfsons. Not fair, but there it was. "Except for the gang of newspeople out there, we're all right, Melissa. Worried, but managing. Thank him for his concern."

"Markus said he'd been trying to find out more about that boat. That you went to Traverse City to find Vicky."

"Yes. She remembered the men, but not much more. Tell Markus we went to Bar Harbor to see *The Wayfarer*. She was there, but we didn't find out much more. No one saw Brian get off the boat. That's why we decided we needed more help—and went to the police."

"*You* did!" Her face changed. "Oh."

"The police find good people too. Did you know that?"

Melissa turned to Sadie and blinked. "Yes. Well." She turned back to Annika. "They were quite a shock. Right on our doorstep that way."

"Indeed." She'd never been angry at this kind woman, but she wasn't going to give the expected apology.

"Yes. Well." She gazed around the room at a loss. "I won't keep you from your pizza, then." She headed for the door, then turned. "And I do hope they find him soon, dear. And clear this all up."

Annika managed to smile through her exhaustion.

An hour later, she helped Sadie into her pajamas and, stripping to her underwear, crawled into bed beside her.

"My animals!" Sadie sat up wide-eyed. "I didn't get my animals!"

"What?" Annika fought the sleep that had already possessed her.

"At Grandma's! I left them there. Don't you remember?"

"Oh … that grandma…" Annika struggled to get her brain in gear. "We'll get them, sweetie. Grandma will keep them safe." *And how are you going to do that now?* She mumbled to herself as sleep took possession once again.

Chapter 21

The jangling of the telephone sat Annika up, staring at the drawings on Sadie's wall. She stumbled into her bedroom and grabbed the phone, memory dragging behind. "Hello?" Her voice was a croak.

"Annie! He's gone for Karl! Your father. He's got a gun!"

"What?" She rubbed a hand through her hair. "Why?"

"He saw it on the news—about Brian, the Wolfsons … I didn't tell him. Didn't have the heart, but the TV … Hurry, Annie! You can stop him. He'll listen to you."

"Mother, calm down. I don't understand—"

"There's no time! I'll come stay with Sadie. Go now, please!"

"Okay. All right, Mom. I'm on my way." She hung up, her eyes sweeping the room for her clothes.

She yanked on yesterday's jeans. Could she leave Sadie? Her mother would be here in ten minutes. She stuck her head into Sadie's room as she pulled on a sweatshirt. She was still in a deep sleep. She'd have to chance it.

She drove through the night toward the Wolfsons. *Heard what on the news? When?* The dashboard clock read 11:40. *With a gun? For God's sake, why?*

Her cell phone rang. She glanced at it. Carmen. Before she could answer it, sirens swooped up from behind her. She braked and pulled over as two cruisers screeched by, headed the same direction. The Wolfson compound.

She pulled out and sped on their tail, arriving before the officers were out of their cars. She ran ahead of them toward the light streaming from the open door of the old stone house.

"God damn it, you heard me! Now, I said!" Her father's voice rang out into the night.

She reached the doorway and stopped cold.

Tom Berglund had Karl Wolfson pinned against the wall, a gun in his chest.

"They killed my baby! Do you hear me? Your boys did that and I'm going to kill them!"

"Dad." Her voice, in a tone she'd never heard before, shot like a command. Her father turned in surprise as the police brushed her aside.

In a heartbeat, they had forced his gun arm up and wrestled him to the floor. His cries of helpless rage filled the night as one of the officers seized the gun and the other pulled his arms behind his back.

Karl slumped into a chair and put his head in his hands.

"Thank God," Carmen cried as she sank to the arm of his chair. "The man's crazy …"

Lightheaded with relief, Annika pushed forward. "Let me talk to him, please. He's my father."

The officer who swung around at her words was Carlson, her afternoon inquisitor. "Oh. Your father?"

"Dad." She ignored Carlson and sank down beside the prostrate man, putting her hand on his back. "Quiet. Please. So you can explain."

He muttered something then lay quiet. "Whyn't you tell me, Annie? You lied. You didn't say the bastard ran away."

"Ran away?" What had he heard? What was the news saying?

"From killing ... feeding that baby drugs, damn it. You didn't know that? You must have. How could you ..." He wrestled in the officer's grasp.

"What baby? Sadie? Sadie's okay, Dad."

"No, dammit, the new one!"

Annika felt lead drop into the pit of her stomach, sitting her back on her heels, robbing her of speech.

"Tom, I think you'd better quiet down and tell us from the beginning." The other officer said without releasing his hold.

"I saw it on TV, Billy—that he was missing, and then I remembered! *I saw them!* Brian and Jonathan Wolfson. That bastard's sons." He yanked his head toward Karl. "But dumb me. Didn't get it until I saw it on the news. Saw that the guys he went with are wanted in a drug investigation."

Annika fought to make sense. Billy, her father called him. Carmen's words floated back. Billy Constantine. Chief of Police. They grew up together. Out to get Karl, she said.

"Where? When did you see them? Brian and Jonathan." The officer was writing.

"I was out fishing." Her father raised his head as far as he could. "By Somer's Cove. Just at dark. My boat drifted around the corner, and there they were. Jonathan handing Brian a package. Drugs." He dropped his head to the floor again. "You can let me up now, Billy—now you have me so I can't strangle that no-good bastard father of theirs."

"That was a damn fool stunt, Tom. You know that." Billy helped Carlson get her father to his feet. "This ..." he took the gun from Carlson, "you aren't getting back. Anyone know you had this?"

"Nope." He stared at his feet and said no more.

"What makes you think the package was drugs?" Karl's voice was a croak.

"I just know damn well it was, that's all. Because it wasn't a week after that my girl lost her baby, that's what. He fed her drugs!"

"Your girl. That would be …?" Billy broke in.

"Me." Annika tried to formulate words. "But that's crazy. Brian wouldn't …"

"Did you lose a baby, Mrs. Wolfson?" Officer Carlson asked, his notebook poised. "When was that?"

This must be some nightmare she was tossing around in. "About six weeks ago, but …" She shoved away crowding memories. "That's just … that had nothing to do with any of this."

"When was it you saw this exchange?" Constantine turned to her father. "How long ago?"

"Just before that. Not a week before she lost that baby. They killed it, I tell you!"

"Dad, no." She knelt before him and put her hands on his shoulders. "I don't know what you saw, but that wasn't … Brian would never have anything to do with drugs." Her words defied the nausea that surged as she spoke them.

"What'd he tell you it was? Huh? To make you take it?" Her father's voice rasped now, his energy spent.

"Nothing, Dad. I took nothing." She saw Billy scribbling. "I swear!"

"Then he snuck it in."

"Okay, Tom," Billy cut him off and turned to Karl who stood leaning against the wall. "What do you know about this, Karl?"

"Not a damned thing, Billy." He pushed himself off the wall. "The Wolfsons don't deal in drugs."

"Hmph," The Chief grunted. "But your boy, Brian, is missing. You know where Jonathan is?"

Karl shook his head. "No idea. Haven't seen him since this morning." His voice challenged the chief to make something of it.

"What time this morning?"

"No idea. I was busy."

"Convenient." Billy snapped. "Did he know we were looking for him?"

"No idea."

Annika watched him. He was clearly shaken. Jonathan knew the police wanted him when he was in Detroit. Who would have told him that if not Karl? The question faded into the confusion.

"Any boats missing?"

Karl blinked. "I'll have to check."

"Mm. Do that and let us know."

Karl looked at his trembling hands.

"Let's go." Billy signaled Carlson. "Nothing more we can do here." He gripped Tom Berglund's upper arm. "Meanwhile we're taking you in for armed assault."

"What? Me?"

"You can't go threatening people with guns, Tom. You're not in Vietnam now." He motioned Carlson to come.

"He had it coming, the yellow-livered bastard."

"That's enough, Tom." Billy shook his arm.

Her father stood, then turned and shot Karl Wolfson a baleful glare before heading for the door. He turned again when he reached it, this time to Annika. "Tell your Mom."

"I will." Annika bit her lip, her hands in fists to stop their shaking.

The three of them stood in the vacuum left by the closing door. Annika stared at Karl and Carmen but could find no words.

"He's crazy," Carmen muttered finally. "Insane, Annika!" Her voice was louder now, and she clutched Karl's hand. "If you hadn't come …" She buried her head in her husband's shoulder.

Annika turned toward the door.

"Annika." It was Karl.

She turned.

"He wouldn't do that. They wouldn't. Brian and Jon."

"Karl ..." She stopped to get control of her voice. "I don't know anything anymore." She opened the door and was halfway out before her brain kicked into gear. She turned to face him. "You and Jonathan fought—at the office the day after Brian went missing. About drugs?"

His eyes went still, then he wiped his lips. "You heard me tell Billy. We don't do drugs."

Annika stared at him, but he didn't flinch, and she could think of no more to say.

"Annika!" Carmen straightened and stood up. "You have to keep him away from here! You have to."

"The police will take care of that, Carmen." She turned and marched out.

Once in the car, she grabbed a blanket out of the back seat and wrapped herself in it to stop the shivering. It wasn't possible. That's all. Product of her father's nightmarish mind. She put her hands on the wheel, switched on the lights and stared at shadows of tree limbs on the empty road. Force of habit took the car home.

Chapter 22

Before Annika reached the porch, her mother had the door open; her face made words unnecessary.

"He's all right, Mom. He didn't shoot anyone." Annika mounted the steps into her mother's arms, and they clung together for a long moment before Annika turned her toward the lighted house. She shut the door behind them and leaned against it.

Her mother pulled away. "I'll make you tea."

"No, brandy. For both of us."

Maggie Berglund threw up her hands. "I'd pass out at the first sip."

"I know." There'd been no alcohol in the Berglund house in Annika's lifetime. "Maybe we both will." She crossed to the liquor cabinet and drew out the bottle and two glasses. "Go sit down."

Her mother rubbed her hands down the side of her jeans and did as she was told, but when Annika offered her a full glass of amber liquid, she stared at it, hands immobile in her lap. "Am I going to need that, Annie? Why?"

"Because I do, and I want company."

A croak of a laugh burst from the older woman. "You always did have a smart answer." She accepted the glass. "All right. Sit down and tell me."

When Annika finished her tale, her mother stared into space without speaking.

"Did you know Billy, Mother? The police chief. Carmen says they grew up together—Karl and Billy and Dad."

"Hm?" She refocused. "Oh. Billy Constantine." She pursed her lips. "They were a threesome."

"Really." So it *was* the man Carmen said was dying to catch Karl out. "Was Billy in Vietnam, too?"

Her mother took a sip of brandy. "He was. Helicopter pilot. Billy always wanted to fly, but that cured him. Came home and never went near a plane again. I teased him about it, once, and about exchanging one uniform for another. He just laughed and said, 'Suits me, I found.'"

"Carmen says he has it in for the Wolfsons—or Karl, anyway."

"There's no love lost in that department, I'd say. Billy's probably got a long memory for being called a pig."

"By Karl?"

"Dunno. By hippies."

"Well, he'll probably be easier on Dad for all that."

"Hope so."

"Did you know Dad had a gun?"

"No." She put her glass down with a sharp click. "But he isn't coming home until I search that house attic to cellar."

"Good. I'll help." She sat back, drained.

"Annika."

She blinked. Her mother rarely called her by her full name. "What?"

"He was yelling that Brian killed the baby ..." Her voice broke.

"That's just … just Dad." But the words lacked certainty. She fought to deny it outright, but the words didn't come. "I can't think about it. Not tonight." She reached for her brandy.

Her mother watched her, sipping her own drink, then finally sighed. "Probably just looking for trouble with the Wolfsons."

Annika agreed, relieved to have the subject closed. "But I don't believe Karl when he says he and Jon didn't fight about drugs."

"Why?"

She paused, remembering that her mother didn't know where her father's pot came from. "Just a feeling. They know something they aren't saying, that's all." She looked at her watch. Three o'clock. "Does Stephanie know about all of this?"

"No. She'd left for work already."

"Okay. I'll send her a text saying you're staying here tonight. I wouldn't want her to come home and find you both gone."

"Oh, I don't need—"

"Yes you do. Because you're going to finish that drink, and you'll be half-crocked."

Her mother gave a half laugh. "I don't need to finish it for that."

"Right. So you can't drive home."

Annika sent a text to Stephanie, then sat in the quiet, studying her mother's face. In her bones, she saw the bride in the picture that still sat on her mother's dresser. A handsome, laughing couple standing in front of a Ford coupe, their first car. At the other end, another picture—her father in uniform, holding an infant Stephanie. What future had they dreamed of then? Which of the lines in her aging face had been caused by the sight of the broken man who had been her groom? Which web was spun from the years of house-splitting uproars, which by her own marriage to a Wolfson, which by Eddy's death?

Shouldn't there be a quotient of grief for each of us, a point where we earn our peace? Margaret Berglund had surely reached that and kept hope alive to boot. Then the miracle had happened. Marijuana. Her husband was back. No longer the man who'd left for war, but at least the man she remembered. And now this mess would probably cut off his pot supply.

Annika bent and pressed her hands to her splitting head, then to her mouth to cover the burst of tears. Once started, the dam that had held them back for days let loose, and she made no effort to stop the torrent. She felt her mother's arms come around her and pull her head to her breast. The woman she was crying for. A hysterical laugh rose and caught in her throat. She sat up and kissed her mother's cheek, then held her tight. "I should be holding you."

Together they lay back against the couch, spent. Annika stared out into the night, but when she relaxed, a wordless dread rose that refused the form of thought.

Giving her mother a final hug, she got up and washed her face, then together they made up the bed in the guest room.

For the second time that night, Annika was wakened by the blare of a telephone, this time, her alarm was buzzing as well. "'Lo?" The fog wouldn't clear.

"Annie? Is that you?"

Reality returned "Steph. Just a moment." She silenced the alarm and sat up, swinging her legs from the bed, anchoring them to the floor. "You want to know what's going on, right?"

"Please."

"In short, Dad went crazy and went after Karl Wolfson with a gun Mother didn't know he had."

"My God," Stephanie muttered, finally. "Did he ... was anyone hurt? Please tell me he didn't find him."

"He did, but no one was hurt. However, they hauled Dad off for assault."

"Off ... to jail?"

"To jail ... for how long I don't know."

"But ... why did he ...?"

"He got a crazy notion ... from the television ... oh, it's too complicated, Steph. I'll fill you in later."

"How's Mom?"

"Pissed. Especially about the gun. I gave her a brandy, and it put her to sleep. Hold on ..." She got up and went to the door of the guest room. Opening it, she saw that Maggie Berglund still slept. No sound came from Sadie's room either. She crept back to her own room and reported as she took in the unperturbed blue water beyond the window, twinkling in the morning sun. As always, its restorative power fed into her veins.

"I'll come get her," Stephanie assured her.

"Her car is here, Steph. I'll drive her, and you can give me a ride home." The mundane act of making a plan returned a sense of normalcy. "And I'd better go get Sadie off to school."

"All right. But keep me posted—about Dad, too."

"You need to sleep—or try to anyway."

"Ha

Keeping her mind glued to the morning routine, Annika pulled on her clothes, went to Sadie and fed, for a moment, on the peaceful, sleeping face. "Sadie?" She shook her shoulder, bringing a soft mutter. "Wake up, baby. School time."

Her eyes opened, and Annika smiled into the questioning gaze. "Good morning." Did she even know her grandma was here?

"'Morning." Sadie sat up and blinked at the apple tree outside her window. "It's Sandy's birthday. I have to make her a card." She jumped out of bed, leaving Annika gaping. "Sandy? It's time to get dressed."

"No, I have to do this first." She opened her box of crayons.

Annika looked at her watch and opened her mouth to give a command, then stopped. Sadie'd apparently awakened to life before her father's disappearance, before yesterday's headlines. Why not give her a few minutes of peace? She left her to her drawing and went to the bathroom.

When she'd showered and dressed, she returned to find Sadie folding her card. "There!" She held it up proudly. "I made her a happy cat. Sandy loves cats."

"Wonderful!"

"I need an envelope."

"Okay, I'll go find one while you get dressed." She started to add a warning to be quiet, that grandma was sleeping, and then changed her mind. *Don't spoil it.*

Ten minutes later, Sadie appeared in the kitchen with her card and her hairbrush. Annika handed her the envelope, then brushed and braided her hair as Sadie ate her cereal. The clock said Sadie was going to miss the bus, but she didn't speak or hurry. "Go get your backpack while I make your lunch," she told her when they'd finished their respective tasks. "I'll drive you this morning."

Annika made herself a travel mug of coffee and set to work. Every minute she spent anchored in daily tasks kept her mind safe. She spared no detail on Sadie's lunch—bread, mayo, cheese, pickles, cherries, cookie— as though she too was inside Sadie's bubble—or cocoon.

A thumping brought her head up. Sadie was dragging her pack down the stairs. "Is it that heavy?"

"No. I just like to." Sadie reached the bottom and swung the pack up and over her shoulders. "Can I go to Sandy's after school? She asked me."

Annika almost laughed. Did she once-upon-a-time live in this world? "Of course. Shall I pick you up there at five?"

"Okay." Sadie struggled to put on her jacket.

"I think you have to take off your pack, Sadie."

"Oh." She disposed of the bag with a practiced shrug and picked up the jacket again. "There. Where's my lunch?"

Dutifully, Annika handed her her lunch box, wondering how long this charade could go on. "Let's go."

She drove along the lake toward town inside a bubble that kept the world at bay. She pulled up at the school. "Have a good day, sweetie."

Sadie opened the door. "And you find those bad men." She marched off, leaving Annika collapsed against the seat.

She caught her lip in her teeth as she watched the small stalwart figure mount the steps to the schoolhouse and disappear. Would Sadie's faith in the grown-up world hold up? She gave a fervent prayer and started the engine.

Once she got home, she found Maggie Berglund in the kitchen, pouring herself a cup of coffee. "There you are. I couldn't imagine where you'd got to."

"I took Sadie to school. That's all." She frowned. Her mother's skin was gray, the lines around her mouth deepened. "How are you?"

"I'll do." She gave Annika a wan smile. "I would have said I didn't sleep a wink, but I woke up so groggy I must have slept a month."

"I know what you mean." She poured herself a second cup. "Let's eat. We'll feel better."

Her mother sank into a chair with a sigh. "Don't feel much like food, Annie."

"I know." She set to work, making oatmeal and cinnamon toast, then set it in front of her.

"Ah!" Her mother smiled. "Look what you did. Our favorite breakfast."

"Yep. Can't fail."

The memory of icy gray winter mornings warmed by the smell of butter and cinnamon filled the kitchen. They ate.

The phone split the quiet. Annika muttered a comment that raised her mother's brows. She reached for the instrument on the counter. "Hello?"

"Mrs. Wolfson?"

"Speaking."

"This is Monika Adams of the Traverse Record Eagle. We'd like to talk to you about your husband's—"

"No!" She cut her off midstream. "I'm sorry, but no comment."

"Well, can you tell us where to find Mrs. Berglund? Your mother?"

"No. I can't." She put the phone down. "We may need to escape, Mother." She went to the window. Too late. A TV truck was parked at the end of the drive.

The phone rang again. She stared at it, willing it to stop but unable to let it ring. "Hello."

"Mrs. Wolfson, please. Steve Mitchell, Detroit News, calling."

Annika slammed the phone down. "The Detroit paper, for God's sake."

"Oh." The lone sound fell from her mother's lips like a stone. "What ... what are you going to tell them?"

"Nothing, Mother. Promise."

The phone rang.

Annika squeezed her temples. "I need this to stop." She picked up the receiver. "Hello!"

"Annika Wolfson, please. Officer Carlson, here."

She sat with a thump. "Speaking."

"Oh." He laughed. "Didn't recognize your voice. Chief Constantine would like to talk to you this morning. Nine o'clock if that's all right with you."

Annika glanced at the clock, the grip of dread returning. Eight-thirty. "All right."

"Good. And we're looking for Mrs. Berglund. Do you know where I can find her?"

She put a hand over the mouthpiece. "It's the police, Mother. Chief Constantine wants to talk to you."

Her mother nodded. "I figured he would. Tell him okay." She rose and picked up their empty bowls.

"She's here, Officer."

"Good. Can you bring her with you?" He sounded friendly and relaxed as though inviting them to lunch.

"All right." She put down the phone and watched her mother load the dishwasher with a rhythm that refused to be broken. As though she'd done this many times.

Calmed, Annika punched in Stephanie's number on her cell phone. "Hi," she responded when her sister answered. "The police want to talk to us."

"Both of you?"

"Both of us, so I'll keep Mom with me. Your house is probably under media siege, anyway," she added, glancing out her own window at the gathering vans.

Stephanie's sigh was magnified by the phone. "I'm not used to this."

"Why would you be? But since you have to go to work, maybe she's better off with me tonight."

"I'm off tonight … but okay, I guess." Stephanie paused. "Take care of her."

"Right." Annika hung up the phone, wondering why either of them thought they were up to that job. She went to brush her teeth.

Fifteen minutes later, Annika opened the garage door and backed out slowly, ignoring the gestures and questions thrown at the closed car windows. Beside her, Maggie Berglund put her arms up over her face as though warding off blows. She put her hand on her mother's leg. "It's okay. Stick out your tongue if you want."

Her mother snorted and lowered her arms, clasping her hands in her lap as Annika sped up and left the crowd behind.

Ten minutes later, they sat together in Chief Constantine's office, listening to the clock tick.

"'Morning, Maggie," The burly chief greeted them as he strode in. "Helluvathing."

"Hello, Billy."

"'Morning to you, too, Mrs. Wolfson." He plopped down a stack of papers. "Now then." He put his hands flat on the desk. "I'm going to have to talk to you ladies separately, I'm afraid. Which of you would like to go first?"

"I will," Annika volunteered.

"No, Annie, let me get it over with." Her mother's voice carried an urgency Annika couldn't deny. The chief was calling for Officer Carlson on the intercom as she left the room.

As Annika sat in the waiting room, her muscles and brain no longer demanded by necessary action, a rush of dizzy nausea overcame her. She put her head between her knees, gripping the arms of the chair.

"Ma'am?" A concerned voice spoke above her. Someone put a hand on her shoulder. "Mrs. Wolfson? Here."

Annika raised her head and took the glass of water the young officer held out. This one looked barely out of her teens. "Thank you." She drank. The panic settled into a lump. She needed to think. Be alone. Not here. She pressed her clenched hands into her lap. *Can't leave Mother. Can't leave Mother.*

Maggie Berglund emerged from the Chief's office looking composed.

"Do you want to see Tom?" Constantine asked.

"Let him stew," she retorted crossing to Annika. She gave Annika's hand a reassuring squeeze. "Your turn." Annika returned the pressure and stood up.

When finally she sat facing Billy Constantine, Officer Carlson in a corner ready to take notes, a stony calm came over her.

"Just repeat to me what happened last night, if you would,"

"My mother called. It was the middle of the night. She said my father had gone after Karl Wolfson, and he had a gun." She told the rest of the story, though the words fought her.

When she'd finished, he nodded. "Where did he get that gun, do you know?"

Annika shook her head. "My mother didn't know he had it, and I certainly didn't."

"So she said," he agreed, shuffling through papers on his desk. "Your dad has a long-time grievance with Karl Wolfson, doesn't he?"

Her jaws clamped. "You grew up with him. And with Karl. I think you know as much about that as I do."

"'Spect I do, but I'm asking you."

"He's never hurt Karl. Or threatened him."

"That may be, but he threatened him last night. How about his story? That he saw Jonathan give your husband drugs."

"A package."

"Mm. What do you know about that?"

"Nothing, Chief Constantine." Her voice carried a certainty rare these days. "Nothing at all. And my husband loathed drugs of any kind. He never had anything to do with them." She spoke as though her words would seal up a hole that had opened. Her ears were ringing and almost blotted out the questions that followed. Was she a swimmer? Was she training for the Olympics? Was Brian her coach? Were they getting along? She folded her hands together, imitating her mother's calm.

"You had a miscarriage recently?"

Her stomach cramped. "Yes."

"When was that?"

"A month ago." She spoke through clenched teeth. "More. August 26th."

"Was that before or after your husband brought that package home?"

"I don't know anything about a package."

"The package Brian got from his brother. Jonathan."

"I don't know when that was. I never saw a package."

"Hmm. Well, we'll be pinning that down. Perhaps it'll jog your memory."

She fought the urge to scream at him.

He rose. "All right. You can go—for now."

She went limp. All? Over? "What about South Carolina? Nils Svenson said Brian got off at the Outer Banks."

He held the door for her. "Bar Harbor police are looking into that. No sign of him so far."

"And the Coast Guard?"

"Nothing there either, as far as I know."

She waited for him to say more. He didn't.

"That's all?

"Yes. Stay where we can find you."

She rose. Tension drained as she returned to the waiting room, and then returned as she eyed the throng of reporters between them and her car.

Chapter 23

Brian

2000

Gym bag in hand, Brian stopped at the window to watch the snow fall against the rosy sky of early morning. Big slow flakes floated onto the lawn, the trees, and the lake below in a silence that held him enthralled. A peace he'd never known descended. On the mantle were pictures of their wedding on Beaumont Bluff, Lake Michigan shining behind them, Jonathan and Stephanie on either side of them, his parents and, by some miracle, hers at either end. He could still feel the wonder of it, gazing into her eyes and seeing that wonder coming back. Around him, the house Joe had given them, a spec house he'd built but not yet sold, warmed him. Perfect, Joe'd insisted. It would allow them to keep focused on the Sydney games. And it was perfect. Away from town and the Wolfson compound, cedar and glass with its own dock, facing the rising sun. He was stretching in the wide open space when he heard Annika's footfall on the stairs.

She came up and put her arms around him. He kissed her, long and soft, without urgency, needing only the moment. Together they watched the first rays of sun clear the forest across the lake and gleam on the untrammeled expanse of lawn.

"Every morning we will do this," he murmured. "No matter what is going on out there, or in here."

"To remind us of who we are, the world we come from," she finished for him.

They turned and kissed again, stretching the moment, then turned for the garage, the car, the pool.

For a half hour they swam together with loose-limbed ease, as though carrying the moment at the window with them, all else forgotten.

"Okay, lazybones." He stopped at the pool end and splashed her. "Time to get busy!" He heaved himself out of the water.

Annika watched, unmoving, as he grabbed his towel and warm-ups, then went to set the time-clock in motion.

He returned to the edge of the pool. "What's the matter?"

She opened her mouth as though to say something, then stopped. "Nothing." She turned away and readied herself for the start.

"On to Sydney!" He yelled, uttering the word that completed the perfection of this day. "Go!"

He watched, lifted by her strokes until he laughed. He didn't even look at the clock for her first few laps. With her times at the nationals, she'd make the Olympic team for sure. "Okay, give me a sprint," he called as she neared the wall below him.

But instead of turning, she stopped.

"Annie?"

She pulled herself up and sat on the edge, gazing out at the water. "I have something to tell you." She gathered herself and rose to her feet and turned to face him.

He blinked, bewildered.

"I'm going to have a baby."

"What?"

She took hold of his upper arms and looked into his eyes. "I'm pregnant, Brian. I'm going to have a baby."

"A baby ..." He couldn't make sense of it. "Now?"

She gave a laugh. "Well no ... in September."

The world spun. "But ... Sydney! August!" He stared without comprehension.

"Brian, don't look at me like that." She spun away, then back. "We're married. It's what married people do! Have babies."

"But—not yet, Annie ... not before Sydney ..."

"Well ... we weren't careful, were we?" His stare registered no understanding. "And I tried, Brian, but ..." She spread her hands in futility.

He didn't answer.

"So I'll keep training, and we'll go to Athens." Her eyes drilled into him, forcing his acknowledgement.

"Athens." His voice sounded stupid, and the word slipped away like a handhold missed. Muted by shock, he watched her bite her lip, turn and dive, swimming with quick, angry strokes away from him. *"Oh no, Annie!"* he yelled without sound. But she didn't stop.

Ten minutes later, he found himself sitting in the dressing room, staring into space. Memory returned and he choked. *No Sydney.* How could it vanish? Like that? The vortex of their years? He leapt up and slammed out of the dressing room, then out of the club, and began to run, the cold bleeding through him like a sieve until he buckled, gasping. *"That's what married people do, have babies."* No! Not us! We go to ... but the word faded off as reality took hold. Shaking, he turned back toward the club. And Annie.

A car pulled up beside him. Their car.

"Come on. Get in," she said. "You'll have pneumonia next."

He climbed in and shut the door. "I'm sorry." His teeth tangled the words. "It's the shock. All the years ..."

"I know. I burst into tears." She pulled out from the curb.

"My stuff's at the club."

She turned back toward the wharf, her eyes fixed on the road. He could see she was fighting tears, but he could manage no response.

By the time he'd retrieved his gym bag and returned to the car, his shock had become a leaden ball in the pit of his stomach.

"We'll go to Athens," she said as he climbed into the car. "But a baby ... we have to let it be wonderful, Brian. We have to."

He gazed at her, at the new light that emanated from her, and `reached for it.

Chapter 24

2007

Once safely enclosed in her car, Annika shut her eyes and counted ten. She opened them to glance at her mother, who sat ramrod straight, jaw clenched, staring out the windshield as reporters tapped insistently on her window. Annika started the engine with a roar. She glanced at her watch as she pulled out of the parking lot. Eleven. The morning was almost gone. "We're getting out of town for lunch."

"No. I need to go home, Annie."

"Why? Your place is crawling with reporters, just like mine."

"I need to make sure there are no more guns. Can't rest until I know."

Annika nodded and felt the muscles in her neck relax. "Okay. So we search." She turned the car toward town. "We're going to have to plow our way into the house, you know."

"Well, I've nothing to say to them. Billy says your father is sticking to his crazy story this morning."

Annika felt her stomach tighten. "But he can't know what was in that package, Mother. He can't." She turned off the main street and approached the house, then honked at the van that occupied the drive. The noise attracted reporters waiting in other cars, and in a flash Annika's car was besieged. She rolled down the window.

"Mrs. Berglund, can you tell us—" "You're Mrs. Wolfson—have you heard from your husband—" "Record Eagle, here—"

"Tell that van to move. We have nothing to tell you." Annika shut the window and sat stony-faced, staring out the windshield. Out of the corner of her eye, she saw the edges of her mother's mouth quirk. Finally, the reporters shrugged at each other and went to knock on the window of the van. The engine fired. It backed out of the drive, and Annika stepped on the gas, scattering newsfolk as she headed toward the back of the house and the detached garage. "Does the old gate still work?"

"I don't know." Her mother glanced at the rusty chain-link that sagged alongside the house. Once upon a time it had fenced in Geezer, the family dog. "I haven't used it in an age."

"Well, we're about to find out." Annika got out and tugged at the post and wire barricade which screamed back at her, causing the mob of reporters to head toward her once again. Thankfully, the gate swung free and blocked their progress. "Please." Her voice was an order, not a plea. "Neither my mother or I know anything—"

A barrage of questions buried her voice. "NO COMMENT!" she yelled as cameras flashed in her face.

Behind her, she heard the car door slam and turned. Her mother was hurrying toward the house. Clenching her teeth, Annika banged the gate latch into place and followed suit. Once in the kitchen, they folded into each other's arms.

"Good Lord," her mother muttered. "They're like animals." She turned away and looked out the back door. "We need to search that garage, you know."

"Not now. We wait until they give up and go away. I don't want to know what story they'll make up if they see us plowing around out there." She turned her mother away from the glass.

Maggie Berglund gave a grunt of assent. "They'll probably think we're looking for drugs."

Annika laughed, expelling the morning. "Let's eat before we tackle this job. Steph is asleep, I hope."

"Not anymore," a voice from the staircase answered. Stephanie emerged in a nightgown, scratching her curls. "Heard you yelling. Did you get rid of them?"

"No, just backed them off a bit. I'm sorry, Steph. We'll be quiet, now. Promise."

"No, no. You need to tell me what happened." She flicked on the coffee pot. "I'll be back in a minute." She disappeared up the stairs, and Annie busied herself making ham sandwiches.

By the time the coffee was done, Stephanie had returned in jeans and sweatshirt, and their mother was cooking oatmeal for her. "Thank you, Mom." She planted a kiss on her mother's cheek, then poured herself a cup of coffee. "Now tell me. Where's Dad? Still in jail?"

Her mother nodded. "Until Karl Wolfson decides whether or not to bring charges … according to Billy. Which is fine because I don't want him here until I know there are no more guns."

"So … why did he want to talk to you?"

"To talk about the quarrel your father had with Karl—as though he didn't know already." Maggie Berglund slapped oatmeal into a bowl and set it before her eldest daughter. "And they wanted to know why he went crazy after all of these years, which I told them I didn't know. And where he got the gun, which I also didn't know but aim to find out." She poured a cup of coffee and handed it to Annika. "And they wanted to know why he thought the package he saw Jonathan give Brian was drugs."

Stephanie put down her cup with a bang. "What? What package?"

"Last night, he claimed he went after Karl because when he was out fishing a while back, he saw Jon give Brian a package," Annika explained.

"So?" Stephanie's brow wrinkled in confusion. "Why did he think it was drugs?"

"He saw on television that Brian and Jonathan are missing, and the men Brian went with might be tied to drugs. And then he remembered seeing the package."

"A bit of a leap, but it sounds like Dad."

"So he decided that Jonathan gave Brian some performance drug and Brian gave it to me, causing my miscarriage." Annika jumped up in protest to her own words and began to pace. "That's why he went after Karl."

"My God. Now that *is* crazy." Stephanie's expression changed from incredulity to horror as the words sunk in. "Oh Annie, that's so awful." She picked up her spoon and put it down. "And what did Karl have to do with it?"

"They're his boys." Their mother raised her coffee cup.

"That's it? They're his boys?"

"They're Wolfsons." Annie laid out sandwiches for herself and her mother.

Stephanie sat silent, toying with her oatmeal, but not eating. "So— do the police believe him—about the drugs?"

"I don't know." Annika sat down. "I told them it was crazy, but ..." She stared at her sandwich.

"But what, Annie? Do you believe it?"

Stephanie's voice penetrated her silence. Annika looked up and met her eyes. "I don't know. I'm trying ... I haven't been able to think straight ... but I can't believe Brian would ... do that." She picked up her sandwich. "No. It just can't be." She took a bite and chewed it, feeling both pairs of eyes resting on her. "The problem is ..." She put her sandwich down. "The problem is that the Sag Harbor police knew the names of the men Brian went with—from a drug investigation. That's when Dad made the connection and … well …The police don't think that's so crazy—particularly since both Brian and Jon are missing."

"Oh shit …" All of the air seemed to go out of Stephanie. She stared at her oatmeal.

"What's wrong, Steph?" her mother asked. "What … oh, no." She put down her sandwich. "Don't tell me. Jonathan is where you get Dad's marijuana?"

Stephanie raised her head and met her mother's gaze. "'Fraid so."

"Oh." It was more a burst of air than a word, and Maggie Berglund sat staring into some future only she could see. "You never told me."

"I didn't need to load you with that." Stephanie reached a hand across the table and laid it on her mother's.

"Maggie Berglund nodded. "Good thing Tom didn't know." She straightened and picked up her sandwich. "Well, sounds like Jonathan's in trouble all right." A few bites later, she noticed Stephanie hadn't resumed eating.

"What is it? You can find another source, can't you?" A new concern entered her voice.

"Sure." Stephanie smiled.

Annika watched her, a new fear rising. Stephanie looked worried—scared. Surely the police wouldn't come after Stephanie, wouldn't come after customers, would they? Her mother was watching her sister, too, clearly not buying the reassurance.

They turned to their food as a distraction, and in the silence, Annika felt possibility seep through the cracks of her defenses, turning her food to paste.

"Well," Maggie said at last, "I guess we'd best get to it."

"To what?" Stephanie's head came up.

"Searching the place to see where Dad got that gun," Annika told her. "And to make sure there are no more wherever it came from."

"Good idea. I'll help." Stephanie rose.

"Shouldn't you be sleeping?" Annika asked

"Somehow, I don't think that's likely." Stephanie gave a dry smile.

"All right." Her mother opened her eyes and pushed herself away from the table. "The attic first."

From a trap door in the upstairs hallway ceiling, Annika pulled down the stairs the way she'd done once a year to get the Christmas ornaments. She poked her head through the opening and peered into the musty dimness. The shape of a crib emerged and the bulk of stacked boxes. "We're going to need a light."

"Here you go." Her mother handed her a flashlight.

Piece by piece, the light took her back to her childhood. Her favorite doll, Melinda, cocked her head from a shelf next to Barney, the raggedy remains of her stuffed beagle. Boxes of school papers were followed by Eddy's bugle and the tricycle that had survived all three of them. On the other side of the attic, marked boxes of Christmas decorations sat next to a dressing table she recognized as her mother's. An old sewing machine and rows of crates, all covered with dust, completed the scan.

"No one's been up here, Mom," she called down. "There'd be marks in the dust."

"All right. Let me have a look."

Annika climbed down and let mother ascend. A few minutes later, she came down, blowing dust out of her mouth. "Takes care of that. I don't think he could manage that trap door and these steps without me knowing, but I'm glad we can cross it off the list."

Two hours later, the three of them had searched the bedrooms, linen and storage closets and descended to the main floor. Maggie insisted on unloading every end table, bookcase, record cabinet and cubbyhole. She stared at the fireplace. "Reach your hand up there, Annie, and see if there's any kind of ledge that would hold a gun."

"Really, Mother," Annika protested, but sank to her knees and did as she was told. "Nope. Nothing." She backed off and brushed her hands.

Her mother sighed and turned away, then spotted the coat closet under the stairs. 'That's the last. Don't know where else to look."

Twenty minutes later, behind a pile of ice skates, Annika found a box of ammunition.

"Ha!" her mother exclaimed. "So that's where it was. Been meaning to clean out that rat's nest for months. If I'd gotten to it, it would have saved us a pile of grief."

"Let's make sure there's nothing else in there." Annika turned back and began pulling out helmets and baseball hats, skates and boots, backpacks and duffel bags. And a shoebox empty except for a bed of oily rags. "I guess this is it. The box for the gun."

Her mother hissed, her hands falling to her sides. She turned for the kitchen, where she sank into a chair. "Why, Annie? Why did he keep it? What demons did he think would come after him?"

Annika sat down and took her hands. "Well, we found it, Mom. You can relax on that score at least."

Her mother made a sound, then pulled out one hand and patted Annika's. "You never relax. They go to war, and you never know them again." She pulled her other hand free and sank her head into them. For long minutes she sat like that, unmoving. Then she sat up. "And there might be more. In the basement or the garage." She looked at the clock. "I can do that, Annie. You need to be getting home for Sadie."

"No, she's going to her friend Sandy's. Let's get it done." Annika rose and went to look out the front window. The street was empty. "Let's start with the garage while we have peace and quiet."

The kitchen clock said four-thirty by the time they'd searched both and emerged holding only a meat-grinder her mother had lost track of years ago.

"That's it, Mom. There are no more, so now you're going to rest." Annika put an arm around her shoulders. "And I need to get Sadie." She turned to Stephanie. "You should be tired enough to sleep now."

Her sister wiped a hand across her brow, leaving a streak of dirt. "I'll shower, anyway. But it doesn't matter. I'm off tonight … or tomorrow … or whenever it is …" The lines of her face, white with fatigue, seemed to collapse in confusion.

"Oh, Steph, I'm so sorry …" Annika threw her arms around her in remorse for far more than Stephanie's loss of sleep.

Her sister laughed, recovering a bit in her surprise. "What for, sweetie? I don't see what you had to do with it." She returned the hug.

"For the whole mess. It's swelling and swallowing everyone." Annika pulled back and straightened. "Speaking of which, Sadie will be thinking I've disappeared, too."

"You've nothing to do with your Dad's feud with the Wolfsons, Annie." Her mother put an arm around her shoulders. "So don't be taking that on, too."

Annika kissed her cheek. "Okay. If Steph'll come with me, she can bring your car home." She turned a questioning gaze to her sister.

"Right." She dropped a kiss on her mother's cheek. "Back soon."

They drove across town, resting in silence.

"What are you thinking, Annie?"

"I'm trying not to. It's all so damned preposterous, Steph. One day I'm swimming in the summer sun, the next I'm … it's like I hit a whirlpool."

"Yeah. Give it time. You'll bottom out, then you can think again."

Annika glanced at her. "That sounds like the voice of experience."

Stephanie nodded. "It was like that after Eddy was killed, and Sean went off ..."

"Sean." The name jogged her memory. "Eddy's friend."

"Love of my life."

Steph's voice had a finality that shocked Annika. The story came alive again, ringing against her skull, robbing her of speech. The silence grew as they passed out of downtown and along the edge of the lake. "I didn't know that," she said finally. "What do you mean—went off?"

Stephanie gave a harsh laugh. "Oh, that was just silly me. I thought he had a thing for me ... you know? But when Eddy was gone ...well, it turned out he'd had another girl all along—" she broke off.

"Oh, Steph ..." Annika put a hand on her leg. "Why didn't I know any of that?"

"No one did, Annie. There was no place for it with the family falling apart—Dad going wild, Mom too destroyed to hold him down."

"And I was off swimming," Annika finished. *Ran away,* her mind blared. She cringed, ashamed.

"You were just a kid, Annie—a ten-year-old." She turned her gaze back to the windshield. "You couldn't have " Her voice faded. "The worst of it was ..." Stephanie stopped again. "... I was pregnant."

Annika swerved onto a beach access and stopped the car. "Oh, Steph. I'm so sorry."

Stephanie nodded without answering.

A vision rose, whether memory or imagination, of Stephanie walking on the beach alone. So alone. She reached over and pulled her sister to her. "What did you do?"

"Went to Traverse City. Took care of it." Stephanie spat the words.

Annika winced. "Alone?"

"Yes."

The word faded into the silence. "That shouldn't have been. Not alone," Annika finally managed.

"I wasn't going to … do it. But I couldn't face the folks … their shame, Dad's rage. I saw what he did to you, and Eddy was gone. It was like I was all Mom had left. I couldn't do it." She turned and pulled back to look at Annika. "But after … that was when I hit bottom." She picked up Annika's hand. "So that's why I know where you were after the miscarriage. That emptiness."

Annika nodded, letting silence settle around them. "That's when you became the glue—the anchor …" Memories sprang up—of Steph with an armload of laundry, Steph at the stove, Steph holding her mother's head. And with them came the familiar feeling that her family was already complete when she came along, their functions established. Whatever role she was destined for, she'd escaped. Flying, flying …

"It pulled me through—being needed." Stephanie's voice brought her back to the present. "It was an escape that turned right, in the end."

Annika turned into the drive of Sandy's house. "What end? There will be other boys, Steph."

"Men, you mean." Steph smiled. "That was fifteen years ago."

"So? It's not too late."

"No, but some things just don't happen." She gave Annie a shove. "Go get your kid."

Annika held her place. "You write beautifully. That must help."

"It does. Like magic, really."

"Magic. I don't think I've ever heard you use that word."

Stephanie laughed. "Go."

Annika obliged. Susan O'Conner opened the door, alarm spread over her face. "Annika. Are you all right?" She waved behind her, as Annika rocked back in surprise.

Then she saw her house in the middle of the television screen, the evening news blaring the story. "Oh. I'm okay." She stopped to recover. "Well, not, but …" she broke off with a half-laugh. "As long as I keep moving, I guess." She smiled. "Thank you, though."

"Do you want Sadie to stay here? She can, you know. And I didn't let them watch—they're up in Sandy's room."

"Mommy!" Sadie raced down the stairs, and Carol raced to the TV switch.

Sadie fell into Annika's arms. "I thought you forgot me!"

Annika raised her eyes to Carol. "I guess not." She smiled. "But thank you for asking."

Chapter 25

"Auntie Steph!" Sadie cried and ran toward her aunt, who had gotten out of the car to greet her. "You came to see us!"

Stephanie and Annika looked at each other in shock, realizing that the visit was indeed an oddity. *Her sister*. What world had she been living in?

"Well, I guess I did. How about that?" Her aunt grinned and gave her a hug.

"Good." Sadie turned and scrambled into the car. "You can see my turtles!"

"You have turtles? Live ones?"

"Yep." Sadie fastened her seat belt. "Three. Grumpy, Bashful, and Sleepy."

"Like the dwarves."

"Ya. But we have to put them in the lake pretty soon. We always do."

But we have to put them in the lake pretty soon. We always do."

"Did they come from the lake?"

"Umhm. The swamp by the shore. Mom and I found them when they were babies. They didn't have a mother."

"I'm sure you were a good mommy. Do you find lots of turtles like that?"

"No. Just these. But other things. Baby rabbits, once. And mice. And skunks, once, but Mommy said we couldn't have those.

"Mm. They stink, huh?"

"Yeah. And we found a baby deer once. Called a fawn. But then we heard a noise and it was the mother."

Annika listened, tearing up. At least there were a few hours she'd shared with her little girl. Warm, alive hours Sadie had held onto. The glass and wood house rose ahead, backed by its tapestry of blue and green, and only her mother's car occupied its drive. "We're in luck. Must be dinner time." She glanced at Stephanie. "You will come in, won't you?"

Her sister smiled. "Wouldn't miss those turtles for the world."

Once inside, the pair headed for the back porch where foundlings were safe from coyotes and human feet, leaving Annika to stare at the caller ID. The Record Eagle. *Not now!* She switched the ringer off and went outside to listen to the rustle of leaves in the autumn breeze, the slosh of water against the pier below interlaced with voices from the back porch. She stood until the seized up muscles in her neck and shoulders let go, then headed for the kitchen.

To be met by the training schedule. She swung away, refusing it.

"Can Aunt Stephie stay for supper?" Sadie asked, trailing Stephanie behind her as she came in.

"No, no, Sadie," Stephanie protested. "Grandma needs me at home."

"Why?"

Annika raised an eyebrow at her sister. Why indeed? "It's pizza,"

"From scratch?" Sadie's face lit up.

"Not tonight. But you can run and get a frozen one from the garage freezer, and we'll fix it up. Do you have homework?"

Sadie shook her head. "We did it at Sandy's. Her mother makes her before she can play."

"Good idea, that," she said to Sadie's back before switching her attention to her sister. "You will, won't you? You said you're off tonight."

Stephanie gave a shrug and grinned, "As Sadie says, why not?"

Annika laughed and opened the refrigerator. "Nothing like a child's wisdom to keep you in perspective."

"No kidding."

"You need to come more often."

Stephanie pulled her cell phone out of her pocket. "I'll call Mom."

A perusal of the refrigerator told her that she would have to brave the supermarket tomorrow, but she did find mozzarella, and the rest were staples she always had on hand.

"Sounded as though she was sleeping." Stephanie put the phone away.

"Good. She does far too little of that." A change in the light and a cool breeze through the kitchen made her glance up to see storm clouds gathering to the west. Good. Rain—maybe even thunder and lightning—that should keep everyone away.

"What are we having on it?" Sadie arrived from the garage, gripping a cheese pizza.

"Maybe we should ask our guest." Annika turned on the oven.

"Oh. What do you like, Aunt Stephie?"

"Just about anything. And you?"

"Hot dogs. And cheese. No mushrooms."

"All right," Annika told her. "There's half a package of hot dogs in the refrigerator. How about olives?"

"Okay. But no mushrooms!" Sadie tugged the refrigerator open.

"Are you grating the cheese this time?"

Sadie nodded vigorously. "You promised I could."

"Steph can help. Wash your hands and go sit at the table, then I'll bring the shredder."

"And a bowl. A big one." Sadie climbed up on a dinette chair.

"Aye aye."

Stephanie took a seat, and Annika leaned against the counter to watch her small offspring thrust the cheese against the grater again and again. Her stomach clenched as the loss of the second child rose unbidden, but she shook it off. This hour was Sadie's.

"That's about enough," Stephanie advised.

"A little more. It takes lots of cheese." Sadie thrust the cheese a few more times. "Okay."

Together they spread the cheese then topped it with the required hot dog slices and olives.

"It should be pickles with hot dogs, not olives." Sadie frowned at the results.

"No, no, not on pizza, Sadie." Stephanie suppressed a smile. "Pizza is Italian, so olives are right."

"Why?"

"Because in Italy, it's warm all year round, and the olive trees love that. So Italians grow and eat lots of olives—and tomatoes together. Like this."

"Oh. Not pickles?"

"Not so much. I think it's ready for the oven."

"Okay. Can I?" She turned to her mother.

"If you're careful. Don't rush." She opened the oven door and pulled out a shelf. Sadie got off her stool and lifted the pizza, then turned and stopped when she realized she couldn't get it onto the oven rack without burning her hands.

"Put it down again, honey, and I'll show you where to put your hands."

When Sadie'd done so, Annika placed her small hands closer together. Her daughter made the transfer successfully, with a little steadying from above, and Annika handed her a hot-pad so she could push the shelf back in.

"There!" Sadie clasped her hands together as Annika shut the door.

"Done. All but the eating." Annika took a cloth from the sink and mopped Sadie's face. Then she crossed the kitchen and closed the window, checking that the back lawn was empty of unwanted life. "Let's build us a fire while the pizza bakes. I think we're going to have rain."

"Oh, goody." Sadie ran for the front room.

"Wait for me!" She peered out the front window into the darkening late afternoon. Smoke from the chimney would announce their presence, but except for her mother's car, the road and drive were empty,. Had the reporters given up on her?

Then she spied the shape of a single car behind the fir tree at the edge of their lot. She picked up her field glasses from their home on the windowsill and could barely make out a shield on its side. A police car. After a jolt of shock, she realized they were here to watch, not come knocking at the door. The press were gone. She could turn on the lights.

"Where's the wood, Mommy? There's no wood."

"Because we haven't had a fire all summer. I'll go out back and get some."

"You and I can lay the kindling while your mom gets the wood," Stephanie chimed in.

Annika picked up the wicker wood basket and went out to the shed. The clouds were thick now, and she shivered in the chill. The lake, roughened by the wind, had turned angry—fall announcing its presence. By the time she got back the smell of pizza was filling the air. She turned the wood over to Stephanie and Sadie and returned to the kitchen for drinks and dishes.

Soon they were settled before a blazing fire, the pizza between them. For the next half hour, Sadie kept a steady conversation about the places they'd explore on her aunt's next visit—shoreline swamps, their woods hideaway, the abandoned orchard ... The list went on. An unreasoning mix of gratitude and remorse rendered Annika speechless as she listened to the inventory of hours stolen from the pool—Sadie's life.

When, sated, Sadie fell silent, they sat watching the dancing flames. When the splatter of rain hit the windows, Stephanie roused and gave a yawn. "Guess I'd better go, if I'm going to beat the storm."

Lightning lit up the room, and Annika laughed. "I think you already lost that one. Take a slicker off the hook by the back door." She stood and put her arms around her sister.

"You come next week, okay?" Sadie jumped to her feet.

"Do," Annika urged. "Friday is pizza night ..." She blew a noisy sigh "Is this Friday?"

"Actually, I think it is." Stephanie chuckled and laid a hand on Annika's cheek. "This has been good."

"More than." She kissed her sister. "It is now a tradition. Sadie keeps close track of those."

"'Bye, sweetie." Stephanie gave Sadie a hug. "I'll be back. It might not be Friday. Your mom will explain about nurse's schedules." With a final pat, she headed for the door.

By nine, Annika tucked Sadie into bed and read her three stories. Two more than the usual, but she wanted to stay here, closeted with *Charlotte's Web*. Her daughter had fallen asleep, but she lingered, watching the apple tree branches wave against the angry clouds.

She woke with a start. Rain pounded against the window, and the wind rattled the panes. Her watch told her she'd slept for two hours. She was cold. When she'd retrieved a sweatshirt from her bedroom and gone downstairs, she rekindled the embers of their fire and got a glass of wine, trying to recapture the afternoon.

But now the room was empty. Memories flooded in. A day. Hot. The sun beating on her head.

"Yes! Better!" Brian jumping up and down on the dock, his arms rotating like a windmill despite the sweat rolling down his face. *"Again! You'll make it yet!"*

"Make it, make it, make it ..." the words drove her strokes faster and faster, legs flailing despite cramping thighs as though he'd taken possession of her ...

Annika jumped up and paced the room until the day became memory again. She willed it to have been a dream, but it wasn't. The cooling breeze off Lake Michigan had failed them as had her body. The heat weighed her down, Brian's yells became desperate. But that day the weight had lifted ... no ... that wasn't right ... more like something was pulling her arms through the water. Brian? No, not that familiar fusing of energy. Strange. Three times she beat the clock. Well ahead of the time she needed. When, with rubbery legs, she climbed out of the lake, Brian threw his arms around her dripping body. *"We're going, baby, we're going all the way!"*

His eyes were alight with an intensity she backed away from. Such joy ... no, not joy. Relief. No. More like he'd been saved. Annika sat transfixed. Something had changed.

A flash of lightning brought her to her feet and to her senses. She stared out at the storm until present reality replaced memory, though it left her limp.

She refilled her wine glass, then stood and watched the wind-whipped lake. Her gaze was on the distant shore, emerging now as the rain lessened. A glint of light below drew her attention. It wasn't repeated, and she was about to count it imagination when a flash of lightening lit up the beach—and a man climbing from a Zodiac.

Brian. Then the moon emerged from the edge of the storm clouds. *Jonathan*. The figure clad in oilcloth climbing up the lawn toward her was Jonathan.

He knocked at the back door, and she stared at it for a long moment before opening it.

"It's me." He shrugged back his hood. "Just me," he added, examining her face. "I'm sorry. I didn't mean to scare you."

She stepped back to let him in, bumped into the kitchen counter behind her and yelped.

"Easy!" He reached out and put a wet hand on her wrist. "You look as though you'd seen a ghost."

She commanded herself into some semblance of order, if not calm. "Where the hell have you been?"

He gave a snort of laughter. "That's better." His eyes searched the room lit only by the dying fire and a single lamp. "Are you alone?"

"Except for Sadie. Sleeping."

He scanned the dark front window. "Are you being watched?"

"Yes. I'll close the blinds."

When she returned, he'd sagged against the kitchen counter for support. "Can I come in?"

"Of course. "

He straightened and shrugged out of his slicker and boots.

"Why are you running, Jonathan?"

"I'm not. Not really. I just need to …" He gestured to the fireplace.

"Warm up. Do you need clothes?"

He shook his head. "I'm dry, except for my hair."

She brought him a towel.

"Thanks." He toweled his wet hair..

She put a log on the fire, then poured him a glass of wine, handed it to him and picked up her own. "Where've you been?" She sank down in a chair, set her glass down and clamped her hands on her knees.

"Camping. Over on ..." He waved his hand toward the lake, "... a spot we used as a hide out at when we were kids."

He wasn't going to tell her more. "And now?"

"And now I'm going to turn myself in to that policeman watching the house." He took a gulp of wine and put the glass down. "But first I need to talk to you."

"About Brian." She, too, took a drink. "And the package my father saw you give him."

Jonathan blinked. "He did?"

"Yes. And went after *your* father."

"Huh?" His hands dropped. "Christ ... what happened?"

"Fortunately, nothing except to get himself arrested for assault. But he had a gun, and he's convinced you gave Brian a package ... of drugs." She forced out the words, confronting them.

Jonathan stared at her wordless.

"Is that true?"

He stood up, walked away, then turned and came back. "Yes."

She collapsed forward, holding her head. *"What? What drug?"*

"Anavar."

The scientific word dropped into the pit of her stomach, ending the week of turmoil. "Anavar," she repeated. "It's an anabolic steroid?"

"Oxandrolone."

"Can it cause miscarriage?"

"I don't know, Annika." He rubbed a hand through his damp hair. "I truly don't. Brian said he'd read up on it, and it was safe—safe for women, he said. When ... you lost the baby he was out of his mind. Afraid it had been the drug."

"He knew I was pregnant."

Jon stared at his hands. "But I didn't, Annie. Not until after. You have to believe that. He didn't tell me. I'd never dealt in anything more than grass, before. I swear. But he was so determined to get to the Olympics— to get you to Olympics—so desperate ... I knew Nils could get it for me, so ... I got it. That's all." He got up and crossed the room to kneel before her, putting his hands on her clasped ones. "And I'm so sorry."

She pulled her hands free and pushed them against her temples.

"He begged to go on that trip to get away. He said he couldn't bear to look at you, knowing what he'd done."

She stared at him. "You were supposed to go."

"Right. I didn't want to. I was scheduled to take a group out, but Nils said their third crew member was ill, and I was it." He sighed again. "That's one of the penalties of dealing in more than marijuana. They have the goods on you."

"So Brian got you into that, too."

"No, no, I did it. Don't put it all on Brian; he just ..." Jonathan's words faded into a helpless shrug.

"Is crazy. To win ..." The words gagged her. "But I can't believe he'd do that ..." She gripped Jonathan's hands. *"He knew!"*

"I couldn't believe it, either. When you miscarried." His words, uttered in sympathy, only served to confirm the truth. Brian the impulsive. Climbing the mast of the old schooner, sailing for Bear Island. Cramps seized her.

"Annika?"

"I need you to leave now. I need to be alone. Please."

There was a long silence, then she heard him get up. "I'll send Mother. She'll help."

"No!" *No Wolfsons!* "Nobody. Please."

Another silence followed. She heard the front door open and close, a burst of voices outside, then nothing.

Chapter 26

Brian

2004

The day was here. The Athens Olympic trials. Brian paced in front of the stands, his ears tuned to the echoing voice of the loudspeaker, as swimmers for the 200 freestyle were called to their marks. Above him the Olympic flags hung from high metal girders. *Made it ... Made it! ... Made it! Athens! Athens! Athens!* his feet said at every step, the rhythm catching him, carrying him through the endless waits between races. So far so good. The times were far faster than he'd anticipated. Nothing beyond what Annie'd made in practice, but enough to set his adrenaline going. Now for the finals. Just one more race.

"Daddy!"

The high voice turned him around. He grinned and waved to the small figure jumping up and down in the stands above. That wasn't enough for Sadie, who scampered out of her seat and down to the rail.

He reached over and picked her up, gave her a hug. Who would have dreamed anything could be so magical as that staccato chuckle against his breast. Or as exhilarating as the first time he'd tossed this soft bundle about in the water, lifting him out of himself. She'd just dropped into his arms one day into the middle of his worry, bringing a laugh from some deep place he'd never known he had.

"When's Mommy swimming?"

"Right now." He kissed her. "She'll wave to you when she comes out. Run back to Grandma now." He put her down and gave her behind a pat, then waved to his mother, who gave him a high sign.

"Well you've all but done it, Brian. Congratulations." Joe slapped him on the back. "You've finally got some family here."

"Yeah. Mom finally rebelled against Dad. Said she was bringing Sadie, and he could stay home if he wanted. By himself, since Jon's off on a trip."

"Good for her. Karl can be his own cheering section for a change."

"Here she comes."

Annie emerged from the locker room and headed toward them. Joe clasped his hands over his head in a cheer.

She came up and gave each of them a kiss. *"Let's go!"* She shrugged out of her warm-ups then turned to step up on the starting block.

"Wave to Sadie!"

"Oh!" She scanned the stands then waved vigorously to the bouncing bubble. Then to his mother.

"On your Marks!"

Annie spun around, stepped onto the block and crouched.

The gun shot the swimmers off the blocks, and Brian's stomach clenched, the years of preparation and frustration collapsing into this single point. Into every stroke, every breath, every turn. The ten swimmers were almost dead even at the first turn. A few had fallen back by the second. Annie was into her rhythm now, a little late, but her stroke looked effortless. He chuckled in relief, breathing his energy into her. As they somersaulted for the final lap, she was in the lead group. He closed his eyes unable to look. Counted five then opened them.

She'd cut loose, as always. His body tensed, then joined hers, stretching, stroking, breathing—and all else vanished. He closed his eyes again as she made the final turn at the far end. When he opened them, one, two, three swimmers were surging forward. A cry caught in his throat. His *Go! Go!* Was lost in the roar of the crowd. One fell back and there were two. The crowd went silent as they hit the wall. The scene froze, waiting for the times.

The numbers flashed on the board above her head, and his ready cheer stuck in his throat. *No. Not right.* He couldn't move.

"A half second!" Joe hissed. *"Damnation!"* He went to Annie, who clung to the wall, staring at the board. "Tough break, sweetie." He pulled her out of the water. "Really nuts." He hugged her, then threw a towel around her shoulders.

Brian spun away, unable to bear the stunned incredulity in her eyes.

Cries of *"Mommy! Mommy!"* were the last thing he heard as the locker room door swung shut behind him.

A timeless space later, he found himself sitting on a wall, looking out to sea. He had no idea how he'd gotten there. He'd run. That he knew. From the scoreboard. *From Annie.*

Hid head fell to his hands. The well swallowed him.

"Hey buddy ... you okay?"

He raised his head and blinked at the man who stood above him. A burly sailor type. "Yeah ..." He looked at his watch. Almost six. Two hours! Where had they gone?

"Know where you are?"

He looked around. "Long Beach." He gave a sour attempt at a laugh. "California. Olympic trials." He gazed down at his red, white and blue warm-ups.

"Yeah? What sport?"

"Swimming."

"You lose a race or something? You were looking sort of done-in there."

"Yeah." He gazed out to sea. "By a half second."

"Damn. That's rough."

"No … it's Annie. My wife …"

"You lose her too?" His voice rose, incredulous.

"What?' Brian's head shot up. "No! Not that!" He was on his feet. "Which way to the Westin?"

"Hotel? Just up that street." He pointed. "Five or six blocks."

"Thanks. Thanks for stopping. Gotta go."

He left his nameless Samaritan and began to run. It wasn't until he was on the elevator that he realized that if he found her, he had to face her. He couldn't. He couldn't not. His brain froze as he left the elevator and walked to the room, put his card in the lock and opened the door.

Annie sat by the window in a terrycloth robe. Her auburn curls, dried without combing, were a rat's nest. She stared at him without moving.

"Annie …"

"Where were you?"

Her leaden tone stopped him halfway across the room.

"I'm sorry. I just had to … I couldn't … couldn't face you … see the shock. It was just too much Annie." He ran to her. Clasped her cold hands. "But just for the moment. And I'm sorry. So sorry. But it was just a bad break, Annie. We're not done." He begged her eyes to change, come to life, see him. *"On to China!"*

Chapter 27

2007

Annika stared at the ashen remains of the fire. She was cold. She pulled the afghan from the back of the couch, wrapped it around herself and pulled her legs up. The rain struck the lakeside windows, angry, insistent.

A pounding at the front door sat her up, blinking into the morning sun. She pushed herself to her feet, stumbled across the room and yanked the door open.

"Your phone is off!" Vicky cried. "I've been calling …" Her voice faded as she took in Annika's face. "Good grief, what's going on?" She came in, closing the door behind her, and led Annika back to the couch. "You look as though … have you been to bed?" Vicky headed for the kitchen without waiting for a reply.

"What time is it?" Annika rubbed her face in an effort to focus.

"Seven-thirty."

"Oh …" She jumped up. "It's late. Have to get Sadie up—"

"It's Saturday, Annie." Vicky finished setting up the coffee pot and came toward her. "Sit down and tell me—all of it."

"It's freezing." Annika wrapped her arms around herself. "I need to turn on the furnace."

"Good idea."

When she returned, Vicky had settled herself on the couch and was patting the seat next to her.

Annika sat and stared at her friend, unable to find the words to begin.

Vicky waited.

"Jonathan came."

"Here? The news said he was missing ..." Vicky stopped as Annika raised a hand.

"He came. By boat. Last night in the middle of the storm. He'd been hiding out in the woods somewhere." The words broke the logjam in her mind, and the story began to pour out, but she stopped when she saw Vicky go white at the mention of the package exchange.

"Oh no. Tell me he wouldn't—"

"He did." She jumped to her feet, a rage deeper and wider than any she'd ever known breaking through the incredulity and shock. "They did and Brian knew!" She picked up a book and slammed it down. Then stared at it. "A performance drug called Anavar."

"Knew ...?"

"I was pregnant. And I lost the baby!" She heard her voice rise and shut it down, glancing at the stairs.

"Slow down, Annie. You mean this was before your miscarriage?"

"Right." She sat down beside Vicky again. "And Brian knew. Jon said he didn't know, which maybe he didn't. We'd just begun to tell people—our parents."

Vicky gave a long hissing sound. "How the hell did Brian get Jon to do that?" Her voice rose in outrage. "And why? Brian hates drugs."

"He was desperate, Jon said. I was too slow. He was afraid I wouldn't make it at the trials."

Vicky let out a long, noisy exhale. "Okay. And you took it?"

"No!" Annika jumped up again. "He snuck it to me!" She caught her voice rising and sat down again and pounded her fists on her knees instead.

Vicky stared, wordless.

"And no, I don't know how. In my cereal? I've no idea, but he did. He told Jon he had."

Vicky reached for her clenched hands and drew them to her. They sat like that, listening to the kitchen clock.

Annika leaned back, letting the anger subside. "Jon said Brian was super upset when I lost the baby—and I know that. He was in a state. He told Jon he had to get away. That's why ..." She choked.

"He went on the trip with Nils and company," Vicky finished for her.

"Right. Jon had clients scheduled, but Nils said they were short-handed, and Jon had to come—in return for getting the drug."

"Oh damn ..." Vicky's voice was barely audible. "Where's Jon now?"

"He turned himself in." Annika stood up and went to get them coffee. When she returned with steaming cups, Vicky was still sunk against the back of the couch.

She opened her eyes at Annika's touch and took the proffered cup. "Thank you." She picked up the remote and turned on the television. "Might as well find out the worst."

"Fontenac police report a break in the case of missing swim coach, Brian Wolfson." The blare of the news anchor's voice bounced from the walls. Vicky turned it down.

"Wolfson's brother, Jonathan, missing since Sunday, has turned himself in for questioning, but denies knowledge of his brother's whereabouts. Investigation into the brothers' connection with drugs continues." He paused. *"Brian Wolfson has now been missing for a week."*

The anchor picked up another sheet of paper, and Vicky turned the set off. "They didn't mention the package—or the baby."

"Thank God. Maybe Jon didn't tell the police."

"He wouldn't—if he could avoid it." She took a sip of coffee. "Go get a shower, Annika. You look terrible."

"I'm sure." She took another gulp of coffee. "All right. I'll do that before Sadie wakes …" She cut off. "Dear God, Vicky, what do I tell her?"

"That her daddy was upset at the loss of the baby. Which is true."

"She doesn't know about the baby. We hadn't told her yet."

"Oh. Well that's good, I guess." Vicky thought for a moment, then shook her head. "Go get your shower. You'll think of something."

Five minutes later, Annika was letting the hot water run over her body. Slowly her limbs released their frozen grip, but the hard ball in the middle of her stomach stayed tight. Her empty womb. Suddenly woozy from heat and steam, she turned off the shower and collapsed on the closed toilet, shaking with tearless rage.

Vicky found her there and helped her dry off and put her robe on, then led her to her bedroom. "Sleep now. I'll take care of Sadie."

Too exhausted to protest, Annika climbed into bed. She didn't expect to sleep, but did.

She woke to the sharp tones of Sadie's voice as she raced to her room for something, then raced back down the stairs. Her watch said it was two in the afternoon. The last of sleep left her, and she turned and buried her head in the pillow to shut out the sun that had found its way to her bed. It did no good. The memory rose of Brian's face, pallid, not meeting her eyes, his untouched dinner in front of him.

"I'm taking a trip." His voice broke the vacuum Sadie had left when she ran out to play.

"What? When?" She dropped her fork.

"Sailing out of Bar Harbor Sunday." He stared at his plate.

"Bar ... *Why?*"

"Need to get away—a break ..." He rose without another word and took his plate to the sink.

Chilled, Annika remembered the drive to the airport, Brian staring at the road, his hands gripping the wheel, his eyes, dark, flat, without emotion, Sadie in the back seat, silenced by the tension, staring at a book.

Annika swung her feet from the bed, rose and went to stare out of the window. The lake, still turbulent from the night's storm, looked like melted ashes. *He's poisoned it.* She clenched her teeth and turned away. *He poisoned me!* Only the sound of Sadie's voice from below softened her mood. She dressed and went down and found them sitting over a game of checkers.

"She's good," Vicky commented, glancing up.

"Daddy taught me." Sadie frowned at the board. "He's better, though."

Annika rubbed the top of her daughter's head. "Good morning, sweetie."

"It's not morning." Sadie looked up at her. "We already had lunch!"

"Guess I must be a lazybones, huh?"

"Aunt Vicky said you were just tired." Sadie turned her attention back to the board.

"There's a list of calls on the dinette table, Annika. I hope you don't mind I turned the phone back on. People are worried about you."

"Sorry. I forgot ..." She crossed to the table, trying to remember why she'd turned it off. The news people. From a far off time, she remembered her quiet pizza dinner with Stephanie and Sadie. She looked at the list headed by her mother's name, followed by the police and a list of news-papers. She sighed and picked up the phone to call her mother. The rest could wait.

"Annika? Oh, thank goodness. I was so worried."

"I know. I'm okay, Mom. I turned the phone off to get rid of the news people, then I forgot it."

"I wanted you to know Karl isn't pressing charges against your father. I'm going to pick him up now."

"That's good news, Mom."

"Mm." She paused, and when she continued her voice was tight, almost shrill. "But Billy says Tom was right—about the package. Did you take drugs, Annie? To go faster?"

Annika's closed her eyes. So Jonathan had told the police about the drug. She glanced at Sadie, still absorbed in her game, and moved out of hearing. "No," she said softly. "He gave them to me without my knowing."

"Oh, no! That's … that terrible! Did he know about the baby, Annie?"

"He did. He knew, but when … when it happened …he …well, he ran away." She sank down on the bench. The words brought back that other day. Athens. The day she failed. And he was gone.

"I don't want to believe Brian—*anyone*—would do that," her mother muttered. "And if he shows up—"

At her mother's words, memory of the missing money struck. "He won't come back." The response came of own volition, without intent. "Not to me."

"No. That's … You wouldn't have him, would you? Oh, Annie, I'm so sorry …" Her voice caught. "Does Sadie know?"

"No. I can't think about that yet."

"All right. I'll tell Tom not to talk about it. She doesn't have to know everything."

"Unless it's blaring on the television," Annika muttered.

"Well, so far so good. Are you okay? I'll come over."

"Vicky's here, Mom. I'm okay, and the police want to talk to me again."

"Oh dear." She sighed audibly. "When will they go away?"

"Just don't tell them anything more."

"Don't worry about that, my dear."

"Good. I have to go. I'll call again, later." She hung up and leaned back against the wall, absorbing the impact of her own statement. *He's not coming back. Not to me.*

Across the room the training schedule danced before her eyes.

Chapter 28

Annika was still sitting by the phone, staring at the training chart, the evil genie that drove their lives, when the door-chimes shook her free of its spell.

Across the room, Sadie jumped to her feet, and Annika rushed to intercept her. "Wait, sweetie, let's see who it is first."

Sadie frowned, puzzled, as Annika looked through the peephole at Carlson's waiting face.

"It's the police, helping find Daddy," Annika told her. "Go on back to your game."

Sadie didn't budge.

"Go on."

Sadie glared, then turned and headed back to the board.

Annika pulled the door open. "Officer Carlson."

He touched his cap in acknowledgment. "Mrs. Wolfson. We'd like to talk—"

"Did you find him?" Sadie was at Annika's side.

Carlson started, then smiled. "Not yet, honey."

"Why does it take so long?" she demanded.

"The world's a big place, Sadie." Vicky's hand was on her shoulder. "And your mother needs to talk to the officer. Come on." She turned the child away.

"Not here," Annika insisted, her voice barely above a whisper.

Officer Carlson nodded. "At headquarters, then."

Annika pulled a sweatshirt from its hook and turned to Vicky.

"We're good." Vicky raised a hand.

"I'll be back soon, Sadie."

The child didn't answer.

Vicky gave Annika a wry smile and waved her off. "Call when you're done. We'll pick you up."

Annika turned and followed Carlson down the steps. The storm had passed, leaving the walks plastered with wet leaves. The sun bounced off a freshly washed world of evergreen and maple. Annika blinked, shocked that all traces of the night could have vanished so completely.

Carlson waved off the approaching press. *Did they never leave?* She reoriented and, as he opened the passenger door for her and tried to get her brain in motion. She felt like a fly caught in a web—she, Sadie, her mother, father, Jonathan —all of them unable to disentangle their feet, to get traction. She looked at the man beside her. "Mother says you're letting my father go. That Karl Wolfson isn't pressing charges."

"True. But he's signed up for rehab. That's a condition."

"That's good. He's been in rehab before. In Traverse." Where was he going to get his marijuana now? Petitions to legalize it for medical purposes had been floating around, but it was still illegal. She sighed. Well, at least her father was home. Her mother would read him the riot act and keep him under her thumb.

"Here we are." He pulled up to the curb and stopped. "Go straight in to the Chief's office. He's waiting for you."

Inside, the receptionist buzzed her through, and she faced Chief Constantine, her mind again a blank. What was she going to say and what not? Her brain refused to look into either the past or the future.

"Sit down, Mrs. Wolfson." Constantine's voice suggested this visit was just routine.

She did so.

He flipped on a recorder. "Interview with Annika Wolfson, September 27th, 2007, 10 AM." He raised his gaze to her. "Jonathan Wolfson paid you a visit last evening."

She nodded.

"Speak up, please. The machine can't record nods."

"Yes. He did."

"Where'd he been, since your husband went missing? Did he say?"

"In the woods. At some camping spot he and Brian had known as children."

"Was your husband with him?"

Annika blinked. "What? …No. Why …? Brian sailed off the East Coast …" Her voice faded in confusion.

"Did you ask whether Brian was there?"

Annika stared at him, wordless. "No," she said finally. "But he would have told me."

Constantine shrugged without comment. "Why did Jonathan come see you?"

Annika went calm, as though a switch had been flicked. "To talk to me before he turned himself in to you."

"Talk to you about what?"

"About why Brian left. Why he went on that sailing trip." The words came easily enough, but she couldn't see ahead.

Billy Constantine waited. "And?"

"He was upset. Brian was. That I'd lost the baby." The words seemed to create their own path, step by step, and she could do nothing but follow the lead of the questions.

"Your father accused Brian of killing the baby. What do you suppose he meant by that?" The Chief's tone remained casual, merely interested.

Her skin grew cold. "He thought Brian gave me drugs. Performance drugs."

"Did he?" His tone didn't change.

"I don't know."

He frowned. "What does that mean? Did you take drugs or not, Mrs. Wolfson?"

"I didn't knowingly take any drugs. I never would and certainly not when I was pregnant."

"Do you know what Anavar is?"

"A performance drug—the Russians used it."

"Have you ever taken Anavar, Mrs. Wolfson?"

"I hate drugs in sports. And so did Brian. He was dead set against them. Always."

"Jonathan Wolfson says he got Anavar from Svenson. Why would he want a performance drug, Mrs. Wolfson?"

"I don't know."

"Is he lying?"

"Jonathan?" She stopped. Was she going to hang Jonathan to protect Brian? "I don't know why he'd lie about that."

"Did your husband know you were pregnant, Mrs. Wolfson?"

"Yes." The word felt like a block of cement. "He knew."

"Did he want the baby?"

"Want …? Oh, he wouldn't … That wasn't … He was upset when I lost the baby—so upset he couldn't look at me. He told Jon that—that he had to get away from …" The rush of words died on her lips.

"From what he did?"

"From me." But as the words settled, they made sense. Finally.

Chief Constantine sat up and drew a pen and paper towards him. "Well we believe your husband got the Anavar for you, Mrs. Wolfson." He picked up a pen and made a note. "If he did so without your knowledge, that's negligence. If it causes harm, gross negligence or assault. And then there's the death of the baby. Do you want to charge him?"

"Charge him?" Annika was disoriented. "Me?"

"You. You think about it and let me know, because, barring charges, it looks as though he left of his own free will."

Annika stared as the words sank in. "And you'll stop looking for him." She looked out of the window. There was nothing to see but a brick wall.

"He's still part of the Bar Harbor drug investigation. They've taken Svenson and Costello into custody. Their ship showed evidence of cocaine and heroin. Whether they confess to giving Wolfson Anavar remains to be seen, and whether they caused your husband harm—remains a possibility, but there's no evidence of that as yet."

Annika shuddered as the chief put in words the thought that had remained half-formed all week. Her rage at Brian didn't include his being thrown overboard. Did it? She shook off the shock.

He rose. "We question why Jonathan kept in touch with those two."

She rose without answering, and walked out numb. She called Vicky, then stood inside the door of the police department, clenching and unclenching her fist. She never wanted to see him again. Never. But charge him? With assault? Negligence, the Chief said. And murder? What did

Michigan law say about the baby? *He killed it.* She saw Vicky driving up, Sadie's face in the back window, and her fists and teeth clenched again.

She ran to the curb, ignoring an approaching reporter, opened the back door and gave Sadie a kiss before climbing in beside Vicky.

"You look sick. What ...?" She broke off at the shake of Annika's head.

"Let's go home."

"Are they going to find him, Mommy?" The small voice was no longer demanding or belligerent.

"I don't know, Sadie. I think we have to just go on day to day and hope Daddy comes home by himself." *And if he does?* She slammed the door on the thought.

"Looks as though you have company," Vicky commented as they approached the house.

Carmen's car sat in the drive, and Carmen herself was coming down the steps. She waved as they turned in, then stopped abruptly when she saw that it was Vicky at the wheel.

Vicky rolled her eyes. "What do you want me to do? Drive off?"

Annika stared at her mother-in-law. "No. I'm done with that." She climbed out of the car and unbuckled her daughter.

Sadie ran off to her grandmother, breaking the newly-formed ice for all of them.

Carmen looked up from the child's hug. "I had to come."

"Yes." The word fell automatically from her lips. "All right. Come in."

"Hello, Carmen." Vicky forced Carmen's attention.

Carmen nodded. "Vicky."

When they got inside, Vicky took Sadie's hand. "We're going out to the dock and check the boats."

"Why? I want to talk to Gramma."

"You go with Vicky," Carmen said. "I need to talk to your mom."

Sadie frowned, confused, but went along.

Carmen sank to the sofa. "I can't imagine how angry you must be," she began when the duo had left the house. "And so am I. Sick."

"Jonathan told you?"

"He did. I'm so mad at both of them, I … and Karl … he can't even speak, he's so furious." She looked down at the hands that clutched the chair arms as though they belonged to someone else.

Annika could only watch her, wordless. What was there to say? What she saw was a mother. Appalled, shaken, but a mother. And a Wolfson. The buried currents that split Wolfsons and Berglunds had surged into full flood at her father's attack, and she and Carmen bore the brunt.

Carmen sat biting her lip. "I just came to tell you that." She got up and took a few steps toward the door. "Karl says you could press charges, especially if the drug … really did that …" She looked a question.

"I don't know, Carmen." Then at the stricken woman's accepting nod, she relented. "But thank you for coming. I appreciate that. And thank Karl for dropping charges against my father."

She nodded. "Karl said to leave you alone. That you probably hate us. But I had to come." Carmen tried for a smile. "Take care."

Annika stood staring at the closed door, regretting her inability to comfort the woman.

"Well?"

Vicky's voice turned her around. "Where's Sadie?"

"Feeding her turtles. She wants to talk to her grandmother. About painting some animals?"

"Oh. Well, she's gone, and this isn't the time. They're in a state over there. Carmen and Karl are furious at their sons. And scared. At least Carmen is. She wants to know if I'm going to charge them."

Vicky sat. "And?"

"The police want to know that, too." Annika started to pace. "I just can't make my brain deal with it. I'm raging inside and afraid I'll do or say something wild—something I can't take back."

The phone rang, and she went over and looked at the ID. "The Record Eagle."

"Let it ring." Vicky ordered. "We're getting out of here."

"Where to?"

"Mackinac Island. I made reservations for us."

"Mac ...You didn't!"

"I did. While you were at the station. You can't stay here right now and neither can I. Plus Sadie needs a distraction."

"Ha! As do we all. Better run tell her the change of plans."

Chapter 29

Annika lay back in her lounge chair on the front porch of the Grand Hotel and let the sun's warmth dissolve her. She was floating in a pool of blue vast enough to release her from all else. If she opened her eyes, the mainland looked shrunken and insubstantial in the distance, with only a thread of a bridge connecting its parts. She'd never been to Mackinac Island. It brought no memories.

They'd arrived by late afternoon yesterday, thanks to Vicky's connections. Sadie's excitement at the boat ride and elegant hotel room had carried all of them through.

"I can't afford this place, Vicky, you know that," she'd murmured. The trip had already dispersed the weight of the morning, leaving her fuzzy.

"Don't worry about it. It's only for one night. I have a friend who found a last-minute cancellation—she gets a deal on it."

Sadie's enchantment was complete. For her, the present was everything—the horse-drawn carriages, the bicycles, the open water, sand and air laden with evergreen. A carriage ride and dinner had ended the day and left them all ready to sleep. A bicycle ride this morning had finished the job of clearing the tension out of body and mind. The porch was quiet. They'd caught a lull between summer guests and fall color tours, and most weekenders were heading for the mainland. Sadie was taking a rare nap in the room above her head, and Vicky, in the chair beside her, seemed asleep.

She was running down a long beach, her bare feet slapping along the water's edge, her arms spread wide, catching the air. She was a bird. A heron. A shape brushed by …

"Come on, silly! Race you!"

It was Brian. Then another raced by. "Look out!" and another.

She laughed and ran after them. The stones cut, the air burned her lungs, but she was part of them, a laughing, shouting mob, racing for a dock, then racing its length to cannonball into the water. She broke the surface screaming. She was holding a lifeless baby …

"Annika!"

She woke to Vicky's face, staring down at her. "Are you all right?"

She rubbed her eyes. "A dream." Around her was the white balustrade of the porch. "I'm sorry. Did I wake you?"

Vicky sat back. "No. I was just dozing. It was like you couldn't get your breath—a gurgling noise." She laughed. "You scared me."

"I was swimming … no, running … with a bunch of kids," she began, chasing the retreating images, "and something happened …" She shook her head. "It's gone … good riddance." She sat up. "Would you like a cup of tea? Coffee?"

Vicky looked at her watch. "Wine."

"Brilliant. I'll get it. Red or white?"

"White. Make it Pinot Gris."

By the time Annika returned with frosted glasses, she'd shaken the worst effects of the dream, though a sense of unreality remained.

Vicky eyed her critically. "You look as though you've had a jolt."

"I do? I feel sort of rocky, but it'll pass." She raised her glass. "Here's to escape. This was a wonderful idea, Vicky."

"And here's to you. You bounce back wonderfully." Vicky raised her glass.

They watched a flock of tiny birds flitting in the bushes beyond the balustrade. Their twitter filled the silence. "What's the very latest we can leave?"

Vicky drew a schedule from her purse. "Eight-thirty."

"Too late. I have to get Sadie to bed by that time."

"Seven?"

"That'll do." Annika yawned.

"Okay." Vicky rose and stretched, "I'll go get us seats. Be right back."

Annika shifted her gaze to the mainland. It no longer looked insubstantial, but the broad stretch of lake protected her. She took a sip of wine and closed her eyes to regain her balance, her sense of well-being. When Vicky returned, they kept their talk within the confines of the island, the heron on the shore, the brilliant flashes of color just emerging, the old fort, the magic of the quiet where the approaching and departing ferry were the only evidence of the motor-driven world.

Sadie's voice floated from above, and they retrieved her for a long walk along the shore, returning only when the sunlight reddened.

"We'd better get packed before dinner." Vicky spoke softly, as though to avoid breaking the spell.

"Why?" Sadie's voice sliced the quiet.

Annika took her hand. "Because we have to leave after supper, Sadie. Tomorrow is a school day."

"I'll go to school *here*!" Sadie stopped, stricken with her beautiful idea. "Do they have a school here?"

Annika laughed. "I don't know, honey, but your home is in Fontenac, and you have a lovely lake and a beach there, too. Two lakes—big ones."

"This is better." Sadie's voice stated fact, but she made no further argument as they packed their bags and went down to dinner. In fact, lost in her own thoughts, she said very little.

It wasn't until they had boarded the ferry and set sail that she broke her near-silence."I have an arithmetic test.

"Oh? Tomorrow?"

"Uhhuh."

"Well you usually do just fine in arithmetic," Annika assured her.

"I didn't do my homework."

Above her head, Annika and Vicky almost broke out laughing at this calamity and transported themselves wholeheartedly into the world of addition and subtraction.

"Mackinac Island is three miles from shore and Fontenac is another fifty miles. How many miles do we have to go to get home?" Vicky asked at one point.

Sadie looked at her in surprise. "What?"

Vicky repeated it slowly.

"Oh!" Sadie put the numbers on her paper and studied them. "Fifty-three!"

By the time they reached shore and drove half the distance home, Sadie was yawning. By the time they reached Fontenac, she was asleep. Annika unbuckled her and carried her in to her bed. When she descended the stairs, Vicky had poured them cider, and was starting the popcorn popper.

"What a lovely idea. I hope the smell doesn't wake her up."

"Oh, oh. Do you think it will?"

"No. She's dead out. But I'm going to go back and shut her door, just in case." Annika turned for the stairs. By the time she came down the second time, she realized how tired she was. "You must be beat, Vicky. You're staying over, I hope."

"I can. I'm not due at work until noon tomorrow."

"Good." Annika picked up the drinks and carried them to the coffee table, then sank down on the couch. Vicky joined her, carrying a huge bowl of popcorn. The room was dim, lit only by the distant light from the kitchen, but Annika made no move to turn on a lamp.

"This is how I treat myself after a long day," Vicky remarked. "When I'm too damned tired to cook."

"I'll remember that. Sadie would love it." Annika picked up a handful.

"Ha. You'll get hauled up for parental neglect."

"Mm," Annika mumbled around her mouthful. "Probably."

Quiet fell as they munched and drank, letting the trip fade away.

"Do you have a plan, Annie?" Vicky's voice came out of the dark.

"A plan." Annika repeated the words as though trying to make sense of them. "No. I'm in a void. I go through the motions—put Sadie to bed, get her up—but my life ... has vanished."

"Are you going to charge him?"

Her voice was gentle, but the words jolted Annika out of the anesthetic. "With drugging me?"

"Or murder."

The calmness of Vicky's tone chilled the room. "I can't ... even say that word." She gazed out at the lake, twinkling in the moonlight. Until this moment, it had marked the end of a lovely day. "All I know is that I don't want him near me—ever again."

"Understood." Vicky put her glass down. "I'll let it go for now, but soon, I think, you're going to need to know ..." She broke off, as though fishing for words. "Whether the drug really did cause the miscarriage."

Annika stared at her, amazed.

"Well it might not have, you know. And sooner or later, that thought will come to you." Vicky took a handful of popcorn as though in defense against Annika's incredulity.

"I suppose …" Annika let the idea sink in. "Come." She stood, led the way to Brian's office, and booted the computer. "This is where Brian looks up stuff."

Vicky pulled up a chair.

Once she had the Internet, she Googled "Anavar." Wikipedia gave them the basics: an anabolic steroid, less powerful and safer than most. She went on down the Google list: "the woman's performance drug!" "Safe for women!" "Sometimes a weight loss drug," "a controlled substance" and on through forums, mostly by men on muscle building.

Only when she paired "Anavar" with "Pregnancy" did warnings flash. Never ever ever take when pregnant. Toxic. Possible cause of birth defects.

They sat back and gazed at the words.

"That should have turned him off," Vicky said finally.

"But he still gave it to me … snuck it to me, knowing I was pregnant."

"If he used that keyword—got to that site. All of the other sites stress its safety."

"And even there it doesn't mention miscarriage as a side effect."

"True."

"All of which is nit-picking. He detested all drugs. But he did it. Period."

"I know. I'm not saying you should take him back, Annika, even if the drug didn't cause it. I'm only looking into the future—seeing that you will want to know."

Annika stared at her glass. "All right. I'll go see Dr. Graves."

The next morning, after Sadie and Vicky had both departed, Annika drove to the doctor's office, where she stared at a waiting room clock that refused to move. The room was mauve, the chairs covered with soft blues and purples, and the pictures on the walls were done in curves—all conveyed the sense of impending motherhood. Its occupants sat in sealed off cocoons. One was very pregnant, stolid in her discomfort, the other frail, haggard with weight loss. Cancer? They brought back her visit after the miscarriage, when she'd sat here, eyeing the happy bulges of other women, clutching her own empty belly. She wanted only to flee. Dr. Graves had agreed to see her on his lunch hour, though his receptionist had made clear that wasn't his practice. Now she sat frozen, trapped by her promise to Vicky.

"Mrs. Wolfson?" The nurse stood in the open door of the hallway to the examining rooms.

Annika stood, only too aware that the other two had looked up, startled and curious. She'd forgotten about the press.

The nurse led her to the doctor's office, and she waited, gazing at the row of family pictures on his bookcase.

"Good to see you." The compassion in the voice behind her turned her head in surprise. Dr. Graves was a big man and bald, well rounded with middle age; his relaxed, unhurried movements as he crossed to his desk and took his seat exuded reassurance. His blue eyes expressed concern and interest. "How are you doing?"

"I'm not sure." She frowned, unable to get her tongue in motion. "You've read the papers?"

"Yes. And been … pretty shocked by it all." He frowned. "I found it hard to believe, in fact, that Brian would run off that way—though I didn't really know him. Or that a Wolfson would be involved in drugs."

She tightened her clasped hands. "They aren't. But Brian asked his brother to get Anavar for me. And he did."

Dr. Graves' face had blanched. "But you wouldn't ..."

"Take performance drugs?" She shook her head. "I didn't, Dr. Graves. I would never take them in any case and certainly not when I was pregnant."

"I didn't think so." His shoulders relaxed.

"But he gave me Anavar without my knowing. He said he did—told his brother that—and I'm sure of it. Looking back, I remember feeling strange when I was swimming. But faster ..." She let a wave of her hand finish the sentence.

"Why would he do such a thing?" He spread his hands. "I assume he knew you were pregnant?"

"He did. And I need to know ... whether the Anavar did it. Know for sure."

He exhaled slowly. "Do you have any idea how long he was giving it to you? Or how much? The dosage?"

"No. How would I know?"

"I should see changes in hormone levels—in your blood tests. Which I didn't, but I hadn't taken one for the three weeks before your miscarriage."

"So you can't tell?"

"There are rarely any 'for sures' in miscarriages. Too many factors involved." He templed his fingers. "I'll do some research, but no steroid is safe for pregnant women. The last thing we want to do is mess with hormone levels."

She sat silent, letting it sink in.

The silence stretched.

Dr. Graves cleared his throat. "Did he not want the baby?"

"I don't know," she acknowledged to herself as well as to him. "But he wanted victory more—it wiped out all else."

"Victory?" The doctor's lips tightened.

"Getting on the Olympic team. Me, that is. I was training when I got pregnant."

"Well, I know that, but …That's unthinkable!" He spun his chair. "Abominable." He stood and went to stare out the window.

"Charge him!" The words shot out as he spun around.

"I don't … But you say you can't be sure."

"No, but you're sure he gave it to you. That's—"

Annika's cell phone cut off his words. She pulled it from her purse. "The school …" she muttered and punched connect.

"Mrs. Wolfson?"

"Yes?"

"This is Ella Simpson, the school secretary. I'm afraid you need to come get Sadie." The second sentence wiped out the uncertain beginning. "Some children set upon her at recess."

"They what? Why?" Annika shouted. "She's hurt?"

"Not badly, but … she needs to go home."

"I'll be right there." She punched the off button and stared at Dr. Graves. "Did you …?"

"I heard. Probably all the press—"

"Oh, dear God …" She jumped to her feet. "I never thought … I have to go. Sorry."

"Of course."

"Don't let that bastard get away with it!"

His voice followed her, setting loose a surge of rage that had been hiding under shock for days. Gravel spurted from her tires as she left the parking lot.

In the school office, she found a bewildered, tearstained Sadie, bandages on one knee, one arm and her forehead. She leapt to her feet and rushed into her mother's arms, saying nothing.

Annika held her close. "How did this happen?"

"There was name calling, then a child pushed her and others joined in. I'm afraid she was down before the teacher could reach her."

"We're terribly sorry, Mrs. Wolfson." The principal's appeared from his inner office. "We wouldn't have had that happen for the world, but I'm afraid with all of the headlines and television …"

His second sentence swallowed the apology of the first, and Annika could only clamp her jaw over her rage.

She simply picked Sadie up and walked out.

"No!" Sadie squirmed to get free. "Not a baby!"

"Sorry." She set her daughter on her feet.

Sadie took off in an angry march toward the door and Annika followed. *How could you let this happen?*

When they reached the car, Sadie climbed into her seat and watched Annika buckle her in without a word. She forced herself to maintain a reasonable speed as she drove, keeping an eye on the silent child behind her.

"Đrughead. That's what they said." Sadie burst out as Annika turned onto the shore road. In the mirror, she saw tears spring to her daughter's eyes.

"Your Daddy's a pothead. A nasty … a druggie."

Annika pulled into the drive and got out. "I'm so sorry, sweetie," she murmured as she set Sadie free. "So sorry …" she muttered to herself, watching Sadie run for the house, tears streaming down her face.

Chapter 30

Brian

2007

"Mister?"

The word came through from a distant place.

"Mister?"

Something nudged his side. He rolled over, clamped his eyelids against the blast of sun off the water. Opened them enough to see a shape against the glare.

"Thought you were dead."

He groaned and sat up, took in the stretch of sand and water, shook his head in confusion, then finally remembered slipping away as Svenson and Costello unloaded *The Wayfarer,* seeking this Outer Banks beach. Then reality hit him in the chest, and he flopped back and rolled away. "Leave me alone."

"Tide's coming in. You're gonna get wet."

"Doesn't matter."

"You Brian?"

"What?" The question brought him to a sitting position. "Why?"

"Couple of men are looking for Brian. That you?"

The frozen state of horror that had driven the last days settled onto him once again—a state without motivation or intent operating on forces beyond his understanding or control. "Tell them I'm not going back. I'm staying here."

"You can't stay here. Look."

He twisted his head around, following the boy's finger. Water flowed between him and land. He was on a spit. He muttered an obscenity and got to his feet, brushing the sand from his clothes.

"This way."

The boy led the way to a spot where they could slosh across then along the beach to the stairs Brian remembered descending in some fuzzy indeterminate past.

"Thanks." He focused for the first time on the small tanned face, the scrambled thatch of blond hair. Sadie's face rose, reaching for him, and a cramp doubled him over.

"You okay, Mister?"

He nodded, taking deep breaths and raised his head. "Not Mister. Brian."

"Yeah?" The boy shrank back. "You with those men?"

Brian frowned, puzzled. "Not anymore. I'm—"

"Well, well, look who's here!"

Dominic Costello stood at the top of the stairs looking down. "Thought we told you to be at the dock at six."

"I'm not going. I'm done."

"No no." Nils appeared behind Dominic. "That's not part of the deal, Brian."

"Why not? What the hell do you care?"

"We told you. You gotta crew for us." Dominic took a couple of steps down toward him. "Come on, we're late."

"You got the stuff—you gotta crew," Nils added. "That's the deal. Now move it."

Brian felt a tug on his shirt and turned.

"You gotta go." His small companion whispered, white-faced under his tan. "They got guns."

On impulse, Brian reached out a hand to the boy's cheek. "I'll be back," he whispered. Then he turned and climbed the stairs, some small sense of purpose appearing from he knew not where.

Nils and Dominic turned without comment as he joined them and headed for the docks.

They marched to the marina parking lot where Costello unloaded boxes marked "coffee" and "sugar" from the trunk of a rental car into one of the marina's loading carts, then down the dock to where the *Wayfarer* sat, sleek and beautiful. "Load those into the hold," Nils directed.

Small details registered, penetrating the numbness that had descended when he'd climbed the stairs and accompanied them. They were making no effort to conceal those boxes, or the contents of the hold. Not coffee and sugar. He'd pried one open. So they'd seen the open box, knew he'd discovered the cargo. Another marker in the black tunnel he'd pitched into when he heard Annie cry out, saw the pool of blood … He jerked away from the memory and slammed the door of the hold.

Voices from above called him to tend the bumpers, the engine fired, and the boat began to move. Nils was at the helm, barking orders. Brian joined Dominic, pulling the covers from the sails, hanging his own noose. Knowing it, not stopping himself.

Then, clear of the marina and the harbor, he watched the main unfurl, catch the wind. They headed north as the sail turned gold in the evening sun.

"Take the jib," Nils ordered.

His body followed orders. His mind flashed scattered bits of the last days as though belatedly trying to gain a foothold.

The terror in Annie's eyes, staring down at the pool of blood.

"No!" Not that. *'No!" Not the baby.*

He grabbed her, hugged her. "No Annie, don't … don't …

It's safe! They said so. Everyone said so. Safe for women …

His mind kept screaming the same words as he sped toward the hospital, as they took Annie away, as he stood before her, knowing what she could not know … ever.

"I'm going, Jonathan! I have to."

"Why? I got the stuff. Not you."

"Because I have to. I can't stay!"

"Why not? What's the matter with you, Brian. What happened?"

"She lost the baby, Jon. They said it was safe and she lost it."

"What baby? What are you …? Oh, my God, Brian. You mean she was pregnant?"

"But they said it was safe. I can't look at her Jon. I've tried. I throw up. Run off and throw up."

Jon sank down and buried his head in his hands. "Shit, Brian, how could you—?"

"Save your breath. It's done. Just get me out of here!"

Concourses and ticket booths, roads and docks slid by without pause, sending him deeper and deeper into the hole, tumbling away …

"Chow's on!" Dominic called from below.

"Set your sail and take the wheel, Brian. I'm going below," Nils ordered.

Brian did as ordered.

"That's our course." He tapped the compass. " Keep it."

Brian stared at the wheel and compass, trying and failing to put his brain in motion.

An hour later, relieved of the wheel and fed, he gazed at the sun setting over the barely visible mainland with the same stupefied inertia.

Another hour passed, and he retired to his bunk.

Voices broken by the wind came through the open porthole above his head brought him out of fitful sleep.

"... going to work ..."

"… has to … knows too mu ..."

"He can't … without … own ass ..."

"It's … dangerous—stupid ..."

"Okay … dump him …"

Impulse without thought or plan sprang Brian from his bunk, up the ladder to the deck and around to the other side of the boat. The wind was up, the sea rough, and only a single distant light showed him the shoreline. Pausing only to eye the tell tale, he slipped into the water and began to stroke.

Chapter 31

2007

Annika woke to the unfamiliar slosh of wheels on wet pavement, the swipe of rain against the window. The globe of a light fixture, water-stained ceiling and the red and gold swirls of wallpaper sat her up, then dropped her. Ann Arbor. Her home for the last month. She rolled over, refusing it. Every morning was like this, a disorientation that faded but never disappeared. She sat up and planted her feet on the floor, then went to the window. The front yard was plastered with yellow, red, and purple leaves. In a month the world had hardened into fall. Across the road, the near-naked limbs of trees revealed the gray waters of the wind-roughened river beyond. The house of a friend of Vicky's away on sabbatical.

"I'll come down on weekends, Annie," her friend had assured her. "And it's on the river—a great location for Sadie."

A mumbling turned her toward the child who would no longer sleep in her own bed. She lay down again and pulled Sadie close, warming the child's body with her own.

Scenes not yet mellowed into memory returned to be relived.

"Where are we going, Mommy?"

"To Aunt Vicky's, baby." Annika continued shoving her daughter's overalls and underwear into a duffel bag.

"Why?"

"Because this town is very upset, and I won't have them calling you names and attacking you." She zipped the bag, then turned, picked Sadie up and sat her on the bed in front of her. "We're going away until they stop."

Sadie's head began to turn from side to side in denial. "We can't. No one will feed my turtles. They'll die."

"I'll ask Grandma Carmen to feed the turtles, but you run feed them now, before we go." When Sadie left, she went to her computer and opened her email. She wasn't talking to anybody, much less a Wolfson.

"Sadie was set upon at school, so I'm going to Traverse City to Vicky's until it's over." She typed in Vicky's phone number. *"Please feed the turtles. Back porch door is open."* She punched "Send" and sent similar messages to her mother and to the school, then went to pack her own duffel.

When she finished, she turned and found her daughter standing in the doorway, silent, watching.

She lay in Vicky's guest room bed in Traverse City, her muscles still frozen by the resolve it had taken to get out of Fontenac. Beside her, Sadie slept, a huge relief from her stolid silence during the trip. In the mirror, she'd seen only the top of Sadie's head, her eyes fixed on the book in her lap; when they arrived, she'd pulled away from Annika's embrace and given only monosyllabic responses to her aunt.

She's given up on us. The certainty sprang Annika from the bed and sent her out to the living room to stare out into the black expanse of Traverse Bay, the sentinel lights of the shoreline. Unchanging, calming.

Screams spun her around and sent her to the bedroom.

"No! You can't!" Another scream. *Don't..."*

Annika gathered up the flailing bundle. "Sadie! Wake up!" She rubbed her back and turned toward Vicky, who stood at the door.

"What can I do?" her friend mouthed.

Sadie started to sob, clutching Annika's neck. "Hot chocolate?"

Vicky nodded and disappeared.

Annika carried Sadie out to the couch, sat the child on her lap and waited until the shivering stopped. "I need to tell you a story."

"I don't want stories!" Sadie buried her face in Annika's neck.

"No. Okay. This is the truth."

Silence.

"Your daddy and I were trying very hard to swim fast enough—get me to swim fast enough—to go to the Olympics, which is a worldwide contest. You know that, right?"

Sadie nodded.

"But I wasn't fast enough—quite—and your daddy thought a pill might help. So he got one, and it did. But that was a mistake, Sadie, because pills are cheating."

Sadie's head came up, eyes wide.

"And your daddy hates cheating." She stopped, at a loss for how to continue. "You know that, too, don't you? From the time you peeked at his cards." She smiled at Sadie's vigorous nod.

From the kitchen, Vicky gave a thumbs up.

"It was also a bad mistake, because I was carrying the beginning of a baby in my stomach—just a little egg, which is how babies start—and I lost it."

"Lost it?" Sadie frowned in confusion. "A baby?"

"The egg of a baby. It came out. You remember when I had to go to the hospital?"

"Yes ..." Her assent was uncertain.

"That happens sometimes all by itself, but your daddy thought the pill made it happen, and he was so upset, he went away. And we don't know where."

Sadie waited for her to continue, her blue eyes deep with attention. "But he'll come back because he loves us."

Annika stared at her, unable to answer.

"He does, sweetie, and we hope he will," Vicky responded for her.

Sadie turned toward her aunt, then back at her mother. "Because even if he made a mistake, we love him." Her tone demanded confirmation.

Annika drew her child close so she wouldn't see her tears. "You miss him, sweetie. And it's hard, not knowing."

Vicky arrived with hot chocolate, and Sadie smiled. Drank.

Annika watched, half bewildered, half relieved. She'd told her. It was done. And the baby seemed to have no reality compared to her father. They hadn't told her yet, hadn't talked about a brother or sister. Was that it? Or she'd simply grasped for her father. Did grown-ups ever understand?

But the muscles of the child she held had gone soft; she drank like a long starved animal. There was no mistaking that relief. She'd taken Annika's hug and tears as assent. It was all just a big mistake. They'd take him back. Annika had accomplished everything and nothing.

~

The next morning the phone rang.

"Jon's home, Annika. I thought you'd want to know." Carmen sounded cautious, as though unsure of her reception.

"They didn't charge him?"

"Oh, yes, with possession. He got fined. But it was a first offence." She paused as though waiting for Annika's response. Receiving none, she went on. "Jon is going down to the Caribbean to find Brian, and it will be over. It was all just a terrible mistake, Annie."

"A mistake." Sadie's word from Carmen's mouth struck her dumb. She raised a hand to disconnect.

"Are you charging him, Annika?"

The words froze Annika for long moments. "I don't know."

—~—

"Mrs. Wolfson?"

"Yes?"

The caller cleared his throat. "Chief Constantine here."

"Yes?" She stiffened.

"A man's clothes—jeans and shirt—washed up on the beach at Outer Banks yesterday."

Annika sat down. She wasn't ready. Not for this. She swung around to Vicky. "Clothes. On the beach—"

"Mrs. Wolfson?"

"I'm here."

"No body, so it doesn't mean too much, but a kid who hangs around the docks said he thought they belonged to a man he met. Named Brian. They're sending them up here for identification."

"I'm not … I'm in Traverse City."

"That's okay. I'll have Carlson bring them down. Give me an address."

She gave it, grabbing for Vicky's hand.

"No trace of your husband on St. John's." Chief Constantine's tone made clear the matter had become routine. "Or in the Outer Banks—except for the clothes. If those clothes tie him to the *Wayfarer,* we'll question Svenson and Costello again. They insisted he jumped ship."

"And keep looking?"

"For the moment. We've sent missing-man notifications out across the Caribbean. Are you going to charge him, Mrs. Wolfson? Criminal negligence or assault, that would be."

Criminal. The word gave a name to it, to the shock, the slammed door, the immovable stone in her belly. It stood Brian in a courtroom, damned him. The first was right, the second …? Years of swim meets rose, the magic of fused energy. The crazy impulses—the sail to Bear Island, her brother's taunt that drove Brian up the riggings, the hours and hours … She'd been as much a part of the race for Gold and all of the other craziness of their lives—more than a part—the center. The sickening rage of his act had dried into the leaden lump of her own collusion.

"The doctor said we can't be certain the drug did it." She paused as she heard in her mind the voices of the chief and doctor rise in protest, but they had no resonance. "No. I won't charge him."

"That sounds like a decision."

"Yes." He was guilty. Nothing would change that. But she couldn't stand up in court and pretend she was an innocent victim. She'd been far too much a part of the race for that.

"Okay. If Jonathan Wolfson's story bears up, he may face a charge of possession—even dealing."

"Yes. I understand." She clicked off her phone and turned to Vicky. "Tell me I did right."

Three days later, she was staring down at the tumbled remains of a duffel bag, Brian's favorite patched jeans and his UM T-shirt. They sucked the breath out of her and she turned away. "Yes. They're Brian's."

She fled to the bathroom and vomited.

And then it had all slipped away, evaporated, leaving Brian out there … leaving her disconnected in Ann Arbor, a place she should know but didn't. She turned away to the ornate dressing table, chest, and headboard, the *fleur-de-lis* of the wallpaper that daily increased her sense of disembodiment.

She had expected the town to feel far more familiar than it did. Now she realized she'd spent her life here between classroom, dorm, and swimming pool, rarely venturing beyond that. Sadie, however, seemed to find some comfort tramping along the shore, some easing of the tension Annika could not ease. And the school was a scant half-mile away. Sadie seemed to take her new classmates in stride, even to welcome settling into the familiar routine. The girl next door, Nancy, had offered to walk with her, and Annika, after a week's hesitation, had consented. The neighborhood streets were full of children walking to school, and though Annika panicked every time Sadie was out of her sight, Nancy, a proud ten-year-old, was as good as her word, and Sadie's conversation, such as it was, was peppered with "Nancy says …"

Saturday. She checked the bedside clock, then looked down at the child. Sadie slept far too much and was hard to waken, but today, at least, they could spend together. "Sadie."

No response.

She put a hand on the child's shoulder and shook her gently. "Wake up or you'll miss Saturday."

Sadie mumbled.

"We can go to the park."

"Yeah?" She rolled over, her eyes lit with a dim spark of interest.

Annika glanced outside again. The sun was trying to emerge. "And if it clears up, we'll go for a canoe ride."

Sadie sat up and looked out the window, an every morning search for the apple tree. She'd stopped asking when they were going home, the gradual seeping away of hope that Annika was helpless to stop.

"So get your clothes on. Blue jeans and sweatshirt this morning." She turned and began to pull out the same for herself as Sadie obediently went down the hall to the room designated as hers. Annika was going to have to insist, one of these days, that Sadie spend her nights there. Not yet. Together they walked each other through the days.

An hour later, they were at the park at the river's bend, searching for turtles to replace the ones they'd returned to the wild on their one brief trip home. As Sadie's sullen silence began to dissolve, Annika relaxed and gazed across the river. The towers of the university hospital rose, bringing memories of the campus behind them. Here Annika regained some connection. Field trips along the river's winding course came back, bringing the same relief and lightness she'd felt as a student. With that had come her obstinate insistence on majoring in environment rather than phys ed—a rare defiance of Brian and her coaches. She'd done it for reasons she'd never bothered to examine, but now it was a reality to hold onto.

"We need one of those."

Annika turned in surprise at the spark of interest in her daughter's voice. In the meadow behind them several children struggled to get their colored butterflies and dragons into the air. "Kites. A good idea. We can do that." She watched the struggle for a minute. "But today the wind is dying, I'm afraid."

"But it's warm now. Can we go canoeing?"

Annika laughed. Sadie was back. Such moments came and went, giving hope. She eyed the river, still rippling but quieter. "You bet. Let's go." The discovery of the canoe livery just down the road from the house had given a spark of promise to the emptiness, a familiar friend in this disconnected limbo. In less than ten minutes, they were checking out a boat, choosing paddles, buckling life vests. In another five, they were paddling upstream. The water wove all into its motion. Annika watched her daughter's clumsy paddling efforts begin to smooth, take on its rhythm. They slid out of the central area, past their house, under the bridge and into open country, and she aimed the craft into one of many reed-filled backwaters where they floated, watching the red-wing blackbirds and water beetles. The sumac around them blazed red, warning of the coming winter, but the sun was warm.

"Well, we'd best be heading back, Sadie. Aunt Vicky is coming this evening."

"Really? To stay?"

"For the weekend, and we need to go to the store before she comes."

"Can we go home with her?"

Annika shrank from the too often repeated question she could not answer. "No, Sadie, not yet. It's too soon." *We've cut loose. We're not going back.* She had to tell Sadie that, but the words stuck. She swung her paddle, turning the canoe back into the stream, where the current picked it up.

"Look, Sadie, a heron." She pointed at the well-camouflaged bird at the shoreline.

"Oh." Sadie stilled her paddle. "But it's too little. And it's not blue," she whispered.

"It's a night heron."

The bird took flight as they floated past, bringing a giggle from Sadie, and returning her attention to the river. Not for the first time, Annika gave thanks for the power of nature to reabsorb and heal.

By the time they returned to the house laden with groceries, there was a car parked in front. Waiting for them? She pulled into the drive, killed the engine, then stopped short half way out of the car. It was Jonathan who emerged, not Vicky.

"Uncle Jon!" Sadie cried, struggling with her buckles.

Pleasure of a familiar face mixed with dread held Annika wordless as he approached.

"Hello Sadie." He grinned at her, then turned to Annika. "My Traverse flight cancelled, so I thought I'd come fill you in on my wasted trip to the Caribbean."

"Oh." She turned away and released Sadie.

"Did you bring Aunt Vicky with you?" Sadie interrupted, jumping from the car.

"We're expecting her for the weekend," Annika explained.

"I know. I talked to her." He glanced at Sadie. "She gave me your address, so I decided to come talk to you myself."

"Good. Come on in." She turned and picked up a bag of groceries.

"Let me." He reached in and took up another sack. "I've been down there for three weeks."

She led the way to the house. "Sadie, go up and get dry clothes on," she ordered as she opened the door.

"I'm sorry to catch you by surprise," Jonathan said as Sadie climbed the stairs. "I called from the airport, but ..."

"I'd left my phone here." She did that too often. Deliberately? "That's okay, Jon. Come this way." She led the way back to the kitchen and began unpacking the bags. "So tell me."

He sat on one of the stools on the other side of the counter. "I scoured five islands and couldn't find any sign of him."

"But if he blended in with tourists and resorters ..."

He shook his head. "Too hot still. Resort and tourist season has only just started. Anyway, I checked the resorts and hotels."

"Could he have used a different name?"

"Sure, but I don't think he would have gone to a resort—not in his state of mind."

"No," she agreed. "It doesn't feel right ... for Brian."

"Annika, has he made any withdrawals from your bank account?"

She shook her head. "No, but he took money with him, Jon. $10,000."

"What?" He sat up. "He did? I didn't know that." He got up and began to pace. "Why? I'd paid for the drug."

"You did?"

"He paid me, Annie, when I gave it to him. If he took that much, he'd open an account ... somewhere, and I checked the banks—showed them his picture."

"So what ... where ...?"

"I don't know. But I don't think he went to the Caribbean, Annie. A white guy, away from the tourist haunts—he'd stick out."

"So he's just ... vanished." She turned and leaned against the refrigerator. The limbo of the past weeks became a yawning chasm with no land beyond. No answers.

"He's somewhere in the Outer Banks. I'd bet on it." He slapped the counter. "I have to get home. One more fishing trip for the season. But Papa hired a private investigator down there to pick up Brian's trail before it goes any colder."

"He left me, Jon." The leaden words flattened his expression. "He doesn't intend ... to be found."

Jonathan got up and began to pace. "I don't believe that, Annie—at least not for good. He'd cool down and come back."

"That's what Sadie says." She mumbled as she heard her daughter on the stairs.

"Aunt Vicky's here! I saw her car." Sadie tugged at the front door.

"Hello, sweetie!" Vicky cried as Sadie threw herself into her arms. "Is your mom—" She broke off as her gaze fell on Jonathan. "Hello, Jon."

Chapter 32

"Vicky." Jon smiled. "I don't mean to bust in on your weekend. I just stopped by to report on my wasted trip to the Caribbean."

"Ah." She waved a greeting at Annika. "No sign of him?"

Jonathan shook his head. "I don't think he was ever there."

"They found a duffel with his clothes on the beach. In the Outer Banks. Chief Constantine called." Annika told Jonathan. She turned to Sadie, whose eyes had gone wide. "But not Daddy."

"So he was there—around there." Jonathan sat down "That's something."

"Is it?" Vicky sounded tired. "The clothes could have fallen off anywhere. All we have is Svenson's word that he jumped ship. As I remember, you used to call that guy a snake."

"I like snakes!" Sadie protested.

"Not this one, honey." He smiled then turned to Vicky. "That he is. But it's a place to start. I'll tell Papa about the clothes."

"Thank him for me, Jon," Annika broke in. "It's nice to know someone's out there searching."

"The police aren't having any luck?"

Annika glanced at Sadie, who was following every syllable, and made a decision. The terror of secrets adults keep had almost cost her

Sadie's trust. "The police aren't going to look much longer, Jon, since I decided not to charge him."

"You did?" The relief on Jonathan's face made clear that her brief text message to Carmen hadn't reached him.

"Charge who? Daddy? What does charge mean?" Sadie's question was more confused than alarmed.

"It means saying someone broke a law. That's more than making a mistake. The police don't go looking for people who make mistakes, only for breaking a law."

"Oh." Surprise lit her eyes. "That's good—isn't it?" Then she frowned. "But they aren't looking for Daddy now?"

"Not for much longer, but Uncle Jonathan says Papa is. He's hired someone to keep looking. And Uncle Jonathan's been looking, too."

"That good. Because Daddy is Uncle Jon's brother."

"He is." Jonathan gave her head a rub and turned to Annika. "Thank you."

"I thought your mother would let you know."

"She probably tried. I lost my phone, worst luck. Bought this throw-away at the airport." He pulled it out of his pocket. "But that's … thank you, thank you, thank you."

"I was going to take Annie and Sadie out to dinner," Vicky said from the couch. "Would you join us, Jon?"

"Goodie!" Sadie exclaimed. "Can we have pizza?"

Jonathan looked at her in surprise.

"What time's your plane?" Annika asked.

"I decided to drive up. Rented a car, but I don't want to crash the party."

"You come," Sadie ordered, marching over to him. "We want you."

"You do?" Jonathan looked from her squared off jaw to the rest of them. "Well, if you're sure …"

"You're family." She reached out and took his hand.

Annika winced. When was she going to tell Sadie she was through with Wolfsons? Not now, while they warmed her cold, empty house. Not now.

"Pizza sound good to everyone?" Vicky asked and received agreement all around.

"*Cottage Inn!*" Sadie proclaimed.

"Ha!" Jon exclaimed. "You know our old haunt, do you?"

Annika looked at her watch. "Dinner time Saturday night? We don't stand a chance downtown. Sadie means the one down the street—a carry-out version."

"I noticed it on the way in," Vicky said. "What do you drink, Sadie?"

"Lemonade."

Forty minutes later, they were settled around the dinette booth, which bore little resemblance to the old pub. But the pizza was the same, and memories began to sprout. Vicky and Jonathan moved from "wet-bottom" sailing on nearby lakes to the inadequacy of those mud-bottom puddles, to a sail trip on Thunder Bay. Annika listened to the easy banter of the two, the way they finished each other's sentences, a bond resurfacing. She watched Sadie's face alight with the laughter of surrounding family. What forces had been at work destroying this? Why had it been so fragile?

"When can I learn to sail, too?" Sadie asked.

There was an awkward pause as they returned to the present. On Lake Fontenac, there would be a dingy or a Butterfly tied to the dock on her seventh birthday and a host of adults eager to teach her. What now? "Not until you're a bit older, honey," She dodged the question in Jonathan's and Vicky's eyes. "Until then, we'll settle for canoeing."

"Until we go home." Sadie bit hard into her pizza.

Annika looked from her daughter to Vicky and Jonathan and shook her head, closing the topic.

"Go up to Delphi Park," Jonathan suggested. "Great water up there."

"For shooting the rapids, you mean." Vicky laughed. "That's for kayakers—macho kayakers."

"Since when? You had a great time playing dodge-boat with me."

"That was then. I've matured." Vicky reached for another piece of pizza.

Silence fell as the word returned them to the present, and the air became heavy with conversation withheld. Not until Annika had put Sadie to bed an hour later did it resume.

"Tell Grandma to be sure to save my animals. I have to paint them when I get home," Sadie had pronounced as Annika took her upstairs.

"Mother's homesick for Sadie," Jonathan told her when she returned.

Annika sat down with a sigh. "My mother likewise. And my father." She knew they expected her to answer the question embedded in their words, but did not.

"Stay as long as you need to," Vicky told her.

Annika stood. "More beer, anyone?"

"That would be good," Vicky answered.

"No more for me. I have to get going." Jonathan looked at his watch, but didn't move to rise.

When Annika returned with beers for herself and Vicky he went on. "I just want to say we really want you to come back, Annie. Mom and Dad are … afraid you won't." He looked a question, his eyes intense. "And I wouldn't blame you if you've had your fill of Wolfsons."

Annika stared at him, both relieved at the uttering of the unspoken and pained at her lack of an answer. "I live day to day, Jon. It's enough. All I can manage."

"I imagine that's so." He stopped, but then went on as though he had to complete the thought. "Mother said it helped her bear Brian's absence—having you there. You're so much a part of him. A necessary part. 'If she's here, his spirit's here too.' That's how she puts it."

Annika felt tears rise. She could find no words, but Jonathan went on as though not expecting any.

"They drove Vicky away, too." He reached for Vicky's hand. "And now they're realizing …" He pulled the unaccepted hand back and took a last swallow of beer. "Dad had lunch with your father at the Vet's center."

"Had lunch? Really?" Annika sat up.

"Really. Just walked up to him and told him they needed to have lunch."

"And my father agreed? Didn't knock him to the floor?"

Jonathan shook his head. "And Mother went to see your mom."

"I don't understand. What does Brian have to do with … all of that?" But even as she said it, she remembered them sitting side by side at the nationals, and Brian beaming, giving her the high sign of victory.

"I don't know really, but you and Brian filled a space that … well, they need each other. It's like they're trying to fill it, to understand … what happened. Dad and Uncle Joe, too."

"That's … incredible—" Annika began, then felt the place where Brian had been open out again and choked.

"I just wanted you to know that." Jon stood up and went to the door, then stopped. "And Vicky, too." He looked a long question at his ex-wife and was gone.

They stared at the closed door, robbed of speech.

Vicky raised her beer and took a drink. "I'll be damned."

"Did you know any of that?"

"No. I haven't been up there since you left." She put the glass down with a sharp click. "I've been pissed. Really pissed. At the whole clan."

Annika started to reply then thought better of it.

"As though they caused the whole mess. Including Jon and me—as though hating each other made them who they are." She sat up again. "No, more than that—made them heroes of some sort—standing against the enemy."

"Except the hate grew old. The passion was gone. It became just … the way things are."

"But you don't want to poke it," Vicky warned. "Or both sides with land on you—the traitor."

"Brian and I just … swam. Paid no attention. Ignored it." But did he? They made their own place, didn't they? Brian with a foot in all camps … was he looking for a place of his own? They made that for themselves. What did the Gold have to do with it?

"But you can bet they never ignored it." Vicky leaned back again.

"My father was enraged—cut me off when I told him I was marrying Brian." Annika gazed out the window, searching memory. "But Carmen and Karl … not so much … they were nice enough … but tentative. Like they were never quite settled in their minds what I was like. As though they expected something to emerge … some mark of the enemy." She laughed. "That's a bit ridiculous, isn't it?"

"No." Vicky stood up and stretched. "They only knew … couldn't understand being neither one or the other, black or white." She went to the window, her face sad. "There wasn't a place between."

"Papa understood that."

"I know. Papa was always sad under that hearty bluff. Marissa, too."

"I guess they were. They kept insisting on those family barbecues."

"On keeping the 'good old days.'" Vicky agreed. "And talked about when Karl and Joe were kids—as though it happened in … another age."

They fell silent.

"Are you going to give him another chance, Vicky?"

She gave a sharp laugh. "I'm not ready to think about that." She turned. "This evening has thrown me back into another time—when we were all brand new."

"It was like that. Except for Sadie, who made me feel very old tonight."

"Well—" Vicky started and stopped, her gaze direct. "Sadie is a Wolfson."

The words jolted, as Vicky knew they would. "You do have a way of stating hard truths." Annika took a deep breath and let it out. "And a Berglund."

"It sounds as though they're trying to make that possible." She reached out a hand to pull Annika up. "And it's time for bed."

Annika grasped her hand. "Jonathan's changed."

Vicky was silent as they climbed the stairs. "He has, hasn't he? At dinner, he was the boy I met sailing, but …" She paused, thinking. "When we were married he came home and went into business with his father and sort of blended back into the Wolfsons … lost something."

"Now he's Brian's brother."

Vicky turned and put her arms around Annika. "Is that it? God help both of us." She released her. "Sleep tight."

"And you."

Chapter 33

The morning was brisk and bright. From the sun-warmed breakfast nook, Annika and Vicky idled over their coffee and watched Sadie, clad in boots and orange sweatshirt, collect red and gold leaves in the backyard. A robin voiced his alarm at her approach and took flight to the back fence. Startled, Sadie laughed and jabbered at him, her words muffled by the glass.

"It's strange," Annika mused. "As though I've wakened in a world I never knew. A place ..." She shook her head. "Or a state of being ..."

"Maybe you have."

Annika laughed. "It's still Michigan isn't it? Ann Arbor?" Her cell phone rang, ending the conversation. She fished it from her jeans pocket and blinked at the ID. "It's Joe!" Her eyes flashed Vicky her bewilderment—struck by the absence of Joe's voice in the last ... how long? "Hello?"

"Annie? It's Joe."

"Yes. I know ..." She paused, waiting for his response, but there was none. "Hello, Joe!"

"I haven't wanted to bother you ... with everything else that's been going on, but ..." He cleared his throat. "How're you bearing up?"

"Okay. I'm okay."

"I've been missing in action since Brian took off. Too pissed at him to do anything, I guess. But I should have called ... come ... and then when it hit the news, I was too pissed at myself for not calling." He cleared his throat. "I don't understand how Brian could have done this thing … whatever the hell it is. Can't get my mind around it. Then Karl showed up and laid into me as though I caused the whole thing—" He broke off. She waited in silence. "I don't know what the hell he's talking about, Annie, but if I did … well, I'm sorry. So sorry."

"No, Joe. You were our dad, our support. Karl just needs someone to blame, I guess."

"Yeah. I guess. I just wanted you to know I'll be happy to fill in for Brian until he comes back. Coaching, that is."

"Coaching." The word sounded incongruous in the fall sunshine of the kitchen.

"Coaching you, I mean." He stopped, then hearing no answer, went on. "I don't mean to rush you. But whenever you're ready …" he floundered, "… I just wanted you to know."

"No, Joe." The word fell from her lips without intention or thought. "No. The race is over."

Her answer was met with silence.

"It turned bad, Joe. Brian got carried away … crossed a line."

"Yeah. He did that all right." His voice faded into tortured silence. "Wanted that Gold so bad … I guess that's what Karl meant, but …" Again the phone went silent.

"Joe?"

"You're the last person in the world he'd hurt, Annie!"

"I know."

"Makes me want to quit coaching forever."

"No, Joe. Swimming—racing—was good for us for a long time."

"That's what I thought. So I thought swimming might help with the waiting." He gave a half laugh. "Help me too, I guess. I miss you both."

"Ah," she muttered as the plea from a man who never pled sank in. "I'm afraid it might do the opposite, Joe."

"Maybe." Silence fell. "Well, just so you know I'm here. You're really okay?"

"Really. And thank you, Joe."

"Yeah. Take care." The connection clicked.

Vicky contemplated her. "He wants you to get back to it. Training."

"No, he just wanted to help, and coaching's all he knows." She rubbed her forehead. "It just ... blindsided me ... so off the wall."

"A month—six weeks—ago, it was all you thought about."

Annika looked out the window where Sadie was now clambering up the apple tree. "Is that why this—sitting in the sun watching my daughter—feels so strange?"

"Could be." Vicky rose and refilled their cups. "Will you go back? To training?"

"No." She let the word lie, unembellished, unmodified, a gavel dropped. "You heard me tell him. The race is over."

Vicky nodded. "I did. Sad in a way."

The backdoor burst open, bringing the autumn breeze and Sadie. "I need to feed the robin."

"Robins eat worms, and I don't happen to have any." She pushed the conversation to one side for the moment.

"I'll go dig some!"

"No, no, we can't go digging up the Carson's lawn. Tell you what. Let's take Aunt Vicky to Delphi."

"What's Delphi?" Sadie climbed into a chair.

"A park up the river," Vicky answered. "Actually, one of a string of parks along the river. We used to canoe up there in the summer."

"Can we canoe?"

Vicky looked at Annika.

"Pretty cold today, sweetie, but we can picnic."

"Is the Dexter cider mill still open?" Vicky wondered.

"Haven't a clue, but we'll pack a lunch and go find out."

The excursion felt like an escape, but as Annika made sandwiches, her mind kept returning to Joe and to the certainty of her response. What had she done? To him? She opened the mayonnaise jar then realized they'd already spread it.

"You all right?" Vicky asked.

"I don't know. That was like a voice from another planet—why?" She turned to her daughter who was pulling cookies from the cupboard. "Run get your shoes on, Sadie. You won't need boots at the park. Your tenny-runners."

"And brush your teeth," she added as Sadie headed for the stairs. As she disappeared from view, Annika turned back to Vicky. "Joe was our father. For years. It was like our parents lived in a place we ate and slept— but Joe was where we belonged. Why would I ... shut him off like that?" She picked up bottles of lemonade and plopped them into the cooler. "Karl showed up and landed on him—blamed him for the whole thing."

"Great. Same old war. New target."

"That's ...too cruel. Mean. And Joe sounded ... so uncertain. As though he didn't know whether I'd talk to him at all. I've never heard that from him. He was the certainty, the guy who knew what it was all about, what we needed to do, where to go, what to eat ..."

"And you needed that." Vicky took the cooler from her and began packing fruit and sandwiches. "Both of you. You were misfits in your own flocks." She zipped the bag. "You found each other, but you were kids. You needed him."

Tears rose in Annika's eyes. "So why did I push him away like that?" She measured coffee into the filter and filled the pot. Vicky said nothing, as though content to let her ponder. "I would have sworn I'd die if I couldn't swim. That I'd explode into a million pieces. But I haven't been in the water for … on the clock … six weeks, you say? It feels like forever." She punched the start button on the coffee pot.

"Maybe you should," Vicky mused. "Maybe it would—"

"No!" The volume of her retort stopped Sadie on the stairs. "No," she repeated more quietly. "It's like … spoiled food."

She turned to Sadie. "Ready to go?"

"Yep."

"Go to the bathroom, then. We're ready as soon as the coffee's done."

Vicky watched Sadie disappear again. "She's a godsend,"

Annika turned, surprised. "You better believe it."

Ten minutes later, they were on Huron River Drive, heading toward the parks that lined the river toward the village that, despite growth, had managed to preserve the region's past. Soon they were surrounded by people bursting from cars, paddling the river, spread out on the meadows, drinking in the last of Michigan's most beautiful season before the cold gray of winter set in.

"Let's go on to Dexter-Huron Park," Annika urged. "Further from Ann Arbor. It's too soon to eat anyway."

The crowds were indeed lighter at the smaller second park, and they spread their blanket near the river's edge. Sadie, predictably, headed for the water.

"I need to take my shoes off."

"Not yet. Let's take the nature trail first. Or eat."

"Nature trail."

"You go ahead," Vicky urged. "I'll guard the goods and have a nap."

Annika waved her assent, and they set off into the woods on the trail bordering the river.

"Maybe we'll see a deer," Sadie called.

"Not if you let her know you're coming," Annika chided.

"Oh." Sadie whispered as she slowed down and crept forward.

The gurgling of passing water, the buzz of insects, and the chirping of small birds were dotted with snaps and crackles from the underbrush. Occasional distant voices of children were all that broke the illusion of wilderness. Annika felt the tension drain out of her, leaving only her senses—the sparkle of leaves in the breeze, the color flashing from a butterfly wing, the flip of a fish snapping an insect from the surface of the water. The smell of the forest. She wondered for a moment at its power but released herself into it.

"Look!" Sadie pointed to a turtle resting on the bank. They stood and watched him for a while, but clearly their presence wasn't important enough to demand action, and soon they went on. Ten minutes later, Sadie spotted her deer, drinking from the river ahead. Her giggle of delight was barely audible but enough to send the doe into the woods.

"That's okay," Annika assured her. "You never see them for long. They can smell us even if we don't make a sound."

"Maybe there are others."

"I'm sure there are, but we need to go back. Aunt Vicky will be waiting for us, getting hungrier and hungrier."

Sadie giggled. "Hungry enough to eat us?"

"Maybe."

"I'm hungry too."

But they found Vicky asleep on the blanket. Sadie knelt and shook her shoulder. "We're here!"

Vicky opened her eyes. "So you are." She sat up. "What a lovely place."

"Did you guard against the bears?" Sadie grinned.

"They must have all gone to sleep for the winter, but I was visited by a woodpecker." She pointed. "Right over there. I'm sure he would have helped himself if I'd given him the chance."

"Did you wave your arms and scare him away?"

"Oh no, I was very quiet. We just studied each other."

"That's a good thing." She turned to Annika. "We missed a woodpecker."

"Maybe he'll come back if we get the food out."

The next half hour was spent consuming their bounty, their only visitors yellow jackets. When the last cookie was gone, Sadie headed for the shore again. "Look!" She ran back to them. "It's a canoe. It's *not* too cold. Can we?"

"We have to go find the cider mill, Sadie. If it's still there, we'll have a treat and maybe get us some apples to take home."

"Yeah?" She gave a long gaze to the river. "Okay. But later we can canoe."

Annika collected picnic gear without answering. The water, the sound of dipping paddles drew her, too, but she wasn't inclined to break the spell that had captured her in the woods.

Twenty minutes later, the heady smell of apples brought their heads up.

"Oh, wow." Annika inhaled.

"I guess the mill's still here."

"Heavenly." Annika turned into the entrance road, and they found themselves among the populace once again. The chill clarity of autumn air loaded with crushed apples and fried donuts fired the festival as they joined the throng waiting to tour the two-century old building. Sadie began jumping up and down, catching the mood. Around them, along the river and wandering the lawn, were beings of all sizes loaded with bags of apples, jugs of cider, donuts and other bounty. "Ooh! Can I have one of those?" Sadie squeaked, pointing to the candy apple being gnawed by a small boy.

"It'll give you a tummy ache," Vicky assured her.

"No it won't. Promise!"

"We'll see. First let's go watch them make cider."

As they approached the open entry shed, the thunk-thunk of presses blotted out everything else. Annika lifted Sadie so she could see over the rim of cauldrons filled with the fruit. After the boom of the presses, the aging room's silence was punctuated only by the crack of barrels being moved. Finally, they were sitting in the tasting room, sipping the result and surveying the rows of sugared donuts in the case across the way.

"We need some of those," Sadie decided, pointing to a row.

"Do you want a donut or a candy apple?"

"Both."

"No."

"A candy apple and donuts to take home."

Vicky laughed. "She's too smart for you, Annie."

"Okay, just so you know the apples under that caramel are sour."

"I like sour!"

"Just so you know." Annika rose. "You stay with Aunt Vicky. I'll be back."

The afternoon sun was still high in the sky when they headed for the car laden with cider, apples, donuts and a sticky child. Sadie allowed herself to be parted from the remains of her apple and sponged down before climbing into her seat. Annika stood, stretched and inhaled air saturated with autumn's bounty before taking the driver's seat.

"Can we canoe now? Please?" Sadie begged as they passed Delphi Park a half hour later.

Annika glanced in the mirror at her over-indulged daughter and stopped the refusal that was on her lips. In Sadie's voice there was something urgent, a clinging to this day. She looked at Vicky, who gave her a thumbs-up. "Okay, we'll see if we can get a boat for an hour." She turned the car and went back to the park entrance.

"There's not even a line!" Sadie cried as they approached.

The canoe racks were nearly empty and the attendant skeptical, but as he shook his head, Annika spotted two boats coming in. "There!" She pointed. "Can we have one of those?"

"Please?" Sadie's chin rested on the counter.

The attendant looked as though he was ready for this Sunday afternoon to end, but he laughed. "Guess you could, young lady."

Soon they were jacketed and on their way, Annika in the rear, Vicky in the bow, Sadie firmly planted in the middle seat. Annika set off up-river, giving in to the pleasure of using her muscles, the rhythm of the pull. Vicky paused in her stroking to raise her paddle between outstretched arms in a cheer. She too rejoiced at being water bourn. Sadie laughed and waved at other canoes, passing on their way back to the livery.

"Faster!" Sadie cried.

And so they sped along for a bit, letting the exhilaration of the day have its way. The sense of flying returned, casting its dizzying spell. "Whoa!" She dug her paddle as Vicky turned, surprised. "Too fast," she muttered and resumed paddling at a more moderate pace. Why? What was wrong with flying? What had risen from the depths to block it? She glanced at her watch and looked around. They were alone on the river now, and the day was cooling. "Time to turn around, anyway."

As the current picked them up, she set a lazy pace, letting the boat drift close to the lily pads, letting the water cast its silence. The buzz of insects, the ping of floating twigs against the rocks, the tapping of a wood-pecker. The blue heron ahead didn't take flight as Annika steered a wide birth around him. Vicky rested her paddle. Sadie put a hand over her mouth to silence her giggle as they passed him.

Annika turned the boat into the mainstream again, and they went on. Her watch said she should set a faster pace, but she didn't. She wanted this peace—her being was starved for it.

"Look! It's a turtle! Swimming!" Sadie flung herself across the gun-wale, reaching for it.

"Sadie—!" She stopped her lunge too late and icy water erased the day. She rose to the surface, choking, to see her daughter, her eyes wide in panic, dog-paddling furiously to reach the overturned boat, but being carried away by the current.

With a powerful whip-kick she was after her, flying as she never had until she grabbed Sadie's life-jacket. Her daughter spun around and flung her arms around Annika's neck, threatening to drown them both. Her mouth full of water, she couldn't answer her cries. Where was Vicky? She pushed Sadie's head aside, and stared at the overturned canoe, saw only a paddle drifting toward them. She caught it. "Sadie! Grab it!" She loosened an arm and turned her. "I've got you. Just hold onto it." She forced her voice to calm, and Sadie responded by reaching one arm for the paddle. She had to catch the canoe. "That's it. You're okay now." Sadie released her hold enough for Annika to turn her head. She pulled the other arm free and put it over the paddle. "Just keep hold of it."

With another whip kick, she got an arm over the back of the canoe and pulled the paddle close. "Grab the boat, Sadie. Let go with one hand—" She pulled one of the child's hand free of the paddle and put it on the gunwale. "Hold on!"

She dove and found Vicky struggling, her head in the pocket of air under the hull, her legs tangled in the bowline. She brought her own head into the pocket long enough to yell "Stop kicking!" then dove and unwound the rope from Vicky's legs. Together they ducked free of the boat in time to see the current pulling Sadie off downstream, screaming.

With a yell, Annika pushed off from the hull, her arms and legs working as though some engine had fired. She reached and reached again. Too soon. And the reaching slowed her. Gave another desperate whip-kick and caught the edge of Sadie's life jacket. *Had her*.

Annika heard Vicky cry out to the approaching livery as Sadie spun and clutched her around the neck, her icy arms threatened to submerge them both once again. "On your back, Sadie. Like floating." She took hold of the arms that were cutting off her breath. "Now!" Her daughter released her hold enough for Annika to duck out of her grasp and flip her over, throwing an arm over her chest. "Gotcha." She grabbed her chin with her free hand, then realized the current had sped up and she had only her legs to fight it. *Rapids*. Where were they?

She swung her head and saw the canoe, out of reach. Vicky, along-side, was trying to right it.

A motor started up, and she saw a boat approach just as she'd decided she had to break for shore before the cold rendered her useless. A moment later a life-ring landed beside her, and they were safe. As strong arms pulled Sadie aboard, she turned to see the canoe drifting past.

"Vicky!" she screamed, pointing to the boat. "Get her! On the other side of the boat!"

The boat turned and sped up to get ahead of the canoe, then turned and let the craft drift into it. They reached the pole to Vicky, who had given up her attempts to right the boat and sagged against the far side. She grabbed the pole, and Annika relaxed. A trembling Sadie threw herself into her arms.

"It's over, baby. All done." She reached out a hand to Vicky as they lifted her aboard.

"Thank God," Vicky muttered, grabbing it and rolling into the bottom of the boat.

"All okay?" the helmsman asked as his companion fished for the bowline of the canoe.

"All okay." Annika waved. "Our thanks ..." She winced at the inadequacy of the word. "Carry on."

"They make it look so simple," Vicky mopped her face with a towel, then wrapped her arms around herself to stop the shaking. "Just flip it over, right? I've done it a hundred times in training classes."

The helmsman laughed as he turned the boat for shore, towing the canoe. "In a nice quiet pool or lake in the middle of summer. Right?"

"Right. That current ... you can't get leverage."

"Yeah. Boat keeps sliding away from you."

Annika let them talk the event away as she rubbed Sadie's back, reliving the sight of Sadie paddling frantically as she was carried away.

In her arms, Sadie's trembling hardened to shaking. "What happened, Mommy?"

"We capsized, honey. A surprise, huh?"

"Why?"

"Because ..." She paused. "Because canoes do that. They're tippy. Remember we've told you about that. Now you know."

"Oh." Sadie fell silent as they approached the livery.

"You paddled, just like we taught you to do," she assured her. "You did right."

"We'll get a blanket for you, kiddo," the helmsman lifted her onto the dock.

Five minutes later, they were all bundled in blankets, cupping hot drinks in their hands.

"Happens three or four times a season," the helmsman assured her. "We even keep dry clothes for folks."

"Wonderful," Vicky exclaimed. "But we owe you a pair of paddles."

"Maybe, maybe not. They have a way of coming home. We'll let you know."

"Did I do it?" Sadie, listening wide-eyed, still sat rigid despite the casual tones of the adults. "Tip it over?"

Annika put an arm around her again. "I don't know, Sadie. It happened too fast to know."

"There was a turtle."

"Yes, I remember that."

"I reached for it ..."

"And I reached for you. But we're all okay now." Annika gave her a squeeze. "And everyone capsizes sooner or later, if they're boat lovers like we are."

"Yeah ..." Sadie's voice faded into acceptance, and she said no more until, dressed in odds and ends, they were back in the car headed for home.

"Did that happen to Daddy?"

The question shot from the back seat, stiffening their newly relaxed spines. "No, his boat didn't capsize, Sadie. It reached home okay."

"But he could fall off." Her voice brooked no argument. "Couldn't he."

"It's not very likely. Your daddy knows boats."

"Someone could push him. The bad men."

"Sadie, we don't know they were bad men. Don't tell yourself that, okay? And if your daddy did find himself in the water, he's a very strong swimmer."

No answer.

"Isn't he?"

Sadie turned to the scenery beyond the window. "Yeah ..."

Chapter 34

By the time they got back to the Ann Arbor house, Sadie had retreated into some private world. After they'd changed clothes, Annika heated soup for them all and made grilled cheese sandwiches, but Sadie fiddled half-heartedly with her spoon and ate little. We've failed her again. The certainty dropped like lead. Worse. Created warmth and safety, then—terror. Again. The experience had been frightful enough for adults trained to cope with it. Annika scraped back her chair and rose. "Come, baby." She lifted Sadie and carried her to the rocker that occupied the corner of the living room. "It's okay to be frightened," she assured her as she rocked. "That was scary. And you were very brave." She felt Sadie softened against her and heard the tears begin. She rubbed her back and let the rhythmic creak of the rockers fill the silence until Sadie slept.

Annika carried her upstairs to bed, tucked her floppy dog in beside her, returned to the kitchen and burst into tears.

Vicky, who was washing dishes, dried her hands and put an arm around her. "She'll be all right, Annie. She's a tough cookie."

Annika shook her head. "It's too much, Vicky, on top of everything else. Just too damn much. How could I have let that happen? Why did I--?"

"No, no, don't think that way. It was a lovely day, and the canoeing was a perfect end ... well, until the end." She laughed.

Annika joined in spite of herself. "You're good medicine, Vicky." She wiped her tears. "And you're right, it was a perfect day. The first in a long time. Can you stay the night?"

"I hope so. I've never much liked driving alone at night."

"Good." Annika rose. "Time for a glass of wine."

"Or so."

They sank into soft chairs in the living room and watched through the trees as the last of the evening sun turned the river gold.

"It almost made me think," Annika mused, "that I could make a life down here."

"Cut loose?" Vicky gazed out the window. "What would you do?"

"Isn't it strange that I've never wondered about that? It's what you're supposed to do in college, isn't it? But I never did. College was just a change of scene for the same thing."

"But you didn't major in phys ed, as I remember."

"True. Environmental Studies." Annika gazed out into the gathering darkness. "I loved the field trips. Like filling me up again after a week of training."

"Well, there you are." Vicky raised her glass.

Annika laughed and clinked glasses with her. "And where exactly is that? What does one do with a degree in the environment?"

"You mean you never thought of that either?"

"Never. I swear. I just liked the escape." She blinked. "There's that word again. Once upon a time, swimming was my escape."

Vicky was silent, watching her with a half smile.

"Before it turned into everything ..."

"Then came Sadie." Vicky grinned.

"Ha. And a different reality." She took a sip of wine. "For me. Not for Brian—until she was there in front of him."

"But I remember him with the baby. He was delighted … and sort of surprised." Vicky put her glass on the coffee table. "That he'd actually created that—or had a hand in it anyway."

"Well put." Annika laughed. "For him, she was a break, a relief from the grind. Life was still the gold medal—but now it included Sadie, too. He wanted to get her swimming. Well, so did I … but differently. For him it was 'get her going, get her going.'" She put down her glass. "That's wrong. So wrong. I think it was the first time I bucked him."

"There needs to be a time for …" Her words faded into a shrug.

"Candy apples."

"And on that note, let's put our sorry selves to bed." Vicky rose and stretched.

"Amen."

Screams brought Annika out of deep sleep, and she bolted out of bed, staring at unfamiliar furniture, confused. The screams came again. *Sadie! Where* … She stumbled into the hall, reorienting as she went, and into Sadie's room where she found her daughter sitting upright, wide-eyed with terror.

"It's okay," she muttered, picking her up. "It's okay. Just a bad dream, Sadie." She nuzzled her as arms clutched her neck, returning them both to the icy water, the relentless current. "You're here, honey. Safe and warm. It's over, baby. You're okay."

Vicky appeared at the door, and Annika gave her a high sign. "Bad dream."

Her friend nodded and went back to bed. Soon Sadie's muscles gave way, and she crumpled into tears. Annika rubbed her back as they let the day fade back into memory. When the tears slowed, she rose, carried Sadie to her own bed and curled up beside her.

In the morning, Annika looked at her sleeping child and was reluctant to wake her. She heard the shower. Vicky was up, and the clock said the day wouldn't wait. "Hey there." She rubbed Sadie's shoulder. "Time to rise and shine."

Sadie opened her eyes, then blinked and gazed around. "I'm here."

"Mm. You are. You had a dream, so I brought you in. And it's time for school."

To Annika's relief, the word sat Sadie up. "Am I late?"

"No. Just time to go find some clothes." She followed her daughter back to her room and together they negotiated jeans and sweater and socks. Then she left her to dress and went down to fix breakfast, relieved that the nightmare seemed to have left no traces.

Sadie was halfway through her oatmeal when Vicky appeared, greeted her, and regaled her with tales of her own first grade.

The doorbell rang as Annika finished packing her lunch, springing Sadie from her seat. "That's Nancy."

"Her new friend and escort," Annika explained to Vicky.

Sadie shrugged into her coat and picked up her backpack, then pulled open the door. "I'm here—!" She stopped, her eyes fixed on the river across the street. "No!"

"What?"

Sadie shook her head.

"Come on, Sadie. We'll be late!" Nancy begged.

"The river! No!"

"It's across the street, honey. You can't fall in. And you've played along the edge, remember? You're fine."

But Sadie shook her head again.

"You go ahead, Nancy. She had a scare yesterday. I'll bring her today."

As Nancy took off, Sadie swung around to her aunt. "We can go home with you."

Vicky's mouth fell open.

"Please? To the lake."

Vicky looked to Annika for help.

"No, Sadie. We're staying here."

The certainty in her mother's voice brought tears to Sadie's eyes.

"We'll walk to school together, so you get used to the river again. Like it was before."

"I don't want to."

"I know, but you can. Today it's important to know that you can."

Vicky reached out and drew Sadie to her. "Your mom's right, honey. That's how you get over scary things. Come on, I'll walk with you, too." She took Sadie's hand and started down the steps.

Annika grabbed coats for both of them and followed. With Sadie between them, they marched to the corner and turned away from the river toward the school.

"That wasn't so bad, was it?" Vicky asked.

"Scary."

"But not too."

Sadie's "yeah" was reluctant and tentative.

By the time they reached the school, she was restored by the promise of movies. Monday was movie day.

"I'll say goodbye now, Sadie," Vicky told her at the door. "It was wonderful to see you."

"You come back."

"I will. Promise." She swept Sadie up into a hug, then put her down and gave her a gentle slap on the behind. "Off you go."

Together they watched Sadie pull the school door open and disappear. "Well, that was a jolt. I thought she'd gotten over it."

"She will—and she'll come out smarter," Vicky assured her. "You did the right thing."

Annika turned for home. "Let's hope so."

In the absence of the cries of children, the steady beat of their footsteps carried them back toward the river.

"It made her homesick for the lake. Me too."

"I know." Vicky gazed at the flow of the water. "But it was a lesson she had to learn—not so rudely, maybe, but if you're going to live here …" She let the words trail off.

"I'll have to turn fear into respect. Not easy." Annika turned onto the front walk of the house that was familiar, but not hers.

"I need to take off," Vicky said as they entered. "I have a meeting with the yacht club's head honcho this afternoon."

Annika, as homesick as her daughter, watched Vicky climb the stairs. She was still standing there when Vicky returned with her suitcase and coat. She put the bag down and put her hands on Annika's upper arms. "Go to campus today. To the career folk. See what's up for graduates in Environment."

Annika nodded as though the words had some meaning.

Vicky shook her. "Reconnect. You can do it."

Annika laughed. "Are you talking to me or Sadie?"

"Both of you." Vicky picked up her bag and opened the door, then reached up and gave Annika a kiss on her cheek. "Bye now."

"Take care, Vicky—and thanks for being here."

Vicky waved as she opened her car door.

And she was gone. Annika stared at the empty street until the morning breeze, edged with the chill of coming winter, turned her back into the house. Carried by the charge of expectation in the air, she washed the breakfast dishes, changed into skirt and jacket, and headed for campus before the empty house could swallow her.

An hour later, she emerged from the School of Natural Resources office empty-handed. In the spring, they said, there'd be fieldwork jobs—mostly geared for students, but things would open up. "Bring your resume."

Resume? What would she put on a resume? She didn't have an employment record, or even an address—or a name. What was her name now?

She stopped at the bulletin board in the hallway. The postings were mostly for internships and research jobs for students, but among them she spotted an ad for a clerk. Part time. She plucked it from the board and went back into the office.

"I'd like to apply for this." She handed it to the receptionist.

"Okay, you do that at Human Resources." She turned and picked up a paper. "Here. This is the official job sheet; it's for a Clerical Assistant. Computer stuff, mostly."

Annika took it, wondering what "stuff" included.

"You're very determined."

Annika turned at the voice to see a tall slim grey-haired woman standing at her office door. "I am. Yes." She searched for words. She was hardly going to tell her her husband had disappeared, and she'd run from home. "I want to get back into it—the environmental area."

"You're a graduate in Environment? From UM?"

"Yes. 1998."

"But this is a clerical job."

"I know, but it will help become familiar with it again. The area."

"I see. And what have you been doing since 1998?"

"Training for the Olympics. It took all my time."

"Training in what?" She looked interested.

"Swimming. I was on the UM team. And the national."

"Really! I was a swimmer myself, once upon a time. Did you make it? To the Olympics?"

Annika shook her head. "Sadly, no. I missed the team by a half second."

"Ouch." She grimaced. "Well, if you got that far you must be a worker."

Annika laughed. "That I am."

"I tell you what. Do you know computers?"

"Yes. I did a lot in school …" She waved a hand, unable to name specifics.

"Okay, wait a minute." The woman disappeared into her office and returned a few minutes later with a letter on School of Natural Resources stationary. "I'm Elizabeth Foley. Take this to Susan Long at Human Resources. Ask for her. Tell her the job posting expires today, and we've only had two interviews."

"Thank you. Really. I appreciate that."

"Good luck." She gave a wave and disappeared again.

An hour later, Annika left campus feeling giddy with relief. She had a job. A place to put her feet—fix her in place. Mornings. Perfect. It didn't pay much, but she could stay in the river house until summer, and she still had savings—some. They could make it.

She needed clothes. Briarwood. Checking her watch, she headed for the mall. An hour later, she emerged from Macy's with two skirts, two pairs of slacks, a supply of tops, hosiery and two pair of shoes. She'd even stopped in accessories and bought a couple of scarves. She was ready.

At three o'clock she stood at the corner where the school route turned onto the river road, waiting for Sadie. She pulled out her cell-phone and texted Vicky. "Mission accomplished. Job, clothes, and a starting time. More later."

Chapter 35

2010

Annika parked her car at Delphi, changed from work flats to sneakers, then went to meet Connie Updike, who was waiting on the riverbank for the canoeing class to emerge around the bend with her daughter, Jessica, and Sadie, its reluctant last member. Jessica, Sadie's best friend since Nancy had gone on to Junior High, had succeeded where Annika's efforts had failed—persuaded Sadie to venture out onto the river again. On visits to Carmen's lake house, the fearless fish had returned, but down here on the river, Annika's urging had been met with a stone wall.

"I don't know how Jessica got Sadie to do this," she told Connie as she joined her.

"Jessie's hard to refuse." Connie was a slim blond with an athletic figure and a spray of freckles across her nose. "She doesn't give up." Her tone was wry.

Annika laughed. "Well, usually Sadie's her match—and getting more headstrong by the year."

"My friends say there's a whole lot more to come."

"I don't think about it. Today's enough." It was a relief to talk lightly of the struggle that had never been a struggle in Fontenac. She and Sadie were no longer in sync. Friends could tell her the change was natural, but she knew better. As she moved from job to job, from clerk to research assistant, slowly bringing her college major to life, feeling more solid by the day, Sadie went through her days in half-hearted, often sullen, accep-tance that didn't change. She only came to life on the weekends she spent up north with her grandparents.

As the boats appeared around the bend, Annika picked out Sadie in the bow of the boat riding just ahead of the instructor's. A tall ten-year-old now, she sat fixed, the paddle motionless across the gunwales. Jessica, tiny for her years, was paddling for both of them. Annika clasped her hands over her head. "Bravo!"

Sadie looked at her and smiled a little. At Annika's second "Bravo!" she picked up her paddle and began to stroke. Jessica raised hers over her head in a silent cheer. A victory. A hope.

Annika watched the canoes approach the dock, her muscles releas-ing the tension that had become their natural mode and let the June sun warm her back as the class moored their boats and climbed ashore.

"I did it." The exultant Sadie was no more.

"You did." Annika smiled, hiding her disappointment at the tone, and reached an arm around her daughter. "How did it feel?"

"Scary. Then okay." She went off to join Jessica as they headed for the parking lot.

Annika followed, feeling punished. Which was ridiculous. But the sense of failure persisted even in the midst of success. She found herself angry at times, and Sadie, sensing it, withdrew. Then she was angry at herself. None of this was Sadie's fault. The confidence Annika once felt in the pool flowed into her work now, lifting her, but Sadie was still the abandoned, uprooted child. For Annika, Brian was no longer an absent presence in every action. Sadie seemed forever waiting and resentful that Annika was not.

"Can we go for pizza?" Sadie ran back, her lively self for the moment. "Jessica and her mom are going to stop at *Cottage Inn.*"

"Sure. Okay. You have it coming."

"Yeah!" She turned and ran back toward the pair.

Annika laughed, absorbing the moment of returning life, feeling forgiven.

As they sat on the restaurant patio chatting with Connie and Jessica, she wished that they didn't have to drive north this weekend. The monthly trips to the Wolfsons or Berglunds, were retarding Sadie's adjustment as well as her own. She'd rented the house out, so Sadie stayed with one set of grandparents or the other. If it was Carmen's and Karl's turn, Annika usually retreated to Vicky's in Traverse City. She could hardly deny Sadie her grandparents, but every trip dumped Annika back into the deadly mixture of pain, anger, worry—and endless waiting that was no longer waiting but a state of being. Time after time it was on her lips to say "We aren't going. We don't live there anymore. This is home." But the crash that would cause stopped her. So month after month, she left it to time to do the work. *Coward.*

The pizza box was empty, and the warmth of the sun fading. "Time to get home, Sadie."

"Yeah." Sadie wiped her mouth and turned to Jessica. "We're going to the lake in the morning. Our real home."

Connie's eyebrows went up.

"Our other home, Sadie," Annika corrected. "That's where the grandparents are," she explained to Connie.

But the next morning, as they crossed from farmland to woodland, that glacier-drawn line that separates Michigan's lower peninsula into north and south, Sadie's words returned. Would she, or either of them, ever reach the point where the sandy woodland lakes weren't their "real" home? Beside her, Sadie sat up, though they were still a couple of hours from Fontenac.

"Will Uncle Joe take me water-skiing?"

"The water's getting cold, Sadie. How about canoeing? You're staying at Grandma Wolfson's. She loves canoeing."

"Mm. We'll see."

Annika flicked a glance at her. This response, with its tone that wasn't quite defiance, was getting increasingly common. Sadie had always lived on the waterfront until the snow flew, and if she ever felt the tension between one Wolfson and the other or between Wolfson and Berglund, she never let on. If Joe came by Carmen's and Karl's in his boat, she'd be out skiing in a flash, cold water or no.

"Sure." Sadie's attention was on the passing scene, now, searching every sign that they were approaching Lake Fontenac.

The sun was high in a cloudless sky as they drove into the village, promising a warm weekend. The tourists flooding the streets for color-tours were still in shirtsleeves. The beaches would be busy, though few would brave the water. Home.

Annika turned onto the lake road, and Sadie began drumming her hands on the dash in expectation, relaxing as they passed Papa's house, as though relieved it was still the same. Annika, despite all efforts to distance herself, shared her daughter's feeling.

She turned into the drive of the old stone house and came to a stop. Sadie jumped from the car, but Carmen didn't come flying out as she usually did. She must be out back in the garden.

Undeterred, Sadie pulled open the screen-door. "Hello? We're—"

Annika bumped into her motionless backside.

Ahead, in the kitchen door, stood Brian.

A sound caught in Sadie's throat. *"Daddy?"*

The word fell to the floor and faded into the shocked silence.

Annika stood fixed in place. There he was. Deeply tanned from some other place, some other life, but it was Brian. The cataclysm of his act struck in a single blow, turning her hot then cold. She struggled to catch her breath. She'd thought him dead.

"Hello, Annie. Sadie."

The voice was Brian's and sent a shudder through her. "Brian."

Carmen crossed the room and took Annika's hand. "He came yesterday. We were going to call, but he said not to."

Annika gave a croak devoid of meaning.

Sadie, still pressed against her, was rigid. *"Where ... were you?"* The words seemed to catch in her throat.

"At ... a place called the Outer Banks. A long way away." His eyes remained on Annika. "Working on fishing boats."

She stared at the features she hadn't seen in three years. The square jaw, dark curls, broad forehead, brow. Only the eyes searching hers were different, not dead, but without sparkle.

"I jumped ship." His paused. "They were about to throw me overboard ..." He stopped again, dropping sentence by sentence as though forced by her silence.

"Bad men!" Sadie burst in the voice of the six-year-old.

Brian looked at her in surprise. "They were." His eyes returned to Annika. "So I got away while I could still swim to shore."

"Oh." She managed the one word of relief. Just the knowing, exploding the fear that for three years had been an unacknowledged part of their days, their only reality.

"You didn't call us." Sadie's voice held tears now, and anger.

"No. I'm sorry for that, Sadie. I couldn't talk to anyone. Not for a long time." He raised his eyes to Annika. "I was too ashamed."

Annika closed her eyes against the answer that so fit Brian.

Carmen put a hand on Sadie's head. Annika noticed that Karl had come to the kitchen door behind Brian. The lines of his face sagged with some combination of disappointment and anger; his eyes searched hers for a reaction. Still she didn't trust herself to speak.

"I went where no one could find me. But in the end, I had to come back. To face you."

She could only gaze at him, the memory of what he'd been coming alive, of his blood joining hers. But that feeling was gone. She was not that Annie now.

"I can't put it right. Fix the damage. I know that. But I can say I'm sorry."

She couldn't speak.

"I don't know how I did such a crazy unthinking thing. But I did. I had to come back. Tell you."

"Where? Papa looked everywhere. Jonathan, too."

"I used a different name. Got a job in a boat repair shop." He looked at Sadie. "You sure have grown a lot, haven't you?"

Sadie nodded. "I thought …" Her voice faded.

"I was dead?"

"Ya." She studied her shoes. Then her head shot up. "You shouldn't ever do that!" She burst into full-blown tears now. "It's wrong! We were afraid! All the time!"

"I know, honey. And I was, too. And I missed you. You and Mommy. Believe me, I did." His voice lost its stiffness, joined her anguish with his own.

Annika tried to turn her daughter toward her to give comfort, but Sadie was frozen solid in confrontation, her eyes a blur of confusion, as though trying to bring together the father she'd longed for and the man in front of her.

"It's okay, baby," Brian said. "I don't blame you for being mad. I tried to make it better though." He flicked a hopeful glance at Annika. "I've brought you a little brother." He reached out toward Sadie. "Come."

Annika's jaw dropped renewed shock. She could do nothing but follow as Brian led Sadie back to the screened front porch. *"Danny!"*

A small brown head appeared over the rise from the beach.

"You always wanted a brother." Brian's words were to Sadie, but his eyes were on Annika.

She could only stare at him in blank incredulity.

"I thought it might help fix … my going away like that."

Sadie gave a short, bewildered laugh. "A real brother?"

The child, who looked to be about eight, reached the porch and took Brian's hand. "This is Danny. Danny, this is Sadie."

"Where did you … where did he … come from?" Annika stumbled through the words.

"He was an orphan who hung around the docks, and … well it's a long story, but I adopted him. He's made my life livable."

Annika shifted her gaze to the child who was watching her, wide-eyed in fear. What must he feel, finding himself in a strange country, a strange house, among strangers, Brian calling him Sadie's brother? She threw off her shock long enough to hold out her hand. "Hello, Danny."

"I've told him he'll be a Wolfson, just like us."

Annika shook her head. No Not me. But her mind, focused on the child in front of her, refused to carry the declaration further. "How can …?" She shook her head and tried again. "What …?" She gave it up and closed her mouth.

"I'm Sadie." Sadie stepped forward. "Do you want to see my sail-boat? It's called *Jumping Jack.*"

A smile broke over Danny's face as he escaped with her to the porch.

Annika followed them with her eyes as they headed back across the road toward the lake. Then she turned away, went inside, and sank to the couch. "Dear God ..."

"Annie?" Brian croaked.

She gave a laugh that half choked her. "It's too much ..." She felt Carmen sit down beside her again and put an arm around her.

"Yeah ..." In that one uncertain word, he sounded like the boy she'd grown up with, reducing her to tears. "I'll go ... tend the kids."

The screen door slammed, and Annika flopped against the back of the couch. "I'm sorry, I ..."

"You're in shock, Annie, and no one can blame you." Annika looked up to see Karl standing in front of her, a glass of water in his hand. "I thought Carmen was going to faint."

"The relief of it ..." Carmen began, but could find no words.

Annika took her hand. "Amen." They sat like that, silent, absorbing for long minutes without words, then Annika rose and joined Karl at the window, watching Brian help Sadie and Danny launch the sailboat. An image from a dream. Some other life.

"I have to go, Carmen." Annika turned. "I need space ... for now. Tell him that."

To her surprise, Carmen nodded in understanding. "Brian will understand. Maybe he needs it, too. He was terrified of the meeting."

"I can imagine." She crossed to the door without correcting the sarcasm in her tone.

"Are you sure you're ready to drive?" Karl asked.

"I'm okay now. Just ... spacey. Vicky is expecting me."

"That's good." Carmen stood.

Annika fled to the car, opened the door, then stopped, staring at Sadie's backpack. Good grief, was she going to run off without saying goodbye to her? She picked it up, along with spare shoes and returned to the house.

"Sadie's things," she explained, putting the bag on the couch. Then on impulse she crossed the room and put her arms around her mother-in-law. "I can't quite make it real, but for you … I'm happy." She felt tears threaten. "Really." She released her and headed for the door. Again she stopped. Brian was down there. She couldn't go. Not now. And she could see the sailboat, Sadie at the tiller, moving along the shore, too far to call. "Tell Sadie goodbye for me Carmen, would you? Tell her I had to go …" She paused. "And I'll come for her tomorrow evening—as usual," she added, nailing down an act from a life that had turned surreal.

"Will do," Carmen assured her.

The afternoon was bright. Too bright. Even with sunglasses, the road glared. Then she was traveling through woods, and the smell of surrounding pines infused her brain. *This is now. Watch the road.* The words failed to anchor her brain, which was hop-scotching between lives. Eventually, the familiar highway calmed her. The flow of emotion returned as shock faded and long-buried tension and fear drained away, leaving her weak. She sank into the new state without question, without thought, letting the miles flow behind her.

By the time she reached Vicky's, rational thought had begun to emerge.

"Welcome!" Vicky opened the door and held out her arms.

Annika went into them with a half sob. "Brian's back."

"What?"

"Brian's back."

Vicky pushed her away, holding her upper arms. "Brian."

"That's what I said. Sadie opened the door at Carmen's—and there he was."

"My God." She closed the door and leaned against it, then shoved herself erect. "We need a drink."

"Please." Annika dropped her suitcase, sank into a chair.

"Are you all right?" Vicky stood above her holding two glasses of wine.

"Thank you." Annika took a glass. "I have no idea how I am. Spinning. I'm so mad—relieved—unbelieving he went three years ..." She took a long swig. "It's a whirlpool."

Vicky took a seat across from her. "Tell me. Where has he been?"

"Somewhere in the Outer Banks. Where no one would find him. Under another name. Working on fishing ships. Ever since ... How could he do that? To Sadie!"

"So he did get off there."

"Not exactly. He said they were going to throw him overboard, so he jumped ship and swam to shore."

Vicky let silence fall.

In the quiet, Annika felt the intervening years—years that had been absent from the scene at Carmen's—return and fall into place. "But in the end, he says, he had to come back and face me."

"And it took him three years—to find the courage."

"Yes." Time slowed, letting words fall into the quiet, one by one as she reoriented herself. "Which feels ... like Brian." Her mind went back to the hours she spent alone after she lost her spot on the Athens team.

"Well ... good for him. And Sadie?"

"In shock. Angry and confused."

"Well, why wouldn't she be?" Vicky picked up her glass and stared into it.

"And that's not all. He brought a brother for Sadie, a boy about seven or eight. Danny."

Vicky blinked. "Come again? A child?"

"An orphan who hung around the docks. He adopted him."

"Annie, that's …" Vicky threw up her hands, searching for a word.

"I know. More than I can take in." She leaned back and took a sip of wine. "Sadie took Danny to see her sailboat. Saved the day … or the moment, anyway. Gave the grown-ups time to absorb the shock. A little."

"He didn't intend to be found, did he?"

"No. I guess it's not hard to get lost down there." She gave a short laugh. "And he had money, remember."

"True.

They sipped wine and gazed out at the reddening light of the harbor.

"There's a great place for crab cakes—practically next door."

Annika blinked as the present took on life. "Sounds good."

They had to wait. By the time they were seated, been served bread, and ordered, Annika began to make sense to herself. "He belongs to a world that's gone, Vicky."

"He does. You've made a new life."

"Have I? It's feeling sort of flimsy right now." She paused as the waitress brought salad. "The relief is so enormous. As though I've been in limbo, waiting … deep down … the whole time."

"I daresay you have, Annie."

Chapter 36

Sunday morning dawned bright, promising to be hot. The sort of day that bloomed people, all heading for the water where their winter-white skins would blaze red by evening. Annika and Vicky wore sunhats as they strolled the beach.

"He hopes I'll come back, Vicky. Which I won't."

"Are you still angry? About the baby?"

"More just ... changed. And very sad. The baby will always be there, between us." She fell silent as they detoured around a group of children screaming and laughing as they splashed each other with frigid water. "Sad for what could have been. For whatever drives him to ... bust things up." She shook her head. "And bringing a brother for Sadie ..." She shook her head. "It's crazy. So crazy. But so Brian. Heedless. Wiping out the black. But it doesn't. Not this time."

"Mm. But he came back to face you. He must have lived a lifetime in three years." Vicky picked up a ball that had rolled to her feet and threw it back to a boy who called his thanks.

The lifetime I started to live when Sadie was born—and he didn't. But we can't just pick up where we left off, Vicky. As though none of this has been real."

"For sure. So just let it rest, for now. Go back to Ann Arbor and your job."

END of the RACE

"And what about Sadie? This is still home for Sadie. There's just no lying to myself about that."

Vicky didn't protest as Annika hoped she would. "School's out in a week," Annika went on. "Then it's my folk's turn ... And what then? When Sadie recovers from the shock, will she want to go to Brian? Brian and Danny and the lake?" She picked up a flat stone and cast it into the water. It sank without a single skip. "Do I just let her be sucked up by the Wolfsons?"

"Sadie won't let that happen, Annie. She dearly loves you. And your folks. Don't make it into a disaster."

Annika put her hands to her head. "Right. I'm giving myself a headache."

"Let's have a glass of lemonade." Vicky changed course toward the street.

After lemonade, they did Vicky's grocery shopping. Then it was time to head north again to pick Sadie up for the return trip to Ann Arbor.

"Thank you for giving me a roost, Vicky. I don't know how I'd get my head straight without you." She gave her friend a hug.

"I love seeing you. Take care and go slow. Okay?"

"Promise."

As she drove, she felt the pull. Toward Sadie, she told herself and knew it was only half the truth. The lake. Her parents. All true. And Brian? Flesh and blood again, not a ghost. A part of her. Standing on the other side of a chasm. Uncrossable. His image turned her to stone. The lost baby was as much a part of her as Sadie.

She drove to her parents as was her habit on weekends when Carmen and Karl had Sadie. They'd have an early supper for her, and she'd retell the story. Every retelling gave it flesh and blood.

"Hello!" her mother called, coming out onto the porch.

Annika went into the familiar arms. "Hello to you."

"Come. Supper's ready." She turned Annika toward the door. "Dad's at the shop, but I'll call him. He'll come in a jiff."

The news of her father's new life as a boat mechanic still made Annika rejoice, even after three years. The house still smelled of pot, and she didn't ask its source. "Does he work Sundays, too?"

"Oh, no. He just fiddles around down there. I think he wants to stay glued to the place, so that other life doesn't get hold of him."

"Well, I know how that is." She sat down at the kitchen table. "Mom, I have news."

She waited until her mother gave her her attention.

"Brian's back."

"Oh!" The expulsion of air sat her down. "Back."

"He's at his folks." Annika reached her hands across the table.

"Oh, my." She shook her head. "I don't know what to say …" She jumped up, went to the stove and came back again. " or how to feel."

"I know. Neither do I. And he brought … adopted a child, a boy of about eight. Danny."

"What? Her mother's brows wrinkled. "A child? With him?"

Annika nodded. "A brother for Sadie. That's what he said."

"Oh, goodness. And how is Sadie with all this?"

"Not sure what to make of it. Confused. But she took Danny off to see her boat. She'll be okay."

"Well, I imagine so. Having her daddy back. When we all thought …" She withdrew her hands and placed them flat on the table, rising to tend a bubbling pot.

"He was dead. I know."

"Your dad may not be so happy, Annie."

"I'm not going back to him, Mother."

"Not?" She turned in surprise. "Really not?"

"Really. What's broken can't be fixed. And I'm not the same person I was three years ago."

"That's true." She turned the flame down under the soup, the traditional Sunday night supper at the Berglunds'. "And I don't imagine he is either."

"No, but I think … he thought bringing a brother for Sadie might fix … things—for Sadie, anyway."

The spoon clattered onto the counter and she turned, her hands on her hips. "Really."

"Really. Is Stephanie here?"

"She is. Go up and wake her. I'll call your Dad." She wiped her hands on her apron, shaking her head.

Annika climbed the stairs and found her sister awake.

"I heard you drive up," Stephanie yawned and stretched.

Annika sat down on the bed. "Brian's back."

"What?" Her arms dropped to her sides. "You're kidding. Back here?"

"Here. At the Wolfsons."

Stephanie studied her face. "So … is that bad or good?"

"To know what happened to him—that's huge." A truck drove into the gravel drive, below, bringing Annika to her feet. "That's Dad."

Stephanie turned away and began pulling her uniform on. "Does he know?"

"Not yet." Fear sharpened the words.

Stephanie put an arm around her shoulders. "Don't worry. He doesn't explode the way he used to."

"I know. But he hasn't come to love the Wolfsons."

Stephanie laughed. "True." She headed down the hall for the bathroom. "Tell them I'll be right down."

"No, tell me about the book. The novel. Has it found a home?"

"Maybe. A publisher in Detroit asked to read it. I'm waiting."

"Hooray!" She gave Stephanie a hug. "I'll keep my fingers crossed."

"And I've found a writers group."

Annika stepped back and looked at Stephanie afresh. She looked younger. Her skin was alive. "You needed that."

"Amen."

A yell came from below.

"See you in a minute." Stephanie gave her a push.

Annika stopped for a moment at the head of the stairs, then descended. Her father faced her from the kitchen door, his hands on his hips. "So he's not dead."

"No." Annika turned to her mother. "Steph says she'll be right down."

"Where the hell has he been then?"

"Somewhere in the Outer Banks." She went to help her mother serve the soup. When Stephanie appeared and they took their seats, she told them the story, which became more a part of her at each telling.

"This boy he brought—from God knows where. Is that supposed to make up for what he did?" Her father's tone was a challenge.

"No. He knows he can't unhappen that."

"Hmph. I should say so."

"But he came to face me. And brought a brother for Sadie."

"So you forgive him?" The challenge had risen to a dangerous edge.

Annika let the question sink into her before answering. It met solid stone. "No." The word sounded true if forgiveness meant erasing the act that had changed them beyond repair.

"You're not going back to him?"

"No."

Tom Berglund picked up his spoon and began eating. "Well," he conceded after a few spoonfuls, "that's something I guess."

"And Sadie?" Stephanie asked. "How's she taking it?"

"I don't know yet. She's angry and confused, but he's back. For her. She took Danny to show off her Sunfish." Annika picked up her spoon and began eating. The rest of the family followed suit, content to let the conversation rest, to let questions wait.

Annika and Stephanie rose to clear.

"You still swimming?"

She turned in surprise at her father's question. "No. Not much."

"Liked watching you." He tore off a piece of bread and wiped his bowl.

Annika stood speechless, an empty bowl in either hand.

"So did I," her mother agreed, saving Annika from a response.

"Maybe I'll get back to it." She knew she wouldn't race again, but spoke to acknowledge the praise.

Her father nodded. "Should."

It was late when Annika headed for the Wolfson compound; Sadie would be late to bed, but the thought failed to alarm her. Her mind had found a place to roost. As she pulled in the drive of the old stone house, she saw Brian sitting alone on the front porch. As she approached, he smiled and waved toward the lakeshore. She turned to see Sadie and Danny on the dock, fishing.

"There haven't been any fish in that lake since I was a kid, but Danny's a fisherman."

"Looks like budding buddyship." She sat down next to him, taking in his brow, his lips, his arm, the crooked toe on his left foot.

The minutes slid away.

"Thank you for coming back."

He turned his attention from her to the lake. "When I saw what I'd done, I fell into the void I'd been fighting all my life—a sucking void—of hopelessness. No ground underneath. But that's the craziness that made me do it, too. Fear of not making it—the Olympics—I could feel the sucking."

"And now?"

"I've been there. Flat on the bottom. Couldn't think. Move. Nothing." He fell silent.

Annika sat listening to the murmur of the children on the dock, her mind combining the energy of the man she knew with the fear, the hopelessness he described. "You were more than that."

He turned to her, his eyes grateful. "Yes. But I had to hit bottom to find that out."

"How did you?"

"Danny found me."

"Found you?"

"On the beach. He kicked me, thinking I was dead." He smiled. "I looked at him and saw Sadie. Life broke through." He fell silent again, as though letting his own words sink in. "That's a strange way of saying it, but that's what happened. Nils was ordering me back on board for the trip home. I knew they were going to pitch me when we got out to sea, but I told Danny I'd be back. That's why I jumped ship in the night, before we got too far out. And I made it."

"That's the kind of confidence I knew. Not the fear."

Brian nodded. "That's when I knew there was something solid— inside. I went to find Danny and got a job at a ship repair shop."

"But you didn't call. They found your clothes—we thought you were dead."

"They must have thrown them overboard—I don't know. But I wanted everyone to think I was dead. What I did cut me off. Forever. It couldn't be undone. Can't be." The voices of children fill the empty air. "All I could do was try again. Differently. And I did, but I couldn't get anchored. I thought time would do it, but it didn't. I had to come back before I could go on."

"Good." She stopped, searching for the words. "You said it can't be undone. And that's true, Brian. It can't."

She waited, watching him as he stared at the children across the road.

"I know that." He looked at his clasped hands then up again. "The race—the Gold—I don't want that back. There was too much craziness in it. But you—you brought me out of the hole over and over, and the joy of you was real, Annie. Always." He turned, reached out his hands and took hers from her lap. "You need to know that. You're the one I've hurt most, you and the baby—" He choked on the word. "It's not forgivable, Annie. I know that. Sadie's the only relationship I can fix at all. I hope."

She looked down at their clasped hands and withdrew hers gently. "It's changed us both. I'm glad you're back, Brian. In one piece. That does fix a lot. It gives us a place to go on from."

He nodded again. "Not forever treading water in the void—" He broke off with a laugh. "There's that word again."

"Dry land and happy to be there. It's enough." The words came from a newfound place of certainty, and she let them settle in silence.

Below, the sun had left the dock and was fringing the tops of trees on the far side. She looked at her watch. "I need to get Sadie home." She went to the corner of the porch and rang the bell, the forever signal to family on the waterfront.

Sadie looked up and waved. Annika motioned her to come. "I'll say goodbye to Carmen and Karl." She went in and found her mother-in-law doing dishes, Karl nowhere in sight. "I'm sorry I'm so late, Carmen."

Her mother-in-law turned, drying her hands. "Doesn't matter to us, Annie, but I know you need to get back."

"I talked to Brian," she began, then changed course. "Or I should say Brian talked. I begin to understand."

Carmen nodded. "I heard you."

"I'm glad he came back, Carmen. But we both know we can't go back together."

"Yes." She put her arms around Annika. "I can't help hoping time will change that—but I understand." She stood back. "I miss you..I never realized what the two of you added to our life."

Annika smiled and returned the hug as Sadie and Danny came up the porch steps.

"Can I stay, Mom?" Sadie banged in the screen door.

"No, sweetie. You know you can't."

"I want to."

Annika blinked at the sudden return of the six-year-old. "There's only a week left of school. Then we'll be back up to Grandma and Grandpa Berglund's."

"I want to come see Danny."

Annika raised her brows. Not her father—Danny. Out of the corner of her eye, she saw Brian disappear down the porch steps. He'd heard. "Maybe—" Annika started to say Danny could come to her parents, then confronted the eternal gulf between the adults and shied away.

"You can come here the time after, just like before," Carmen assured her, filling the breach. "And maybe you can stay longer, since school will be out."

"Can I?" Sadie turned to Annika.

"It can probably be arranged," Annika conceded. "But right now, you need to go collect your things."

Sadie ambled off, in no hurry.

"Annie," Carmen began in a low voice, "we'd love to have her for the summer. You know that, don't you?"

Annika smiled, but the future rushed in with hollow certainty. "Let me think about it." There was nothing to think. As she shepherded Sadie to the car, the certainty was unanswerable. Sadie was being swept into the Wolfsons.

A week later, Annika headed for Ann Arbor with an empty car. She should feel free. She told herself that over and over. Like Vicky. It was only for the summer. She'd get used to it. She could go back if she wanted. Brian would be ecstatic. But none of it cut the aloneness. She'd cut herself adrift.

Every weekend, Annika fled her empty house. She went to the fireworks on the Fourth of July. She went to summer concerts. She joined a group of singles at the Unitarian Church. She went hiking with the Sierra Club. She limited her calls to Sadie , who was bubbling with news of her father and brother to once a week. And ended the call in tears.

She drove north to visit once, then once more, a visitor at both the Wolfson's and her own parents' house.

July became August and she confronted the prospect of bringing an unwilling Sadie home. Was it home? She didn't sleep. Or woke from sleep in a rage. Sadie was her child! All she had left! How dare they just swoop her away! The man who destroyed her baby! How dare he take possession! It was *wrong*, damn it. Just *wrong*!

But when she imagined Sadie's face, torn away time and time again from water, forests, father, family—new brother—she couldn't imagine committing the act. Or facing the resentment that would grow and grow. The injustice rankled until her life circled in a cage of her own creation.

She poured herself into her job, taking on more and more of the research, spending hours in the library or before a computer screen. But despite her efforts, the topics carried her further and further from her love of the land. She realized she was in the field less and less, and she'd gone as far as her degree would take her. Then, stale and stiff she went to the pool, swimming lap after lap, slowly nursing herself back to life.

August was half over when she returned from the pool to find Vicky sitting on her doorstep.

"Hello, stranger."

Amazed and wordless, Annika threw her arms around her. "Hello yourself!"

"What have you been doing, anyway. You never call."

Annika winced at the edge in Vicky's voice as she unlocked the door. "I've been cutting myself off. From the north country and—everything." She let Vicky precede her into the house. "But I'm so glad to see you," she mumbled, fighting tears.

"Why? I mean why cut yourself off?" Vicky put down her overnight case.

"Because if I don't, I'm likely to do the wrong thing."

"Meaning?"

"Go back to Brian. To get Sadie back."

"To get ...? Sadie is your child, Annie!"

"She's also a child returned to the lakes and forests of her home. To the father she thought she'd lost. To Danny, who she bosses like a typical big sister"

"Ah." Vicky's face relaxed in understanding. She looked around the room, which had failed to acquire any personal touches. "I think we should go to dinner. A good dinner."

Annika laughed. "Sounds perfect."

A half hour later, they were settled at a table and had ordered food and drink. Annika stared at Vicky, acutely aware of her relief and of the isolation she'd fallen into.

"You haven't asked me why I came," Vicky commented. "Uninvited."

"Ouch. Why did you come?"

"There's a business in Traverse City. A small one that rents sailboats and kayaks and takes people on pontoon boat tours. That sort of thing. The manager is an old friend of mine, and he wants to retire."

"And?"

"How would you like to take a flyer? Come into business with me? I want to run nature tours around TC, and you're perfect for the job."

Two weeks later, Annika and Vicky had settled on a plan to take over the Northland Water Tours and Rentals and started house-hunting in Traverse City. The owner, Bud O'Conner, planned to depart for Florida as soon as he sold the business. He offered his bungalow, but it was too small to accommodate both of them plus Sadie—and maybe sometimes Danny. Two days after they'd settled the business deal, they rented a house near the elementary school, registered Sadie in a fifth-grade class and returned to Vicky's condo exuberant and exhausted. They'd just sunk into soft chairs and put their sore feet on ottomans when the doorbell rang. Vicky groaned and roused herself.

"Papa!" She stepped back in surprise.

Annika rose to her feet.

"Hello, Vicky." He hesitated, as though unsure of his reception.

"Come in!" Vicky stepped back with a smile. "Long time, no see."

"Well, that's what I'm about," he said, stepping into the apartment. "Hello, Annie. I was hoping I'd find you here. I heard you two were going into business."

Annika nodded, jolted by the intrusion of a Wolfson into the brand new present.

"We are," Vicky answered. "In fact, we were just celebrating. Can I get you something? Beer, wine, lemonade, iced tea?"

"Ah. A glass of lemonade would be welcome, thank you. It's a hot drive today." Markus Wolfson lowered his heavy frame onto the couch. "I came to invite you both to my Labor Day barbecue." He let the statement rest in silence as he accepted the frosted glass from Vicky. "Thank you."

Annika and Vicky looked at each other, each waiting for the other to reply. When neither did, Papa went on.

"Melissa and I've never been happy with the way Karl and Joe split the family ... but you both know that." He took a drink. "I don't believe in messing with my children's lives, but God's mercy has brought Brian back. It's time the Wolfsons learned how to heal their hurts, and I've told them so."

"Them. All of them?" Vicky sounded doubtful.

"Yep, and the others join me in hoping you'll come—both of you." His voice held its usual force, but his eyes pleaded.

Annika gazed at him. She had always liked the down-to-earth head of the Wolfson clan, but now she was viewing him from a different place. Outside. "All right, Papa. I'll be there." She turned toward Vicky. "Speaking only for myself, of course."

"I don't know how I can refuse, Papa. I'll make it."

"Ahh! I thank you, ladies. Thank you!" The old man rose and spread his arms wide. With a laugh, they rose and went into them.

"You're staying in town, I hope." Vicky said, pulling back.

"Mm. Missy made a doctor's appointment for me when I told her I was coming. She fusses about the old ticker."

"Good. We'll take you to dinner and fill you in on the new venture we're embarking on."

The next two weeks shot by like a released rubber band, the demands of the moment driving all need for thought away. Annika turned slowly in their new living room, eyeing Vicky's couches plus Annika's rocker and the mix of pictures retrieved from the lake house and Vicky's condo, plus a couple of new additions from Ann Arbor art fairs. It was decidedly new, and she felt energy surge. She was ready.

Vicky backed through the screen door, her arms loaded with groceries. "You're here! Good." She dumped a sack into Annika's waiting arms and followed her into the kitchen.

"What time are we expected tomorrow?"

"Time?" Annika froze in the act of putting eggs in the refrigerator. "Oh." She gave a short laugh. "The picnic. Two o'clock."

Vicky raised her brows. "Don't tell me you've gotten cold feet."

"I have, but there's no choice, since I have to collect Sadie, which puts me in the middle of the soup in any case."

Vicky laughed. "Good, because I'm counting on you to help me through."

"Sadie says they invited my folks, too."

"Really! A regular United Nations." Vicky spilled potatoes into the sink. "That should keep you busy, at least." She picked up the peeler. "At least Sadie is okay. She seems delighted with everything that's happened—especially moving to Traverse City."

Annika smiled at the memory of Sadie's quick tour of their new quarters, which included the nearby school, park, and river.

"I can go back and forth all the time," she'd exclaimed. "Maybe even take the bus, huh?"

Annika had been so delighted at the return of the old Sadie, that she hadn't argued.

~

A little after two the next afternoon, Annika and Vicky, carrying potato salad and wine, stood at the top of Papa Wolfson's wide lawn, viewing the scene.

Halfway down the lawn, Karl stood at the barbeque pit, turning chicken on the spit. Papa stood at the other end, tending the smoking grill and yelling instructions to Brian who stood between them, wrapping ribs in foil. Brian caught sight of them and waved. His smile was wide, but he didn't leave his post.

Maggie Berglund and Carmen chatted as they laid places at the picnic tables. Carmen burst out laughing and shook her head as though at a punch line.

Down by the water, Joe and Tom Berglund occupied lawn chairs, deep in conversation, Tom nodding sagely from time to time.

A lone sunbather occupied the dock. Suzanne, Joe's wife, and she was calling to the bright zodiac that was approaching—Jonathan with Sadie and Danny in the stern.

"Yooo…!" Sadie yelled and waved so hard it rocked the boat. "Mom! Here!"

Annika waved. "I'm going to be okay." She turned. You?"

"Just in time!" Melissa called as she emerged from the house carrying lemonade.

"Just fine," Vicky answered. "Good people."

Behind them another car rolled up, and Stephanie emerged, carrying an apple pie and a six-pack of beer. She grinned. "Hello, you two!"

"Aha!" Vicky exclaimed. "Just the lady I was looking for. Come, let's help Melissa." She beckoned Stephanie.

Annika waved them on their way and headed for the shore, where Sadie had leapt to the dock and was running toward her.